DIFFERENT

"This is a heart-opening, wisdom-packed, edge-of-your seat adventure. Through masterful storytelling, *Different* left me in awe of how relationships, careers, and stubborn problems do change when we are open to life's gifts."

> – Dr. Cheryl Kasdorf, author of *Antidote to Overwhelm*

"Written by the world's next great inspirational novelist, this book is a MUST READ. It changed my life for the better and I'm sure it'll do the same for you as well."

> – Tom Bird, bestselling author and writing coach

This book is much more than a well-written novel; it will make you ponder your own life mission. The characters and story are so vivid and memorable and will remain with you long after the last page is read. If you love a novel that digs deep into your soul and makes you think about the world and spirituality, then this book has it all. Highly recommended.

> – Reviewed by Lesley Jones for *Readers' Favorite*

"A soulful and engaging novel about the mysteries of life that should be read far and wide. It will take you on a journey of discovery."

> – Cathy Byrd, author of *The Boy Who Knew Too Much*

"Couldn't put it down! Datta Groover has woven together an impactful story about family, love, trauma, insight, healing—and so much more. It kept me guessing until the end."

> – Stephanie McHugh, professional stand-up comedian

"This is a journey of discovery that you will want to make without any expectations except that it will be a wonderful experience, and trust me, it will be. The characters are great. They are real people, here in our real world, facing real problems, and they are lovable and likable. The plot fits the scenario perfectly. Datta Groover is a master of weaving all the elements of a story into a modern masterpiece."

– Reviewed by Ray Simmons for Readers' Favorite

"*Different* is an emotionally engaging ride all the way through. I loved the richness of this story and that I couldn't predict what was going to happen. I highly recommend this book if you are looking for an uplifting read with a little edge."

– Amy Kennedy, director of The International Artist^{TM}

"Captivating and intriguing, *Different* delivers unexpected twists while deeply satisfying my desire as a reader to be inspired. I loved the exploration of family dynamics and the profound effect of secrets. Beautifully written!"

– Karen Collyer, professional book editor and author of
Shame, Guilt, and Surviving Martin Bryant

"Datta Groover's *Different* is an absorbing, inspirational novel that explores marital conflict, secrets, a family at risk, and the special abilities of a borderline autistic child who doesn't speak."

– BlueInk Reviews

DIFFERENT

DATTA GROOVER

Deep
Pacific
Press

LOVELAND, COLORADO   MELBOURNE, AUSTRALIA

ISBN: 978-0-9832689-4-9 (Paperback)

Library of Congress Control Number: 2018966311

This is a work of fiction. Names, characters, businesses, places, events, locales, and incidents are either the products of the author's imagination or used in a fictitious manner. Any resemblance to actual persons, living or dead, or actual events is purely coincidental.

Front cover images by Shutterstock.
Cover design by Patrick Knowles.

Printed by Steuben Press in the United States of America
and by Ingram Spark in other countries

First printing edition February, 2019

Deep Pacific Press
117 E 37th St. #580
Loveland, CO 80538
www.DeepPacificPress.com

DEDICATION

I dedicate *Different* to my dear friend, editor, cousin, and prize-winning, *NY Times* bestselling novelist Mary Freeman Rosenblum.

Thank you for your friendship, your professional advice, your absolute honesty, and your love. Thanks for all your great suggestions for *Different*, for watching over me through this process, and for your massive contribution to the writing world and the world in general.

I will miss you always.

CHAPTER ONE

Frank sat bolt upright, tangled in bedding. How'd he wind up on the floor? Soaked in cold sweat, senses on high alert, he scanned the room. Something moved around the end of the bed toward him in the barely visible light. He fumbled with the drawer on his nightstand, then relaxed at the sound of Sofia's soothing voice.

"Hey, it's all right. Just a bad dream." She gently rubbed his back. "Same one?" When he didn't respond, she tried again. "Frank? Breathe, *cariño*. Everything's okay."

Frank exhaled. "I can't stand the thought of you and the kids—" he began, then leapt to his feet, startling his wife.

"Frank, they're fine." But he was already halfway down the hall.

She was probably right, but he had to be sure. First the girls. Both Lisa and Jodie slept soundly. Farther down the hall in Sam's room, he stood for several minutes watching their five-year-old sleep. It calmed him and helped soothe the terror of the nightmare. Funny, though. When Sofia put him to bed early that evening, Sam had grabbed his favorite stuffed bear—the one he never went to sleep without—and slipped past her, then ran out of his room over to where Frank sat checking his email at the dining room table. He solemnly looked at his father and put Little Bear in his lap. "Why, thank you, Sam," he'd said, but when he tried to hand the stuffed toy back to his son, the boy shook his head and ran back to his room. As if he knew his dad was about to have a rough night. So Little Bear slept with Frank and Sofia that evening.

When he got back to bed, Sofia greeted him sleepily. "Everything okay?"

"It is now." He climbed under the covers and nestled close to his wife. "What would I do without you?"

"You'd be hopelessly lost," she murmured before drifting off to sleep.

Frank lay staring at the dark ceiling, thinking about the recurring nightmare, his heart still beating faster and harder than normal. In the past, Sofia had suggested he get help with the dreams, but she couldn't know some things were beyond help. Those dreams were based on what could never be fixed or undone. He'd willingly give up his own life for the safety of any one of his family members. If and when that time came, however, he might not have a choice.

He sighed and rolled onto his side. A minute later, he was sound asleep.

Sofia didn't mention the dream the next morning. She had only kind and soothing words for him—as usual the day after a nightmare. As if they were like any happily married couple: deeply in love, caring, and affectionate with each other.

Over the next couple of weeks, however, things slowly and inevitably drifted back to normal. The way they always did.

Frank checked his watch and slapped the steering wheel. Damn! Late again. When he'd arrived ten minutes behind schedule last time, Sofia took it as a lack of commitment to their marriage. Wasn't taking time out of his workday to show up for counseling proof enough of his commitment? She didn't understand that leaving work wasn't simply a matter of shutting down his computer. If he had exposed wiring or anything like that, he had to "make it work or make it safe," as the sign on the wall at the shop reminded him.

The day hadn't gone well. The mistake had been telling his crew about the counseling. Everyone gave him a hard time—even Jason. They teased him all day, and though Frank tried to laugh it off, the teasing bothered him. He even had some ugly thoughts. What if they couldn't make things right? What if their marriage didn't pan out? Frank experienced dark moments when his mind went there.

HR had announced another round of updates to their employee handbook that morning, for the second time that year—and it was only February. That meant another useless meeting to discuss all the new changes. Working for Lake Oswego Public Works had other downsides as well. Everything had to be politically correct and checked at least three times, then discussed ad nauseam. Which today put him far behind schedule.

Portland traffic worsened each year, and he hated how much it slowed him down. Especially today. A freezing drizzle and the gray Portland sky made everything feel even slower. Burnside would most likely be jammed, so he'd have to cut across on Fourteenth Street.

No point in trying to explain any of that to Sofia. He'd still get a black mark for being late. Of course, she had to choose a counselor in the Pearl District rather than someone close by. He knew it was for the "greater good of their relationship," as she liked to put it, but still. Getting away from work was never easy. Too many people depended on him.

It'd been over a month since the last nightmare. The subject probably wouldn't even come up. Not that it had anything to do with their relationship, anyway. Digging up the past meant a lot of wasted time. For him, the best therapy meant being home in the garage working on his quadcopter. But if this counseling business helped their relationship, it was a good thing. He just had to keep telling himself that.

After ten minutes of not advancing even a full block, he activated the flashing yellow lights on his roof. With no police in sight, he crossed the solid white middle line into the empty oncoming lane and took an illegal left turn at the next corner. If a cop stopped him, he'd say a utility emergency had just come up. That line had saved him from a ticket on more than one occasion.

When his GPS told him he'd arrived, he saw no place to park save for a public garage the next block up on the right. Better than nothing. He stopped even with the entrance, his right blinker expressing his intent to turn, waiting for the constant stream of pedestrians—bundled up against the cold and wet—to take their sweet time passing by so he could turn in. Did any of them think to stop and wave him in? No, that would be way too courteous. His irritation increased by the second. Finally, he got a break. He revved the dirty white City of Lake Oswego pickup and made the sharp right into the garage. Unfortunately, the truck slid sideways on the slick sidewalk at the last moment and hit the edge of the entrance full-on. The impact was hard enough to deploy his airbag and slide his .45 auto out from under his seat into plain view. He grabbed the pistol and hurriedly stuffed it back under the seat, moments before some guy in a two-piece suit and holding an umbrella knocked on the window.

"You okay, bud? Want me to call someone?"

Frank waved him off, reversed, and renegotiated the turn. He moved forward slowly and found a parking space without further difficulty. Feeling as though he'd taken a hard punch in the mouth, he checked himself in the rearview mirror. No blood showed, but the airbag had scuffed his cheek and bruised his lip. The yellowish powder on his face made him look jaundiced. He had a slight headache, which seemed normal under the circumstances. He got out and examined the damage to the truck's front left corner: bent bumper, smashed headlight, and some serious wrinkles on the fender. The office manager wouldn't be happy, but that was why they had insurance. He locked the truck, checked his watch, and ran for the exit—already ten minutes late.

On his way to the counselor's office building on the next block, he ran past a homeless man camped on the sidewalk, bundled up against the cold drizzle, a young girl sleeping in his arms. His cardboard sign said "Combat Vet—please help" in black marker. Frank waved encouragement to him as he ran past. Sometimes that was all you could do. He shook his head as he walked across the lobby. Portland had a massive homeless problem that the city seemed unable to fix. He punched the *Up* button on the elevator and checked his pockets. Uncle Gino had fought in Vietnam and told him horror stories not just of the war, but of some of the things veterans went through when they came home. And this guy had his daughter with him, who appeared to be around Lisa's age. Surprising that Child Protective Services hadn't picked her up. They frowned on children living on the sidewalk.

The elevator dinged and the doors opened. He stepped inside and hit the fifth-floor button, but right before the doors closed all the way, he stuck his hand out, opening them back up. Swearing under his breath, he ran back into the lobby and out onto the sidewalk. He handed a ten-dollar bill to the veteran, who looked at him incredulously at first, then mouthed a silent "Thank you."

Waiting for the elevator a second time, Frank noted he was now more than fifteen minutes late. He was definitely going to get an earful about this—if not now, then later.

Grateful for the men's room outside the counselor's office, he ducked in and washed off the airbag powder. He looked at his face in the mirror as he dried off with paper towels. He was ready for this. Tossing the used towels in the trash, he opened the door and took a deep breath.

CHAPTER TWO

Sofia looked up and gave her husband a tight smile as he walked into the waiting room. "Glad you could make it, Frank."

He did his best to smile back. "Got stuck in traffic. It's getting worse all the time. And the drizzle didn't help at all."

"I noticed that myself."

"I had to wrap things up at work." He felt like he was telling his third-grade teacher why he was late to class. "If I just took off and left wiring exposed, that would be dangerous."

"And I couldn't just take off and leave Sam. So I gave myself plenty of time. He's with Nonna Eve, in case you were wondering."

"Got it." He motioned toward the inner door with his head. "Any sign of Steve?"

She shook her head slightly. "I told you he'd be on vacation this time, remember?"

He looked through the stack of periodicals on the side table, pulled out a year-old edition of *Sports Illustrated*, and gave her a glance before leafing through the magazine. "When did you tell me that?"

"Couple of weeks ago. I said he wouldn't be available, but that he had arranged for somebody he trusted to fill in for him."

He didn't mind her being right, but her tone of voice indicated she wanted him to know precisely how right she was. And who goes on vacation in

February? "Okay then, any sign of Steve's replacement?"

"Not yet," she answered.

He smiled. "So I'm right on time."

Her eyebrows rose. "Sure."

They sat in silence for several minutes before she asked what happened to his lip. Frank rubbed his forehead. "It's a long story." He'd tell her about the truck later. Or not. After another couple of minutes, he looked up from his magazine and sighed. "Do we really need to be here?"

"We discussed this, and you agreed that our session with Steve was worthwhile." Sofia frowned. "Besides, a little help goes a long way."

"Maybe." He glanced at the clock on the waiting room wall. "But I'm missing time from work."

"And *I'm* missing time getting Sam's lessons ready for tomorrow. Besides, we need to—"

The tall, young redhead who opened the inner door caught Frank by surprise. She must be the counselor's assistant.

"I'm Kim." She extended her hand. "I'll be your counselor today."

He tried not to look shocked as he shook her hand. Were they giving out therapist licenses in high school now? "Frank MacBride, and this is my wife—"

"Sofia. Pleased to meet you."

She took them to her session room and motioned toward a small sofa and some comfortable-looking chairs. "Please sit wherever you like." Sprigs of fragrant lavender in an enameled porcelain vase adorned a coffee table. French doors provided a view of a small balcony with three pigeons walking across its Spanish terrazzo tiles. The male was apparently trying to impress the two females, who pretended to not pay attention. Frank smiled. Not so different from humans.

Kim adjusted her glasses and wasted no time getting down to business. "So, what brings you in today?"

"My wife," said Frank.

She looked at Sofia. "How about you?"

"Well … that's our problem. Or part of it."

"How so?"

Sofia sighed. "He jokes all the time. He's funny, but sometimes things need to be serious."

"And how does that affect your marriage?"

"Isn't it obvious? I mean, how can you have a serious discussion if your husband always makes a joke of everything?"

Frank frowned. "I lighten the mood. Is that so bad?"

Sofia examined her glossy pink fingernails. "It can be. When we talked about you flirting with other women, what did you say? That it was nothing. You made it a big joke."

They'd had a conflict on Valentine's Day the week before. Trying to make her happy, he took her out for dinner and a movie, where he might have flirted with the nineteen-year-old who took the tickets. Before that, he'd joked with their waitress. Neither of which was a big deal. The argument that followed, however, didn't end well.

"*Amore mio*, sometimes it's good to take some weight off."

Sofia folded her arms across her chest. "And sometimes it's good to be serious. For example, when we talk about you flirting."

"But that's the whole point. It's not serious."

"Not to you, maybe."

Frank shook his head. She wasn't getting it. "No, not to me. It is you I wake up next to. You are my chosen one."

"So why am I not enough for you?"

"You *are* enough for me. I just play. It means nothing."

"It sounds like 'play around,'" said Sofia.

"No." He waved a finger at her. "Not me—never. You could be less suspicious, you know. That would make everyone happier."

She looked at their counselor. "See? He doesn't think it's a big deal," she said with a quaver in her voice.

Frank frowned and hoped she wasn't going to play the emotional card. "Because it's not a big deal." He turned to Kim. "We go in circles around this. She brings it up a lot."

Kim nodded and turned to Sofia. "How often does he flirt?"

"All the time. The prettier she is, the more likely it happens. And they always seem to be younger than me." She paused. "It's not just that he does it. It's the whole energy of it."

Frank rolled his eyes. "Not this again."

Her eyes flashed. "Correct me if I'm wrong, but isn't that why we're here? So we can talk about things in front of someone who can help us?"

He gave her a thin smile. "It's just when you start talking about energy and stuff. I'm not into all that New Age woo-woo lingo. It's vague enough to prove anything you want."

Sofia shook her head. "I'm not trying to prove anything. Energy is not something invented by what you call 'New Age.' It's real and has real effects."

"Tell us how you feel when Frank flirts with other women," said Kim.

She closed her eyes and drew a slow breath. "I feel that he's not taking me or our relationship seriously. Especially when he does it often."

"Is there any truth in what she says, Frank?" asked Kim.

He said nothing for a beat, watching a starling that had landed out on the balcony railing. "First of all, age has nothing to do with it. She worries because she's older than me by not even two years, which also means nothing. Sofia is a natural beauty and always will be."

"But do you flirt all the time?" persisted Kim.

"Not always. I don't know why she says that."

"Almost always—at least whenever you can," said Sofia.

He lifted both hands in a palms-up gesture. "I'm half Italian. It's what we do. It doesn't mean what you think it means."

Kim smiled. "Well, the flirtatious Italian man certainly is a cliché. More importantly, though, are Italians faithful?"

He shrugged. "I don't know. Probably most of us. I think no less so than other cultures. Maybe more than some." He frowned and nodded at his wife. "No different from Spain."

"I'm Catalan."

"Catalonia is in Spain, no?" Frank asked.

Sofia shook her head. "Yes, but not the same. We are independent. You know this."

"You mean you *wish* you were independent."

Kim cleared her throat. "Are you faithful?" she asked Frank.

"Of course!"

She turned to Sofia. "Is he?"

She glanced at her husband before answering. "I have no reason to think otherwise."

"Which is not actually answering the question."

"Yes, I think he is sexually faithful—if that's what you meant."

Kim nodded. "That was what I meant. We'll get back to this." She turned to Frank. "What do you want? What really brought you here?"

He took a deep breath. "Sofia thought we needed help."

"And do you think so?"

"Maybe. I don't know." He paused. "Things can always be better, right?"

"Usually, yes. So are you here because she got you to agree and you're doing it to make her happy, or are you here because you also think things could be better?"

He looked at the ceiling and thought about it. "Maybe both. I want our relationship to be better and I want to make my wife happy." His eyebrows raised. "And I want what's good for our family."

"I get that." Kim nodded. "You mentioned on the intake form you have a 'special needs' child."

"That would be Sam, our five-year-old," he said.

Sofia leaned forward. "He's borderline autistic. He functions well and interacts well—considering he doesn't speak."

"At all?"

She took a deep breath. "No. He's never said a single word, and no one can tell us why. The so-called experts say it has something to do with his autism, but they're just guessing. He only makes eye contact when he wants to—which is rare—and he doesn't like being touched. He's loving, but not in a physical way."

"Yet you say he interacts well."

"It's hard to explain, but yes, he does."

"Is he challenging?"

Frank said "no" the same moment his wife said "yes." He recovered quickly, however. "But she would know better." He motioned toward Sofia. "She spends all day with him."

"All day?"

"Yes, she teaches him. Homeschooling." He chuckled. "Home kindergarten, to be more precise."

"I see." She turned to Sofia. "Do you enjoy that?"

"Of course. My major at Portland State was education, and I minored in psych. I worked as a guidance counselor at Ben Franklin High before the kids were born. So I have the tools and training."

"Which doesn't mean you enjoy it."

"But I do." She paused. "It's not how I envisioned using my training, but it's a perfect arrangement. They would eat Sam alive in kindergarten. Besides, his math skills are already at an advanced first-grade level, almost second-grade."

"Do you worry about him being able to interact with peers?"

"Oh, no. He's quite close to his sisters, and to Frank and me. The risks and dangers of public school overpower the benefits. He'd be way too easy a target."

"What dangers are we talking about?"

"Mean teasing, bullying. That sort of thing."

"Sure. And you know peer interaction differs greatly from family interaction, right?"

"I do, but the indicators are there," said Sofia.

"Indicators?"

"That he could interact well with his peers if he chose to."

"Yes, but it generally takes lots and lots of practice."

Sofia frowned. "It's kind of a touchy topic for us. We've had quite a few well-meaning people give us advice on what we should do with Sam." Sofia held her hand flat above her head. "I'm up to here with it."

"Okay. We don't have to talk about that now—or ever if you don't want to."

Kim smiled. "What attracted you to Frank?"

"Well, when he's not getting on my nerves," she nodded toward her husband, "he's adorable, confident, and funny. He can fix just about anything. Mostly, though, I love that he has such a huge, sensitive, generous, and vulnerable heart. I'd see him around campus encouraging others, always giving a kind word. He made people feel special. I wanted him to make *me* feel special."

"Did he flirt then?"

"Even more back then. He was a champion at it! He'd also joke with other guys. Everybody loved him. He was one of the more popular students at PSU during my time there, and for sure more social than academic."

"In what way?"

Sofia glanced at Frank, who slowly shook his head. "He almost failed his classes. He was enrolled in second-year engineering, going for an associate's degree, but he almost didn't make it."

"Why?"

"Well, for one thing, he was quite active socially. Parties, hanging out, fun things." She paused. "And he had his football. That took a lot of time and kept him in the spotlight."

Frank frowned. "Hopefully it wasn't all bad for you."

"It was great, but I don't know what would have happened with our relationship if you hadn't achieved your two-year degree."

"Wow. Nice of you to finally tell me."

"Just being honest. She asked for our story."

Kim nodded. "I did. Anything else you want to say about Frank, Sofia?"

"Well …"

"This is the time to talk. Frank, are you okay to hear what she has to say?"

"Of course."

Sofia took a deep breath and looked at the floor. "Sometimes I feel like I married my father."

"What?" Frank's eyes widened. "You mean your super-critical father who hates me? And everyone else, as far as I can tell." He looked at the ceiling. "So I'm critical and mean?"

"You're *not* like him in many ways. You're not critical. Or mean. Not at all."

He shook his head. "Then why would you say that?"

"It's just that he loves being in charge. Like you."

Frank frowned. "It's not like I boss you around."

"Sometimes you do."

Kim shifted in her chair. "Thanks for sharing that, Sofia. Anything else?"

"Well, sometimes …" She looked Frank in the eye. "It seems to be all about you. Even when you are protecting or providing for us. Or being generous. Just like Papá."

Frank was stunned, even though part of him could see the truth in what she said. "I guess it's good we came here. So we can get all the dirt out in the open."

Kim shook her head. "It's not dirt, but I do think it's good to get things out in the open where you can talk about them." She paused. "Even when it's not comfortable. It took a lot of courage for Sofia to say that."

He discreetly checked his watch. Still ten minutes to go. "If you say so."

Kim smiled. "I do. Now tell me about Sofia."

He remained silent for a while. "I love my wife, even when she is brutally honest. I love her because she is smart, beautiful, and sexy. I love her because she has given me—given us—three very special children. I love that she lets that beautiful dark blond hair of hers grow long, though I know she would cut it shorter if not for me. I love that her eyes are a shade of green I've never seen on anyone else." He looked at his wife and sighed. "She inspires me to be a better man, and I have to say, she's kept me happy these sixteen years, challenges and all."

Kim nodded. "She sounds perfect."

Frank wagged his finger at her. "Not perfect. But perfect for me." He paused. "But she worries too much. She sees all the ways things can go wrong."

Sofia frowned. "One of us has to."

"Maybe, but many times that means you think you're the one who's right. And I wish you wouldn't worry so much." He turned to Kim. "I want to do more to make her happy."

"That would be nice," said Sofia. "I mean, sure, you try. But maybe if you tried harder to not pay so much attention to other women—"

Frank raised his hands in exasperation. "I told you—"

Sofia rolled her eyes. "I know, it's your Italian blood. It's what you do."

"That's part of it, yes." He looked at the counselor. "You see? This is what happens."

"What if you paid less attention to other women?" Kim asked.

Frank shrugged. "I don't know. I can try, sure. But really, that means less than she thinks."

"Maybe so. But you see it upsets her, right?"

He took a deep breath and looked at his wife, tears welling in her eyes. "I guess."

Kim sat a little straighter. "Does it upset her or not?"

"Okay, it does. Yes."

"And you said you want to make her happy, right?"

"Of course."

"Then I want you to do something. For sixty days, make a conscious effort to flirt less—or not at all. When you come in again, you can let me or Steve know how that went."

Frank gestured with his palms upward. "Sure, I can try that." He looked at his wife. "If that will make you happy, *amore mio*, I will do it."

"That would thrill me, *cariño*."

Kim glanced at her watch. "We've come to a great stopping place. We're a little past time, but that's fine. The main thing I want you to take away is the awareness of your love for each other, and the huge amount of commitment you both bring to this partnership. Sure, you have work to do, but work is what it takes to build a great relationship." She stood. "Does that make sense?"

They both nodded. She took a thin book out of one of her cabinets and handed it to Sofia, who looked at it with curiosity.

"What's this?"

"A journal. I want you to write in it at least once a week until I see you again."

"Thanks, but I really don't have time."

"Frank made a concession today, and he's going to do something that's hard for him." She nodded at the journal. "I want you to do something hard as well. Write your thoughts, feelings, and observations. Keep that where no one else can get to it. A locked box would be perfect, so you can write without holding back. Once a week, at least ten minutes, and that's all. More often if you feel like it. Some people do it every morning when they first wake up and love it. All you need do is to keep that pen moving across the paper."

"I don't know."

Frank smiled. "I know. Let's switch. I'll write in the journal ten minutes every week, and you don't flirt with any women. Easier for everyone."

Sofia tried not to smile. "You see what I put up with?"

Kim nodded. "Just try it. Do we have a deal?"

"I guess." Sofia looked uncertain. "Will I have to share this with you?"

"No. You don't have to share it with anyone. In fact, I don't recommend it. The main thing is to write without holding back—which is a lot easier to do if you know no one will see it." She held the door open. "Steve or I will see you both the last Tuesday in April at four thirty. Just let us know in the next week or so who you prefer to meet with. We're not attached either way—we only want what's best and most comfortable for you both."

CHAPTER THREE

SOFIA'S diary. THIS IS PRIVATE. CLOSE IT NOW! And how did you get past my lock, anyway?

March 3, 2011

Who writes in diaries past the age of thirteen? So she called it a journal. Still, isn't this for pre-teens? But I gave my word in front of Frank. I will do this once a week as I promised, for two months—more if I feel like it. Not that I will feel like it. Is this what they teach people in counseling school? And when did she graduate, anyway ... last week? What if I have nothing to write about? Keep moving your pen across the paper, she said.

Next weekend I get to visit my parents, where I'll have a golden opportunity to hear about all the things I'm doing wrong. Papá has already made a big deal about the fact that they're flying me down to Sacramento. Like it's more than a drop in the bucket for them. Wouldn't it be nice if they'd come up occasionally to see their grandkids? No, Papá is too old to travel, Madre says. She always makes excuses for him. I guess it'll be good to get away, but I wish I was going somewhere nice. Not Sacramento, and definitely not with my parents.

I got to spend quality time with Nonna Eve this week. She's who I want to be when I grow up! She invited me over for tea and had me drop the kids at my sister's—which she'd pre-arranged with Maria. And she read me poetry! Nothing deep, but still. I don't know if Madre ever read anything to me, what to speak of poetry.

Sitting across the kitchen table from me, Nonna Eve took my hand and gently stroked the back of it with her other hand. I felt so loved! She then told me right out of the blue that the biggest pain is that of an unfulfilled life. How did she know what I needed to hear? As if she knew what happened at Ben Franklin. But teaching Sam fulfills me. Sure, it would be nice to be doing it on a grander scale, but at least it's more or less the same work I'd planned on doing. I'm so glad Nonna Eve gets me. I'm blessed to have the best mother-in-law on the planet. Frank better not ever leave me—but if he does, I'm keeping his mom.

Was the session with Kim helpful? I don't know. Maybe. In the past week, Frank has been trying. We went skating with the kids at the Clackamas Mall Thursday evening. They say Tonya Harding practices there, but I've never seen her. Whenever some beauty would walk or skate past, he'd pretend to not notice, even when they noticed him. Which happened a lot. He's trying to make me happy, and that by itself feels way better.

The counseling session went well, I guess. Probably worth going back. As long as she focuses on Frank and our relationship and stays out of all my past family drama, it'll be fine. Will it help our relationship? Maybe. Will it help Sam speak? I don't see how, but time will tell.

Speaking of time, my ten minutes are almost up! That's close enough for me!

The day had gone unusually well. Before work, Frank volunteered an hour at the Southeast Senior Center. Nonna Eve's idea, of course. "We're all going to be there one day," she'd say, "so we might as well rack up credits now." He put in an hour a week, sometimes more if they had extra maintenance issues. He never felt he had the time to spare beforehand, but afterward was always glad he'd helped. The residents there knew him as "Eve's boy," since Nonna Eve volunteered at least three or four times a week and knew everyone on a first-name basis. A lady named Carol had cried when Frank changed her light bulb. She thanked him repeatedly and kept calling him Blake. He gently corrected her the first couple of times, but eventually he gave up. For her, he could be Blake, whoever that was. Or had been.

On his way from the Senior Center to work, other drivers seemed more courteous than usual, and traffic was lighter than normal. His day at Lake Oswego Public Works went smoothly, with things falling into place the way they seldom did. He'd almost made it to quitting time without a single problem. At the moment, however, something was off. Maybe it was the sound of the motor, vibrating at a slightly different pitch. Or the faintest hint of an acrid odor that didn't quite belong with the subtle but familiar mix of water, ozone, and lubricating oil. Maybe it was the sound of the water rushing through the massive pump. Or maybe he was just going nuts.

"Hey, Jason."

"What's up, boss?"

"Come look at pump three."

"Sure." Jason sauntered along the catwalk and squinted at the monitor panel displaying the vitals of a pump-and-motor combination the size of a minivan directly below them. He scratched his head. "Looks good to me."

"I know it *looks* good, but something is off."

"Oh, I get it! You're doing your Pump Whisperer thing again." Jason laughed. "Or is it simply because you're just closer to the action than the rest of us?" At five foot five, Frank received a fair amount of good-natured teasing about his height.

"Funny. You know this is important."

"I do, and I also know the swing shift is coming in at five thirty. If there's anything seriously wrong, they can handle it. I don't hear, see, feel, or smell anything off with it. There's nothing to worry about."

"What kind of attitude is that?"

Jason shrugged. "It's the kind of attitude that keeps me from seeing trouble when there isn't any."

Frank sighed. "And what if over thirty-seven thousand people were left without water? Would you worry then?"

"I sure would, because that would mean both backup pumps would be offline and the entire fail-safe system—that cost the City of Lake Oswego at least fifteen years of both our salaries put together—would have been a colossal waste of time and money." He studied the digital readouts on the monitor panel. "The vitals are all looking healthy, chief." He shook his head. "No need to worry. It's all good."

"Don't give me that 'It's all good' crap. It's my job to worry. You know that. I'm tagging this." He pulled a *Check or Repair* tag out of his shirt pocket.

Jason buried his hands in the front pockets of his coveralls and frowned. "Seriously? You know that means we're not going home on time."

"Yeah, I know. But we can't take the chance." He began writing on the tag. "Sometimes I wonder what would happen if I—" His phone rang. He pulled it out and looked at the numbers scrolling across the screen. "It's my wife." He watched it ring twice more.

"You gonna get that, or what?"

Frank stared at his phone for another ring before he hit answer.

Sofia smiled and wiped the inside of the dining room china cabinet while Adele sang "*Someone Like You*" on her boombox. She found it funny that when properly motivated, something that would ordinarily drive her crazy became almost fun. The Petersons were driving up from Salem on the weekend for the first time in ages, and here she was getting the house ready as though she actually liked cleaning.

Spring had arrived early, and flowers around the neighborhood were already in full bloom—a rare occurrence for early March. With the open windows letting in a fresh breeze, she inhaled the mixture of fragrances in the air. There had been a brief but intense rain earlier, putting all those negative ions into the air. It was one of the things she loved about Portland. Many days were rainy in the morning and heavenly in the afternoon. Or vice versa.

Sam walked in, his eyes brimming with tears. She didn't notice him at first, but once she did, her heart melted. "*Querido*, what's wrong?" She opened her arms to him, and he jumped in to give her a tight hug, which worried her even more, since he normally avoided hugs. "Sam, what is it?"

Tears flowed silently down his cheeks.

"Are you hurt?"

He paused and slowly shook his head. The tears came faster.

"Oh, Sam! What happened?"

No response.

She took him in her arms again and rocked him back and forth, which used to help when he was a toddler. He smelled faintly of peppermint soap. "Oh, Sam, I wish I could help."

In a strained voice, he said "Moe."

Sofia frowned. She had waited five long years for this moment. He'd just spoken his first word, but she didn't feel the relief and joy she had anticipated. It was the proof they'd been waiting for that he was a normal boy and would speak and grow up like other people and have a normal life. But something was wrong. She'd seen him upset, and she'd seen him cry, but not like this. Nothing like this.

"Who is Moe? Do you mean 'more'?"

He didn't look at her or move except for his increasingly desperate sobs. She called Frank and was almost ready to give up by the fourth ring when he finally answered. "Hey, Sofia, what is it?"

"Can you come home now?" She hated how she sounded but had no choice. Frank would know what to do if he could see the situation for himself.

He didn't answer right away. Sofia was about to ask if he was there when he finally responded. "What's wrong?"

"I don't know. It's Sam."

She heard his sharp inhale. "Do we need to call nine-one-one?"

"No, nothing like that. He just said his first word, but he's crying and—"

"No way!" Frank paused. "So why's he crying?"

"That's what I can't figure out. He said, 'Moe,' but he won't tell me what that means." She sighed. "Or he can't. I don't know what's going on, but I need you here. Please." Frank was the rock in the family—great at calming her down and finding the best thing to do.

"I would, but I've got a pump going weird on me, the control circuits for an entire section are open, and—"

"Can you come home, please?" She didn't want to sound desperate, but they really needed him there.

"I have no idea what's going on except—"

"Me neither. Please just get in your truck and drive. Your son needs you." She paused. "And I need you. Something is not right."

He sighed. "Okay, I'll have Jason tag this pump and I'll be there in fifteen."

She hung up and turned back to her son.

Tears still gliding down his face, he looked at her with a sadness a five-year-old shouldn't be capable of.

She wiped his tears with her palm. "What do you need, Sam?"

He shook his head again. "Moe."

She'd always known in her heart that the speech pathologists and other experts were wrong. The ones who said he'd never speak. That if he was going to talk, he would have done so by now. She knew in her heart he'd speak eventually, and her hope rested on that day. Which was today. But now that it'd happened, she almost couldn't bear the fear and anxiety rising inside her. Not exactly the happy moment she'd imagined.

She heard Frank's City of Lake Oswego pickup truck pull up to the curb less than ten minutes later. He almost ran through the front door, then knelt by his son. "What's wrong, buddy?" he asked, frowning.

"Moe."

Frank glanced at his wife, who shook her head.

"I don't know what you're trying to say, Son, but I want to understand.

Can you tell me more?"

"Moe."

"What's he trying to say?" asked Frank.

"I have no idea."

They couldn't get to the bottom of the boy's sadness and grief. They'd once had a beagle puppy named Tracker that got hit by a car when he went off following the scent of who knows what. Someone had left the gate to the backyard open. They never figured out who, but the result was that the little beagle had died violently. All three kids were heartbroken, especially Sam. He grieved for what seemed like ages. The family took him to see other puppies in the following weeks, but when they'd ask if he wanted this one or that one, he'd just shake his head sadly. Eventually they stopped asking, as there did not appear to be any replacement for Tracker as far as Sam was concerned.

But she'd never seen anything like this.

"I know," suggested Sofia, "Let's call Nonna Eve. She knows him better than anyone."

"Good idea." Frank pulled out his phone and dialed her number. After a half-minute, he gave his wife an exasperated look. "She never picks up."

"Can you leave her a message?"

"That's exactly what I'm about—Hey, Mamma, call me when you get a chance, please. I think we need your help on this." Nonna Eve always knew what to do.

After more than an hour of trying to comfort Sam, they'd made no progress either in consoling him or in finding out what was wrong.

Lisa walked in the door, fuming. "Thanks for missing my game, Mom. You promised me you were—what's going on? Why is Dad home?" She looked from Frank to Sam to Sofia. "What happened to Sam?" Sam ran to his sister and gave her a bear hug. Lisa frowned and silently mouthed to her parents: "What happened?"

Frank and Sofia simply shook their heads. Jodie walked in a moment later with her cello and a reproachful look on her face. She, too, changed when she saw Sam. Sofia suddenly remembered that she was supposed to bring them home right after Lisa's game. She shook her head at Frank. "I'm such a bad mother."

"No, you're not," he said, putting his arm around her. "You're one of the best moms on the planet." He nodded at Sam, his arms still locked tightly around Lisa. "You saw an emergency, and you dealt with it. Sam needed your full, one hundred percent undivided attention, and that's what you gave him. The girls understand. Don't be so hard on yourself, because you're amazing." He nodded at Jodie. "How'd you two get home?"

"We got a ride from Mr. Riley."

"Who?"

"Mr. Riley, the orchestra teacher. He saw us waiting out front in the pickup zone."

"You could have called."

"Not when we don't have cell phones," said Lisa.

"Any adult you asked would have been happy to let you use theirs, I'm sure."

"Whatever."

Their son was inconsolable. He joined them for dinner, but he wouldn't touch his food. Everyone tried to cheer him up, but nothing worked. He'd cry, then stop for a while, then his eyes would fill with tears and he'd start again. Frank and Sofia had a short strategy talk about it after the meal, but they couldn't come up with any ideas or solutions. Just after 8 o'clock, Frank got a call from Beth, one of Nonna Eve's best friends.

"Do you have any idea where Moe is? She was supposed to meet us for bridge an hour ago and hasn't shown. That's not like her to just—"

"Who?" Frank's heart raced. "I'm sorry, *who* are you looking for?"

"Eve. We call her Moe. It's our little inside joke. You know, from *The Three Stooges*." She laughed. "I'm Curly, and—"

He almost dropped his phone. "*Sofia!*" he yelled.

"What happened?" she called out from the other room.

He speed-dialed Nonna Eve's number, but she didn't answer. "I'm running over to Mamma's."

"What's going on?" But he was already out the door and halfway across the lawn.

CHAPTER FOUR

Frank pulled up in front of his mother's darkened house, where her beloved red Subaru was parked in the driveway. They'd tried talking to her just last month about living in a retirement community, but she wouldn't hear of it. She loved her space. Besides, she was healthy, fit, and spunky. She'd had a checkup in the past two weeks. Everything was fine, the doctor said. Her exact words were, "You'll probably outlive us all." And Nonna Eve had been delighted to tell Frank and Sofia that. Just her style: sassy and defiant, with an attitude you'd never expect from a seventy-one-year-old. So they let the retirement community idea drop.

His heart beating wildly, Frank ran across her freshly mowed lawn, rang the doorbell, and without waiting, pounded on the door. No answer. He thought she might be out with a friend and just forgot about her bridge game.

He had the back door key in case of emergency, and he walked around the house to unlock it. "Mamma," he called as he came inside. "Mamma, where are you?" He turned on the living room lights, and there she sat in her favorite recliner, a *People* magazine open in her lap, chin resting on her chest.

"Mamma?" Walking across the room seemed to take forever, as if time had ground to a halt. He placed a shaking hand on her cold and stiff shoulder.

He called 9-1-1 and was surprised at how calm and matter-of-fact he sounded when they answered. The woman who took his call was all business, but she was apparently trained to be compassionate as well. "Police and an ambulance are on the way. Will you be okay until they get there?"

When he called Sofia, however, he found himself unable to speak.

"Frank, what is it? Is everything all right? Are you there?"

"Sofia, Mamma's dead."

After a few moments of silence, she finally spoke. "Oh, Frank, I'm so sorry."

"You know, I was afraid of this, but thought I was being irrational." He tried to steady his voice. "I just called nine-one-one."

"You wait right there. We'll be right over."

"I'm not so sure it would be such a good idea for the kids to see her like this, especially with the police and paramedics here."

"Is there any chance that she might be—"

"No, definitely not. She's—she's been gone for quite a while. At least a few hours."

"I'll get someone to watch the kids and be right over."

"Okay. See you soon."

Five days later, on their way home from the funeral service, the family rode quietly in their Chrysler minivan. The only sound was the windshield wipers clearing away the pouring rain. Sofia reached over and put her hand on Frank's arm. "Nonna Eve was such a wonderful soul."

"Yeah. She was pretty amazing." He took a deep breath and sighed. "She lived a good but far too short life." He paused. "Though if she had written her life as a script, it would have ended just that way: a quick heart attack, with no one around her bedside worrying and taking care of her for weeks or months."

Sofia nodded. "I know. She was always thinking of others." She closed her eyes. "That was such a beautiful service. I loved how you explained that Evelina meant 'giver of life' and was a role she fully embraced." They traveled in silence for another minute or two. "That is so true. She brought life wherever she went." She looked at the three sad faces of her young children in the back seat and felt a powerful wave of love. For them, for Nonna Eve, and for Frank.

"Sam?"

He looked at the back of her seat with sad eyes.

"How did you know?"

He turned and stared out the window at the houses, cars, and trees they passed. Finally, he simply shrugged.

Frank kept his eyes on the road and slowly shook his head.

SOFIA'S Journal. THIS IS PRIVATE. CLOSE IT NOW!

March 26, 2011

Missing Nonna Eve. The past three weeks felt like three years.

At times I envy Frank. He's so sure about everything. The Catholic church has all his answers. At least most of them. But I don't think it can tell him why God took Nonna Eve away. Was that kind and merciful?

I loved Nonna Eve, but Frank absolutely adored her. I hate to see him so sad.

My parents sent me a card. They didn't call. They sent me—not Frank, not our family—a sympathy card. Signed 'Mom and Dad,' as if it would mean more with those words in English. Of course in Madre's handwriting. Probably Papá didn't even know she sent it. Since he turned ninety, he tries even less to connect. It used to embarrass me that Madre was so much younger. Now I'm glad. He gets crabbier every year, and I don't know if I'll miss him when he's gone. Should I feel bad saying that?

How did Sam know about Nonna Eve? He felt profound grief before anyone else even knew she'd died.

Last week he made a drawing for Frank. It was a picture of Nonna Eve's house with her waving from the front porch. Very simple, yet it brought up so much emotion in me. Frank cried when Sam gave it to him. Sometimes our little boy seems so grown up it's scary.

Frank rubbed his jaw. Nothing had gone right all day. In the two months since they'd lost Nonna Eve, *so* much had not gone right. He and Sofia still had their ups and downs. It'd been more up than down lately, but their challenges had not evaporated. Kim had said it would take time and patience to work things out.

And now the new boss wanted to see him. Not his immediate supervisor. The big boss, Mr. Mathews, the one who oversaw all the hiring and firing. Rumor had it he was quick to do either, and he fulfilled that prophecy when he fired half the admin staff his first two weeks in the position. Frank wondered if he was next.

When he knocked on the opened door, a tall black man with salt-and-pepper hair and a neatly trimmed goatee stood up from his desk and smiled. "You must be Frank MacBride."

"Yes, sir."

"Jim Mathews, and don't call me *sir*." He motioned toward a small sofa and sat back down. "Close the door and have a seat." He muted the soft classical music coming from the speaker on his desk and picked up a clipboard. "Sorry to hear about your mom. I understand that was unexpected."

"It was." Frank paused. "Thank you."

"And that was around the time you tagged pump three to go offline."

"The same day, yes."

Mathews flipped to the next page on his clipboard. "You played ball for Portland State as a sophomore. Is that right?"

Frank nodded. "Wide receiver."

"And you turned down a full two-year scholarship so you could come work for us."

"I was kind of done with the whole college scene by that time, and I wanted to start my real life." Frank smiled. "My wife was due to graduate at the same time, which made it an easier decision. How about you—did you play?"

Mathews tapped a pencil on his desk. "Only in high school. Got some offers to play college ball, but it wasn't the direction I wanted to go. Something we seem to have in common."

"Right."

He looked at Frank over the top of his glasses. "Life is too short to do what we're not called to do, know what I mean?"

"Definitely."

"Anyway, I wanted to give you some time before we talked."

That was exactly what a kind person would say before firing someone. "I appreciate that." Frank tried to keep a neutral expression on his face. He liked working there, and he couldn't afford to start a new job search.

"Do you know how much it costs to take one of the main pumps offline?"

"Not exactly. Maybe eight or nine hundred dollars?"

"Close. About nine hundred and fifty dollars. That's including the tech analysis, but not a biopsy if required." Mathews tapped his pencil again. "As it was in this case."

"I noticed they had stripped it down."

"Correct. So what's your guess for the total cost of all the tech analysis, strip-down, and offline time?"

"I don't know, but I'm sure it was substantial."

"Substantial would be an understatement. Our total costs on that unit, including preventative repairs—based on *your* trouble tag—were over sixteen thousand dollars. That's a lot of money, MacBride."

"Yes sir, but sometimes I have to make what I feel is the best call in any particular—"

"I heard the nickname around the shop for you is the Pump Whisperer."

"I may have heard that now and again."

Mathews leaned back and clasped his hands behind his head. "And what do you suppose that twelve-hundred-horsepower motor-pump combo cost the city of Lake Oswego in the first place?"

"To be honest, sir, I don't really—"

"There we go with *sir* again." Mathews smiled thinly. "Okay, I'll tell you.

Each one of those high-efficiency pumps cost over ninety thousand dollars, plus installation, mounts, controls, shipping, and so on. That's well over a hundred and twenty thousand dollars per unit. If the pump goes down, parts of it are salvageable, but the cost would still be, at the minimum, somewhere between seventy and eighty thousand dollars." He raised an eyebrow at Frank. "You with me so far?"

Frank nodded.

"When you tagged that motor, we took it offline and tore it down. We found a little micro-arc in one of the windings that burned right through the temperature sensor. That would have kept it from shutting down and protecting itself when it overheated. Which was happening when you noticed something was off. Anyway …" He waved his hand in the air. "The bottom line is that you saved the life of that motor, and probably the pump itself. If it had frozen up with that volume of water going through it, I'm confident it would have damaged the impeller as well." He smiled again. "So you just saved us somewhere between eighty and a hundred thousand dollars. Maybe more."

Frank breathed a sigh of relief. "You could have started with that and worked backward."

Mathews' laugh was deep and warm. "I know, but what would have been the fun in that? At least we have a happy ending, right?"

"I guess."

"You guess right. But tell me something. How did you know the motor was failing?"

Frank shrugged. "I just knew."

"Jason says if there's something wrong with just about anything, you'll find it."

"Maybe."

"Maybe? What do you think I'm going to do about our little scenario?"

"I really wouldn't know, Mr. Mathews."

"Call me Jim." He walked around his desk and shook Frank's hand. "Effective this current pay period, I'm giving you a fifteen percent raise."

Frank's jaw dropped. Fifteen percent? Did he hear that right? "I don't know what to say."

Mathews laughed. "'Thanks' would be a good start."

"Of course, thank you *so* much. That's very generous."

Mathews tilted his head slightly. "It's a matter of paying you what you're worth. Good thing we don't base your salary primarily on your driving skills."

"Very good thing. But those benders weren't all my fault."

Mathews grinned. "Sure they weren't. Anyway, the raise is already yours."

"I can't tell you how much I appreciate that. My wife will be very happy."

"She better be damn near ecstatic." He walked over and opened the door. "Hope you're happy as well."

"Definitely."

"Good. By the way, this Thursday I need you to help Portland Municipal with their signal-control system on the MAX light rail. I'm loaning you out for the day. You know, good neighbor relations and all." He winked. "Besides, you can bet your booty they'll have something we'll want sometime soon. We may have all the talent, but they have the money and material resources."

"If you say so."

"Oh, I definitely say so."

Frank called his wife on the way home—hands-free, of course. "I've got some good news for you."

"That's great, because after the day I've had, I *really* need some good news."

"Why, what happened?"

"Many things. Jodie was upset because she didn't do as well as she thought she should have in orchestra. You know how she sets her bar so high. I'm sure she was much better than any of the other cellists—probably better than *any* of the kids in the orchestra. And Lisa had some bad experience with a boy."

Frank drew a sharp breath. "What do you mean? What kind of experience?"

"I couldn't really find out. I walked in the room as she said something to Jodie about some 'stupid boy,' but then because I'm within hearing range she clams right up. I tried to ask her, but she wouldn't tell me. You know how stubborn our kids are."

"Yep. I'm sure they get it from my side of the family."

"You know good and well they get it from both of us," she said.

"I do, but I wasn't going to say that out loud. How was Sam today?"

"He was the most challenging." She sighed. "It's been hard for him since Nonna Eve passed away. He's smart and learns so fast—but only when he wants to. Today, he was mostly inattentive and would just drift away mentally and sometimes literally walk away in the middle of what I was trying to teach him. And he had a few of his little silent temper outbursts. Nothing huge, but there were at least two or three times when he just got really mad—without any reason I could see. He hid twice. One time I couldn't find him for twenty minutes. And of course, when he doesn't look at me, it's hard. Especially when he tunes me out, like I'm not even there. I know I'm supposed to be okay with it, but some days I'm not up to the task."

"My sixth sense tells me this is probably not the best time to bring up—"

"If you're about to mention putting him in special needs school next year, then your sixth sense is right. You should listen to it."

"Got it."

"Anyway, I'm sure you didn't call to hear me whine. You said you had some good news. I'm *so* ready for that."

Frank pulled up to a stoplight a few blocks from home. "I'm only five minutes away. I'll tell you when I get there. Get the kids together, and I'll make an announcement."

"You sure you don't want to give me a hint? Maybe as insurance that I won't kill anyone before you arrive?"

"I love the way you're so funny under stress. I'll see you in a few minutes." He hung up and smiled. She's definitely going to like this.

The announcement didn't quite go as planned, however. Lisa and Jodie were both sullen and withdrawn. Sam paid no attention to anyone. The first words out of Sofia's mouth were, "That's great, but weren't you due for a raise anyway?"

Frank looked at his family and managed to smile. Some days were simply easier than others.

CHAPTER FIVE

Sofia apologized before Frank left for work the next day. She usually came back around and took responsibility when she'd been moody, and he was grateful for that. It wasn't like he was free from moods, either. Plus, she had Sam on her hands all the time and the girls before and after school. Like Nonna Eve used to say, "All's well that ends well."

He hummed and tightened the last two screws on the control box cover. The day had gone well. The MAX Light Rail people treated him like a celebrity of sorts. He'd just finished installing new fail-safe circuitry at Rockwood Station in Gresham and had completed all his assigned tasks for the day. They'd let him knock off nearly an hour early, though he'd still receive a full day's pay.

Good thing, since a light drizzle had started, and he would've had to stop for safety reasons anyway—finished or not. Working with high voltage while wet was not his idea of fun. It would have increased his level of stress, and of course his chances of dying. Thinking of Sofia and the kids was what usually reminded him to play it safe. Occasionally Jason or one of the other guys would tease him when he was particularly cautious, but Frank didn't care. He wanted to be around to see his kids grow up.

After packing up his tools, he waited for the next Portland–bound train, which would take him to the Lloyd Center so he could get his car and head home. He looked forward to seeing his family, and he had a significant case of what Sofia called "the warm and fuzzies" despite the cold drizzle.

A train going the opposite direction discharged its passengers. As it pulled away, what he saw on the platform across the tracks nearly stopped his heart: a man with a shaved head and mustache, wearing a brown leather bomber jacket. He seemed to be looking for something. Frank stared open-mouthed, and the hair on the back of his neck stood at attention. He hadn't seen Belgian Pete since Italy.

As Pete walked toward the exit, he glanced in Frank's direction and froze. Just then Frank's train pulled in, breaking the visual connection between them. With his pulse pounding in his ears, he grabbed his toolboxes, boarded the train as quickly as he could, and made his way to the front car. He sat in a forward-facing seat, trying to slow his breathing, and discreetly looked back over his shoulder. Belgian Pete—or someone who looked exactly like him—was nowhere in sight. Moments seemed to take hours before the doors closed, and the train began to pull away just as Pete stepped out onto the platform Frank had occupied less than fifteen seconds before.

With elevated levels of adrenaline still running through his veins, Frank checked his watch at least twenty times in five minutes. He was two stations away from the 99th Street Transit Center. He could change to the red line. That would still get him to Lloyd Center and make him harder to find. Just in case Belgian Pete had phoned ahead. He thought of the ruthless killer and shuddered. What are the odds? He desperately hoped that wasn't really him.

With a growing sense of dread, he watched houses and cars pass by. Maybe it was time to tell Sofia about Italy. He sighed. She'd be furious, and it would raise her anxiety level significantly. Better to get his family to safety first and tell her later.

Frank was adamant. They had to move to a safer place. Thieves had broken into their van twice in three months.

Sofia frowned. "So why is that such a big deal?"

"Because I want my family to be safe. Isn't that a good enough reason?"

"It depends. Apart from the safety issue you're suddenly bringing up, I thought you liked it here."

"I do. I have a great job, I like the people I work with, and I like Portland and Lake Oswego—I just don't think this area is safe enough. Too many dangers in the big city." He told her he wanted to take them south, almost to the California border, to a little town called Ashland. Supposedly more beautiful than Portland, and much safer.

She'd heard of it. Her half-sister Maria had visited there the previous summer. She'd loved the plays but hated seeing all the "ungrounded bohemian types," as she put it, who hung out everywhere within city limits.

"No way I'm moving to that hippie town," she said.

"But the schools there are great. The best in Oregon."

"So you say. And where's the proof of that?"

"Well, I would say SAT scores, teacher credentials, retention rates, percentage of students who go on to college—I would consider all that proof."

She shook her head. "I'm not moving to some dead-end stoner town. That's the last thing I want for our kids."

Frank frowned. "Do you hear yourself? You see all the negative influences here? You think there aren't hundreds of times more stoners here?"

"They're not all stoners. Plus, you just got a raise." She shook her head. "We're not moving."

"We need to think about it."

"I've thought about it. Besides, if we moved, I'd want to be closer to Madre."

"I thought you hated Sacramento."

"Not that close. Maybe the Bay Area or something."

"*Amore mio*—my electrician's license is for Oregon only. In California they don't pay nearly as much because there's no license required."

Sofia folded her arms across her chest. "Which brings us back to where we started this delightful conversation. I say we stay right here."

Frank struggled to keep his mind on work over the next few weeks. Sofia was dead set against moving—which she'd made abundantly clear. But they had to go. Staying in Portland would be too risky, in case that really had been Belgian Pete looking for him back in Gresham. His first order of business was to keep his family safe. If it was only his safety at stake, he might risk it. But as he'd learned from bitter experience, the Mob sometimes went above and beyond, either to set an example or to not leave witnesses. His only choice was to drag Sofia kicking and screaming out of the Portland area. They were due for a change, anyway. Wherever they ended up, she'd eventually adjust.

He looked at his phone for a long minute before he rang Klamath Falls Public Works. By the end of the day, he'd also called public works and utilities in Bend, Eugene, Roseburg, and Medford. He'd start with the private sector the next week if he didn't get any bites.

Kim smiled as Sofia sat on her couch. "I'm glad you could make it. It's fine that Frank couldn't get free from work. It's usually better anyway having a solo session with each of you between couples' sessions. Steve was totally good with you making the switch, and I'm honored that you both chose to work with me. From your email, it sounds like things are a bit up in the air for you and Frank."

"Well, they're a little better now, but a few weeks ago he suddenly announced that he wanted to move. Even though we're all happy here." She grimaced. "The worst part is that it didn't seem to matter to him what I thought."

"Would you like to tell me more about it?"

She explained Frank's proposal to move and how insistent he was, though he'd finally agreed to stay. As they talked more about it, Sofia offered that when she was sent away to Catholic boarding school, she'd lost all her friends. She wrote to them, but they all trailed off pretty fast in one of the more painful experiences of her life.

"Why were you sent away to school?"

Sofia shrugged. "Just something my parents thought would be good for me."

"Okay."

Sofia looked through the French doors at the overcast Portland sky. She could tell Kim didn't believe her, but she wasn't about to get into that part of the story.

"Have you been journaling?" Kim asked.

"Not really. I've only written a few times since I saw you last." She smiled with half her mouth. "I'm sorry."

Kim waved her off. "Don't worry about it. Look, just write whenever you feel like it. Was it good for you at all?"

"It was good. I don't know—I just got busy."

"Anything to do with things coming up that you weren't comfortable with?"

"Oh no, that wasn't it at all. I was just busy and then kind of forgot."

"Sure." Kim paused. "So getting back to the school thing."

"Okay."

"What was school like for you?"

"Oh, I don't know. Somewhere between awful and horrible."

"That bad, huh?"

"Worse."

"Want to tell me about it?"

Sofia paused. Her time in school, both public and private, wasn't something she liked to think about, much less discuss. And then there was Ben Franklin High and Carl. "Well ..."

"Only if you're ready."

Sofia stayed quiet for a long while, then sighed. "In secondary school in Barcelona, I had this perv teacher, Mr. Mateu."

Kim tapped her pen against her hand. "Did he ... do anything to you? Touch you in any way?"

"Not exactly, but he had this twisted thing he did. He'd asked this girl named Camila to stay after school. Mr. Mateu told her that her skirt was too short, and to make his point, he tugged on her hem. While supposedly scolding her, he shook it and eventually lifted her skirt enough to get a peek underneath. She told the principal, but nothing happened. Either he didn't believe her or didn't care."

"And how did that affect you?"

"All the girls were upset about it, but I got really worried when Mr. Mateu told me to stay after a month or so later."

Kim looked at her with concern. "What happened?"

"The same thing that happened to Camila."

"Did you tell the principal?"

"Of course. I was so mad. But he did nothing about it."

"That must have been hard for you. Did you tell your parents?"

Sofia swallowed. "No way was I going to tell them. I was afraid my father would go ballistic and that he might take it out on me."

"Had that happened before?"

"Oh, yeah. To my mom and me, at different times. He definitely liked to shoot the messenger."

"So nothing ever happened to this Mateu perv?"

"Well …" Sofia examined the ceiling.

"Whenever you're ready," prompted Kim.

She took a deep breath. "I waited a few days and went back to the principal, who told me I had an overactive imagination and that Mr. Mateu had been a respected teacher in the Barcelona school system since before I was born."

"What did you say to that?"

"Well, nothing more to the principal. But I was furious. That night I told my dad, who just looked at me and didn't say a word. At best I expected him to get mad at Mateu, and at worst, that he'd hit me. But nothing happened. He just stared at me."

"He would hit you?"

"Sometimes. Anyway, the very next morning there was a substitute teacher in Mr. Mateu's class. He told us our regular teacher was away on business and he would be taking over the lessons meanwhile."

"Sounds like your dad had some clout."

"That would be the understatement of the decade. We never saw Mateu again. A full-time replacement teacher took over two weeks later."

"I see. How did you feel about that?"

"Scared. I was already afraid of my father. But I also felt protected. Like no one could do me any harm. Or so I thought."

"What do you mean?"

Sofia turned red. "Oh, nothing. We live in a dangerous world, right?"

"You don't have to tell me if you don't want to."

"There's nothing to tell."

"There's no shame in saying things that happened to you as a child. Even if you think they were your fault."

"I told you everything." Everything I'm going to tell you, that is.

"Okay, that's fine." Kim smiled and stood. "I see Frank next month, and you both when?" She glanced at the calendar on her smartphone. "Looks like the last Tuesday in July." She didn't notice—or at least didn't mention—the tears brimming in Sofia's eyes.

CHAPTER SIX

On her way home, Sofia held the wheel tightly, wishing the trembling would go away. She'd told Kim more than she had wanted to.

She relived one particular incident from her past often. It could have been worse—at least she understood that intellectually. It all started innocently enough. Staying after school for soccer practice, she'd showered, changed, and wandered out to the far reaches of the playing field, passing time before the busses came to pick them up. The other girls were still in the locker room or waiting out front. Sofia, though, preferred to walk and daydream.

She jumped when she heard a voice call out "¡Hey, guapa!" *Hey, beautiful!* She saw three boys leering at her from the doorway of the field house, where they stored the off-season athletic equipment. She looked straight ahead and walked faster, but one of the boys grabbed her arm. "¿A dónde vas, guapa?" *Where are you going, beautiful?*

She tried to pull away, but the boy was too strong. Another boy grabbed her other arm. "¡Dejalo ir!" *Let me go!* she yelled. But they just laughed and pulled her inside the field house.

By luck, Pedro Rovira, the boys' soccer coach, happened to come by to get some equipment. Or maybe he'd seen them grab her. He yelled at the boys, who scattered in different directions. The coach was kind and asked if she was hurt. With tears in her eyes, she shook her head. He offered her a ride home but first told her to straighten up her blouse. She did the best she could, but it had a small tear and a button missing. As soon as she got in the house, she'd change it quickly before her parents noticed.

On the way home, she managed to stop crying. I have to get it together. Papá will be furious!

Pedro pulled in to their circular drive and stopped by the front door. As they got out of the car, she wished she'd asked him to let her out a block away. She thanked him and tried to think of a polite way to get him to leave without taking her to the front door, which suddenly opened.

Her mother frowned at them. "Hija, what are you doing?"

"Um, the coach gave me a ride home."

Coach Rovira gently took her arm and walked her to the door.

Her father appeared in the doorway as well. "What are you doing with my daughter?"

"I gave her a ride home."

"Why?"

"Well, some boys were rough with her after school, and—"

"What do you mean, *rough*?" Eduardo asked, eyeing the tear in her blouse.

Her mother put her hand to her mouth and gasped.

Rovira made a placating gesture. "Nothing to worry about. I arrived there in plenty of time to—"

"Plenty of time?" Eduardo looked at his daughter. "You'd better tell me this is not what I'm thinking."

"As I mentioned, I got there in time," said Mr. Rovira.

Her father's neck reddened first, then his face. The storm Sofia knew so well was coming, yet he sounded almost calm. "Thank you for intervening. Will these boys be punished?"

"If we can figure out who they are, of course." The coach didn't see the volcano under the surface. How could he know?

"Of course. Sofia, inside. Thank you, Mister … ?"

"Rovira. I'm the boys' soccer coach at Sofia's school."

"Good day to you, then." He opened the door wide for his daughter. The moment she walked past, he slammed it shut, her mother barely getting out of the way.

He put his reddened face inches from Sofia's. "You were standing out."

"Papá, I was not doing anything." She wanted to step back and put distance between them but knew better.

"You have to be normal."

"I am normal."

He slapped her hard enough to turn her head. "You are not." He pointed his finger in her face, almost touching her nose. "Your skirts are too short and your hair is too wild. We see the results. You attracted the attention of that teacher, Mateu, last month. You flirt with boys. Big surprise they come after you. Like a pack of lusty dogs chasing a bitch. Is that what you want? You want to be their bitch?"

"I don't flirt with them."

He slapped her again. "You don't talk back to me, do you understand? Now tell me, have you been violated?"

"Eduardo, please!"

He jabbed a finger in his wife's direction. "*Stay out of this, Isabel!*" he yelled. He turned his attention back to Sofia, her face now streaked with tears. "Well?"

"No. Mr. Rovira got there in time."

"*In time* again. I hear that a lot this hour. Go now to your room."

"But, Papá—"

He raised his hand again. "Do you want to test me?" She cringed, and he slowly let it down.

"No, Papá, I'm going."

Ten minutes later, he opened her door without knocking. "Get ready to go."

"Where am I going?"

"To see the doctor. I've made an appointment with Dr. Cardona, and he'll see you right away."

"I told you, Papá, they didn't hurt me. I'm fine."

"Then it will be a short visit. Your mother will drive you."

On the way, Sofia tried to talk her out of it. "Why are we doing this?"

"To make sure you are okay."

"I told you, Madre, I'm fine. Nothing happened."

"We just need to make sure." She paused. "It's your father's idea."

"You should be sure already. I told you." She sighed. "Podem parlar Català?" *Can we please speak Catalan?*

"No, your father forbids it."

"But he's not here, is he?"

"Hija! Mind your manners and respect your parents."

"You grew up speaking Catalan. *Your* parents spoke Catalan. You respect them, no?"

Her mother's hands tightened on the wheel, but she remained silent. Isabel was fifteen when she lost her parents in a car accident. Sofia knew she was causing her pain, but she didn't care.

"You should take my word for this," said Sofia.

"We do, hija, we just want to make sure."

Sofia huffed and looked out the window. "So you keep saying. And what if you found out the worst?" She faced her mother. "What would you do then— send me away like you did with Maria?"

"Your papá and I are just trying to do what's right," Isabel said, but her face betrayed a flash of anguish before returning to neutral.

Sofia looked back out her window, and they traveled in silence for several minutes. "You didn't answer the question," she said.

As soon as they returned home, Sofia immediately stomped up the stairs toward her room.

"Hija, come here," her father called.

She hesitated before complying, then came back down and stopped in the doorway of her father's study, where she glared at him.

Eduardo looked at his daughter haughtily. "You know we had to do this."

"I don't know that. I told you nothing happened. Mr. Rovira told you nothing happened." Tears again welled in her eyes.

He waved her comments off. "He's a loyalist liberal. He wouldn't know how to find his ass with both hands."

Her mom appeared beside her. "Is everything okay?"

"Of course. Dr. Cardona called when you left the office." He smiled thinly. "You see, hija, it all checks out. We know your story is true, and all is forgiven."

"Forgiven? There is nothing to forgive, Papá. Except maybe those boys. Yet I was the one punished."

"You put yourself in danger. You trusted loyalist liberals to protect you and look what happened."

"Papá—"

"We have a new plan for you. Santa Angelina in Manresa."

Sofia suddenly found it almost impossible to breathe. "Please, no! That's a super strict place. Maria hated it there."

"She did not! She got a very strong background for her university studies, which is why she's doing so well."

"She still hated it. I don't want to go there."

Her father looked at her sternly. "You will find that in life, there are many things you don't want to do, but you do because you have to." He made a wide, sweeping gesture. "You think I like living around all these loyalists? All these bleeding-heart liberals?" He shook his head. "Of course I don't. But I have to. They should have taken things further after the war, gotten rid of them all. But you, hija, we will get you away from these liberal influences. Santa Angelina is one of the best girls' schools in Spain. You will be safer and more protected— both from communist ideologies and from boys who have absolutely no understanding of respect."

"But, Papá, I am safe here. I will be more careful, I promise."

Her father nodded. "You *will* be more careful, wherever you go, wherever you are. This will help you remember, always. Santa Angelina is a good Catholic school. The best. You will get first-class training there."

Tears streamed down her cheeks. "Please, Papá, don't send me there."

He dismissed her with a wave of his hand. "No more argument. Your mother will take you up this weekend."

SOFIA'S Journal. THIS IS PRIVATE. CLOSE IT NOW! I mean it!

June 15, 2011

I haven't written here in three months. Where to begin? The session with Kim yesterday brought up a lot for me. Maybe too much. She thinks I have a hidden reason for not having Sam in public school. What hidden reason do I need? The boy doesn't talk.

When I tried to tell Frank about it, we had another argument about putting him in school. He doesn't understand how dangerous school can be. Not in the way it was for me, but still …

When I told him Sam wasn't going to public school, he asked, "If school is so dangerous, why'd you let our daughters go?" He doesn't understand that Sam is more vulnerable. I'd tell him about Ben Franklin and Barcelona, but then he'd probably say I was projecting my fears onto Sam. Then he brought up special needs programs again, as if they're some magical solution. We can't afford the private programs, and the ones run by the state—no way I'm putting Sam into those.

Kim got me to promise that I would write about anything I don't want to tell her about. Fine. I almost got gang-raped in high school. My father forced me to go to an old drunk doctor who checked to see if I'd lost my virginity. What a humiliating experience! And even with proof that nothing happened, Papá still shipped me off to that horrible Santa Angelina.

Okay, Kim, you happy? That is something I will never tell you. Or anyone. Do I feel better? Maybe just a tiny little bit. I don't know. Some days I think about telling Frank these things, but I don't know if he'd understand.

Speaking of secrets, some days I wonder if he's hiding something. I'd probably know if he was having an affair, but they say the wife is frequently the last to know.

I still have dreams that he leaves me. He still flirts, but only when he thinks I won't know. He doesn't understand how that just makes it worse.

Trying to read to Sam again today was a total failure. For a few minutes he seemed to be paying attention, but then he walked off and hid in the laundry room. I knew he was somewhere close, but what's the point in finding someone who doesn't want to be found? It's not just a game for him. I don't know what it is.

I don't think he saw me cry. Is there a reason he won't let Frank or me read to him?

I wish I had some answers.

Frank knocked on Jim Mathews' open door. His boss wasn't smiling this time. He looked up and frowned. "Have a seat, MacBride." He stared at Frank. "Guess who I got a call from today."

"No idea, Mr. Mathews."

"Ron Wyden."

"The congressman?"

"None other. Can you imagine what he wanted?

"No, sir."

"You. I got a congressman asking for you."

"What?"

"Yeah. Seems you had talked to some public works supervisor down in Eugene a couple of weeks ago. Ring a bell?"

"Um—"

"A very well-connected public works supervisor, whose cousin just happens to be mayor. Seems he looked you up, found out some things he liked, called his cousin, and asked him to move you there." He shook his head. "Which you apparently looked into right after I gave you what I thought was a very generous raise."

"It *was* very generous," said Frank. "But they called me out of the blue. All I told him was that I'd consider it. You know, to not be rude. I never said I was ready to move there."

"That's not the story I heard."

Frank leaned forward. "That's because they didn't want to come out and admit they were pirating other municipalities' people."

"Right. So you didn't mention to this public works supervisor you were looking for a safer place to live?"

Frank felt his cheeks grow warm. "Maybe I had a bit more of a discussion with him, just to get rid of him."

"Right." Mathews tossed the pencil he'd been holding onto his desk. "You know what they say: 'No good deed goes unpunished.' You could have said something to me, you know."

"I'm sorry. It's just that I've been feeling the Portland area isn't safe for my family."

"Isn't safe? Don't you live in Southeast? It's one of the safer urban places in the country."

"I know, but—"

"Look, save it. The congressman asked that I let you go, and he had me call the Eugene Public Works supervisor—some ambitious tool named Kingston. Eugene is going to match what we paid you pre-raise and pay moving expenses." He shrugged. "They said they'd give you the fifteen percent once you showed them what you're worth. Anyway, I still have Jason and Diego. Apparently they've got nobody worth beans. Their supervisor is a real stick-in-the mud far as I can tell, but that's what you get."

"I'm really sorry about this—"

"I would have rather heard it from you, that's all." He arranged some papers on his desk. "You may choose to ask yourself whether you really want to work for someone who disregarded your request to not call your current employer." He shrugged. "Who knows? Maybe it was intentional to mess up our working relationship in case you were just dipping your toe in the water." Mathews shook his head. "Anyway, give them a call and work out the final details. I expect at least two weeks from you, three if you can manage—but only if it won't mean another call from a politician."

CHAPTER SEVEN

Sofia didn't take the news well. "I can't believe you did that behind my back!"

"I was putting out feelers."

"We agreed that we were staying here."

He raised his palms in a helpless gesture. "I'm just trying to do what's best for our family."

"What's best for our family is staying right here."

"But—"

Sofia frowned. "Isn't this something we're supposed to work out together?"

"It is, but now my hands are tied."

"How is that? Just tell them no."

"It's not quite so simple."

"Sounds simple to me."

He shrugged. "Not really. I mean, Wyden asked Mathews to let me go, and now he's pissed at me. He offered me a generous raise, and my response was to look for other work."

"My goodness, when you say it like that, it sounds really bad," she said sarcastically.

"Sofia—"

"Frank, I don't want to move. This is not your decision to make. We decide together."

He shook his head. "Even if we didn't move, I'd have no choice but to look for another job."

"Why am I not jumping up and down with joy?"

"Look, I'm sorry, but I kind of lost my job."

"I think 'kind of' doesn't fit in that sentence." She frowned. "And you didn't exactly *lose* your job. More accurately, you threw it in the trash. Had you honored our agreement, we wouldn't be in this situation."

He rolled his eyes. She didn't understand, but he wasn't about to tell her the whole story. Not now. "Okay. I did the wrong thing. I should have told you about my continued search." Time to improvise. "But I only asked around." He paced the room. "I don't know why these people in Eugene took it further. It's a better job, anyway."

"In what way?"

"More potential for advancement, for one thing."

Sofia frowned. "Sorry, I'm confused. Did you not get an unexpected and significant raise less than two months ago, right here?"

"I did, but—"

"So they would pay you more than that in Eugene?"

"Not exactly."

"Here we go," she said.

"Hear me out. They would start me at the same rate as before I got the raise, pay all our moving expenses, and as soon as I'm in place and doing everything as promised, they'll bump it up fifteen percent. At least." He gestured upward. "And the sky's the limit."

"Right. You're saying you're going to take a fifteen-percent cut in pay until you prove yourself. Instead of staying here. And what if that pie-in-the-sky raise never happens?"

"It's virtually automatic."

"I love the word 'virtually.' It's the perfect loophole."

Frank exhaled audibly. "Well, at this point, our hand is forced. Everyone here in town in my line of work will know that Mathews let me go. They'll want to know why. The answer will not impress them. Eugene is our best option."

She shook her head in disgust.

"Besides, there are upsides to this," he said, "apart from the job itself."

She folded her arms across her chest. "Enlighten me."

"We'll be in a safer place, with less traffic and noise."

"Okay."

"And Paul Peterson works there."

"Yeah, but he and Janice live in Salem. And it's not like you hang out with him much, anyway."

"Just trying to come up with positives," said Frank.

She shook her head. "I would say you're stretching for positives. Really stretching."

Kim looked at Frank over the top of her glasses. "You don't particularly want to be here, do you?"

"Sure I do. Part of the deal I made with Sofia was that I'd see you on my own."

"Which is great, but not the same as wanting to be here."

He shrugged. She was right about that.

She nodded slightly. "Okay, then, let's dive in. Any nightmares lately?"

What the hell? "She told you about them?"

"We have a transparency agreement to talk about anything that comes up for either of you, remember? The nightmares scare her as well—she just doesn't show you that."

Frank nodded silently and stared out the French doors, his mind far away.

"We don't have to talk about that if you don't want."

He shook his head and turned back to her. "I don't want."

"Okay, then." Kim cleared her throat. "On a scale of one to ten, how committed to your intimate partnership are you?"

"Ten."

"On the same scale, how committed is Sofia?"

"Nine. Or eight."

"Why does she get a lower score?"

"I don't know." He focused on a pigeon strutting across the balcony. "Sometimes she's not very happy with me."

"And how do you know that?"

"Simple. She tells me."

"She directly says she's not happy with you?"

He looked out the window again. "Not like that." He paused. "She's always saying things like 'you need to do this better, you need to do that better.'"

"What kind of things?"

"Anything and everything. No matter what I do, there's always some way it could be better. Or should be better. If I mention work, I should ask for a raise. They don't pay me enough. Or at home, I don't spend enough time with the kids or with her."

"What about your love life?"

"That's one area I think she's never complained about." Frank smiled. "If there's one thing I know, it's how to make a woman happy in the bedroom. But if she didn't like anything in that area, she would tell me." He shook his head. "Probably every single day."

"Do you feel criticized?"

"Sometimes. Some days I can't do anything right. And even if I do something right … For example, I worked very hard on my first drone project. It's a quadcopter I built from scratch with spare parts. Things we threw out at work, and that kind of stuff. If you bought it, it'd cost hundreds of dollars. But I built it," he said as he snapped his fingers, "with mostly recycled parts. And a few things I bought. So, this takes me months. Because I work full-time. I'm a family man. I'm a husband. I do all these things and I've only got a little time for hobbies. After working on this about five months, I get it going and take the family out for the maiden voyage." He nodded. "I take it up, and it flies magnificently. The kids are literally jumping up and down, chasing it back and forth, and everybody's happy. Sofia, though, she's just watching and frowning. I land it and say, 'So, what do you think?'" He looked at her with a pained expression. "You know what she said?"

Kim shook her head. "No idea."

"She said 'How much did that cost?'" He raised both hands in a frustrated *I-give-up* gesture. "I mean, later, she said she was proud of me for making such a wonderful thing, but that wasn't her first response, if you get what I mean."

"I do." She shifted in her chair. "So tell me, Frank, what do you know about—"

"Every time I share an idea with her, it's always cold water first. Splash! Always what's wrong with it. Always the way it won't work. If I ask her, 'So you think that was a stupid idea?' she'll say something like, 'Oh, no, that's a brilliant idea.' If I ask why she couldn't say that first, she just shrugs and says, 'I'm just trying to help.'"

"I see. I can understand why that might be difficult for you."

"*Difficult* is not quite the right word. I think a more accurate word would be …"

"Painful?"

"Yes, exactly that. Painful. I talked to her about moving. I want her and the children to be in a safer place. Does she appreciate that I care? That I want them to be safe? No!"

"It sounds to me like you need to talk about the move with her more."

Frank shook his head. "No way!"

"Why not?"

"Because we're definitely moving, and she's not happy about it. I'm not bringing *that* subject up again unless I have to."

"I see." She nodded and paused. "So, what do you know about her childhood?"

"Well, her father—Eduardo—cheated on her mother. Pretty often, the way Sofia tells it. They had plenty of money, but I don't think they shared much love and warmth. He's older than Sofia's mother by something like thirty years. Maybe more. His first wife died a year after they married, leaving him a new baby to care for—Sofia's half-sister Maria. He remarried almost immediately. They eventually sent both girls away to Catholic boarding school, which they hated. Not that Eduardo cared. He's always been grouchy, and the older he gets, the meaner he gets."

"Anything else?"

"The sisters have a funny relationship. They adore each other, but neither of them would ever say it. They argue about anything and everything, but in truth they're inseparable. When Sofia was pregnant with Jodie, Maria moved to Portland from LA. She's a forensic accountant and can work from wherever she wants. She said she moved there for business, and she conveniently found a place a few blocks away from ours. She helped her sister a lot then, and still does. Plus, she's very close with our kids, who love her." Frank smiled. "They call her Auntie M—you know, from *The Wizard of Oz*."

Kim nodded. "Sounds like she's a positive force in your family's world."

"She is."

"And when you move, that's something they'll lose. Or at least have far less of."

"I'm not so sure about that. Sofia told me she called her sister the other day to talk about moving, and Maria hinted that she might prefer Eugene herself. In an offhand way, of course."

Kim made a note on her pad. "But she didn't say she'd actually move there."

"No, but that's how she rolls. She'll hint at something, but not come out and express it directly. Especially if it's affectionate or loving. She'd rather have a root canal than say something like, 'Oh, I would miss you so much. Maybe I'll move to Eugene as well, so I can be near you and the kids.'"

Kim thought for a few moments. "From everything I've heard from Sofia, it sounds like they were there for each other growing up."

"I think so, mainly Maria being there for Sofia. She's at least eight years or so older. Maria was sent away when Sofia was something like eight or nine, and they didn't see much of each other after that point. I know Sofia wasn't so happy in Barcelona, and she had a hard time socially. Her father was a huge fan of Franco, even though they lived in a region not very favorable toward that brutal fascist. I think that made Eduardo a little paranoid. I also have a sense he physically abused her."

"Why do you say that?"

"At times she suddenly stops talking if we're having a conversation about her childhood, especially about her home." He smiled thinly. "Sometimes you can tell a lot by what people don't say."

"Tell me about it." She rolled her eyes. "You think she had it pretty rough?"

He nodded. "Definitely. And I don't even think the physical abuse was the worst part. From what she says, she suffered a lot of emotional abuse as well. For example, even though they lived around people who spoke mostly Catalan, he forbade Sofia or her mother to ever speak that language. They could only speak Spanish around him. In the schools, everyone spoke Catalan and learned Spanish as a second language. It must have been weird for her."

"What else do you know about Sofia's relationship with her father?"

"I don't get the sense he was sexually abusive, but how would I know since she hasn't even told me about the physical abuse? I know he was an absolute dictator in his home. He ruled his family the way Franco ruled his country.

"Sofia told me he was always getting into somebody else's pants. I think his wife tolerated all his affairs out of fear of him."

"You mentioned in our first session that he's critical."

"Saying he is critical is like saying the Pacific Ocean has some water in it. Eduardo is one of the most critical people I've ever met." He shrugged again. "When he heard I was Catholic, he was happy she was marrying me, but when he heard I was Italian, that changed everything. He's very racist. I can do nothing right in his eyes. Nothing."

"What about her Catholic boarding school?"

"All I know for sure is that they were pretty mean. A bunch of sexually frustrated nuns, to hear her describe it. Taking out their frustrations on young girls, rigidly adhering to rules that didn't all make sense."

"Would you say it was a pretty critical environment?"

"I would say it was an *extremely* critical environment."

Kim closed her eyes for a moment and took a deep breath. "What if that was her experience of love as a child?"

"I wouldn't call it love. I would call that control. Both in her home and in that stupid isolated and restrictive school."

"But that's the problem. People have different ways of expressing love, and some express it in ways that don't seem like love at all. A person may be hypercritical of her partner because she feels it's the best gift she can give to help them be a better person. Same would go for her child or student."

"I don't think there was much love in that school. Those nuns were cold people."

"You may be right about that. But what if their motivation was love for and dedication to God? Maybe they felt what they gave to Sofia was an extension of that love?"

"Then I would say that's a pretty twisted concept. I think you show love for God by showing love for others, not by hitting the bare thighs of young girls with rulers."

She nodded. "I agree with you. But not everyone has the same understanding." She paused. "What I'm getting at is when she's critical, it's her way of saying, 'I love you.'"

Frank scratched his head. "That would be a bit of a stretch."

"Sure it is." She leaned forward in her chair, elbows resting on her knees. "I'd like you to do something for me during the next month."

"What's that?"

"Every time you feel criticized by Sofia, I want you to say to yourself, 'She's saying she loves me.' Can you do that for me?"

"I can try."

"Don't try. Do it. Then see what happens. Maybe in a month you'll tell me I was crazy, and that it didn't work at all." She glanced at the clock and stood up. "And who knows? That scenario might just change. My belief is that it will. Just give it time, patience, commitment, and a bit of work." She smiled warmly. "Thanks for coming in today, Frank. We made progress."

"If you say so."

CHAPTER EIGHT

SOFIA'S Journal. THIS IS PRIVATE. CLOSE IT NOW!

July 22, 2011

I'm upset. Wait, let me rephrase that: I'm so fucking pissed off I could scream. I didn't want this move, and I certainly did not ask for it. The last time I journaled, I didn't even know we were going to move, but here we are in a new town with no friends, no connections, no family. Maria said she was going to look into moving here, but who knows if that will work out. I'm not holding my breath.

Frank started his new job at the beginning of the week. He doesn't think he's going to like his new boss, from what he's seen so far. Yet he loved his old boss. The guy was great, he gave him a huge raise, Frank respected him, and he liked the work there. And we both loved Southeast Portland! So of course we had to leave!!!

The move was so much harder than I expected. Why is it always like that? Even when you think a move is going to be hard, it always turns out to be even harder.

If Nonna Eve was here, I know exactly what she'd say.

"What's the silver lining in that?" Maybe if I just stare at the clouds long and hard enough, a silver lining will magically appear. I'm not holding my breath for that, either.

Frank is annoyingly upbeat, mainly because he's trying WAY too hard to be positive. The kids seem okay. Jodie is a little mopey, but apparently the new school where she'll start next month has a good music program and a really good orchestra director.

Finding a house was simple. The rental market here is much easier than Portland for sure. I wonder why? Oh, I know! Because no one wants to live here. We have a lease with an option to buy, which I hope we never need because I WANT TO MOVE BACK TO PORTLAND.

Taking a lot of deep breaths and reminding myself everything is going to work out. Eventually. I just have to make sure I don't kill anyone before that happens.

"I got your memo, Mr. Kingston."

Jeff Kingston looked up from his desk and motioned Frank into his office. "Have a seat. And what's with this *Mr. Kingston*? You can just call me *sir*." He gave Frank half a smile. "Just kidding. People around here call me Jeff."

Frank nodded. That's not all they call you.

"So how was your first week?" Kingston asked.

"Not too bad. I'm learning the ropes. Everything's on a much bigger scale than Lake Oswego." He shrugged. "But I'll be fine." He glanced at the gigantic moose head on the wall to his right. Weird.

"What was it like working in Lake No Negro?"

"Excuse me?"

"Don't tell me you don't know Lake Oswego's nickname? Not too long ago, the city charter barred blacks, Jews, and other minorities from living there. And I think blacks only make up something like half a percent of the population there now."

"I really wouldn't know. My old boss there is black," said Frank.

"So I heard. They are probably trying to change their image. Affirmative action and all that crap."

"I'm sure Mr. Mathews was the best man for the job and they hired him on the basis of his qualifications."

"Relax. I just wanted to make sure you know we're open to everyone down here."

Frank frowned. What's that supposed to mean? That he doesn't hold being Italian against me? "Sure."

"If you haven't figured it out already, I run a tight ship around here," Kingston continued. "I expect punctuality, honesty, hard work, and subservience. Ha! Kidding again. Everything but the subservience is real, though. I also insist upon write-ups, which is no joke. Most importantly, I expect that my instructions are followed to the letter. Do I make myself clear?"

"Absolutely."

"You can see what happened to the last employee who didn't follow instructions." Kingston grinned and gestured at the moose head.

Frank forced himself to smile. The man was definitely humor-impaired.

Kingston leaned forward. "I'm going to tell you this because you'll hear it anyway. The mayor of Eugene is my cousin, Dave Kerby." He tapped his finger on his desk. "Which was how I pulled strings to get you here, as you already know. Our great-great-grandfather was Simon Kerby, who helped draft the original city charter. He made a trust that anyone in our family's direct line gets a slice of after working in a 'leadership capacity' for the city, as he put it, for at least seven consecutive years. Besides Cousin Dave, we have a lot of family working for the city, and we all embrace family values." He leveled a stare at Frank. "Long story short is that I always get what I want. Always."

Frank had a picture in his mind of how things would go in their new town. He'd have a new and more exciting job with interesting challenges and problems to solve. The girls would be happy with their new school, and Sofia would have made new friends. They'd all have made new friends.

Yet six months later, none of that had materialized. The girls weren't happy with their school, Sofia hadn't made any new friends as far as he could tell, and she obviously missed her sister. She wasn't even close to happy. Work was okay, but there was a lot more red tape to cut through, and his new boss was annoyingly obsessed with procedure. Frank still hadn't received his promised fifteen-percent increase, even though he'd definitely proved himself. There had been a little fender-bender with the company truck, but that could have happened to anyone.

It seemed that something came up almost weekly with at least one of the kids. Once it was Jodie complaining that one of the trombone players didn't like her because he always teased her. Sofia had tried explaining that probably meant he *did* like her, but her daughter didn't buy it. Another week, Lisa was convinced her math teacher had it in for her, which she said had nothing to do with the fact that she hated math. One day, Sam apparently decided he wouldn't eat meat or fish ever again. He simply refused. Frank had tried playing tough with him, which seemed like a good idea at the time. He would occasionally give him nothing else, but for those meals Sam would fast, leaving the table with nothing in his belly. After three episodes of that within a two-week period, Sofia put a stop to it. "That's enough," she'd said. "He wants to be a vegetarian, and we're going to let him."

Not long after, Lisa announced that she also had decided to be a vegetarian.

"Are you sure, Leese?" Frank had asked her. "For an athlete in training, you really need to monitor your protein intake."

"Dad, I'll be fine. That's just a myth that you need all that protein. Most people get far more than they need. Besides, plant protein is higher quality than animal protein anyway."

"Who's been talking to you about that nonsense?"

Lisa shrugged. Frank frowned at Sofia, who gave him a "Don't look at me!" face.

The running bug had bitten Lisa the year before, just two months after her tenth birthday. She loved to run and was the fastest player on her soccer team by a good margin. She'd run daily after school, and when she could talk her dad into it, they'd run together. Sam always wanted to go with them, but they told him he was too young. After all, six-year-olds didn't normally go out running. One day, three months before Sam's seventh birthday, Lisa asked Frank if her brother could run with her.

He considered it. "I guess so, but be very careful. Make sure you hold hands before crossing any streets, and stay in the neighborhood. And whatever you do—"

She rolled her eyes. "I know, Dad … don't talk to any strangers or get near their cars."

A few months earlier, Jodie and Lisa had been walking to a nearby park when a man in a dark blue Cadillac pulled up and offered them a ride. He knew their names and said he lived across the street and down a bit, but the girls had never seen him. So they declined. When they told their dad, he took Lisa and rang doorbells up and down the street, asking if anyone nearby drove a Cadillac. They only got one positive response, and it was for a pale pink Mary Kay Cadillac. Neither did they come across the man they'd seen or figure out how he'd learned the girls' names. Frank filed a report with the police, but as far as he knew, the man was never located.

"Better safe than sorry," Sofia told their girls. "You made the right decision." She didn't mention that nothing like that had happened in Portland, but Frank knew she had to be thinking it. They went through all the trouble and anxiety of moving to Eugene mainly to be safer. But were they? He'd been beside himself with worry. What if something terrible happened to their kids? He didn't see how he could live with himself. It took him hours to get to sleep that night.

When Lisa took Sam out for their first run together, they were only supposed to be gone for ten minutes, but they stayed out more than twenty.

Frank smiled at the sight of his two happy kids, both breathing heavily. Lisa was beside herself. "You wouldn't believe how fast he is! I mean, there's no way he can keep up with me, but I thought I would have to be practically walking.

Sam is superfast for his age. Plus, he's got great stamina for a little kid."

Sam glared at his sister. He didn't like being called 'little'. He was slight, not as heavy as most boys his age, and not as tall, either.

From then on, every time Lisa would leave to run near the house, Sam stood by the front door, ready to go. At first she'd say, "No, sorry, you can't keep up with me." But he persisted, asking in his silent, endearing way, brown eyes pleading his case. Eventually, she began saying yes.

Soon she did her fast running at the school and slower workouts near the house with her brother. She came up with a system where she would run ahead two hundred yards or so, then jog in place while Sam caught up. It never took long. His speed and endurance impressed Lisa—and she was not easily impressed by anyone or anything.

CHAPTER NINE

Except for an occasional sigh, the gentle sound of light rain hitting the roof, and the hiss of tires on wet pavement through downtown Eugene, the inside of the car was fairly quiet.

Lisa stared out the passenger window at the rain and groaned. She was sick and tired of all the doctors, testers, and specialists. They never once did anything that could make a difference, except to stress everyone out, especially Mom. "What's this place we're going to?" asked Lisa.

"Pacific Assessments."

"Didn't we already go there, like, a year ago, when we first got here?"

Her mom's grip on the steering wheel tightened. "We did, but this time it's for a different set of tests. We need to find out why Sam isn't reading."

"I can tell you that," said Lisa. "It's because he's only six."

"He's almost seven, and he understands things way more than most kids his age. He's just not reading."

"Whatever. I don't see why Jodie and I can't just stay home. I'm sick of going through these tests. They always say the same thing. 'Oh, what a bright little boy you have. He's so intelligent, so creative, and he really *cares* about other people.' If I hear that one more time, I'm going to barf. I guarantee you today they'll tell you he'll be reading soon. 'Don't worry. Just bring him in again next month and have your credit card ready.'"

Sofia took her eyes off the road long enough to give her younger daughter a quick glare. "Look, I couldn't get a sitter, and—"

"Who says we need a sitter? Come on! Jodie's almost thirteen. That's old enough to babysit. Besides, we're not babies, and we don't need someone to—"

Sofia slapped her hand on the dash. "Lisa! I'm tired of your whining. You think I enjoy all these tests? You think Sam likes them? None of us do, but we have to go, don't we? Believe me, I don't want you to have to come with us any more than you want to be here. Maybe less so. But sometimes I have to make the call. That's what parents do. Understand?"

"I wish I didn't understand," Lisa said quietly.

"What was that? I couldn't hear what you mumbled."

"Nothing!"

In the back seat, Jodie gave Sam a little smile and shook her head. Her brother just frowned.

By the time Sam's testing was complete, they'd been at Pacific Assessments over an hour and a half, and were all pretty cranky when they got in the car.

"Listen, kids, I'm going to drop you off at Hendricks Park."

Lisa folded her arms across her chest. No one ever asked her what she wanted. "If it's all the same to you, I'd just like to go home now."

"Well, if it's all the same to *you*, I'd rather you stay with your brother and sister so you can keep an eye on each other."

"It's going to rain again any minute."

"We don't know that. If it rains, I'll come pick you up. That's why we got you a cell phone. You won't die if you get a little wet. It's been well over eighty all day, so it's not like you'll catch cold. Otherwise, I'll come get you at six. We all need a little fresh air and separation. Just make sure you three stick together." Sofia took a deep breath. "Right now, I need some alone time. I don't have to look into my crystal ball to tell you that's exactly what I'll get."

Lisa knew better than to argue with their mom when she got in that kind of mood. As they got out of the car, Sofia told them to be careful, and she'd see them at six.

Lisa looked at her watch and sighed. That gave them over an hour to kill.

She could see that Jodie wasn't happy about being at the park, either. She would probably rather be practicing her precious cello. Sam was the only one who didn't seem to mind. He loved being with them, and that wasn't so bad.

They were all on the swings, the girls complaining about grown-ups in general, when Jodie noticed Phil Hollinger coming their way. "Neanderthal at two o'clock," she said, nodding in his direction. They all gave him their full attention. Word around school was that Phil had been held back early on, as he was a year older than the other eighth graders. Not liked by the other kids in school, he seemed determined to make life difficult for everyone. A few days back, he'd knocked a stack of books out of Bruce Keenan's arms, just to be mean.

Lisa stopped swinging and got Sam to stop as Phil walked toward them. Lisa took her brother's hand and walked in the opposite direction. They hadn't gone more than thirty feet when Phil started in. "Hey, cutie, where you going with the retard?"

Lisa turned around, her face flushed. "He's not a retard. He's twice as smart as you."

Phil laughed. "Yeah, I don't think so. You're both stupid, but he's not even smart enough to talk." He walked faster. "Hey, don't go so fast. I just want to play some retard games with you and Rain Man."

Jodie jumped off her swing and walked purposefully toward Phil. "You just shut up."

"Well, what if I don't?" He took a step toward Jodie. "You gonna beat me up, geek girl?" He smirked at her. "Didn't think so. I always wondered what's it like to live with someone too stupid to talk. We should get to know each other so I can get an idea of—"

Jodie slapped him. He was trying to laugh it off when she punched him in the eye.

"You little bitch!" He reached for her, committed to the fight. But Jodie pulled his hair and twisted hard. "Ouch!"

Phil hit back, but Jodie had caught him off guard. Lisa and Sam watched, open-mouthed, too far away to help. They'd never seen their sister fight anyone in her life, boy or girl. Phil was also surprised, but not for long. In obvious pain, he pulled back his fist to punch her, now in full fighting mode. Lisa watched as if it all happened in slow motion. She ran toward them, Sam right on her heels, knowing they'd never get there in time.

Jodie told them all later that she'd remembered something she saw in the movies when she kneed him between the legs as hard as she could.

He crumpled to the ground. Lisa couldn't believe her eyes as her sweet older sister who never got mad at anyone kicked him hard in the ribs.

"Ow! Stop it!"

Lisa and Sam looked at each other with total disbelief. Jodie had taken a few hits—and she would surely have bruises to show for it later. At the moment, however, she looked pretty good.

Other kids in the park had run over to watch, and a small crowd had gathered. Phil groaned, sat up, and glared at the three MacBrides standing together. "I'm going to get all three of you."

Jodie looked at him defiantly. "You sure you want to try that?"

"You people are crazy!"

She put her hands on her hips. "We people don't like bullies who bother people. You stay away from my brother." She narrowed her eyes. "And my sister." She nodded to her surprised siblings. "Let's go, guys."

As they reached the entrance to the park, Lisa turned around to see Phil looking at them sulkily. "I think you made him mad, Jodie."

She nodded. "Yep, I think I did."

"Don't you think he's going to come after you in school?"

"Not really." She looked meaningfully at her younger sibs. "One thing Nonna Eve used to say is that you need to stand up to a bully or they'll never leave you alone. You might get a black eye once, but they'll never bother you again. Bullies mainly go after people who are weak and let them get away with being bullies. I don't think Phil got away with anything today."

Lisa smiled. "He sure as hell didn't. He's the one with the black eye. Still, let's call Mom to pick us up early just in case he gets a second wind. If you tell her there are bullies—"

"No! Don't tell Mom or Dad anything about this, okay? They wouldn't understand." Jodie was scuffed up but didn't have any bruises on her face. She might just get away with keeping it secret from their parents.

"Hey, you're the hero of the hour, so whatever you say goes." Lisa checked her watch and grinned. "And you've still got another forty-seven minutes before your hour expires, so enjoy it while you can."

"That's my little sis." She gestured at Lisa's phone. "Just tell Mom we're all tired and can she please come pick us up. That'll work."

Sofia arrived ten minutes later, much calmer than when they'd seen her last, and almost apologetic. On the way home, Lisa gave her sister a knowing smile. Jodie's secret would be safe.

But they underestimated the power of social media. Someone had videoed part of the fight and posted it on Facebook.

Tami, the mom of one of the girls on Lisa's soccer team, saw the post. Phil had punched her son Ricky earlier that spring, but he wouldn't go to the principal about it. For Tami, this was better justice. By dinnertime that evening, Sofia had received two more calls from grateful parents. She had also been amazed by the video. That was her calm, cool, and collected Jodie sticking up for her brother.

She texted Frank at work and told him he had to watch the fourteen-second video clip before he came home. When he arrived, he sat down with the rest of the family.

"What happened out there, Jodie?"

The three siblings glanced at each other.

Jodie swallowed. "Well. This mean boy named Phil was teasing Sam, and I made him stop."

"Teasing him? How?"

"Well, he called Sam retarded. Right in front of him." She glanced at Lisa. "And us."

"So you hit him?"

"Well, kind of. I mean, yes."

"And was that the right thing to do?"

She shrugged. "I don't know. Maybe not. But I'm glad I did. He had no right to tease Sam."

"No, he shouldn't have done that." Frank cleared his throat. "You know, violence doesn't always help things. Sometimes it makes them far worse. What if you'd broken your hand? You wouldn't be playing cello for a long while if that'd happened."

"I know, Dad." She examined her feet. "Am I grounded?"

"Grounded? No, that would be punishment. We should reward you for sticking up for your brother and giving that bully what he deserved. My official line as a parent is that violence should be used only as a last resort, but off the record, I can't tell you how proud I am of you."

All three kids beamed.

"… and so is Mom. Just don't make it a habit. I think you learned a big lesson today, princess."

She looked at him curiously. "What's that?"

"You may not be bigger than someone, but you can always win if you know where their balls are."

Sofia giggled. "Frank! That's no way to talk to the kids."

The air conditioning had gone out for the second time in a month. They'd talked to the landlord about it, but nothing had happened apart from a quick, temporary fix. Sofia rolled onto her side and faced her husband.

"Are you awake?"

"Mmph." Frank sighed. "I am now. What's up?"

"I'm hot."

"I know. But there's not much I can do about it tonight. We'll get portable fans tomorrow."

"Do you think Jodie's obsessed with her music?"

"Somewhat."

"Does that concern you?" asked Sofia.

"Not at all. Getting enough sleep concerns me. I have to replace a transformer disconnect tomorrow, and I'll be working twenty-seven feet off a concrete floor."

"Hey, sorry I woke you, but don't get all grumpy on me."

"Okay, how's this? Do I sound less grumpy now? Should I apologize for being woken up?"

"Please. This is important."

He rolled over to face her. "Okay. What was the question again?"

"The question is whether our daughter being obsessed with her music is a problem."

Frank rubbed his face with both hands and yawned. "No, not really."

"Not really? If she misses one day of practice, she thinks something has gone seriously wrong."

"While I agree that she's a little obsessed, I also know that every single person who's ever been genuinely successful in their area of expertise has been a little obsessive. I mean, look at her hero, Yo Yo Ma. From everything I've heard, he's been obsessive about playing his cello since he was nine. She's not close to that level of obsession, and even if she was, I'm not sure that would be all bad."

"Yeah, but with some people, obsessive behavior takes over their life. Like Howard Hughes. They say he was utterly obsessive-compulsive," said Sofia.

"I don't think that's the case with Jodie. She's not what I would consider obsessive-compulsive. Howard Hughes was socially dysfunctional. Or non-functional. Whatever they call it. Yo Yo is a better example. He's pretty balanced in his social interactions. He lets obsessiveness work for him, not against him. I think people like that are able to cross the line between a normal life and an extraordinary one." She couldn't see clearly in the minimal light from the clock but thought she heard a smile in his voice. "If there's one thing we're learning as parents of this crew, it's that our kids will be extraordinary, no matter what anyone does." He rolled back over. "I'd love to talk more, but I have to get my rest for tomorrow. I know you'd feel bad if I fell twenty-seven feet to a concrete floor or became a crispy critter. Or both."

She gave his shoulder a squeeze. "Being a bit dramatic, are we? You'll be fine." She sighed. "Sorry, you know how I worry."

"I sure do. Good night, beautiful."

"You know, Sam sat outside her door again."

"Huh?"

"When she practiced today. He sat in the hallway with his eyes closed."

"Okay. Not sure why this can't wait until morning."

"It can wait. I just wanted to tell you. It's so sweet, really." She sighed. "It's touching that Sam loves listening to Jodie, even when she's only doing exercises."

"It *is* sweet. Very sweet. Now good night."

CHAPTER TEN

Frank had been dreading the office holiday party and the related stress. Not that he hated parties—quite the opposite, actually. He liked them, and he liked most of the people he worked with. But Kingston would be there.

"We definitely need to do this, right?"

Sofia leaned into the mirror as she applied her eyeliner. "You'll be fine. Remember how you enjoyed yourself last year?"

"Well, yes. But Kingston and I have been kind of going downhill since then. He's such a prick."

"He certainly is. But you're a bigger man than he is." She fixed a steady gaze at him. "Plus, Maria's babysitting the kids, and you've promised to take me out. Not only that," she said, brushing on mascara, "I've got half my makeup on, so you're not weaseling out of this."

"I guess I can just stand on the other side of the room from him."

"You most certainly can." She turned back toward him. "You interact with him on a daily basis, right?"

"Yeah, well, I *see* him every day. When I get there and when I punch out. If you want to call that interacting."

"You know, if you feel that strongly about him, maybe you should actively look for other work. As your beloved and committed wife, it's my highly objective opinion that you'll never be happy working for somebody who's an absolute jerk. What did you tell me he said to you last Monday? In front of all your coworkers, how you disappointed him?" She raised her eyebrows. *"After you saved the day by replacing that bad motor doing an emergency shift on the weekend."*

"Yeah, well, I think he was having a bad day."

"Seems his *life* is a bad day, if you ask me." She frowned. "Why are you defending him?" She turned back to the mirror. "Didn't you just say he was a prick?"

"Believe me, I would much rather work for almost anyone else, but there aren't many opportunities in town, and this pays well—"

"It pays okay. It does *not* pay well."

Frank hated getting into this loop. "Sofia, look, I know it's a tough situation. We spend so much on help for Sam and—"

"I thought we agreed we *had* to do that. Has there been a change in plans I don't know about?"

"No. Of course we're going to give him everything we can. I know it has to happen, but it raises our overhead significantly."

"And if you had a job that paid decent money, we wouldn't have a problem with that overhead, would we?" asked Sofia.

Frank folded his arms across his chest. This is her saying she loves me, at least according to Kim. Sure didn't feel like it. "I'm open to any specific constructive suggestions you may have," he said, "but for now I *have* a job that pays a decent salary."

"That pays enough for us to just *barely* get by."

"And around we go. I need not remind you that our original plan was for us both to work," he said.

"No, you certainly don't. I remind myself of that often enough. Pretty much daily. But right now the kids need me, and Sam … well, he's going to need me for a while. Longer than we thought."

Frank shook his head slightly. "I know. I get it."

When they lost Nonna Eve, they also lost the world's best babysitter. Sofia was deeply grateful for Maria, however, who'd found a job and moved to Eugene eight months after the MacBrides. She adored her nieces and nephew, and they loved her. She didn't have any kids herself—or a permanent partner—and claimed she preferred it that way. Sofia had her doubts about that, but despite their differences, she adored her sister.

Sofia loved her kids, but it felt good to be out of the house and around other adults occasionally. Even if it meant having to be at the City of Eugene Parks and Public Works holiday party.

It wasn't so bad, apart from the din of people trying to talk louder than the music. There was also the mixture of perfume, scented oil, and fake pine spray someone had generously applied to the tree on the far end of the room. But otherwise, she was happy to be there. She knew a few people, and she could see Frank having a good time despite Jeff Kingston.

His wife, Andrea, was already half-loaded by seven thirty. The open top few buttons of her blouse displayed a good bit of cleavage. Her husband seemed genuinely embarrassed, to which she appeared completely oblivious. Most likely it was precisely what she wanted, along with plenty of attention from everyone else in the room. She cozied up to different men, who seemed uncomfortable—as did their wives—though they did a pretty good job of downplaying it. Not only was she the boss's wife, she was very attractive. According to Frank, she'd been Oregon's representative in the Miss America pageant a dozen or so years before. That would make her around thirty-one or -two. She certainly looked the part of the beauty queen and apparently enjoyed her little game. If Sofia remembered correctly, she'd also made a scene at the holiday party the year before.

Sofia sipped her drink and watched the drama unfold. How interesting.

Then Andrea started in on Frank, which Sofia found downright amusing—at first. After all, he was the most handsome man at the party, at least in Sofia's biased opinion. He only got on her nerves when he got bossy with her. Or flirted with other women.

The opening strains to "I'll Take you There" by the Staple Singers started off loud, and Andrea leaned over to say something to Frank, apparently on the pretense of needing to be closer so she could be heard, her breasts almost touching him. Well, so much for almost. She was all over him. She noted his willing participation in Andrea's little act.

He was enjoying himself! Sofia suddenly felt far away, as if she'd just separated from her body and was observing from a distance. Kingston also noticed the interaction between Frank and the former Miss Oregon. Sofia could see him reddening from across the room.

"Sofia, good to see you." She turned to see Paul Peterson, their friend and supervisor in the Eugene parks department.

"Paul, how are you? Where's Janice? I haven't seen her yet, and hoped—"

A loud crash captured their attention as Andrea stumbled into and knocked over a small table. Frank caught her gracefully. A carefully planned move on her part, if Sofia had ever seen one. Frank helped her upright as Jeff Kingston strode over and grabbed his wife's arm.

"That's it, we're out of here." He glared at Frank and stormed off, pulling his loudly protesting wife along with him.

"This can't be good," Sofia said to Paul.

"I'm with you on that," he answered.

She couldn't help noticing a trace of a smirk on her husband's face, however. That's what he enjoyed—upsetting Kingston. She frowned and shook her head. Just like little boys on the playground.

Sofia drove home that night, as she'd only had a single glass of wine compared to Frank's three or four. Especially since a light snow was falling, and the wetness on the roads was supposed to turn to ice any time.

"How about that Andrea Kingston?" said Frank. "She made quite the scene."

Sofia didn't take her eyes off the road. "She sure did."

Frank looked over at his wife. "I'm hearing some undertones there. You think I had something to do with that?"

Some things weren't worth the battle. "That's not for me to judge. You know whether you did or not. Let's just say you enjoyed yourself and leave it at that."

"Okay."

Sofia motioned to the red envelope on the dashboard. "What'd they give you?"

"Probably some tacky Christmas card. Excuse me—holiday card. Maybe we'll get lucky and it'll be a picture of Jeff Kingston on his last fishing trip." He picked up the envelope and tore it open. "Yeah, just as I thought. The card's nice, though. It's a photo of our entire team out in front of the shop—*mamma mia*, there's a check in here."

Sofia glanced over. "That's a surprise. How much?"

Frank squinted at the printing. "I can't tell. Mind if I turn on the light for a moment?"

"Not while I'm driving at night through snow on a slippery road."

Frank opened the glove compartment, allowing light to spill out onto his lap. "Oh my God, this is for a thousand dollars!"

"You're kidding me!" They could use the money.

Frank laughed. "*Amore mio*, I am *so* not kidding you. There is Jeff Kingston's signature, large as life."

Sofia took a deep breath. "Good thing he signed that before the party."

"Yeah, very good thing," he said happily.

She shook her head. Her husband apparently missed the irony.

CHAPTER ELEVEN

Early in their marriage, Frank had wanted the family to attend mass every Sunday. Over time, though, their attendance became less frequent. Some Sundays Frank or Sofia felt tired, other Sundays they were busy, and sometimes they simply made other plans. Or Frank wanted to work on one of his projects in the garage or fly his quadcopter. By the time they'd moved to Eugene, they only attended a few times a year. Spiritually, she felt fine on her own without the help of any priest or church. She'd experienced her fill of that while growing up. However, she saw their marriage as a source of mutual support, and if Frank felt it was a good thing for the family, she was behind him all the way. Besides, she liked Father Keith, who offered Mass at St. Mary's most Sundays. Maria's complaints about his untraditional ways only made him that much more appealing to Sofia. That and his smoothly shaved bald head. Maria preferred the older priest, Father James. Something about him being more in tune with the Catholic Church itself was how she'd put it. Sofia knew that was Maria's way of saying Father Keith was way too liberal.

Back in Barcelona, not attending church hadn't been an option. Eduardo insisted they attend Mass every Sunday, lest they wind up like so many people in the world with no moral compass. In the days of Franco, he'd say, people had never gotten away with all the nonsense they do these days. She remembered her mother asking him if they could skip one Sunday, and his reaction was as if someone had doused him with a bucket of cold water. That was positively out of the question, and off to church they went. Sofia never liked the priest there, or the way he looked at her and her friends. Maybe she'd just imagined it, but she felt uncomfortable every time she walked past him.

She found their current church schedule more to her liking. They attended every Christmas and Easter without fail, and usually—but not always—one or two Sundays in between. That Christmas morning had been wonderful, their second without Nonna Eve. The year before, grief had bubbled up whenever someone mentioned her name.

They followed their unspoken agreement: no talking about their birth family, and no politics. Sofia didn't think Barack Obama was a perfect president, but she'd grown weary of all the criticism she heard from her sister about him. Maria had always been their father's favorite, probably because she'd so readily adopted his worldview. But she loved her older sister dearly. Her favorite moment of the day had been the presentation of Maria's gift to Sam: a bright red T-shirt with big white letters saying "Communication is Overrated!!" Sam pulled the shirt out of its wrapping, held it up, and looked quizzically at the lettering. When his aunt Maria told him what it said, he put it on with great enthusiasm—right over his pajama top. Everyone laughed wholeheartedly, while Sam ran into his aunt's arms and hugged her tightly.

They'd attended the eleven a.m. Mass, which had just ended, and Sofia looked forward to a cozy and quiet afternoon with the family.

First, though, Frank and Sofia hung back and asked Father Keith about Sam. The kids waited in the van with Maria. Frank had suggested it that morning to Sofia, and she'd asked him if he wanted to talk to the priest alone. "No," he said, "I want you to be there with me. You're the best bullshit detector I know. We need to understand what's going on with Sam."

In Frank's mind, surely God knew, and perhaps this priest had half a clue. He asked Father Keith if Sam's condition could be the work of the Devil.

"Well, I can't know God's intent, and I certainly don't know what the Devil has in mind—if there even is such a being. I see the references in the Bible to Satan as more metaphor than anything else." He smiled. "Not everyone in the

Church agrees with me on that. Do I think your son is evil? No way! I've seen your son in God's house, with God's children. He is the opposite of evil, as far as I can tell. Is he being influenced by some evil power? I am just as sure not. I can't pretend to know what God's plan for your son is, but when I see him in all his goodness, I think it must be something wonderful."

Sofia had been half-expecting some worn-out Catholic rhetoric. "Thank you," she said with tears in her eyes. "That was beautiful."

A few days later, Lisa's friend April came over so they could do their Christmas-break homework together. Sofia had long held strong opinions about Jess, April's "hippie" mom. She'd seen her dropping her daughter off at school, with her multiple bracelets and long-flowing African-patterned skirts. And sandals. Always sandals. When Jess came to pick up her daughter at the MacBrides' that day, she met all the kids, but she was most impressed with Sam. "Oh," she said to Sofia, "he's so present and wise. This one's an old soul." Sofia wasn't sure what that meant, but it sounded good. Hippie or not, Jess gained credibility—right up to the point in the conversation when she said Sam was a healer.

Sofia didn't know how to respond to that. "He's a what?"

Jess stared at Sam, who sat at the dining room table, focused on his drawing. "He's a healer. It's clearly written in his aura."

Fortunately, Sofia stood where Jess couldn't see her roll her eyes. "Um, how do you see that?"

Jess put her hands on her ample hips and nodded toward Sam. "It takes practice." She made a square with her hands and looked at him through it. "No doubt about it. Awesome energy. He's been practicing it for many lifetimes."

Sofia shook her head. There were so many fruitcakes in the world, and now she had one loose in her house. She glanced at her daughters, who hung on every word. They should have a debrief after this. "Thanks for that, Jess. It's good to know—"

"And his work here is not yet done."

"I'm sure it's not. After all, he's only seven." She drew a deep breath. "Thanks for letting April come over—"

"He took birth seven years ago this time around, but he's an old soul."

"So you said." Sofia felt the onset of a headache. "Well, Jess, good to finally meet you …"

Jess looked at Sofia with an intensity that caught her off guard. "I didn't *let* April come over. She's drawn to where she needs to go."

Sofia made a conscious effort to not roll her eyes again. "Sure. Aren't we all?"

Jess shook her head. "Oh, no. Like Thoreau said, people live lives of quiet desperation. Most of us don't follow what we're called to do. We do what we're told, or what we think we're supposed to do. Whatever will earn us approval or happiness."

Sofia nodded. "Right." Anything to get this woman out of her house.

Jess turned her attention back to Sam. "April feels drawn to your family," she said as she nodded, "because she is also an old soul."

"Undoubtedly." Please just shoot me now. Sofia nodded toward Lisa and Jodie. "I'd better get the kids ready for dinner. Thank you so much for coming over."

"You're welcome. It's what I do."

"Sorry?"

"It's what I do," Jess said enthusiastically.

It was April's turn to roll her eyes. She'd apparently heard variations of this conversation before.

Sofia shook her head. "Okay, well, this has been great, but—"

"I help people see things they're blind to."

"Like a seeing-eye dog," said Lisa.

Sofia tried to keep a straight face. "Lisa!"

Jess laughed. "No, that's kind of true." She looked at Sofia earnestly. "It's the role I play."

Along with the role of chief nutcase. She opened the door for them. April promptly went out, but Jess hung back. Once Sofia's girls had left the room, Jess moved in close, apparently to share one more bit of hippie wisdom. Sofia didn't know if she could stand more. Her head throbbed.

Jess whispered something she couldn't quite hear. "Sorry, what was that?" Sofia asked, more out of politeness than caring what she had to say.

Jess glanced around to make sure no one was within earshot. "I said, there are things you should know."

"What kind of things?"

She pressed a business card into Sofia's hand. It said only *Jess Heartsong* above her email and telephone number printed on a rainbow background. "We should have tea, or coffee or something. I have concerns."

Sofia stared at the card. "About what?"

Jess glanced around the room again. "This is not the time." She waved and walked out the door. "Call me!"

"Sure," said Sofia. She frowned and closed the door. That wasn't going to happen, yet she couldn't help wondering about Jess's concerns. They were probably something ridiculous.

Frank was the last one in the Public Works shop on New Year's Eve. He'd volunteered since he and Sofia were staying home anyway, and he'd still get home by around six thirty. As he locked the main gate on his way out, his phone chirped with an incoming message from a number he didn't recognize.

(541) 555-0183: *Happy New Year!*

Frank: *Thanks. Same to you. Who is this?*

(541) 555-0183: *Andrea Kingston. Thanks for catching me at the holiday party*

Frank: *You seemed like a good catch to me*

(541) 555-0183: *I'm a great catch*

Frank: *I can only imagine. How did U get my number?*

(541) 555-0183: *Jeff's phone, of course*

Frank: *Got it. Well, have yourself a great year*

(541) 555-0183: *You can bet on it!*

Frank got in his car shaking his head. How in the world did a gorgeous woman like that wind up with a chooch like Kingston?

The first thing Frank did every morning when he arrived at the office was to check his email. On this particular day, he found a forwarded email from Jeff Kingston in his inbox.

From: jeff.kingston@eugene-or.gov
Sent: February 3rd, 2013 9:17 AM
To: frank.macbride@eugene-or.gov
Subject: FW: City Maintenance and Management Exposition and Conference

MacBride—make plans to attend. JK

--------------------- Forwarded Message ---------------------
From: expo@deeppacific.com
To: jeff.kingston@eugene-or.gov
Subject: City Maintenance and Management Exposition and Conference

CMMEC is proud to announce our seventh annual maintenance and management conference and expo in the Portland Metro Marriott's Conference Center February 23, 2013.

We have all the latest technology you need to make your job easier and more efficient. Register by February 16, and get two free coupons for the hotel's all-you-can-eat buffet.

For more information or to register, click here:
https://www.ExpoCenter.org/events
See you then!

------------------- End Forwarded Message -------------------

Frank knocked on Kingston's open door.

"Can I help you with something?" The man seemed irritated.

"Yeah, boss, I was just wondering about this expo in Portland."

"You're going."

"Sure, I saw the email. I just wonder if it wouldn't be better to leave me here to hold down the fort, so to speak."

"Remember when I said I expect you to follow my instructions?"

"I'm not refusing, just discussing."

"One thing you will learn about me, MacBride—because you obviously haven't figured it out on your own—is that I hate wasting time. I hate idle chitchat, and more than that, I hate talking about things that have already been decided." He raised an eyebrow. "Will there be anything else?"

"I guess not. Should I register myself?"

"If you know what's good for you, yes."

Later that week, Frank called Jason—his friend and former co-worker from Lake Oswego—and mentioned he was going to the expo.

"That's great," said Jason. "We can hang out."

"You're going too?"

"I am. Mathews went last year and said it was one big party with a few sales pitches thrown in. They will try hard to make us happy because they want to sell us lots of state-of-the-art technological stuff. Some of it is actually cool—saves time and stress. We also get to meet other people who do what we do and exchange ideas and work out problems and stuff. Plus, he said he wanted as many of us as possible to go because of the frequent-flyer miles."

"Frequent-flyer miles?"

"For every employee a supervisor brings, they get some crazy number of miles, like ten thousand miles per man or something like that."

"Now I get it."

"Get what?"

"Well, my new boss insisted I go, even though we don't have someone to cover for me when I'm gone. But the frequent-flyer miles thing makes sense. He was a real jerk about it, too."

"Well, forget him. This will be fun. You're not driving up with him, I hope?"

"Nah. He didn't offer, and I'm not going to volunteer. I'll make the most of it. I'm trying to put Portland in my rearview mirror, but it keeps popping up in front of me."

"Oh, that hurts. I'll try not to take it personally. Anyway, I'll see you in— what, two weeks?"

Not if I can find a way out of this. "Yep. See you then!"

Chapter Twelve

Bad enough he had to come up for a stupid trade show, Frank didn't like being forced to socialize. He was going to make the most of it, though. He sipped his wine and took in the surroundings at the Cowboy Cafe. Not bad for a Marriott. Their themes were usually more plain vanilla. Jason was trying to impress the barmaid, who seemed to be humoring him. Jeff Kingston appeared to be enjoying himself with a city planner from St. Louis. Frank had met her earlier in the day and understood Jeff's interest. She had to be pushing mid-forties, judging by the professional info sheet at her booth, but she looked a good half-dozen years younger. Plus, she had what Sofia would call an "irresistible personality." Kingston hung on her every word. How ironic that his wife was a former Miss Oregon, a stunning beauty who wasn't far from being in as good shape as she'd been when she won the title at nineteen. He scanned the room and saw her sitting at a dark corner table—looking right at him.

Four glasses of wine later, Frank felt pleasantly buzzed. More than that. Borderline drunk, really. He'd learned everything he ever wanted to know about his boss's wife and then some, including how she got cheated out of the Miss America title. It was racial bias, she explained. They'd wanted a "woman of color," as they liked to call the winner.

"Are you sure that was it? I mean, you're talking high stakes. There's no shame in not taking first place against *that* kind of competition."

"Are you serious? Take a good look." She held both hands straight out to her sides, palms up. "Honestly, do I look like someone who would lose a stupid beauty pageant?"

"Not really, no."

"Do I look like someone who loses at anything?"

Frank gave her a wry smile and shook his head. You look like someone who's had a few glasses of wine too many.

She leaned across the table. "And that's not even considering the charm and talent categories."

"Of course." He smiled thinly and planned his escape. "Well, thanks for the company, but I need to—"

"Jeff told me to coordinate with you to carry materials back to Eugene. Which is code for lots of printed brochures that'll hit the recycling bin before they're even looked at."

"My car's almost full as it is."

"I'm sure you'll figure it out. Or if you'd rather, I'll just tell Jeff you need his help."

"Pass on that."

"Smart choice. What's your number again?"

He gave it to her and she called it. "Save it as Andi. A-n-d-i."

"Thought you went by Andrea."

"I do, but I let my friends call me Andi." She tapped Frank's leg lightly with her high-heeled sandal. "Annie Oakley at four o'clock." Frank was still trying to figure out what she meant when a staff member in a white cowboy hat, low-cut top, short tasseled skirt, and cowboy boots approached their table.

"Howdy, pardners. Y'all ready to get your giddy up?"

Frank laughed. "What did you just say?"

She smiled warmly. "We're gettin' some cowboy karaoke started up here in the next ten minutes and need you to giddy on up and have fun."

"Oh, thanks, but no. I don't sing." He nodded toward Andrea. "She might, though."

She shook her head. "Not me, pardner. Jeff gets enough stage time for both of us."

As Annie Oakley walked to another table, Frank glanced around the column that partially blocked the view of his boss. "Speaking of which, looks like your husband took off."

She waved her hand dismissively. "He left with the Spirit of St. Louis while you were talking to that cute little cowgirl." She took another sip of wine. "I believe you were admiring her breasts at that precise moment."

Frank forced himself to laugh. "Um, I have no idea what you're talking about."

"I'm sure you don't. Just like you probably didn't notice how much she was into you."

He shrugged. "Maybe a little."

"Maybe nothing. I'm sure she wouldn't mind a little rodeo with you."

Frank felt his cheeks grow warm. Someone once told him that people blush when there is an element of truth in what's being said. He held up his left hand. "Then it's a good thing I'm already spoken for."

"It would take more than that ring to stop her. Trust me on that."

Time to change the subject. "So you don't mind your husband's interest in that city planner?"

She smiled and shook her head. "Not at all. Bet you fifty dollars he had something amazing to show her on the expo floor."

He frowned and checked his watch. "Isn't that locked up?"

"Correct. So she'll be quite impressed that he has the key." She laughed. "Right now, Prince Charming is probably wondering if her pencil skirt would be easy to unzip. Either that or he's offering to walk her back to her room."

"Sounds like you know the plan by heart."

"Let's just say I know his MO."

"And you don't care?"

Andrea looked at him over the top of her wineglass. "Honey, I gave up caring a long time ago. Besides, we have an open marriage. He can do whatever he wants." She glanced at her watch. "Though I'll bet you another fifty dollars he won't score with her."

"What makes you say that?"

"Because he's not charming enough, and she's not driven enough." She looked at him mischievously. "A girl's gotta have a reason for sex," she winked, "while a guy just needs a place."

Frank laughed. "Wasn't that—"

"Billy Crystal in *Princess Bride*." She pointed at him. "Now, *that* was a classic."

"Definitely." He nodded. "But I don't think that's where it's from. It was in *When Harry Met Sally*. Or maybe he said it live."

"*Princess Bride*."

"Okay." Whatever. "*When Harry Met Sally* was a classic, too."

"I'll say." She gave him an amused look. "They sure got that 'friend' thing right."

"Friend thing?"

"How men and women can never be friends."

"Oh, I don't think that's what—"

"Anyway," she interrupted as she glanced at her watch, "this princess better get going. Jeff will be all keyed up after his failed attempt to get Miss St. Louis into bed."

"You sound pretty scientific for someone who's had four or five glasses of wine."

"It's all about experience, if you know what I mean." She smiled and stood. "I'd ask you to walk me to my room, but we both know how Jeff feels about you, so why poke the sleeping dog?" She giggled. "Or kick the sleeping snake, more like it."

Frank sighed as he stood. "I hate it when you're right."

She laughed. "Honey, I'm always right." As she walked past him, she ran a finger across his bicep, leaned in close, and whispered in his ear, "Let's do this again sometime."

He smiled and admired the curve of her neck as she passed by.

Frank's head spun as he opened the door to his room, but overall he felt good. He turned on the TV and flipped through a few channels before killing it. Same old garbage.

He'd had fun down in the Cowboy Bar. Sofia didn't loosen up like that. The difference was that he trusted Sofia and was fully committed to their relationship. He wouldn't trust Andrea any further than he could throw her.

His room phone rang and he glanced at his watch. Already 10:45. Sofia usually called earlier, and on his cell phone. He picked up the phone with a flourish. "Hey, beautiful."

After a moment of silence came a giggle. "Howdy, pardner."

"Oh, hi, Andrea. I thought you were my wife."

"It's *Andi* to you, and I can assure you I'm not, but thanks for the compliment." She giggled again. "Listen, Jeff needs you to sign an order he's making to buy some remote current monitors from Fujitsu."

"Now? It's almost eleven o'clock. I'm sure it can wait until morning."

"I'm sure it can, too, but you know Jeff. When he wants something, he wants it. And as you are no doubt painfully aware, he loves to see people jump at his command."

"Okay, I'll be right up."

"He's just started a shower. He wants me to bring them to you."

"Okay. Please make it quick. I don't plan to be up long."

"What's your room number?"

He told her, and she knocked a few minutes later. "May I come in?"

He opened the door wide. "Of course." He frowned as she walked past. "Where are the papers I'm supposed to sign?"

"Oh, that was merely an excuse to come down and say 'Hi.'"

"I also feel the need to leave when I'm in the same room as your husband."

"That's funny, but we're not exactly in the same room."

"What do you mean, 'not exactly'?"

"We always get adjoining rooms. It keeps the peace—if you follow me."

"I can imagine." He frowned. "So you lied in order to gain unlawful entry to my room?"

She looked at him innocently. "I know. That's bad, right?"

"Very bad."

"I guess I deserve a spanking."

"That's *really* bad."

"Is it?"

She closed her eyes, sat down, then flopped backward onto the bed.

"You okay?" Frank felt a mix of danger and excitement.

"Sorry. I felt a bit dizzy there for a moment."

"No worries. Wine will do that to you."

"I just need to recover." She sighed. "Do you think I have nice legs?"

Frank took a deep breath. "I guess."

She pointed at him and frowned. "You don't guess, you know. I saw you admiring them downstairs."

He shrugged and smiled. "Guilty as charged, your honor."

"And I was honored that you looked. Anyway, enough excitement for one evening. I'll leave you in peace." She reached her hands toward him. "Help a girl out, will ya?"

He took her hands and pulled, but she let go and flopped back on the bed when she was halfway up. "Whoopsie." She batted her eyelashes theatrically. "I think y'all will have to put that strong back of yours into this if we're going to get me off," she said in a fake Southern drawl.

"You mean get you up."

She batted her eyelashes again. "That's what I said, darlin'."

Frank shook his head and smiled. "Y'all are just helpless."

She closed her eyes. "That wasn't even close. Just stick to your sexy Italian accent, okay?" The Southern belle in her had apparently receded into the shadows.

"*Bene. Come desideri, signora.*"

"That's what I'm talking about. Whatever you just said was damn sexy." She stretched out her arms toward him. "Now help me up, pretty please."

Frank put his arm under her back and pulled her into a sitting position, but she didn't let go. "Just give me a moment," she whispered. She turned her head slightly so her cheek touched his.

Two sets of alerts went off in Frank's head. One was a "run away while you can" warning, and the other was an "opportunity is knocking" alert.

She slowly released him from the hug and held both of his hands. "You know what I'd like right now?"

"I have no idea." *You're probably going to ask for a foot rub.*

"I'd like you to speak Italian to me," she said as she gently rubbed her thumbs on the backs of his hands, "as we're making love."

"Um, I don't—"

"Slow, passionate, delicious love that neither of us will forget as long as we live."

"Oh, I don't have any condoms."

"Whatever shall we do?" She put her hand to her cheek in mock distress. The Southern belle was back. "Oh, wait—I know." She pulled a small box out of her purse. "I brought these in case someone got lucky. Looks like you're about to get pretty damn lucky, cowboy."

"You sure this is a good idea?"

"Trust me, this is not only a good idea. It's a once-in-a-lifetime opportunity." She lay back on the bed and slowly pulled up her skirt, revealing tiny leopard-print panties that barely covered anything. "Now giddy on up."

CHAPTER THIRTEEN

Frank lay on his back, feeling pleased with himself, the effects of the wine mostly gone. His bedside clock told him Andrea had been in his room over an hour and a half. He turned on his side to face her. "You awake?"

"I am, cowboy." She stretched like a big, noisy cat. "Just trying to get motivated enough to go back upstairs." She moved closer to him so her nose almost touched his. "That was awesome."

"Yeah."

She gave him a gentle kiss before sitting up. "I want to end all my Friday nights this way."

"You and me both. I mean ..."

"I know what you meant. You want this with that cute wife of yours."

"Yeah."

"I get it." She clicked on the reading lamp next to the bed, stretched again, and began singing softly, "Nobody does it better ..." but apparently that was all she knew of the song. She put on her skirt and panties and looked around for the rest. "Have you seen my bra?" She ran her hand under the covers until she nudged Frank's side. "No keeping souvenirs, now."

"Wouldn't dream of it."

"Liar!" she said playfully.

She found her bra and thanked Frank as she began putting it on.

"What for?"

"You know." She smiled warmly. "For making me feel like a natural woman."

"*Certamente! Sono al tuo servizio.*"

"Whoa! You keep talking like that, you might *never* get me out the door." She shook out her blouse. "This thing is hopelessly wrinkled." She put it on anyway. "I love your confidence. Jeff is so … I don't know. With everything he does, it seems he's trying to prove himself."

"I've noticed."

"Everything is about validation with him," she said.

"Well, when you go up, please wake him and tell him I said 'Hi.' That should help him feel validated."

She pushed his shoulder. "You are one funny boy. Where were you when I was looking for a suitable husband?"

Frank put his feet on the floor. "Probably at PSU, learning how to make circuits do what they're supposed to do."

"That's a good school. I'll bet you never got beat up."

"Of course not! Why would you say that?"

"Jeff got mugged twice at UCLA, and threatened more than that."

"I've heard that school has the highest rate of campus violence in the U.S."

"And he attracted it right to him," Andrea said, "like a fucking magnet."

"It wouldn't have anything to do with him having a chip on his shoulder, would it?"

She laughed. "Probably. I know when he attended high school in Fresno, he fought all the time."

"Really?"

"Oh, yeah. To hear him tell it, you might think he was a super badass, but I believe he suffered a lot of pain. I know his mom was big—at least three hundred pounds, from the photos I've seen. She did things for the school, probably trying to make up for her drunk and useless husband. Jeff didn't want either of them anywhere in sight, but she insisted on helping at the school. His dad hung around outside the liquor store three blocks away from the school half the time. Jeff got teased mercilessly about both of them, and he frequently raised his fists in response. I think once the other kids learned how easy it was to upset him, they made a game of it. Despite what he says, he mostly got the crap beat out of him—both by kids at school and by that worthless father of his."

"I had no idea!"

"No? Ever noticed his teeth? Half of them aren't even originals."

Frank frowned. "No kidding."

"Yeah, once his dear daddy was stone drunk and hit him in the face with a metal wastebasket, knocking a bunch of his teeth out. His mom told the hospital he fell out of a second-story window and landed on something hard."

Frank frowned. "I almost feel bad for the guy."

She finished her second shoe and stood up. "You shouldn't. No one's making him be a dick." She straightened her blouse and checked herself in the mirror. "We all have bad things in our past," she said, fixing her lipstick. "The responsibility is on us to overcome them."

"What bad things happened to you?"

She put her lipstick back in her purse and made sure she had all her things. "Nothing worth talking about."

"Fair enough. So his story about being part of a multigenerational family that founded Eugene is just a load of BS?"

She walked to the door and paused with her hand on the knob. "Oh, no, that's all true. His father just wanted to tap the trust fund without working for it. Great-Great-Grandfather Kerby set it up so any family would have to work in a leadership capacity for seven years for the city to get part of the trust. Which means in another few years, we'll be filthy rich. We already get some of that on a monthly basis." She winked at him. "No, his father got in a fight with the trustees when they wouldn't bend the rules and give him a lump sum, so he pulled up stakes and left with his big wife and little baby Jeff. They moved in with her family in the hills outside Fresno. He doesn't talk about it much, but I know they were poor as dirt. Pretty crazy, really, since all his father had to do was work for the city for seven years to hit the jackpot, and even then he would have gotten a generous monthly stipend. I think hard headedness is in their genes. Anyway, talking about Jeff and his family makes me sleepy." She opened the door and blew him a kiss. "See you 'round, pardner."

Frank turned out the light and tried to relax, but sleep wouldn't come for a couple of hours. He didn't want to think about Jeff Kingston, but his mind gave him no choice.

As he loaded his suitcase and the large number of brochures Andrea had given him that morning into his pickup, his phone chirped with an incoming text message. He got in and started the engine before looking at it.

Andi: *u made me such a happy girl last night. u r fantastic!!!!!*

Frank deleted the message and tossed his phone onto the passenger seat. She'd seemed aloof when he'd arrived at her room that morning to get the material, with Jeff muttering and packing suitcases in the background. Yet she'd given him a wink that spoke volumes.

His phone chirped again about halfway through Salem. He knew he probably shouldn't look at it while driving, but the road was open with no one around, so what did it matter?

Andi: *r u one of those guys who takes advantage of helpless women and runs away?*

Frank pulled in for gas at the next station, and while they topped off his tank, he texted back.

Frank: *Sorry, just busy with all the pack-up and departure, then driving.*

Andi: *I'm not busy at all. Jeff's driving, not being fun today.*

Frank: *I get it.*

Andi: *I bet u do. U aren't as talkative as last night*

Frank: *Just stopped for gas. Thanks again. It was fun.*

Andi: *It was SO much more than fun!!!!*

Frank: *Sure. Well, I'm going to start driving again.*

Andi: *c u later, alligator.*

Frank: *Later.*

On the drive home, Frank thought about the previous night. It wasn't like he'd planned what happened. That would be different. He never saw himself as a man who'd cheat on his wife. Millions of people had affairs—particularly when alcohol was involved—and especially one-night stands.

It had been kind of thrilling to have slept with his boss's beautiful wife, and it gave him a nice little ego boost. Was that so bad? It had been a good one-off thing, and it might even spice up their own love life. Andi was right—it was her husband's own fault. He was the one who chose to be a dick. She was more than Kingston could handle, anyway. She'd probably made up all that stuff about her husband's past, though. Andrea Kingston was a master manipulator and storyteller, without a doubt.

The important thing now was to act normal. Sofia must never find out.

When he arrived home, she greeted him at the door. "So, how was it?"

He hugged and kissed her before answering. "Oh, you know. Pretty boring stuff. How'd it go here?"

"Not boring, that's for sure. Lisa's team won her practice game. She made two of the three goals herself."

"That's great."

"I'll say. She downplays it, saying the other kids passed to her, but she's getting good. Jodie went to a sleepover at a friend's house and came back unhappy."

"What happened?"

"No idea. You think she'll tell me?" His wife smiled at him.

He opened the refrigerator and looked around. "Do we have anything to eat? I'm half-starved."

"Talk about a one-track mind!" Sofia laughed. "Make that two-track if you include sex. Didn't they feed you there?"

Frank felt his ears getting warm. "I don't know if it counted as food." He pulled out a tub of dip and closed the door. "Everything was pretty ordinary. Too much of Jeff Kingston for my liking, and lots of people trying to sell me every tool, software product, and technology gadget you can imagine. All designed to make life easier." He gave her a twisted smile. "But you know what I think?"

"I'll bet I'm about to find out."

"I think all this technology does the opposite of what it's supposed to."

"Meaning?"

"It ultimately makes life more complicated and stressful."

"I couldn't agree more," she said. "Speaking of complicated and stressful, I don't know what they made you do there, but you look exhausted."

"Tough schedule. I also didn't sleep well. Too much noise and commotion."

"Sorry to hear that, but I'm not surprised."

"Yeah." He looked around. "Where's Sam?"

Sofia shook her head, her smile suddenly gone. "He's been in a bad mood all day."

"Really?"

"Really." She sighed heavily. "He climbed into bed with me late last night and was so sweet. He hasn't done that since he was two. The weird thing is that it felt as though *he* was taking care of *me*. Like he didn't want me to be lonely. But today he's just been mopey. He won't do any schoolwork, and every time I've tried to engage him, he just hides somewhere. I don't want to push him. He's just not himself."

"Weird."

"I know. Sometimes he seems so grown-up, and other times …" Her eyes glistened with the threat of tears.

Frank wrapped his arms around his wife and held her tightly. "Sam's just different. Everything is going to be fine." He hoped he sounded more sincere than he felt.

Chapter Fourteen

Sofia lay in bed unable to sleep. What a long day! It was good to have Frank back, but something seemed off. He was nice but distant. Maybe because he was so tired. If anyone threw a party at the expo, he definitely would have been at it. Not that those public works people seemed like partying types, but you never knew.

She sighed and quietly rolled out of bed so she wouldn't wake her husband. Standing in the doorway of Jodie and Lisa's room, watching them sleep, she thought about love. About the Valentine's Day idea of love. The Hollywood idea of love. The happily-ever-after fairy-tale idea of love.

This, however, was true love, pure and simple. Watching her girls sleep. Wanting the best for them. She loved her husband, she loved her girls, and she loved Sam.

Walking down the hall to her son's room, she opened the door to find an empty bed. She checked the bathroom but found it unoccupied. She marched down the hallway. No sign of Sam in the kitchen or laundry room. She'd never figured out why he liked to hide, and he'd never done it at night before. Disturbed, she took the steps down to check the family room. She checked his favorite hiding places around the house and tried to think of new ones he might have recently discovered. No luck. Her heart raced as she turned on lights. Walking through the house, she called his name but got no answer.

Lisa came in, her eyes sleepy. "What is it, Mom? Where's Sam?"

"That's what I'm trying to figure out."

Frank walked in, scratching his shoulder. "What's going on?"

"I can't find Sam! He's not in his bed."

"He has to be around here somewhere. Remember the time we found him under the bottom shelf of the linen closet? That was quite a scare."

"I looked already. He's not there." Her voice broke. "I don't think he's in the house."

Frank checked Sam's bedroom window but found it closed and latched. "Lisa, wake up Jodie," he called out. "We need to search everywhere, and fast."

Jodie joined in the hunt, but still no Sam. Frank motioned toward the front door. "Let's look outside. Sofia, you check the back with Jodie, Lisa and I will search the front."

Looking everywhere they could think of, they found no sign of him.

They spread out and searched up and down the street, checking backyards and looking over neighbors' fences.

Frank gave his wife a worried look as they gathered back in the living room. "We need to call the police." He called to make the report and was still on the phone as Sam walked in the front door.

Sergeant Kinzer, the duty officer who took the call, reminded Frank to keep the doors locked and suggested they have Sam checked to see if he was a sleepwalker. He also suggested they get an alarm system. "You can set the system to chime whenever a door or window is opened. Or you can have the alarm go off when the door is opened without first disarming the panel. Make sense?"

Frank thanked him and hung up. He knew what his next home project would be.

Sofia hugged her son. "Oh, Sam, where did you go?"

He looked at her with his beautiful brown eyes and said nothing. As usual.

"You must never, ever leave the house again without our permission," warned Frank.

Sam nodded. He didn't seem defiant or unaware of what was going on, nor even look guilty.

Frank woke before five the next morning and lay in bed staring at the ceiling while Sofia slept soundly beside him. Guilt felt like a physical weight on his chest. Sam going out had nothing to do with what happened in Portland—it couldn't. Yet what were the chances that would happen the same night he got back? And Sofia said he'd been in a bad mood all day yesterday. Maybe this was God's way of punishing him.

His workday dragged along until about two thirty in the afternoon, when he parked his pickup in St. Mary's lot, which was empty save for a couple of older sedans parked by the parish. Opening the front door of the chapel, he found the dimly lit interior comforting. The only light came through the divinely inspired stained-glass windows. The faint aromas of frankincense and myrrh along with traces of extinguished candles reminded him of Italy, when his mom would take him and his brothers to confession every week and Mass every Sunday without fail. Even as an adult, she'd frequently ask him if he'd confessed his sins, and he'd routinely go just to make her happy. Not that he ever had much to confess. Until now. Checking the parish schedule online, he found that Father James manned the confessional from two to four that afternoon. Which would be perfect. He'd be in and out before anyone else knew where he'd gone.

After waiting in the booth for what seemed like an hour but couldn't have been more than a few minutes, the window slid open. "Forgive me, Father, for I have sinned. It has been several years since my last confession. I accuse myself of the following sins ..."

He recited a condensed version of his story with Andrea and immediately felt better, as though a weight had been lifted off him. That changed dramatically once the priest spoke, however. He asked Frank to commit to fifty-nine Glory Be's and fifty-nine Hail Mary's, twice around his rosary. All well and good, but instead of Father James, Father Keith occupied the other side of the confessional. He would undoubtedly have recognized Frank's voice.

He almost didn't hear the priest ask if he would agree to sin no more.

"Of course," Frank finally responded.

"It's never 'of course,'" said Father Keith. "It must be a conscious and deliberate decision on your part. In this society of loose morals, this act is widely tolerated and considered almost acceptable. But not in the eyes of God. You have bedded another man's wife and betrayed your own wedding vows. That is a mortal sin, for which you have asked forgiveness." He paused. "Fortunately, our God is merciful, and he has forgiven your sins."

Frank thought he was supposed to say something else, but for the life of him, he couldn't remember what. All he could think about was whether Father Keith knew it was him. He mumbled his thanks, left the booth, and had his truck started less than a minute later. Priests were sworn to secrecy around confessions, and with the seal of the confessional, it was one hundred percent safe. So why didn't he feel safe?

As he came out of the shower one morning a few weeks later, Frank's phone chimed with an incoming text message from Andrea.

Andi: *We should meet for coffee.*

Frank: *I don't think that's such a good idea.*

Andi: *Honey, we need to talk. I promise to keep all my clothes on. ;)*

Frank: *Okay, fine. Let's meet, but please don't text me. What if my wife had seen that?*

Andi: *So? You could tell her u r working on good company relations. We need to sign you up for a recovering Catholic guilt-management course.*

Frank: *What makes you think I'm Catholic?*

Andi: *The rosary on your hotel room table was a pretty strong hint. No worries, I am cool with it. Jeff's calendar says u r at the east pumping station all morning. I'll meet you for coffee at 11 at the Starbucks on Delta, just north of Beltline. P.S. Learn how to lock your phone!*

Frank tried his best to focus on work the next morning, but he worried about the upcoming meeting with Andi. When he arrived at Starbucks at 11:02, she wasn't there. Maybe she wouldn't show.

He sat reading the paper and inevitably opened to the comics, his favorite part. By almost quarter-past, Andrea still hadn't shown.

He sighed with relief and started for the door only to meet Andi on the way in. She looked even more attractive than the last time he'd seen her.

She raised an eyebrow. "Just where do you think you're going?"

"I didn't think you would show."

"Honey, I always show. I just got a little caught up. Wanted to look my best, you know?"

"You certainly look great." He motioned toward the table where he'd been sitting. "Why don't you have a seat while I order. What would you like?"

"I'll have a double mocha latte."

"Are you sure?" *That is wrong on so many levels.*

"Of course, silly. It's fantastic."

He got back to the table with her chocolate-milk coffee and a cappuccino for him. He sat down and leaned forward. "So, how's your day going so far?"

They made small talk for a few minutes. She was surprisingly easy to be around. More so when sober than when she'd had four glasses of wine. Finally, she got to the reason for calling the meeting.

"Look, I just want to put this out on the table so there's no weirdness between us."

Frank nodded. "Good idea."

"Please don't get me wrong. That was the best sex I've had in ..." She paused. "Well, ever. You really know how to make a girl happy, don't you?"

Frank smiled and shrugged.

"Anyway," she continued, "I just didn't want you to feel there was any expectation that we had to—you know—keep going."

"Oh, no, I didn't have any expectations of the sort." *But I was sure as hell worried that you would.*

"On the other hand, we both have a lot to offer each other," she said. "So I propose we keep things open. No conditions, no expectations, no obligations. You've got my number, and you can call or text me anytime."

"Sure."

She stretched back in her chair and smiled playfully. "Whenever you feel a little adventurous, just text me a time and place."

This was an opportunity to close the door—the perfect time to say, *You know, let's just leave it at that.* He also weighed the risk of offending his boss's wife. Besides, it had been a two-way street, and all she was asking for was to leave the door open. He could do that, no biggie. "Sounds good to me."

She smiled and sipped her coffee. "Okay, then." She stood, leaving her half-finished cup on the table. "I've got to get home before the plumbers arrive. They're installing my new ice maker today." She smiled as she turned away. "I'll see you around—hopefully."

"Yeah, see you later." He watched her walk through the door and considered how nicely her slightly stretchy slacks fit her. Just before she went out of sight, she turned and gave him a quick smile. Frank shook his head. *That is one beautiful woman!*

CHAPTER FIFTEEN

A few days later, Jeff told Frank they were going to Reno for the EnviroCity convention in a few weeks. CMMEC was also hosting this conference.

"Is that necessary? I mean, we just went to their expo in Portland two months ago. We might find something new we didn't see there, but—"

"The focus of this convention is environmental—hence the tag *EnviroCity*. It's a whole other focus. If it wasn't necessary, do you think I'd be going?"

"I meant for me."

"You expect me to carry all those brochures back? Plus, you can investigate stuff, talk to people. You know, things like that."

While you're adding up your frequent-flyer miles and seriously hoping to meet another cute city manager. Or cute anything. Frank shrugged. "Okay."

"And we're flying—courtesy of the city of Eugene—so we'll be there and back in a day and a half."

Sofia had learned over the years to count her blessings. The bigger the obstacles in her path, the more important to remind herself of all she had to be grateful for. A challenging but fulfilling marriage, a comfortable home, and healthy kids with no major issues—except for Sam's communication shortcomings.

Lisa had stayed home from school—which was not like her. No one liked being sick, and Lisa was no exception. She had a fever and complained of pain all over. The fever hadn't started until late morning, but even before that there was no doubt her daughter wasn't well. She'd lamented missing soccer practice at least three or four times during the day. Her team needed her, she said. Apparently, she also needed the team.

Jodie, on the other hand, if given the chance, would stay home from school so she could practice her cello, read, or do research on the internet. Was that such a bad thing? Sofia didn't think so. Not that Jodie was a liar. She simply tended to exaggerate when she didn't feel well. Nonna Eve had once said, "We don't choose our children's destinies. We look for the sparks, then fan the flames. And we learn as they learn."

Checking on her daughter every half hour, Sofia reflected on what she was supposed to be learning right then. Parenting could be tedious, difficult, and thankless, anxiety-laden work. But parenting was also a chance to practice unconditional love. A chance to put someone's needs so far ahead of your own when the situation calls for it that the entire world takes on a different perspective. Sure, sometimes things were tough. Like now. But she wouldn't trade what she had for the world. She sighed. This was what she signed up for.

After dinner, when she checked on Lisa, she noticed her temperature had climbed to a hundred and three. She called their pediatrician in a panic, but she said not to worry. "Give her Tylenol every two hours and keep checking her temperature."

Sofia wanted that temperature to break. She kept telling herself it was only a fever, nothing to worry about. But a voice in her head told her it was more serious. Hours later, her temperature still hovered around a hundred and three. She again called the pediatrician, who again told her not to worry, but they should call her back urgently if her temperature reached a hundred and five. If they couldn't reach her, they were to take her in to emergency without delay.

There would not be much sleep for Lisa's parents that night, just lots of little naps. They set the timer on Sofia's phone to go off every thirty minutes. Frank went on the hour, Sofia on the half hour.

Sofia checked on Lisa around eleven thirty and found Sam standing next to her bed. She gave Lisa her Tylenol and carried Sam back to his room. "Hey, young man, you need your sleep. Lisa will be fine."

When Frank came back from his midnight check, he mentioned that Sam was there again.

Sofia groaned. "What if he catches whatever she has?"

"Well, if that's going to happen, he probably already has. Plus, if I know that boy, the only way we'll keep him out of there is by putting him under lock and key."

Sure enough, Sam was in her room again at twelve thirty, standing guard over his sister. Lisa's temperature remained at just over a hundred and three. Sofia placed a damp washcloth on her daughter's forehead and let it cool her for a few minutes before she went back to her own bed, feeling frustrated and helpless.

She didn't return until nearly four in the morning, almost breathless with guilt. Her phone had run out of battery, so no timer, and they'd both slept through their turns.

Sam was standing next to Lisa's bed, smiling gently in the dim glow of the night light. Sofia's eyes filled with tears. How could her little boy care so deeply for his sister? He's special, this one. She put her hand on Lisa's forehead, which was noticeably cooler. When she took her temperature, it came out almost normal. Sofia closed her eyes and sighed loudly, relief flooding through her. She sat on the edge of Lisa's bed as tears of happiness poured down her face. Thank God!

Sam's embrace caught her by surprise. He held her tightly, then let her go, giving her his adorable lopsided smile.

She was a soggy mess—but she just didn't care. Waving good night to Sam, she had almost left the room when she noticed a sheet of paper at the foot of Lisa's bed. Sofia frowned and picked up the picture of a pair of elephants and their baby, obviously drawn by someone with a lot of heart. She showed the drawing to her son. "Did you draw this for your sister?" she whispered.

Sam nodded and his smile deepened.

"Is this Lisa?" she asked, pointing to the baby elephant.

Sam nodded.

Sofia didn't even try to hold back her tears. She couldn't remember feeling so much love. Ever. "Is this Dad and me?"

He nodded again.

"So where are you and Jodie?"

Sam pointed to the air on either side of the drawing. She started to pull him into a hug but let go when she felt his resistance. He needed to be the one to reach out. "Oh, Sam, you are one in a million." She'd seen some great drawings he'd made. Not typical for someone his age, but nothing extraordinary. These elephants, however—they were special. Not just for a seven-year-old. They were special, period.

She went back to bed, leaving the elephants with Lisa. As she climbed in, Frank rolled over. "Is everything all right? How's her fever?"

"Her fever is down to ninety-nine. And everything is amazing."

Frank checked on their daughter again at five. Lisa was sleeping peacefully at her normal temperature with Sam's Little Bear tucked in next to her. Sam had gone back to his room and was also fast asleep.

The next morning, Sofia felt as though a weight had been lifted from her shoulders. Not only had Lisa made a quick turnaround, she was touched by the poignancy in Sam's drawing, which someone had taped to the wall next to Lisa's bed.

She called Maria and filled her in.

"My little nephew has so much heart," her sister said.

"I know. He amazes me in so many ways. Do you know he's never lied to or misled us?"

"You can't mean never."

"Not once."

"Well, that's hard to believe. All kids lie at some point, don't they? How else do they learn to be honest?" Maria asked.

"I understand what you're saying—but not Sam. He's different."

"That's wishful thinking on your part. Lying is a normal part of psychological development. You know that—you're the one with the fancy degrees.

Understanding the difference between telling the truth and lying has to be learned through practical experience. It's something we hopefully learn as we mature—which most of the men I dated never *did* learn. I don't know why I keep attracting them. They all seem so different at first, but then a few months into the relationship, I realize they are carbon copies of each other. They all seemed so honest, and by all external measures appeared to be capable of a committed, monogamous relationship. But they've all been cheaters and liars."

"Like Papá."

"Well, no. They were all thoroughly different types of men," said Maria.

"Except in that one critical area."

Maria sighed heavily. "You know, I'm not in the mood for being analyzed by my baby sister right now."

"Fine with me. We don't need to go there." Sofia paused. "I don't know. Some things seem so good on one hand, while other things just aren't working. Like Frank's job, and that horrible boss of his. And then there's Sam. So sweet, so smart, so present—but he doesn't say a word. Ever. And he's still not reading."

"I understand, Sofia. But I agree with Nonna Eve."

"In what way?"

"That he's going to be just fine."

"I wish I could be so sure."

A week later, the day before their trip to Reno, Frank got a memo to see his boss.

"Change of plans." Kingston leaned back in his chair. "My wife wants to go to Reno, and since she's on the books as a contractor, that works for me. I'll be gone tomorrow and Friday, back on Monday." He leaned back and looked up at Frank. "Are you good to hold down the fort until then?"

"Assuming we don't have any forest fires, tsunamis, hurricanes, tornadoes, or lightning strikes to our transformers, I think I'll be able to handle it."

"Is that supposed to be funny?"

"Yes, particularly since it's not that likely a tsunami would make its way this far inland."

"Whatever." Kingston didn't crack a smile. "I want to ask you something, and I'm fine if this doesn't work for you. There will be no repercussions and no problems if you decline."

"You've definitely piqued my curiosity."

"I've got some wiring and fixtures that need to go in at the house. You're going to log your hours as general city maintenance, and don't mention the address of my house or anything like that on the worksheet." His eyes narrowed. "Are you okay with that?"

"Sure."

"You'll have the house all to yourself. Get started first thing in the morning so you make sure you get everything taken care of. I can show you what needs to be done. We're leaving for the airport around nine. Will that work for you?"

"How about if I show up at eight thirty?"

"Right. I'll see you then." He scribbled the address on a piece of paper and handed it to Frank. "Don't be late."

CHAPTER SIXTEEN

Frank rang the doorbell of the Kingston residence at 8:27 the next morning. Andrea answered the door, smiled warmly, and opened it wide. "Oh, honey, the electrician's here," she called out, not taking her eyes off Frank. "Welcome to our humble abode," she said softly as she made a grandiose sweeping gesture and bowed slightly.

More of that prize-winning cleavage, Frank thought as he walked in. I'm glad she won't be here while I'm trying to work. That's one distraction I don't need.

Jeff came down the stairs, buttoning his top button. "Oh, there you are."

"Yes, sir," he said, glancing at his watch, "right on time, as promised."

"Andrea, you remember Frank MacBride from the Christmas party?" There was no mistaking the edge to his voice.

She nodded. "I do."

"Nice to see you again, ma'am."

"The pleasure is all mine. But if you call me *ma'am* again, I'll ask my husband to fire you. *Ma'am* is for old ladies." She smiled. "I think you were up at the maintenance expo in February, weren't you? I believe you carried all the brochures back."

Frank noticed Jeff paying close attention to the conversation. "Yep, that was me, representing the great city of Eugene along with your husband."

Jeff nodded and rubbed his hands together. "Right. Let's get down to business. I'll show you what needs to be done. And remember, it has to be perfect, because it's for the sole purpose of making my wife happy. And as we know, 'Happy wife, happy life.' Isn't that right, dear?" he asked as he walked out of the room.

She winked at Frank as he followed Jeff. "You got that right, baby."

It took Jeff fifteen minutes to show Frank what he needed to do. "Andrea!" he called.

"I'm right here."

"Have you seen my wallet?"

"In the basket on the little table in the hall."

"How about my phone?"

"With your wallet."

"What about the plane tickets?"

"On your phone."

Frank breathed a sigh of relief once they left and immediately got to work. The Kingstons' house had to be worth close to a million. Must be from that monthly influx of family money, because there's no way they could afford it on a public works supervisor's salary, and Andrea didn't seem to have a paying job.

The work Jeff had laid out was fairly basic. Running a new switch leg, installing a couple of outlets, and changing out some light fixtures. Who could say what Andrea had in mind asking for these things, but that was one mind he had no intention of getting inside.

He was on a ladder, replacing a light fixture in the master bedroom, when he heard the front door open and close. "Honey, I'm home!"

What the hell? Frank walked out of the room to see Andrea beaming up at him from the foyer. "What are you doing here?" he asked.

"I live here, silly!"

"I know that, but I couldn't help noticing you left for the airport less than forty-five minutes ago. With your husband, if I remember correctly."

She started up the stairs. "Well, the most terrible thing happened! We were getting ready to check in and I suddenly felt utterly nauseous. I had to go to the women's room three times. Jeff hates being around anyone who feels even the slightest bit sick. So he handed me the car keys and told me to go home and rest and he'd see me on Sunday. Once in the car, I instantly felt so much better, but by then it was too late to catch the flight." She grinned wickedly. "Don't you just love it when people are so predictable?"

"It all depends what I'm predicting."

"You're cute. And funny." She took his hand and led him back into the master bedroom. "Come help me make the bed."

"You sure that's a good idea?"

"Are you kidding me? It's a great idea. For lots and lots of reasons." She sat on the edge of the bed and patted the space beside her, though Frank remained standing. "One, much bigger bed. Two, much more comfortable bed. Three, it's the middle of the day, which I find incredibly sexy, don't you?"

"Um—"

"And four, we're both stone-cold sober." She began unbuttoning her blouse. "Trust me—if you liked me drunk, you're going to *love* me sober. You're about to get treated in a way you'll never forget."

"Maybe because we're not drunk, we can decide this might not be the best thing."

She motioned to the sheer lace bra beneath her fully unbuttoned blouse. "Surely you're not trying to say no to this?"

"Kind of. Even though you're the most attractive women I've ever seen up close."

"Why, thank you."

"But I'm married, in a committed relationship, and we have three kids."

"That sure didn't stop you before."

"I was drunk before. *We* were drunk before."

"Aw, that's so sweet. I almost feel like I'm back in high school. 'It meant nothing. I was drunk.'" She smiled and untucked his shirt with a quick movement. "You knew what you were doing. All we need now is a repeat performance. This time while we're sober. In broad daylight." She raised an eyebrow and grinned. "Which works for me in a big way!"

He took half a step back. "I appreciate the offer, but I—"

"I get it. You're a man of integrity."

"I try to be."

"Of course you do! You're thinking of your wife. And your marriage. How virtuous!" She reached behind, unclasped her bra, and let it fall into her lap. "Remember these?"

"You're a hard woman to say 'no' to."

"Honey, I'm damn near impossible to say 'no' to." She lay back on the bed and did one of her cat-like stretches. "I'm going to let you take it from here, cowboy."

Jess's card had been on the side of the refrigerator for well over a year. It occasionally crossed Sofia's mind to call her, but she didn't until her desire to talk to someone outside the family outweighed Jess's quirkiness. Her sister was great—to a point. But family stuff would come up unfailingly, and somehow Maria always brought politics into the discussion. She was perfect for babysitting, though. Not only did she have a great relationship with the kids, she worked from home and had plenty of room in her apartment.

Sofia left Sam with her that day and met Jess at the funky little coffee shop she'd suggested. She enjoyed herself more than she thought she would, and Jess seemed pleased to have been asked out. Sofia wasn't about to tell her she was her only choice. In the nearly two years they'd lived in Eugene, she'd met no one she could call a friend. How pathetic was that? She'd gotten together with Janice a few times since the move, but now that they lived farther apart, it was harder to make happen.

"You know, your son is very special."

Sofia smiled. "What makes you say that?"

Jess widened her eyes and gave a funny shrug. "I just know these things. His gifts are really close to the surface, if you know what I mean."

Here we go again! "I'm sorry, but I have no idea what you mean."

"Look, I know you think I'm a fruitcake."

You hit the nail right on the head. "Not at all."

"It's okay, I'm used to it. I know I drive April nuts—but part of it is her preteen thing. You know, where they're always embarrassed by their parents."

If I were April, I'm sure I would have died of embarrassment long ago. "Right."

"So with Sam, well, he's got the same set of gifts we all have, but his are more accessible. That's what I mean by closer to the surface. April told me he knew when his grandmother had crossed over."

"That's true."

"So how did he do that?" Jess asked.

"Believe me, I have no idea."

"I think you do."

"Excuse me?"

"I think you do have an idea. He connected with his grandma beyond the bodily level. What else could it be?" She looked meaningfully at Sofia. "Sam is very tuned in."

"Well—"

"He knew the way we all do. You know how you're aware of what your husband is feeling, even when he's in the other room?"

Sofia shrugged. "Maybe sometimes."

"It's the same. Sam's ability to connect on a psychic level is highly acute." She smiled. "Maybe his grandma's was, too." She glanced at Sofia, and her smile swiftly faded. "Sorry that I'm freaking you out, but I have to tell you again that he has an amazing power as a healer."

"And you know that because ..."

"Because I see it in him. Trust me—he will surprise you, that one."

"He's surprised us many times already. But that doesn't—"

"He's been working on it through many lives," said Jess.

"Oh, please!"

"It's true."

"So you said when you came over Christmas break. But that's just your belief. I don't buy that reincarnation stuff."

"Why not? It absolutely makes sense."

"How in the world does it make sense?" Sofia shook her head. "That we come back as a fly or a gopher or something random?"

"That's the point—it's not random. Our soul goes on to the next lesson in a logical, progressive fashion. Or sometimes it repeats an old lesson until it's fully learned."

"Our soul? I don't know. I mean, my parents raised me Catholic, but I'm not sure how much of that I believe now."

"Okay. So what's the difference between a living body and a dead body?"

"Well, a dead body is no longer alive."

"Exactly. But all the ingredients are there." Jess pointed upward. "Except one thing."

I think I know what's coming. "What's that?"

Jess became more animated by the moment. "The soul." Her eyes widened even more. "That's the only difference."

"Okay." Maybe it's time to make a graceful exit.

"So why is it such a stretch to think that same soul can't find itself another body to live in?"

Sofia sipped her coffee and discreetly checked her watch. "But all that's just guesswork. I mean, no one's ever seen a soul, right?"

Jess shrugged. "You don't have to see something for it to be real." She gestured at the space around them. "You can't see oxygen, but it's real enough. We'd die pretty fast without it."

How did I get myself into this? "I don't know. It's a bit 'out there.' If reincarnation were true, I think more people would believe it."

"You've heard of *Scientific American*, right?"

"The scientific journal? Of course."

"You can hardly get more mainstream scientific and less 'out there' than them. So here's an eye-opener. When you get home, google 'Scientific American Reincarnation Stevenson.' It'll blow your mind. They wrote about the work of a guy named Ian Stevenson, who chaired the Psychiatric Department at the University of Virginia and scientifically documented over two thousand cases of kids who remembered previous lives, hundreds of which were substantiated by direct, irrefutable evidence. The *Scientific American* article makes a strong case that understanding reincarnation will revolutionize the way we see things. The article proposes it will be the next major scientific 'discovery.' Which is funny because there's nothing new about it."

They sat in silence and sipped their drinks. Finally Sofia spoke. "I know the Church is totally against the idea of reincarnation. I tried to talk with Frank about it once, and he got pretty upset."

"Institutionalized beliefs never made something true or not. Ever heard of the Council of Nicaea?"

"No."

"It took place more than three hundred and twenty years after Jesus' birth, called by the Roman Empire."

"Okay." Sofia wondered where Jess was taking this.

"All the leaders of the different branches of Christianity were forced to accept certain standards—to make it easier for the Romans to rule. You know, a standardized plan. Part of that plan was to declare reincarnation and preexistence of the soul to be anathema."

"To be what?"

"Anathema—cursed or blasphemous. Even *talking* about reincarnation meant the death penalty. Before that, reincarnation was a widely accepted belief in the Christian world."

"I doubt that." Sofia shook her head. "There's a conspiracy theory for just about anything you can think of these days."

"Oh, this is not a theory. It's not even disputed fact. Just look it up. Everything I just told you is simple history." Jess smiled and sipped her tea. "Except the part about Sam being a healer. I hope it's okay I shared that with you. You probably think I'm fruitier than ever."

Definitely! "Not at all. This is fascinating."

"Well, since I'm already out on a limb, may I have your permission to say something about your husband?"

Sofia abruptly set her coffee on the table. "You know, let's leave it at that."

"I'm sorry. I do that sometimes. I put my nose where it doesn't belong. I need to learn to let people discover things for themselves."

Sofia stared at her. Discover things? I will not lose it or waste another minute on this discussion. I will stand up, wish this self-proclaimed fruitcake a nice day, and walk to my car. Or not. "What do you mean by 'discover things'?"

Jess's forehead wrinkled. "Oh." She looked over her shoulder as if someone might be sneaking up on them. "I need to learn to let insights come to people on their own. That used to drive Kevin crazy. He's my ex. I'd give him all this information he didn't necessarily want, and—"

"What insights are we talking about?"

Jess waved her off. "Oh, they're not even true insights, really. I sometimes just have a sense about things."

"Do you?"

"Sometimes, but that sense is not always right." Jess's words came faster. "I've been told I need to learn to keep things to myself." She began gathering her things, knocking over her hand sanitizer before stuffing it into her macramé handbag. She picked up her keys with a slightly shaking hand. "Thank you so much for meeting me for tea"— she motioned at Sofia's cup —"and coffee. It was a pleasure to see you again. April is always so happy when she comes back from your house and—"

"What is your insight, Jess?"

She sighed. "You know, sometimes I speak without thinking, and I apologize—"

"You're just making it worse," said Sofia. "Say whatever you have to say, and I will feel free to let it go in one ear and out the other."

Jess's eyes darted from side to side before she closed them and took a deep breath. "I think your husband may be having an affair."

"You have *got* to be kidding me!"

"I'm not. The morning of the day I came over to your house, I had this—"

Sofia stood up. "I meant you've got to be kidding me that you're actually saying this. Shame on you! Just what I need is some psychic wannabe telling me her visions of my husband being unfaithful."

"That's why I tried not to say anything."

"You should have tried harder."

Jess rubbed her temples. "This is the kind of thing Kevin would tell me."

Sofia grabbed her purse and keys from the table. "Maybe he was onto something!" Jess seemed close to tears, but Sofia was too mad to care. She glared at her new could-have-been friend and walked off.

CHAPTER SEVENTEEN

May 5, 2013

It's 2:27 a.m. Can't sleep, may as well write. Haven't done this in forever. Well, we did it! We're homeowners! Instead of rent payments, we now have mortgage payments. Frank said we'd be crazy not to. It feels a little weird paying two hundred twenty-three dollars more per month for the same place we've been renting for the past two years. I have to be honest, though—something feels good about it. I'm sure it'll work out for us in the long run.

It's been seven months since Sam went out. I wake often and check on the kids, especially him. I don't think he'd ever sneak out again, but that was too scary. Scarier than the eleven minutes we lost Jodie at the state fair. Sam was missing for almost an hour, which felt like a day. Funny how time can stand still and how fast things can change.

Lisa has been complaining about April not coming over, and I feel so bad I could cry. I wish I hadn't insulted her mom. Even if she is a crazy wannabe psychic.

Now she's not letting her daughter come over because of me. I just got so angry. She had no right to say that about Frank. I really don't think he'd go that far.

He's been weird about Portland since before we left there, though. Why'd we leave in the first place? Why can't we go back? When I bring it up, he's adamantly against the idea. He won't even talk about it—which is not like him. He hated going to that expo, and when he got back, he was different. Nicer to me, but ... I don't know, strange. Was there another woman in his life when we lived there? Did it end badly?

Today I came right out and asked him if he'd had an affair. He looked quite shocked, and he couldn't believe I'd asked him that. Maybe it was my imagination, but I thought he got a little bit too defensive. Someone told me once that defensiveness is a way of saying, 'I believe at least part of that, but I'm not ready to face it now!' Don't know if that's true, but maybe.

He asked if there would ever be a time when I fully trusted him. I felt bad. My fault for letting Jess inside my head, though I still wish I hadn't yelled at her. I feel bad on many levels. Sometimes I feel like a rat in an electrified maze that takes all the wrong turns. So tired of getting my nose shocked!

From: AndiKing117@gmail.com
Sent: June 12, 2013 2:38 PM
To: frank.macbride@eugene-or.gov
Subject: Wassup?

Frankie,

You never write, you never call. What's a girl to do? Two months is way too long.

I get that you needed space, and I was happy to give it. Hope it's been good for you. I've been doing well with my space too, doing a lot of reflection and introspection. It feels so good. Know what I mean?

I know you'll be pleasantly surprised with the understanding I've come up with.

I'd love to tell you all about it, but I don't think it would come across as well over email. Let's meet for coffee, same place, 2 p.m. Tuesday.

See you then! Don't be late. You know how much I hate to be kept waiting.

~Andi

From: frank.macbride@eugene-or.gov
Sent: June 13, 2013 11:03 AM
To: AndiKing117@gmail.com
Subject: Wassup?

Hi Andi,

Thanks for your offer to meet over coffee. I look forward to hearing about your understanding. I also felt a little incomplete with the way we left things.

See you at 2 p.m. Tuesday, at the Starbucks on Delta.
Best,

Frank.
P.S. I don't go by Frankie.

"Hey there, Andi."

She stood and gave him a hug. "Good to see you, Frankie."

He let go of her and took a step backward. "I told you I don't go by that."

"Aw. I bet I'm the only one who calls you that."

"Yes, you are."

"Then it can be my pet name for you."

"Listen—"

"I'm just teasing." She smiled mischievously as they both sat down. "I must admit, though, you *are* fun to tease. Jeff goes ballistic at the slightest little thing, so I can't tease him at all. He's not as much fun." She picked up a cappuccino with foam from the table and handed it to him. "Is that what the doctor ordered?"

"That works, sure."

She sipped her mocha latte and raised an eyebrow. "'That works' is all I get? You know I got it exactly right."

Frank took a deep breath and forced himself to smile. No self-respecting Italian would drink cappuccino in the afternoon. What did that say about him? "Yes, you did, thanks. I appreciate you remembering." At least she didn't get him that mocha nonsense.

She giggled. "Look, you can relax. I've got great stuff to tell you."

"I'm all ears." Frank started on his cappuccino.

"Well, I've been having these dreams."

"You should know my dream therapist's license expired last month," he said with a wry smile.

"Look, everyone, Frank's back!"

"I've been here the whole time."

"Sure. So these dreams," she said as she leaned toward him, "well, they're pretty erotic—are you okay if I share them with you?"

Frank took another sip of coffee. "Sure, go for it."

"Okay. So, I'm on my way home from the spa, and I've just had a Brazilian wax. I mean the real deal."

"I'm with you so far."

She took a gulp of her coffee. "I'll bet you are. So I come in to tell Jeff, but before I can even open my mouth, he throws me over his shoulder, carries me to the bedroom, tosses me on the bed, and ties me down with soft restraints. All very unlike Jeff."

"I believe you."

"Of course, I'm highly excited and enjoying myself immensely. My dream must have fast-forwarded, because I'm suddenly wearing almost nothing. I'll let you use your imagination for that part."

"*Grazie!*"

She giggled and continued. "And then, just when I'm a hundred percent ready for him, he walks out of the room." She raised both hands, palms up. "And just leaves me there, all hot and bothered and absolutely nothing I can do about it. Is that weird or what?"

"Yeah, I guess you could say it—"

"And the weirdest part starts with him doing that in the first place. I mean, not to get into too much detail, but I would say my husband has no imagination when it comes to anything, especially lovemaking."

"I'll take your word on that."

"You're so funny! That's one of the things I love about you."

Frank set his half-finished cappuccino on the table. "Thanks again for the invite, but I really need to get back to work. I've got a big agenda this afternoon—"

"Are you kidding me? We just got here. You're not the only one with an agenda, you know." She lifted an eyebrow. "Plus, you haven't heard the whole story."

"Sorry, I thought you finished."

"No, silly, I always let you know when I'm finished, remember?" She winked at him. "Anyway, so he goes out of the room, and I'm wondering, 'What the hell?' And then the door opens again and I'm thinking, *Okay, he was just teasing me.* Only it's not him, but you."

"Oh …"

"And then you do your Italian stallion thing, just like in *Rocky*, but better."

"I think Rocky was celibate in that movie. Plus, he was a fighter, not a lover."

She laughed so loudly, some of the other patrons turned to look. "You are so funny. That is such a turn-on."

"So you've said." He nodded. "Well, that was some dream. I want you to know I'm honored to have been part of it."

She giggled. "Oh yes, you certainly were part of it. A very big part, if you catch my drift. And there's more to the story."

Why am I not surprised? "Tell me."

"My therapist suggested I talk to you about this and—"

"You told your therapist about us?"

She reached out and put her hand on his. "Relax, she's totally on our side, and besides that, she's sworn to secrecy. You know, professional ethics and all that. Anyway, she told me I should tell you about it, and to invite you to do a reenactment, so to speak. As a way of closure."

As if a therapist would ever suggest something like that. "Maybe we should cool it. I think my wife suspects."

"No, we're already cool. Let her suspect." She giggled and stretched. "Or just tell her you're sleeping with someone younger, prettier, and much more fun."

"You're quite sure of yourself."

"I know." She leaned back, crossed her legs, and gulped her latte. "I'm also sure this will be a great afternoon." She glanced at her watch. "Jeff's not home for over three hours."

"Um—"

She leaned across the table and whispered, "Look, you've done the righteous protest thing, and it's cute—but I know you want me. I'll park on Maple Street, outside the East Pumping Station. Park your truck inside, then come out and get in my SUV. I'll have you back in plenty of time." She stood up and extended her hand. "In case anyone's watching." After they shook, she started toward the door, then stopped and walked back to him. "Just so you know, I've already started."

"Started what?"

"The reenactment. I was at the spa Friday afternoon." She smiled. "Getting waxed."

He waited for a minute or two, cleared the cups and napkins from the table, and headed toward the East Pumping Station. Once he parked, she drove him to her house and pulled into the garage. When they walked inside, she looked at him and smiled. Her face registered surprise as he smoothly swept her off her feet. Her arms around his neck, she looked at him admiringly as he carried her up the stairs to the bedroom. "You know how to surprise and delight a girl, don't you?"

He set her down on the bed, began unbuttoning his shirt, and smiled. "You're not bad at coming up with a few good surprises of your own."

She smiled as she pulled off her skin-tight jeans, revealing sheer boy-shorts that left nothing to the imagination, then laughed at Frank's expression. "And you are so fun to surprise."

CHAPTER EIGHTEEN

Four months later, Frank hummed as he came through the front door after work. Sofia gave him a playful swat as he walked past. "And just what are you so happy about?"

"Well," he said as he smiled, "next Tuesday is my annual performance review. It's been nearly two years since I started here. As you know, the deal was they'd start me low and raise me as I proved myself worthy." He nodded. "Which I definitely have. I haven't been late one day in the past six months, and I've had no major errors or write-ups." He ticked off each point on his fingers. "I've gotten several positive comments from the City Council about my work, and Eugene finally adopted my idea for the recycle program."

Sofia frowned. "Which many people didn't like."

"Well," he said and shrugged, "you can't please everyone."

In the spring of the previous year, Frank had proposed to the Eugene City Council they standardize garbage rates citywide and reward people for recycling by charging them much less for smaller garbage containers, and considerably more for larger containers. It upset many people, and it took over a year to put in place.

"Anyway, I'm just saying it's not a sure thing," she said.

"But it *is* a sure thing."

"How do you know Kingston won't get in your way?"

"There's nothing he can say. It's all quite straightforward. I've been waiting for this raise a long time."

"That's the understatement of the year."

The morning of Frank's performance review, Sofia woke an hour earlier than usual, determined to play it cool. When he got up, she tried to not let him see how excited she was. That way, if the worst happened, he wouldn't think he was letting her down. At least not as much.

She gave her husband a smile she hoped was full of encouragement and support.

He kissed her on his way out the door, then asked for another for good luck. She happily gave it and felt a huge swell of pride and affection as she watched him get in his pickup. "May all go well, *cariño*!" She waved to him as he started the engine. "Wait!" she suddenly called out. He looked at her with curiosity as she ran across the lawn, then leaned in the window and whispered in his ear. "Just want you to know I'm wearing my lucky thong today."

"Your what?"

"You know, the lacy lavender one someone special gave me for my birthday."

"How could I forget?" He laughed and gave her another kiss. "Thanks for the image, *amore mio*!" He waved and drove off.

The day took longer than usual to go by. Sam was good, but time just seemed to drag. She must have looked at her phone a dozen times. She knew she shouldn't call—Frank would give her the news in his own way, probably in person. Besides, they'd most likely hold the review at the end of the day, when he came back to the office after a day out in the field.

When Frank's pickup pulled up after work, however, she immediately knew something wasn't right. He should have been out of his truck and bouncing across the front lawn. Instead, he sat in his truck for a few minutes.

He finally came in and gave her the bad news: Kingston had postponed the performance review a full month.

"How is that? Wasn't this scheduled since last spring?"

He shook his head. "Something in the city rules says the supervisor holding the review can postpone it up to thirty days under certain circumstances. When I asked Kingston why, all he did was repeat the reference without saying what those circumstances were. And he made it exactly thirty days."

Sofia shook her head in disgust. "That's it! Time to look for another job."

"As we've talked about before, there aren't any other open jobs around here at my skill level. I can get a position as a maintenance electrician over at the Weyerhauser plant, but that would be a big cut in pay, not a raise."

"But you would eventually get raised to something reasonable."

"It would take years to get even close to my current pay level." He frowned. "And even then, I doubt I would make it to the same level. I mean, the reason I make what I do is because I'm good at different things, especially at solving problems. That's what they hired me to do, and I do it pretty much beyond everyone's expectations. Except Kingston's. No way I'm gonna win with him."

She shook her head. "Look at the stress this is causing us."

"I know. I think of it almost every single day. But I'm not worried about my stress. You know me. I like to roll with the punches, and I'm good at that." He stroked her hair. "It's you I worry about. It's *your* stress that bothers me."

"Why don't you complain to his boss—that guy in the City Council who oversees him."

"You mean Rick Wilson?"

"Yeah, him. Why don't you tell him what's going on?"

"He's a career politician, first of all. I really don't think he cares as long as the city—and the voters along with it—don't go up in flames." He sighed and rubbed his forehead. "We've gone over all this before."

Her voice hardened. "I know we have. I was there, remember? And now, thanks to your investments drying up, we're at a point financially where we've never been. We need to review our options. You should file a formal complaint about Kingston to Wilson."

"That would only make things worse."

"Worse *how*?" She shook her head in disgust. "The only way it could be worse would be if Kingston had you thrown in jail."

"Trust me, things can always get worse."

"Well, you trust *me*, Frank MacBride, things can always get worse at home, too."

With that, she stormed out of the room.

Fifteen minutes later, Frank slid his phone into his pocket and called out to his wife, "I'm taking a walk around the block."

No answer. Maybe she was in the bathroom. He pulled out his phone a few houses away and called Andrea.

"I was hoping you'd call one of these days. It's been months since I've heard a word from you," she said.

"Did you say anything to Jeff about us?"

"Not really."

Frank drew a sharp breath. "That's weird, because he's suddenly become more hostile. He just postponed a performance review I've been counting on, one that I needed for a raise."

"I might have mentioned that you sometimes flirt with me."

"Why would you say that?"

"Because it's true," she answered.

"Seriously, can you please tell me why you said that?"

"It just came out in conversation. Maybe because I've been missing you."

"That's a great way to show it."

"It was a great way to get your attention," she said.

"It worked."

"Plus, it's fun making him jealous. He gets so steamed."

Frank realized he'd stopped walking and started moving again. "I'm glad you're having fun. But listen, my job is at stake here, and—"

"Oh, relax. I didn't tell him we've been intimate."

"I don't know why you'd say anything at all."

"I told you, silly. I'd love to keep going back and forth about this, but I have to get going. Why don't we meet for coffee and discuss things further?"

"I don't think that's a good idea."

"Same place as last time. Starbucks on Delta, tomorrow at two thirty."

"I have to work."

"I know, but you'll find a way to be there."

"Look, Andrea, I really can't—"

"Don't be late. You know it's bad luck to keep a girl waiting." She hung up abruptly.

The next day, Frank briefly considered showing up and explaining to her in the clearest possible terms they were done. But not following her command was probably the best way to end it. That was a language she'd understand.

Sofia sighed, put her book down, and rolled over to face Frank. "You know, Sam's not picking up sign language. He's so stubborn. Almost like he doesn't *want* to communicate."

"They say that's one of the potential issues with autism."

"I know. I just don't know what to do about it."

Frank sighed. "Sometimes there's nothing you *can* do."

She took a deep breath. "Yeah, but …"

"But what?"

"I worry about our kids. I mean, what if they forget to pay their bills or maintain their marriages?"

"You're assuming they'll even *get* married. Who knows? They might be so wrapped up in their lives, they'll bypass the whole relationship deal altogether," said Frank.

"Are you trying to worry me more? Besides, that doesn't describe our kids. They're too loving, too caring, and too attractive. They'll all find partners. Although …"

"What?"

"I worry most about Sam."

"Sam will be fine."

"I know, but how would he be in an intimate partnership?" she asked.

"That's something we won't know for a long time, so I suggest we not worry about it yet." He reached over to switch off his bedside lamp. "Good night."

"I just see them all so … focused," she said.

He yawned. "Which is funny, because most parents worry that their kids are not focused enough."

"Do you think our kids are obsessive?"

"Are we back to that topic?" He smiled. "They are, but not in a bad way. Like with Jodie and her music. It serves them pretty well, I think."

She sighed. "Maybe. Papá always says you can't name one highly successful person who isn't at least a little obsessed."

"That sounds like something your father would say."

"Don't you start on Papá."

"I'm agreeing with him. Look at Thomas Edison. He was famously obsessed. He would work on something for days or weeks and hardly take time to eat or sleep."

"Are you justifying obsession or telling me things aren't as bad as they could be?" she asked.

Frank thought for a moment. "Maybe a bit of both. It's a matter of degree. Did you know that Edison set aside one day per year to be with his family?"

"You're kidding."

"No, that's what he did. He changed the world with his incredible, amazing inventions, but I don't think he was such an ideal family man. And if he hadn't been so obsessed, he never would have accomplished the magic he did."

They lay in silence for a few minutes.

"Can I tell you something?" asked Sofia.

"Of course! My primary purpose in life is to hear you out, answer every question, and satisfy every want." He rolled back to face her. "Within reason."

"You're funny! Remember when I had coffee with the mom of one of Lisa's friends last spring?"

"No, but I'll take your word for it."

"She said that Sam was 'tuned in' to people."

"Okay. Let me guess. Was that the one you call the 'hippie mom'?"

"That's her. Jess. She also said Sam was a healer."

"And you believe that?" Frank asked.

"No. I told her she was a wannabe psychic. Which is why her daughter doesn't come over anymore. I don't think she's allowed. I haven't seen her once since spring."

"Ouch. But Leese will make other friends."

"I hope so. But what do you think about this healing business?"

"That Sam could be a healer? No way. He cares about people, sure, but this whole idea you can heal people with mystic powers or whatever is bonkers," Frank said.

She lay quietly. "I've read about people who do exactly that. There are hundreds of documented cases."

"Bogus!"

"I've read dozens of testimonials. People with incurable conditions—like stage-four cancer—have been helped by healers," said Sofia.

"Sometimes just believing you're cured can cure you. Don't they call that the power of positive thinking?"

"Maybe. But can you just 'believe' an aggressive tumor away?"

"It could be all sleight of hand. Then you pay people to give testimonials."

They lay in silence as Frank's breathing gradually slowed.

"What about Jesus?" Sofia asked.

"Huh?"

"What about Jesus? Didn't he heal people using God-given powers?"

"Well, yeah, but that's why he's Jesus," Frank replied.

"Okay, but if we're all created in the image of God—"

"Sofia, I would love to discuss this further, but right now I'm just too tired."

She stared at the dark ceiling for a minute or two. "Sorry."

But he was already snoring softly.

Chapter Nineteen

At breakfast the next morning, the girls talked about the school talent show that Lisa was thinking about entering.

"You should definitely do it," said Jodie. "There's nothing so much fun as failing in front of the whole school."

"Well, I'm actually going to practice my dance, which is how I plan to *not* repeat my sister's pathetic performance from two years ago."

"Good of you to bring that up, Lisa," Jodie said, her voice tense, "because that was almost as bad as it would be if I had tripped walking out to my starting position on the hundred meters for track team tryouts."

"You don't trip because you never get out there. You never race, you don't compete, you don't even try—"

"You're crazy. I just don't try the things you do."

Lisa smirked at her sister. "That's right, you go for the safe things. Where you won't get hurt."

"You think performing in front of a live audience is safe? What planet did you just fly in from?"

Frank slapped his hand on the table. "Stop it, you two!"

Sofia shook her head. "I wish you girls would be more supportive of each other," she said. "One day it will be just you two to care for each other." She paused. "Along with Sam," she added, glancing at her son. "You can all take care of each other." She stumbled over her words. "I mean, later on, when Dad and I are no longer around." She turned to Sam, who focused carefully on his oatmeal. "See what you're missing by not going to school? All this opportunity to bicker—"

"Mom," said Lisa. "Sam couldn't exactly bicker anyway, could he?"

Sofia's eyes slowly filled with tears, and then she practically ran from the room.

"Nice going, Lisa," said Jodie. "That was mean."

Lisa looked at Frank. "Dad, a little help, please!"

He shook his head. "You're asking for help after you upset your mother that way? You've got to be kidding me." He threw down his paper and went after his wife.

The orange armed light on the alarm panel next to the bed was a huge comfort to Frank and Sofia. Mainly it was a comfort to Sofia, since Frank slept through almost anything. She'd wake up and look at the panel long enough to focus on the glowing orange "Armed Stay" icon on the display. Then she'd go back to sleep, knowing her son was safely in bed. It became such a part of her nightly ritual that she didn't give it a second thought. She'd wake up, check the panel, and drift back off.

One night, instead of the orange "Armed Stay" icon, she found the green "Ready" icon glowing. She climbed out of bed and went to check on Sam. His bed was empty. Of course.

She shook Frank, who sat upright, suddenly wide awake. "What's going on? What happened?"

"Sam's gone."

"What?" He too saw the green "Ready" icon on the panel.

They searched the house. Sofia wondered aloud whether they should call the police.

"I'll drive around the neighborhood first. Let's give it ten minutes, then we'll call." He sighed. "They'll think we're cranks."

"I don't care. It's freezing out there. "

"I know. We're making the call if we don't find him in ten."

Nine minutes later, Frank came back in. No sign of their son. He called the police. Kinzer was on duty again that night. His first question was whether Sam had something warm on.

"I don't know."

"Is his jacket—or whatever it is he wears in the cold—still there?"

"Just a minute, let me check." He put his phone down and checked the hall closet. Sam's jacket was gone. That was a relief. As he picked up the phone, Sofia mouthed something to him. He looked at her crossly and covered the phone with his hand. "Sorry, I'm no good at reading lips. What are you trying to say?"

"It's in the dryer."

"What's in the dryer? Look, I've got to finish up with the police here and—"

"Sam's jacket. I washed it this afternoon, and it's in the dryer."

Frank slowly brought the phone back to his ear. "Officer?"

"Still here."

"Looks like he doesn't have his jacket."

"All right, we'll send a couple of cars over there right away. But make this stop. It's dangerous for your son, and it wastes our resources."

Frank didn't like being scolded. "We installed an alarm system so we could tell whenever he'd go out."

"And how's *that* working out for you?"

"Well, it was disarmed, so it didn't go off."

"Yeah, that's the funny thing with alarm systems: they have to be set to work."

"Well, I did set it," said Frank.

"You sure?"

Kinzer's parental tone put him on edge. "Of course I'm sure. I do the same thing every night."

"Does he have the code?"

"No, only my wife and I have that. Even our daughters have no way of turning that on or off."

"Then check the history."

"How do I do that?" asked Frank.

Kinzer cleared his throat. "Well, just about every alarm system made within the past twenty years has a means to log in and find out what time they got armed and disarmed and by who. Find the online manual from the manufacturer, and it will tell you exactly how to do that."

"Great idea. I'll do that in the morning, but first I need to find my son."

"Of course. I've already dispatched two cars to your neighborhood. This is top priority since it's so cold, which clearly presents an additional risk to his safety."

"Believe me, I get that. I'm going to drive around, too. My wife will stay here."

"Make sure you take your phone with you. You said you have daughters?"

"Yes."

"How old are they?"

"Twelve and fourteen."

"I suggest you leave one—or both, even better—at home, and you and your wife both drive around. Do you have two cars?"

"Yes, a pickup and a van."

"Then get them both out there. The more eyes open, the better. Make sure you all stay in contact and that your ringers are on. Let us know when you find him."

Frank hung up and turned to Sofia. "You could have mentioned Sam's jacket before."

"I didn't think of it until you looked in the closet."

He rolled his eyes. "Fine, but next time try to think of things sooner, okay?"

"Why did this suddenly become my fault?"

"I'm just saying we need to be more on top of things," said Frank.

"Let me know when the lecture's over so we can find our son."

With the girls waiting at the house and Sofia out in the van, Frank drove around Eugene for over an hour before his phone rang.

"Any sign?" Sofia asked.

"Not yet."

"Why does he do this? And tonight, of all nights—it's so cold out there. He might catch pneumonia."

"I have no idea, Sofia. There are so many things I don't understand about our son."

"I know. That's why this is so frustrating."

"Let me call you back. Someone's calling in." He switched calls. "Frank MacBride here."

"Mr. MacBride, this is Officer Collins, Eugene PD. I found your son, and he's fine. Dispatch had warned that he might be improperly dressed for the cold, but he was wearing a man-size down jacket. Everything is good—he's warm and toasty."

"Oh, thank God. Where are you?"

"About four blocks from your house. I think he was on his way home. He won't talk to me, but dispatch said that is to be expected."

"He doesn't talk. To anyone." Frank paused. How many times had he said those exact words? "Well, thank you so much. I'll call my wife and tell her to meet you there. I'm over near the Interstate, north of Beltline, so it will take me longer to get home. If you're not still around when I arrive, thanks again."

By the time Frank pulled up, the policeman had left Sam with Sofia, who was the only one still up.

He looked at his wife with exasperation. "What are we going to do?"

"I wish I knew."

The next day after work, Frank logged in to the alarm system with his laptop and checked the history.

"Sofia, look at this," he said, studying his laptop screen.

"What am I looking at?"

"This is yesterday's log from the alarm system."

"So, what does it say?"

"It says I armed the system at 9:03 and you disarmed the system at 12:14 a.m."

She frowned at the screen. "That's impossible. "

"Doesn't seem likely to me, either, but that's what the system says. What time did you discover the system was disarmed last night?"

"I think it was around 2:15 or something like that."

"Have you given the code to Sam?" he asked.

"Of course not. We agreed on that, remember?"

"I know, it's just—this is so weird." Frank rubbed his temples. "How about the girls? Have you ever given the code to them?"

"No! And I don't like your tone. Specifically what are you accusing me of?"

"I'm not accusing you of anything. I'm just trying to be sure," said Frank.

"Maybe you could try to be sure in a different tone of voice."

"Sorry, I'm just—"

"Let's ask Sam."

They watched Sam playing with his Legos in the family room for a few moments. He was so happy, so innocent, so apparently free of cares and worries. Frank knelt down in front of him. "Sam, did you disarm the alarm system last night?"

He nodded without looking up.

"How did you get the code?"

He stared at his Legos and didn't move.

"Did someone tell you the code?"

He shook his head.

"So how did you get it?"

More silence.

"Sam, we need to make sure you are safe. Do you understand?"

He nodded.

"You know it's dangerous for an eight-year-old to go out by himself at night, don't you?"

Again, Sam nodded.

Frank threw his hands up. "So work with us on this please, Sam. Mom and I really want you to be safe. It's the most important thing to us in the world."

Sam glanced at Frank, then Sofia, and nodded again.

CHAPTER TWENTY

When Frank got back from work later that day, he reprogrammed the alarm system with more complex codes and new master codes. He told Sofia her new code quietly, when Sam was in another part of the house. "Whatever you do, don't write it down or tell anyone, especially Sam."

Her eyes narrowed. "Are we doing this again? Of *course* I won't. Do you think I'm crazy?"

"No, you know very well I don't think so. But we have to be very careful to make sure our dear son doesn't get out and wander the neighborhood again."

"I get it. I know we have to be careful. I'm just not having a very good day."

"Yeah, I think I know exactly what that looks like." He put his hands on her shoulders and gave her a gentle squeeze. "We'll figure this out."

"That would work for me."

Sofia loved that Sam learned things fast—at least the things he *wanted* to learn. He was only eight but already doing math at a fifth-grade level. She watched her son, absorbed in his numbers, and for the thousandth time she wished his language ability was at least a fraction of his math skills.

"Do you want to go to school one day, *querido*?" she asked. He nodded, his brown eyes shining and hopeful.

She doubted that would ever happen, though there were options. Jane, one

of the state liaisons for the homeschooling program, told her about OSNIP, the Oregon Special Needs Integration Program. They had kids with special needs in some of the same classes with other students in the mainstream public schools. She still couldn't imagine how that would work. Even if he spoke perfectly connected sentences, how would he survive the other kids in school? He was too sensitive, too caring, and too small. Bullies picked on kids least likely to fight back. When she'd worked as a guidance counselor, there had been so many examples of kids who were mean to each other. Cruel, even. School was a dangerous place. And there was the reading thing. He still wasn't reading, nor would he even let himself be read to. That by itself would be a serious problem.

"Ready for geography, *querido*?

Sam nodded, eager to please.

She brought out the globe. "Okay, point to where I was born."

He turned the globe to Europe, picked out Spain, and pinpointed Barcelona.

"Well done. You found Barcelona, Spain." She couldn't help wondering how many eight-year-olds could do that. Probably not many. She couldn't remember whether they'd ever talked about Frank and where he was born. Might as well try it out.

"Where was Dad born?"

He again went to Europe, then Italy, and pointed to Milan.

She smiled. This boy doesn't miss much. "That's good, *querido,* your father is half Italian, but he was born here …" She turned the globe and pointed to Chicago.

Sam frowned, spun the globe back to Italy, and emphatically pointed his finger again at Milan. He had a defiant, almost angry gleam in his eyes. She thought it best not to push the point. She'd let Frank talk to him. Maybe he'd believe it if he heard directly from his dad. "Good job at finding out where I was born, Sam." She pointed again at Barcelona. *Always focus on the positive—* that's what the homeschool manuals suggested. All kids had their little quirks, beliefs, and tantrums. Rather than insisting on them getting something right, it was always better to go back to a point of agreement.

"Where do we live, *querido*?"

He spun the globe back to the U.S. and pointed to Eugene.

"Great." They were back on track. "And where were you born?"

He spun the globe and pointed to Nepal.

She gently corrected him again. "No, sweetie, you were born in Portland in the Good Samaritan hospital." She gave him her warmest and most gentle smile. "I know, because I was there."

He spun the globe back, jabbed his finger at Nepal, and glared at her.

Surprised, she tried again to correct him as gently as she could, but he stomped off to his room and slammed the door.

Sofia contemplated throwing something against the wall. Which was exactly what her mother did back in Barcelona when she felt frustrated. Many days when Sofia got home from school—before she got shipped off to Santa Angelina—she would discover pieces of broken plates in the living room or kitchen. They never discussed it, but both girls knew what was going on. Sometimes they heard their parents talking in hushed tones about other women in her father's life. The pattern repeated itself, and everyone expected it. She was angry at her mom because she did nothing about it. Though in hindsight, what could Isabel have done? Other than leave her cheating and abusive husband.

The frustration Sofia felt with Sam's situation was different. He could be difficult with his hiding, his temper, and randomly losing attention. He still didn't speak, and the growing possibility was that he might never read or write. She saw no solution, but she wasn't about to give up, either. She was in it for the long haul, no matter how difficult.

At the moment, it felt *very* difficult.

CHAPTER TWENTY-ONE

Sofia met Frank at the door after work and let him know about the flare-up with Sam earlier that day.

He frowned. "What happened this time?"

"I asked him to point out places on the globe when we were doing geography, and he got mad when I corrected him. I thought it would be good for you to talk to him, since the upset was over your birthplace."

Frank became still. "What do you mean?"

"I asked him where I was born, and he pointed to Barcelona. When I asked him where you were born, however, he pointed to Milan, Italy."

Color drained from his face. "No!"

"Hey, it's not that big a deal. He just got it wrong. I pointed to Chicago, but he kept spinning it back to Milan. And he got furious with me."

"Then what?" he asked hesitantly and sat on the couch.

"Well," she continued, not sure of what was going on, "I asked him to show me where we lived, you know, just to calm him down. He pointed right to Eugene. But when I asked where he was born, he pointed to Nepal, of all places. I tried to explain, but he got absolutely steamed. He ran to his room and slammed the door. It's way too early for him to start his teenage years, if you ask me." She shook her head. "I'm not sure what's going on with him, but sometimes I think maybe we treat him as though he's a little too special, know what I mean?" Her husband didn't appear to be listening. "Frank?"

He covered his face with his hands.

"Frank, what's going on? Are you okay?"

"Yeah. Um, no. I need to think. And walk. We'll talk when I get back. Just give me fifteen minutes. Or half an hour."

"Frank, what the hell?"

But he had already left. She noticed Sam watching her from the hallway. She asked him facetiously, "I suppose you know what this is all about?"

He nodded, but she was stumped.

Her husband came back almost an hour later. "Sofia, I'm ready to talk."

"You're scaring me."

"I love you, I love our kids, and I am a hundred percent committed to this family."

"Are you trying to put me at ease? Because it's not working."

Frank rubbed his temples. "I know." He cleared his throat and called out. "Lisa? Jodie?"

"Down here, Daddy!" responded Jodie.

"I'm going to have Sam come down with you. Can you all stay down there while Mom and I talk?"

"What's going on?" asked Lisa.

"Don't worry about it. This is grown-up stuff. Everything is good. We just need to clarify a few things," said Frank.

Once in the master bedroom, Sofia asked, "So what's going on?"

"Sofia, please sit down."

"I will not sit down until you tell me what the hell is going on. You putting things off is just making me more anxious—"

"I'm not putting things off. I'm trying to tell you. This is just very ... difficult."

"Is there someone else?"

"What? No, of course not. How could you think that?"

"Well, I could very easily think that the way you are carrying on right now. What did you do, kill somebody?"

He didn't say a word.

Her hand involuntarily covered her mouth. "You didn't!"

"No, I didn't. But my father did. And my uncles and my cousins did. I don't know if anyone knows how many people my family killed."

"What? Your uncles? You told me you didn't have any uncles other than Gino."

"Well, that's sort of true. Any uncles I had are dead, as far as I know. Let me tell you some things that are true, but I need to also tell you why. Please wait to hear the whole story before you ... do anything." He looked at her with sad eyes. "Do we have a deal?"

She nodded wordlessly.

"Okay, the first problem is that Sam's right. I don't know how, but he's right."

"What do you mean?"

"I mean I was born in Milan."

"You're kidding!"

"I wish I was. My father double-crossed and stole from a government official in Milan, who was very well-connected with the Concino family. That official vowed to have every one of us killed—including my three uncles, Pops, me, Nonna Eve, and my two brothers. The three of us were under twenty. I was seventeen, Patrizio fifteen, and Joe only ten."

"You have two brothers you never told me about?" She sat down hard on the bed. "This is unbelievable!"

"Had. I *had* two brothers. Mamma took me to the hospital with an ear infection. She thought it would be a quick turnaround, but they made us stay overnight. She was furious about that, because her brothers were coming over for dinner with their families. The only person who knew where we were was her friend Cara." He swallowed. "It saved our lives. They killed everyone in the house. We didn't know until we got back from the hospital. I'll never forget the sight of my brothers lying in their blood, next to Pops and Uncle Alessandro." He stared at the wall. "I never saw the bodies of my other uncles. Or my aunts. We got out of there as fast as we could."

"No!" She looked at him and frowned. "That's why you have the nightmares, isn't it?"

He closed his eyes. "Yes. Sometimes I see what happened, and sometimes ..."

"What?"

"Nothing. The government guy's name was Luigi Henrico—he was a low-level minister or something—and he wanted to send a message that people would understand so they'd fear him."

"And you would have been there but for dumb luck." She shook her head in disbelief. "So what happened then?"

"Cara's family had connections. We hid out a few days while they made fake documents for us." He took a deep breath. "And that's only part of the story."

She waited patiently for him to finish. "I'm listening."

"Mamma went to a storage space where Pops would occasionally hide things. It was ordinary but secure, and she had the combination. She found fifty gold coins stashed there. We used them to pay for the documents and travel, and—" He looked at her sadly. "There was no investment. I would just sell the gold when I had to."

"So that was another lie."

"No, it was part of the same lie. Believe me, it was only to protect you."

"This is incredible!"

He shrugged. "We went to France, where we got new U.S. passports on the black market. It took a while, and Mamma pulled strings to get those. I don't know how. Once we arrived here, she contacted an old friend of my father's, whom he'd said to look up if she was ever in trouble. That was Uncle Gino. Not actually my uncle, but a dear family friend who got us established here."

"Uncle Gino is not your real uncle?"

"No, and Gino is not his real name. We had to keep everything double insulated as far as we could. I'm not sure of the extent of that double cross or even all that was done—Mamma didn't know herself. But obviously my father upset some powerful people."

"Who knows all this?"

"Me, Gino … and Mamma used to know. And now you." He sighed. "And I wasn't born as Frank."

"Seriously?"

"Seriously. Uncle Gino said it was important that we change our names." He shook his head. "Now you know why I live in fear."

"I get it. At least now you're far away from them. Plus, it's been a long time. Doesn't seem like there's any chance they'd find you."

Frank sighed. "Unfortunately, not too long before this all happened, Pat and I got caught stealing."

"Pat?"

"Patrizio. My little brother. It wasn't a big deal, and I don't remember what we stole, but the local police chief was in the pocket of the Concino family. Normally, they don't fingerprint teenagers for a minor offense, but they fingerprinted Pat and me. I think it may have come from Henrico to send a message to my father. Not sure what kind of minister he was, but it had something to do with the police. They were trying to squeeze my dad. Maybe thinking he would pull up stakes and leave everything behind. Not my father. From everything I remember about him, he was one bullheaded man. He was furious about that and just increased his operations. He also went back on an agreement with Henrico. The police squeezed him more, which pissed him off, so he stole some of Henrico's gold. Which was a fatal mistake."

"The fifty coins."

"Exactly. It was like kicking a hornet's nest. Uncle Gino told us to not contact anyone back home for any reason. Not that we had much of anyone left, really. Maybe a distant cousin or two. One side effect of the whole mess is that my fingerprints in my old identity are somewhere in the system. Police agencies all over the world share that kind of information. So if I ever got fingerprinted here, they could connect me with my previous identity. I could be deported and sent back to Italy."

"But surely they wouldn't do that. You have a family, a life, and a job here."

Frank shook his head slowly. "How I wish you were right. But let me tell you how governments work. They don't care. They have their rules and regulations. And there's an even greater risk. I have no idea how the Concino family is operating these days, but if they are still in with the police in Italy, and they found me, and I was enough of an interest for them—"

"Don't talk like that. You haven't been fingerprinted since you got here all those years ago. I'm sure it's not going to happen now. And even if it did, it doesn't mean they would make the connection." She snapped her fingers. "So that's why you keep a gun, isn't it?"

He nodded.

"… and why you've never gotten a concealed-carry permit, even though you carry it with you in the pickup, concealed." She took him by the shoulders and turned him to face her. "You'd be in a lot of trouble if you got caught with that."

"I would, but not as much trouble as I'd be in if I got caught by the wrong people without it."

"What a mess!" Her mind spun. "So how in the world could Sam—"

"There's no possible way he could know. Unless he got lucky. But that kind of luck is one out of millions. And you said he got mad?"

"Yes, mad and insistent. He kept turning the globe back. He was furious with me for trying to tell him you were born in Chicago."

"He couldn't know—but apparently he knew." Frank frowned. "Not like I ever talked about it around him—or anybody else."

"No, you sure didn't. Though you should have, at least to me."

"Like I said, that was for your protection."

She didn't know whether she should be mad. "So you're not half Italian?"

"No, baby, I am the real deal. Full-blooded one hundred percent Italiano."

"We're not even MacBrides, then, are we?"

"No, sorry. That and my father being Scottish was all part of the story Uncle Gino helped us come up with. He thought it would make us harder to find."

"Why didn't you tell me later, after we married or maybe after a kid or two? Once you realized I was clearly committed to this relationship."

"Because I knew you'd worry. Always looking over *your* shoulder. Wondering if the Concino family will ever find me. Just too close for comfort. And it's why we had to leave Portland."

Sofia's mouth dropped open. "What are you talking about?"

"One of their guns saw me there. A dangerous guy named Belgian Pete.

At least I think it was him. That's why I had to get us out of town as fast as possible."

"And you didn't think for one second to tell me why, knowing how upsetting the move was to me?"

"I did consider it—many times. I thought it would have made you more upset."

"That doesn't give you an excuse to withhold critical information from me. I was upset, but knowing the reason would have made it easier. Like we were doing it together."

Frank looked genuinely remorseful. "I know. I'm sorry. But I swear on Mamma's soul that my first wish was to protect you and the kids. I would rather die than let anything happen to any of you."

"Am I supposed to be good with being lied to?"

"My beloved wife whom I adore, I have never lied about my feelings for you, my commitment to you, or my commitment to our family."

She looked into the face of the husband that she thought she'd known for fifteen years but now was not so sure. She believed him but had also believed he was born in Chicago and other things that weren't true. "So what about Sam being angry about his birthplace?"

"We both know he was born at Good Samaritan in Portland, not in Nepal. We both saw him come into this world. Maybe the whole born-in-Milan thing was just God's way to make me finally tell you the truth. Otherwise, it makes no sense."

"So many things make no sense. But here's something that does. I'm driving to Sacramento tonight to stay with Madre and Papá."

"I need to work tomorrow," he said.

"Actually, you don't. That's what sick days are for: when you piss off your wife and need to cover with the kids. I have to do this. I need time to think, to feel, and to see if I can make sense of the new reality I found myself thrown into. Plan to take tomorrow and Friday off. I'll be away at least for the weekend."

"At least?"

"Yeah, at least. I have to sort things out in my head. This is quite the hot potato you tossed in my lap. Right now I need space."

"Right. Just please don't doubt how much I love you," he said.

She gave him a hard look, then went to say goodbye to the kids.

Jeff Kingston was not gracious when Frank called in to request two days off. He told him it was a family emergency, and when Kingston pressed him for details, he stood within his rights and wouldn't say more. Kingston didn't like hearing 'no,' but Frank was beyond caring. The relationship with his boss had gone to hell a long time ago. Though, as Andrea liked to hint, things could always be worse.

He watched Sam do his lessons. He had to improvise with the curriculum and figure out with Sam's help where they were up to. Yesterday had gone well, and today had been another good day—up until around lunchtime, when Sam got upset about something, though Frank couldn't figure out what. Even with his girls who talked perfectly well, they sometimes wouldn't tell him—or didn't even know themselves—why they were not happy.

Sofia returned late Sunday afternoon. The kids all rushed to hug her while Frank stood behind them, waiting. Before even looking at her husband, she sent the kids to watch TV down in the family room.

"I told my father."

"Sofia, we needed to keep that private."

"I only told him you had broken my trust."

"Great, now he'll think I had an affair."

"Believe me, that would not lose you any ground in his eyes. Maybe even gain some. But that's not the point. He asked me some important questions, and they all have the same answer."

"That doesn't sound good," said Frank.

"Well, hear what he asked. 'Do you love me? Do you love our kids? Are you committed to our relationship?'"

"Do I want to know your answers?"

"I think you already know they are all yeses. I didn't tell him you are also sometimes a pain in the ass."

Frank rubbed his forehead. "I'm sorry I lied to you. I felt I had to. But now you know everything, and I won't lie to you anymore. That's all I can promise."

She nodded. "There's just one other thing you need to know."

"What's that?"

"No sex for a month."

"I hope you're kidding."

"Only time will tell," she said with a gleam in her eye.

Chapter Twenty-Two

Hi there, this is Jess's phone. You know what to do at the beep and I will get back to you soon as I can. Thank you so much for calling and make yourself a blessed day!

"Hey, Jess, this is Sofia, and I wouldn't blame you if you never want to talk to me again. I want to apologize for being nasty to you last May. I was already afraid of what you said about Frank, and that just totally triggered me. What you said about Sam and healing and reincarnation are very interesting. Fascinating, really. Anyway, I'm fine if you don't call me back, but I would love you to. I want to be your friend, if you're open to that.

"I know you haven't been letting April come over because of me. I don't blame you for that one bit. If someone talked to me that way, I'd also be concerned about letting my kid go over to their house. You have my absolute promise I would never say anything against you to your child.

"Here I am rambling on like a crazy woman. I guess all I need to say is, please forgive me."

Looking through the paperwork in his inbox at the Public Works office one morning, Frank found a performance review memo scheduling him at three o'clock that very afternoon with Kingston. Odd—two days earlier than the rescheduled date. He checked his online work manifest for the jobs to be done.

A battery needed replacement at the computer backup station across the hall, some breakers needed replacing in the office main panel, a security light needed a ballast changed out at the heavy equipment lot, and one of the ventilation motors at the water treatment plant had been making a funny noise. They were each labeled *Urgent, High-priority*.

Frank shook his head. Kingston loved to put an "urgent" stamp on things. A few of the items looked somewhat urgent to him, especially the water plant motor, but not everything on the list. Since when was replacing fully functioning breakers an urgent task? He had to do all urgent issues in the order posted on his work manifest, as clearly outlined in the policies and procedures manual. On the work description for the heavy equipment lot, he saw instructions to call Kingston's minion Barry to let him in the gate. It annoyed him that Kingston had never cleared him to have a gate key code in over two years he'd been working there. He was pretty sure it wasn't an issue of trust, but of Kingston reminding him who was in control.

When Frank finally got through most of his list and arrived at the lot, he called Barry—who told him he was running late and would arrive as soon as possible. An hour and seven minutes later, he showed up to let Frank—who by then was well behind schedule—through the gate. When asked what had taken him so long, Barry just shrugged. Frank knew the answer, but why would Kingston go to so much trouble to harass him? Some things just didn't make sense. He didn't reach the water treatment plant until after one o'clock, and he hadn't even stopped for lunch.

When he checked the digital logs on the whining motor, he found it way out of its normal parameters, drawing far too much load current. The overload protection had not shut it down and signaled a remote alert as it should have. It would be a long afternoon. He replaced the motor controller and looked at his watch. *Damn!* He had to get things wrapped up and back to the office before the performance review. It was already 1:57, and he still had to test everything, determine why the motor made noise in the first place, and troubleshoot the alert system. He called Kingston to let him know he'd be late for the three o'clock review, but his call went directly to voice mail.

"Hey there, boss. I'm sorry, but I'm stuck with this ventilation motor. It was running on overload but not shutting down, so I decided to replace the motor controller and the current sensors. I've already got the controller replaced, but I still have to install the new current sensors and find out what caused the whine in the first place. Once I make sure it's all good and back online, I should be there for the performance review around three thirty or three forty-five. Four o'clock at the absolute latest."

He knocked on Kingston's office door at 3:39.

"Come in."

Frank walked in, sighed heavily, and sat across the desk from his boss. "You wouldn't believe the day I had."

"You're late, MacBride."

"I know. That's why I left you a voice message. Didn't you get it?"

"I did not."

"Well, I called you just before two and—"

"Listen, MacBride, we're already behind schedule, and I have more important things to do. Let's move along." He opened a binder and began writing.

Frank leaned forward. "What are you doing?"

Kingston glared at him and continued writing, saying nothing for a few moments. "You'll get a copy of everything. I'm saying you have issues organizing your schedule. You have difficulty being on time and meeting commitments. You couldn't even show up on time for your own performance review, even though your tasks for the day were all clearly assigned ahead of time."

"Now, hang on a damn minute. I had to work with that motor at the treatment plant because it was a potential burnout."

"And that you argue with me every chance you get."

"Hey, I'm only trying to—"

"See, that's exactly what I'm talking about." Kingston smirked. "And we're about finished here." He glanced at his watch. "Since we started late, we don't have as much time as we would have, but oh well."

"What the fuck are you talking about? I haven't even been here five minutes. You haven't mentioned my attendance record, my peer interactions, my completion of jobs, how few callbacks I've had compared to everyone else, and—"

Writing again, Kingston's smirk deepened. "Excessive use of profanity in the office." He looked up and smiled thinly at Frank. "Are you still here? Would you like to throw in some racial slurs while you're at it? I think a few of those would round out your review nicely."

Frank drew a deep breath and suppressed a desire to leap over the man's desk and grab him by the throat. Sofia was right. Time to look for a new job. The problem was, it would have to be somewhere other than Eugene. And even then, he was sure this buffoon of a boss would give him as negative a recommendation as possible. As he left the office, he turned and faced his superior. "I know you want to get rid of me."

Kingston looked up at him and cocked his head to the side. "Whatever gives you that idea?"

"Look, if you'll agree to give me a positive recommendation, I'll quit in two weeks. I won't make a fuss or cause any trouble. I'll just go. You'll be happy and I'll be happy. Or at least happier. This is obviously not working."

Kingston turned his attention back to his binder and read aloud as he wrote. "Threatened to quit, and hinted he might cause a lot of trouble if I did not comply with his demands." He looked back at Frank. "Anything else?"

"Are you going to fire me?"

"No, and you will not quit, either. Trust me when I say I'd destroy you." He leaned forward. "You know what they say about keeping your enemies close."

"Look, there's no need for us to be enemies."

"You don't want to be enemies?" Kingston asked.

"No."

"Too bad you didn't think of that before coming on to my wife."

Frank sat in his pickup truck on the Public Works lot, staring out the windshield. Sofia would be eager to hear the news, happily anticipating the raise they'd been waiting for all this time. She wouldn't like what he had to report. Whether she said it out loud or not, she'd be thinking he'd already received this raise back in Lake Oswego two and a half years earlier. Back when he had a boss he liked and they lived in a place they liked. Yet he'd insisted they move, forcing the round peg of their family into the square hole of Eugene. For what? Because he'd thought Belgian Pete was after him. More likely that wasn't even him back in Gresham. At least now Sofia knew the reason for their move. He sighed and started his truck. Time to face the music.

She was livid when he told her what had happened. "I can't believe that small-minded bastard. What's his problem? Why does he have it so *in* for you?"

He shrugged. "Beats me. You were there at the Christmas party, and I know he got really upset with me over that, even though it was his basket case of a wife who was the problem."

She sighed. "Maybe he thought you enjoyed that. Who knows?" Maybe he noticed your little smirk and knew there was something personal going on that had everything to do with him. "We don't know what's going on behind the scenes there, either. For all we know, every time they have a fight, she might say something like, 'I bet Frank MacBride wouldn't do that; I bet Frank MacBride is nice to his wife; I bet Frank MacBride lasts longer than ninety seconds.'"

He felt his cheeks warming and hoped she didn't notice. "That's funny, Sofia. Anyway, he was on my case long before the Christmas party. It's just that it's gotten worse since then."

She sighed. "We were counting on that raise."

"I know," he said. "But we'll think of something."

Sofia shook her head. "It's just so damn unfair."

"Well, whoever says life is fair is lying." He raised an eyebrow. "I think we know that one pretty well."

Frank took a walk around the block after dinner that night and called Andrea. "Why, Frank, how sweet of you to call."

She must think she's being cute. "You know my job is in jeopardy, right?"

"Why, I'm doing fine, thanks for asking. And how are you today?"

"Come on, Andi. This is a huge problem for me. Why did you tell him?"

"Why did you stand me up a month ago at Starbucks?"

"I never agreed to show up. That was you bossing me around, and I don't like being bossed around."

"Did I damage your fragile male ego?"

"Not at all. I just didn't feel I had to show up." Frank drew a deep breath. "And it's not fragile."

"I see."

"I wanted you to get the message that it's over."

"But it's not."

"It is!"

Andrea spoke slowly. "If it was over, we wouldn't be having this conversation, would we?"

"You know what I mean. The physical part."

"That's not over, either. I still want you."

"Andi—look, why did you tell Jeff?"

"I didn't."

"I wonder why he dramatically increased his level of hostility toward me."

"Because he read your texts on my phone."

"Are you kidding me?"

"Don't worry. I had erased the most incriminating ones, just in case of this exact scenario. He still doesn't know our little secret. Can you imagine what he'd do?"

What had he gotten himself into? "You left your phone out where he could find it, didn't you?"

"I can't believe you think I'd do that on purpose. I had it locked, but he must have figured out my password. Maybe he looked over my shoulder. I don't know. He's a very suspicious guy. What can I do if he violates my privacy?"

"Well, you could start by deleting *all* our texts, Andrea."

"Andi. Because we're friends with plenty of benefits, remember? We should get together to work this out. Just text me a time and place, and we'll take it from there. Don't forget, it's not nice to keep a girl waiting. Oh, looks like Jeff just pulled up. Maybe I should get off the phone—what do you think?"

Frank immediately hung up. *"Fuck!"*

CHAPTER TWENTY-THREE

From:intuitivejess2344@gmail.com
Sent: December 3, 2013 3:07 AM
To: sofiamb@AOL.com
Subject: Thank you

Hey there, Sofia.

Thanks for your beautiful message. Sorry to take so long to get back to you. I should have put a vacation message on my phone, but I didn't think about it. That's pretty spaced out, isn't it? I've been in Europe now for almost two months. Big surprise, right?

Of course I would forgive you, but there's nothing to forgive. I did the wrong thing, and I assumed you didn't want to have anything more to do with me. The same week we met for tea, April was visiting her dad and he found a couple of joints in her backpack. When he asked, she said I gave them to her. The sad part of that is I haven't smoked in years, so how would I give weed to my twelve-year-old daughter? I don't even drink. I don't do any of that stuff, because it just clouds me up, you know? But I did back when Kevin and I met. He's assumed that since I'm obviously lost without him, I went back to where I was before.

Anyway, he's senior partner in his law firm now and gets people whatever they want, right or wrong, as long as the price is right. He went to court and asked for full custody of April. He made up other stuff about me that was very hurtful and not true. It didn't help that I was busted for possession twice back in college. He got everything he asked for. I only get to see my daughter whenever he wants. Which is practically never. It's been one of the saddest times of my life. I asked my parents for a loan. They'd never liked Kevin and were pretty sympathetic. I know they never expect me to pay them back, but I will when I can. So here I am traveling, which has been life-changing for me.

They say the best way to find yourself is to get lost. Have you ever heard that? It totally resonates with me. I feel so much better than I did before. If I ever write a memoir, I could call it Lost and Found. Ha!

Ten days ago in Barcelona I thought of you. At a coffee shop talking to some travelers from Scotland, we discussed Gaudi architecture and other amazing sights there, and without thinking I said, 'My best friend grew up here.' So there you have it.

I push people away. I don't try, but it's what I've always done. Thanks for not staying away.

With love,

Jessica
P.S. Sorry for the long email

Frank had been trying to connect with Jason in person for weeks. They finally met at a cafe in Salem and ordered a couple of beers. After a few minutes discussing work, how much everyone at Lake Oswego Public Works missed Frank, and how much less fun his new job was, Frank explained the situation with Andrea.

"It's like a scene right out of *Fatal Attraction*. And I'm Michael Douglas."

"When's the last time you got it on with her?"

"Months ago. Back in June."

"Is she good in bed?"

"Jason, this isn't funny."

"Who's being funny? I need the whole story. All the sordid details."

Frank took a deep breath. "She's very good."

"As in better than Sofia?"

Frank sighed. "Let's just say more enthusiastic. And," he examined his fingernails, "she made me feel good."

"How?"

"Like she cares. It's weird. On one hand, she's the most self-centered person I've ever met. But she does things that make me forget that."

Jason leaned forward. "Enlighten me. How does she do that?"

"Well, for example, she got herself a full Brazilian wax, just for me."

"You're kidding! How many times had you slept with her up until then?"

"Twice."

"Damn! I was married to Katie almost twelve years and I couldn't even get her to give herself a decent trim. You poor guy!" He took a long swig of beer. "So what are you now, forty-five?"

"Thanks for that. I'm only forty-two."

Jason smiled. "Close enough. Welcome to your midlife crisis."

"I don't think—"

"Some guys get a hot new car, some take up skydiving, others have affairs." He gestured at Frank. "It all makes perfect sense. How'd you get yourself into this in the first place?"

"With an innocent-enough conversation in the Marriott Cowboy Cafe at the expo. Things just kind of progressed from there."

"Hang on—not the hottie you were talking to off in that secluded corner?"

"It wasn't exactly secluded, but yeah, that's her."

"There are worse problems to have, you know. I mean, your wife is pretty hot, make no mistake, but that woman is movie-star gorgeous." He shook his head. "I don't think I would have said 'no' to her. Brazilian or not."

"She was Miss Oregon at one time."

"That's easy to believe." Jason leaned in. "So tell me why this is a problem?"

"You know damn well. First of all, because I'm married with three kids, and second, because she's my boss's wife."

"Right, just testing. Um, do you have her number? Maybe I could take her off your hands and solve both our problems."

"Now you're being downright hilarious." Frank scratched his head. "Look, I know I blew it, but …" He watched a couple walking past the cafe's front window. "I don't want this to mess up my relationship with Sofia."

"Sounds like someone has a different attitude these days." Jason leaned back. "When we worked together, you didn't seem to care so much, the way you'd hit on anything that was female and halfway cute."

"I wasn't hitting on them. It was harmless flirting."

"I see. Well, that's *completely* different."

Frank fidgeted with his wedding ring. "Anyway, things change."

"Apparently so. And I understand why it's a problem. Just tell Miss Oregon it's over."

Frank shook his head. "I did, and it is. That's what I was saying before. She not only threatens me, she makes good on her threats. A few months ago, she told her husband I flirt with her just because I stopped seeing her."

"Hell hath no fury, right? That's not good. Especially considering what an asshole your boss can be even when he's *not* provoked."

"Exactly. But it gets worse. A few weeks later he got into her phone and read her texts with me. Or so she says. Bottom line is that things went from bad to worse between the boss and me in a hurry."

"Yikes!"

"And she's hinted that she could tell him we've slept together."

"That would be what we refer to in technical terms as being in deep shit," said Jason.

"Which is why I wanted to see you."

"What do you think would happen if you told your wife?"

"If I told her, she might walk." Frank sighed. "With the kids."

"That's not likely, is it?"

"I'm not sure. I lied to her once about something big, and when she found out, she took off the same day," said Frank.

"But she came back, right?"

"She didn't come *right* back. It took her four or five days."

"What did you lie to her about?"

Frank squinted at his friend. "I'd love to tell you, but then I'd have to kill you."

"Funny. What was it?"

He stared off into space. "I really can't tell you."

"You can tell me you cheated on your wife, but you're holding back something more secret than that?" Jason leaned back in his chair. "This has got to be good."

"If I told you, you'd understand why I *can't* tell you."

"Whatever."

Frank sighed. "It's the reason I had to meet you here in Salem, even though it meant I had to wait another week to talk to you."

"Oh, so you had an affair back in Portland. And you're worried that you'd run into her." He smiled and shook his head. "What makes you think I wouldn't understand that?"

Frank took a deep breath. "That's not it."

"It's okay, you can tell me. Anybody I know?" He smiled. "You were quite friendly with that beauty in accounting. What was her name? Sue, or Mary Sue? I saw you hitting on her pretty much every chance you got."

"Sue Ellen, and I didn't have an affair with her or anybody else there." He took another deep breath. "And I wasn't hitting on her."

"So who was it? Some bohemian hottie you met at Whole Foods?"

Frank rubbed his forehead. "No, I honestly didn't have an affair with anyone anywhere until this thing happened with Andrea."

Jason shook his head. "So don't tell me, then." He looked at his watch. "Anyway, I should get back." He picked up his beer and stood. "You started by asking me what I thought. Don't tell Sofia. Break off all contact with Andrea. If that messes up your work situation and you get fired, then go out and look for a new job. But don't let her hold you hostage with her threats." He turned to go. "I'll see you around."

"Jason, please sit down." Frank glanced around to make sure no one was within earshot. "There are people who want to kill me," he said as quietly as possible.

"Yeah, me too. Couple of former girlfriends and my ex-wife. Not to mention my third-year high school English teacher. I used to cut up in his class all the time and—"

"I'm serious." Frank reached across to where Jason's beer bottle had been and put his palm flat on the table. "Please. Sit down and let me tell you about it."

Jason sat. "I hope you're kidding!"

"I wish I was. Better you don't know the details, but the long story short is that's why I had to get out of town with my family."

"You must have truly pissed somebody off. I understand why you didn't want to tell me." He shook a finger at Frank. "Now it makes perfect sense why you left Portland. We were all scratching our heads about that. You had it good. You were happy, your wife and kids were happy, you made decent money, and if you ask me, Portland is a lot better than Eugene."

"I know." Frank shook his head. "And I don't even know whether it was the right thing to do. Summer before last, some perv in a Cadillac tried to pick up my girls when they were two blocks from home. Don't know what I'd do if something like that happened." He bit his lower lip and exhaled. "I'd die if anything happened to my family. And I have these nightmares where the worst happens."

Jason stared out the window. "Man! That sucks." He nodded at Frank. "But look, you were trying to do the right thing. You made the best decision you could with the information you had at the time." He leaned back in his chair. "You're asking me what I think, right?"

"Of course."

Jason finished his beer in one long swig. "Okay. You've been known to worry occasionally."

"So you've told me. Many times."

"Maybe you overreacted in Portland. Too late for that now, but I still wouldn't consider moving back if there is any risk at all. The main thing is that you need to stop second-guessing your decision to move. Going forward, every time you feel protective or that you have to do the right thing, ask yourself this: 'Am I doing this for me, or for them?'"

"I'm always doing it for them, of course."

Jason shook his head. "Not necessarily. We can think we're doing things for someone else and feel all good and righteous about it, but it's really for us. So we feel better about ourselves."

"What are you, a therapist all of a sudden?"

"Better believe it." He winked. "But here's the thing: so much can happen to any of us at any moment. A drunk driver can swerve into our lane or we can get some rare—or not so rare—terminal disease. You're an electrician. You could get juiced by fourteen thousand volts or fall off a ladder and break your neck. Or come down with leukemia. Any one of those things is more likely than you getting taken out by someone you've pissed off.

"Same thing with the safety of your family. You'll always be careful, but there are no guarantees in this world. There is no way to protect them one hundred percent. It's just not possible."

"If only it was so simple."

"Maybe it's simpler than you think," said Jason. "Anyway, that's the way I see it. What else are friends for, right?" He glanced at his watch. "I really do have to run." As they both stood, he gave Frank a hug and a light slap on the cheek. "Call me whenever you want so we can talk more about this.

Meanwhile, don't tell Sofia about Miss Oregon if you know what's good for you."

"Right."

Jason scratched his chin. "And don't expect her to be as enthusiastic about sex when she's taking care of three kids. Four kids, including you. Besides, she's around you all the time with day-to-day family stuff. That can definitely decrease sexual polarity, you know."

"Tell me about it."

Chapter Twenty-Four

As they got ready for bed a couple of weeks later, Frank asked Sofia if she was okay.

"I'm fine," she said. "Just stressed with Christmas shopping and everything."

"Are you sure?"

"I think I would know."

"Okay, just asking," said Frank.

He was walking on eggshells again, which Sofia found irritating. "Sorry, I didn't mean to snap at you like that. I had such an intense day. Everything I said to the girls just came out wrong. Plus, I get good ideas for presents, but have to work around a severely limited budget, which is frustrating. The worst thing is that all this fruitless testing with Sam drives me nuts, and I'm upset he isn't reading. He can read numbers, so why not words? What Lisa said last summer is so true. All we hear from them is, 'We don't know; we can't tell; we need to run more tests.'" She sighed. "'We have no freaking clue' is what they should say. Instead, they tell us we need more testing, go to this therapist or that one. All for more than we can afford. When you were cashing in the gold coins, it helped cover the testing expenses. But now they're all used up. Worst case is when we have to ask my parents for help." She sighed. "Which they rarely do anymore, and always with a comment or two. You know what I'm talking about."

"Believe me, I do. Which is why we stopped asking."

"Anyway," she said, putting her arms around him. "I'm sorry. We're on the same side, and I'm grateful for how much you help with the kids, among everything else. Honestly, I have no clue how single parents manage. I couldn't be doing this without you." She kissed him gently on the cheek. "You'd better never leave me."

"Well, that's not likely to happen, unless some hot movie star offers me the opportunity to share her life, bed, and salary with her. I've heard Jennifer Lawrence has been making inquiries. Apart from that, I'm here for the long run."

Sofia laughed and punched him in the arm. "For my part, I will try to not snap at you, unless you really deserve it." She smiled seductively. "Fortunately, I know just how to make it up to you for my momentary lapses in inter-spousal interactions."

"And you think you can make it all better, just like that, huh?" He shook his head. "Do you really think I'm that easy to manipulate?"

"Yep, I sure do."

That night, Frank's phone rang at 12:43. He woke in a panic, thinking it was Andrea.

"Frank MacBride?"

"That's me."

"Sergeant Kinzer with the Eugene Police Department."

"What's wrong?"

"I apologize for calling so late, but we just received a complaint from someone over in Parkhill who said they heard a noise in the house. When they went to investigate, a small boy was inside and took off running. I know it's far-fetched, but since your son has these, um, wandering habits, we thought maybe—well, we don't know it's him, but since he might possibly fit the description …"

Frank glanced at his alarm panel. The orange "Armed Stay" icon was lit, which meant everybody was home.

"Nope, all good here. Besides, Parkhill would be too far for him to walk."

"Right. Well, sorry to disturb you. Just thought we'd check."

"No, I appreciate you checking," Frank said with a yawn. "We never figured it out, but we're relieved that it finally stopped."

Sofia, Frank, and Sam ate breakfast one morning as the girls got ready for school. Sofia liked how the homeschooling was going. Not only did Sam enjoy it, when she'd had him tested on his progress week before last, he was in the ninety-fifth percentile statewide in math for his age. Sure, it might be easier for her if he was in public school, but that wasn't an option. Not for Sam.

"Remember Beth?" Sofia asked Frank out of the blue.

"Um ..."

"Nonna Eve's friend."

"Of course."

"You'll never believe what she told me."

"What's that?" asked Frank absently, without looking up from his paper.

"Remember when I told you that her son Jeremy had stage-four lymphatic cancer?"

Sam stopped eating and suddenly became very interested.

Frank finally looked up. "Um, not sure. When did you tell me that?"

She frowned. "About six months ago, but since you listen selectively, you may not have heard a word of it."

He folded his paper and set it down. "Sorry, teacher, I'll try to pay more attention in class from now on."

"Anyway, I met him a couple of years ago," she continued, attempting a smile, "and he's a very nice man—"

"Who's a nice man?" asked Jodie as she came in and sat down.

"Beth's son, Jeremy," said Frank, "and your mom is saying 'is' instead of 'was,' so that's probably a good thing."

Lisa walked in as well. "What are you talking about?"

"Someone named Jeremy," Sofia said, "and I'll tell you if I can get a word in edgewise. This could have been a very sad story, so you all need to hear it." She tucked her hair behind her ear, a sure sign she was excited. "Anyway, they had given him four months at most to live—only two if he didn't get chemo *and* radiation therapy."

Frank shook his head. "That's rough."

"He wanted to spend his last two months with as full a life as possible, rather than his last four sick as a dog. His family was split on that. Beth fully supported his decision, but his dad—her ex-husband—insisted he should fight it. Jeremy chose to not fight."

"I get that," said Frank. "I mean, it's his choice, right? He should be able to decide how he wants to live the rest of his life. Hell, we all should." He paused. "How old is he?"

"Don't know, exactly—somewhere in his mid-forties."

Frank frowned. "That's too bad."

"Not really. Here's the good part. Beth said he's testing clean."

Frank took a long sip of his coffee. "Meaning he's in remission?"

"No—meaning he's got no more cancer cells in his body."

Sam looked from one parent to the other, as if watching a ping-pong match.

Frank's eyebrows went up. "How'd he do that? One of those fancy alternative cures?"

"Well, no, that's the strange part. He wasn't on any cure at all."

"How's that possible?" asked Frank.

"Like I said, he'd given up and just wanted to live his last days without being a burden to anyone. Pretty much threw in the towel. Then one day he felt better, and when they tested him last week, they said he was clean. As in done with the cancer. I have this image in my head of all those docs in white coats, standing around, scratching their heads."

"No way!" said Lisa.

Sofia smiled. "Yeah, isn't that something?"

Frank nodded. "I'll say! If they could only figure out how some people can dodge those kinds of bullets, then maybe they could find a cure for all kinds of cancer." He glanced over at Sam, who had been watching him intently. He smiled at his son, who returned a shy smile before going back to his breakfast.

"That's not all," Sofia continued. "Beth told me about another miracle that happened last fall with Joyce Clemens."

"She's married to the philanderer with the electronics store who does the cheesy TV ads, right? Dave Clemens? Get Clemens, not lemons!"

"That's him. Well, not anymore. I mean, they *were* married. Joyce had leukemia, and while you never know how that one will go, it's never a good thing. They said because she was so close to all those electromagnetic fields in the store, she was more susceptible."

"Yeah, like us electricians. More of us die from leukemia than the next two causes combined."

"I know." She frowned. "Are you trying to worry me?"

"Never." He smiled sheepishly. "I'm glad you care." He cleared his throat. "So what happened with Joyce?"

"She's good. The leukemia is gone without a trace. Normal red blood cell count."

Frank nodded. "That's great news, and it supports my theory that when people truly believe they are being cured or will be cured, then they magically are. Most times their body just knows what to do based on what their mind tells it, and then it puts things in place. You know, the power of positive thinking and all that." He gestured with his palms up. "Makes a lot of sense, scientifically speaking."

Sofia looked doubtful. "Okay, I get how that would make sense in certain situations. But it wouldn't explain either of the two cases I just mentioned. Jeremy was certain he was finished. Stage-four lymphatic cancer? What are the chances of surviving that? The doctors directly told him he had no chance, and he believed them. They mentally prepared him to die. And with Joyce Clemens, not much difference. She was about as ready to die as a person could be—in a whole other sense. She hated her life. She had an unhappy marriage from the beginning. Some people had even said getting terminally ill was a hidden blessing for her, because she suffered way too much with that man. Once she got over it, she got over him. After she'd been better for a few months, she filed for divorce. He played the victim role big time. 'Oh, poor me. I stood by her during her time of greatest need, and as soon as she gets better, the ingrate just dumps me. For no good reason.' He doesn't mention all the times he cheated on her. He didn't even try to keep it a secret. I think it made him feel powerful, rubbing her nose in it like that. Guess he thought she'd always tolerate it." She smiled at her husband, who looked thoughtfully off into space. "And now, according to Beth, she's happier than she's ever been."

She turned to her girls. "You two! The MacBride bus is leaving in ten minutes, so you better get a move on if you don't want to walk to school."

Jodie got up, but Lisa stayed put.

Frank sipped his coffee. "Better get going, Leese. You don't want to hold up the show."

"Um, yeah, I just have something for you to sign." She pulled out a folded-up, worn-looking paper from her backpack and handed it to him.

He frowned. "What's this?"

"It's a request for a conference with my math teacher, Mrs. Birchard."

Frank and Sofia exchanged a meaningful look. He unfolded it and shook his head. "This is for tomorrow morning."

"Sorry … I should have shown it to you earlier."

"Yeah, you should have. This is dated last week!"

Lisa looked at the table and said nothing.

"This is for eleven o'clock," he said to Sofia. "Are you free then?"

She shook her head. "Can't do it. Sam and I have an appointment at ten thirty with the Home School Cooperative."

"Any way to change it?"

"I wish. I had to set this up three months ago, and it has to happen before the end of the month, or they say they'll revoke our permission. They are probably bluffing, but who knows? Maybe I could tell them we have a public school conflict." She frowned at her daughter. "Why didn't you bring this up before, Lisa?"

She gave her mom a tight-lipped smile and shook her head.

Frank sighed. "We have load tests at the treatment plant tomorrow. With, I think—" he said as he counted on his fingers, "at least four, maybe five other people involved."

"Can't any of them fill in for you?" Sofia asked.

"Unfortunately not. A licensed electrician has to be present to get the certification. That's me, so I need to be there. Plus, I know what I'm doing more than any of those guys. If anything went wrong with one of those motors down the road, it would be a massive problem that would come back to haunt me. Which is why we do the testing in the first place. Kingston would hate me if I asked to reschedule."

"Doesn't he already hate you, Daddy?"

"Yeah," added Sofia, "it's not like he's going to delay your raise, is he?"

He didn't need the reminder. "No, of course not. But giving him any excuse to keep denying me is not in our best interest." He turned his attention to his daughter. "Promise me this won't happen again, Leese. Once an appointment is made that involves either of us, you better let us know as soon as it's set. That way we might have some kind of negotiation room, time to reschedule things—or something. This is unacceptable."

Lisa continued to stare at the table.

Sofia picked up her daughter's plate. "You better run and get ready. I'm not waiting for you. We have to get you both to first period on time."

"Who's going to the conference with Mrs. Birchard?" Lisa asked.

Frank glanced at his wife. "We don't know yet."

CHAPTER TWENTY-FIVE

Sofia worked hard to not lose it with this teacher, who apparently did not like her daughter. Lisa wasn't even allowed in the conference, which made no sense at all. She had to miss one of her other classes just to sit out in the hall.

For the third time, Mrs. Birchard explained something Sofia already understood. "Lisa could be the best student in the class. If she only tried harder—"

"But she's a B student."

"She's a B minus student," the teacher corrected. "And she should be an A student. She's one of the smartest girls there. But she doesn't apply herself."

"She does."

"What do you mean?"

"Well, she probably applies herself more than ninety-nine percent of the kids you teach. She applies herself in a big way to soccer and to dance, and she spends at least four to six hours per week running and working out. She also gets As in some of her other classes. Like history, for example—and I know Mr. Jenkins has a reputation for being a tough teacher. My older daughter went through his class two years ago and had a hard time with it."

"Which is further proof she could do better in math. Mrs. MacBride, it's fine that she gets good grades in history, but is history going to help her balance her checkbook? Is dancing going to help her figure out how much tax she owes? Or what a loan payment on a car would be?"

"For goodness' sakes, she's a B student—"

"B minus!"

"Okay, fine! She's a B minus student, but as you said, she's smart and capable. What you don't see is that she is highly motivated. If you could compare her with every single student in her class ten years from now, she'd not only have a higher retention rate than most or all of them, she'd have figured out more on her own."

"I think I see the problem."

"You see *what* problem?" Sofia tried to calm herself.

"You spoil the child. You obviously see her through a magical set of rose-colored glasses that don't—"

"Magical? Are you putting me on? I don't need to hear your judgments about what you think is obvious. You're teaching kids to be more concerned with grades and how they appear in terms of the status quo rather than what they're learning in terms of usable skills."

"*Now* who's sounding judgmental? Math is a very usable skill. Especially compared to soccer or dance. Or history."

Sofia stood up. "I think we're done here."

Mrs. Birchard appeared unruffled. "Now, Mrs. MacBride, many parents have a hard time hearing constructive criticism about their children, but—"

"Constructive criticism I can take. Demands for conformity are something else. I have a problem with people who try to fit my kids into a tight little box." She closed her eyes for a moment and took a deep breath. "I know you're trying to do the best thing—we just don't agree on what that is. It would be great if Lisa got all As in your class. And you're right about one thing—she could totally do it if she wanted to. But here's something I want you to know." She searched for the best way to phrase it. "Better yet, let me ask you this: how many hours a week on average do you think kids in this country watch television and play video games?"

"Well, I'm sure it's a lot, but I don't see what that has to do with our discussion."

Sofia sat back down. "Kids in this country watch at least forty-seven hours of television or video games on average per week. Depending who you ask, some say it's significantly higher than that, over fifty-five hours. Do you want to guess how many hours a week my kids watch or play?"

"I'm sure I don't see the relevance of—"

"Four hours." She folded her arms across her chest. "That's it. No more than that. They can watch one age-appropriate movie as part of that four hours, and if they want to play video games, that also goes within the four-hour time. Per week! My kids have interests. They do things. They will be successful in their lives not because they conform to some classroom standard that is later converted into a boring job, but because we've encouraged them to do what they love and put their whole selves into whatever that is. I'm sure you know math remarkably well. But my suggestion to you is to not keep trying to fit square pegs into round holes." She stood and picked up her purse.

"Mrs. MacBride, progress in mathematics is something that can be measured in a very logical and straightforward way. It is a good sign—"

"Mrs. Birchard, human beings—and their lives—are not always logical and straightforward. I appreciate your time and that you care enough about Lisa to have asked me to come in. Thanks again for talking to me, and I hope you will consider what I said."

"And I hope you will consider what *I* said."

"I will," she said over her shoulder as she walked out the door. Lisa looked at her tentatively from her seat in the hallway. Sofia frowned at her. "You ready to go, Leese?"

She nodded. "Am I in trouble?"

Sofia looked at her daughter for a long moment and shook her head. "No. Far from it. Come on, let's get out of here."

"I've still got classes, Mom. Third period starts in fifteen minutes."

"That gives us a good ten minutes to talk. Mostly so I can tell you how proud I am of you."

"Really?"

"Yeah, really. And also to try a little harder in math. It'll come in handy someday."

Sofia normally looked forward to Saturdays, especially when she'd had a tough week. Frank would go to his gun range and practice firing at paper targets. It was his way of letting off steam. He'd usually take the kids, who she suspected didn't enjoy the shooting as much as they enjoyed being with their dad. It gave her some quiet time. Unless there was a soccer match or a concert. But those usually took place late afternoons or evenings, so Saturday mornings were mostly peaceful in their house. But today they were all going on a picnic. No shooting practice for Frank; no peace and quiet for Sofia. As she pulled her cross-trainers on, for at least the fourth time that morning she asked herself why she'd agreed to go.

Frank and the kids had been excited about this for days. The Petersons were coming, and they'd all have fun. She knew that, but she also needed her alone time. Besides, you never knew what the weather would bring. In Oregon, weather was a roll of the dice, with rain being the most likely outcome.

Frank had asked for the following weekend off when he saw the forecast, but Kingston denied it. He didn't give a reason, simply saying it wouldn't work and that they needed him on call. The only reason he'd gotten today off was because he had applied for and got it approved six months previously. Before things had gotten so much worse at work.

Paul had told them he knew a great spot near the base of Mount Hood. He said it was a beautiful undiscovered little regional park.

"Looks like we lucked out," said Sofia as they pulled into the parking lot. It was unseasonably warm, with deep blue skies and some scattered clouds—and no sign of rain.

"Yeah, I guess we did. Good thing, too, since the boss from hell wouldn't let me take any other weekends off."

"Don't get me started."

"No, I definitely don't want to do that." He looked at her slyly. "At least not in that way."

She looked out the window and smiled. It would be a great day after all. She opened her door as soon as they stopped and turned to their back-seat passengers. "Girls, both of you keep an eye on Sam. I want you all to stay together, and no one goes out of sight without checking with a grown-up first."

Lisa rolled her eyes. "Yes, Mom."

"Anyone see the Petersons?" asked Frank.

"Isn't that their car over there?" Sofia pointed at a dark green Jeep Cherokee in another part of the lot.

They met up at the public restrooms, according to plan. Sofia was happy to see them, especially Janice, who also seemed glad to be there.

"There's a great clearing down that path." Paul pointed at an opening in the bushes. "If we're lucky, we'll be the only ones there. Most people go for the visible spots near the road. They don't want to take a chance on the unknown."

Janice laughed. "But not Paul Peterson, Park Department innovator and master explorer. No, he'd much rather spend his available time boldly going where no human—with half an ounce of common sense—has gone before."

"You say that like it's a bad thing," Paul said with a mock-hurt expression.

The path was longer than Paul had remembered, but just as they were ready to turn around, they came to a beautiful clearing with picnic tables and no people.

"See," he said. "People don't come down here much."

"Wonder why that is?" Janice asked sarcastically.

They settled in and relaxed in the peaceful atmosphere. Things went fine until Sofia heard the girls arguing loudly on the other side of the clearing.

"Yeah, well, it was my idea," said Jodie.

"I saw it first," answered Lisa.

"I don't care, it was still my idea."

"Girls!" Sofia frowned as she walked over. "What are you arguing about?"

"Well, I suggested we collect rocks to take home and put in a big bowl in the living room," explained Jodie. "Small rocks, of course. Then Lisa finds a great rock she wants to keep for herself. Even though we had an agreement."

"We did not have an agreement. I never said, 'I, Lisa MacBride, promise to never collect another rock for myself as long as I live.' In fact, I—"

"Where's Sam?" Sofia looked around anxiously, then back at the guilty looks on her daughters' faces.

"It was Jodie's turn," said Lisa.

"Was not!"

"Was too!"

"Stop it, you two! *Frank*!" she called out. "Did either of you see where Dad went? Maybe Sam followed him."

The girls shrugged and shook their heads.

"Oh, *Frank*!" When Sofia wanted to, she could really belt it out.

She heard his faint reply before he came back into the clearing with all four Petersons. "I was showing them the stream I found," he said, looking around. "Where's Sam?"

"That's the problem. The wonder girls here were supposed to be watching him, but they were more interested in arguing over rocks."

"It was Lisa's turn to watch Sam," said Jodie.

"Cut it out," Frank admonished. "We need to find him immediately and talk about what happened later. He can't have gone far. Paul, Janice, are you and the kids able to help?"

"Do you have to ask?"

Frank started off toward the tree line, at a different direction from where they had just come. "Let's go. Stay within sight of the person on either side of you."

Sofia found him in a small clearing, staring at two chattering squirrels near their nest about fifty yards away. "Frank! Here he is!" she called out before turning to Sam. How could they ever be angry with this child? "Oh, Sam, you have to let us know before you go off like that." He wasn't listening to her. "What is it?"

He pointed at something on the ground beneath the squirrels' nest, barely visible but moving. Then she noticed his eyes brimming with tears.

"Sam, are you okay?" He stared at whatever it was. "What's that?" She moved forward, but Sam grabbed her hand with a surprising ferocity. "What is it?"

He pointed again at whatever was on the ground, and then to the squirrels' nest and the very animated squirrels on either side, just as Paul walked up with Janice.

"He keeps pointing at something on the ground," said Sofia. "It looks like a baby squirrel."

Frank and the others joined them in the clearing.

Paul put his hands on his hips. "I think you're right. We see that a lot in the field. The baby falls out of the nest, and for some reason the parents won't get it. Sam's right in not letting you get near it. The closer you come, the less chance they'll save it." He shook his head. "Right now that's not looking likely."

"But it's their baby. Why don't they just go get it?"

"Hard to say. Sometimes the squirrel pup is too big for the parent to lift." He shrugged. "More likely it damaged something internally when it fell. Animals have a way of knowing these things—don't ask me how. I've seen it both ways. Sometimes they get it back in the nest in a few seconds, and sometimes they leave the poor thing to die. It's usually one thing or the other. They're extremely upset and may keep this up for a while. I've seen them go on for hours before they suddenly quit." He squinted at the baby squirrel still writhing on the ground. "Pretty sure this one won't make it."

Frank sighed. "Well, that's too bad. Maybe if we go back to the clearing and leave them in peace, it'll have more of a chance."

He placed a hand on Sam's arm. "C'mon, Son, let's go."

But Sam wouldn't budge.

Frank frowned. "Come on, Sam—let's give them some space."

Sam reluctantly agreed, but as they walked away, one of the squirrels rushed down and picked up the baby in its mouth and carried it back to the nest.

"I'll be damned!" said Paul. "I've never seen that happen. Once they give up, they don't change their minds." He scratched his head. "At least not that I've seen before now."

CHAPTER TWENTY-SIX

After a few minutes of trying to get both sound and video functioning properly, they finally got secure video conferencing working on Sofia's laptop.

"Hi, you two."

Sofia leaned toward the webcam. "Hey, Kim."

"Are you both okay doing this over the internet?"

"I think so," said Sofia. "But couldn't we just use Skype for this?"

"It's not considered secure enough for professional counseling," explained Kim. "The ideal thing would be if we were all in the same room, but this is as close as we'll get for now."

"Works for me," said Frank.

"So how's everything in the house of MacBride?" asked their counselor.

Frank glanced at Sofia. "We're fine."

His wife smiled thinly. "We've worked through some things."

Frank leaned forward. "She still has dreams where I leave her."

"Is there anything you can do to make her more secure about your commitment to her?" asked Kim.

"Honestly, I don't know. She knows I love her, she knows I'm committed—"

"How does she know you're committed?"

He raised both hands in a gesture of helplessness. "If she doesn't already know, I have no idea what I can do to convince her."

"Okay." Kim nodded. "That's something we can work on. What else is up for you guys?"

Frank frowned. "We still go round and round about putting Sam in public school."

Sofia shot him a sharp look. "He doesn't speak, hates to be touched, won't read or be read to, and won't look anyone in the eye. How could things turn out well for him in that scenario?"

"There are special needs programs that could work out well for our son. But we won't know if we never try, will we?" asked Frank.

"Probably not," answered Sofia.

"Don't feel you have to come to agreement on everything right away," said Kim. "You've made a big step just acknowledging that you disagree. Insignificant as it may seem, that's actually huge."

"Why is that?" asked Frank. "We've known we disagree on this for years."

"Knowing something and acknowledging something are two different things. Trust me when I say you're making progress."

Sofia nodded hesitantly. "Okay." If this was progress, it sure didn't feel like it.

"How's the journaling going, Sofia?"

"Not as regular as I'd like. But I still write every once in a while." Maybe once or twice a year.

"Have you practiced what I suggested?"

"You mean about writing what I don't want to speak about? Sure." Sofia shrugged. "I mean, I could probably do more of it."

"Great. I encourage you to do so."

She nodded. "Okay." It was probably not going to happen. Once was enough.

They did their best to work through some of their issues with Kim's help, but by the time they finished, Sofia wondered if it had been worthwhile. At least they'd tried, which counted for something.

Sofia parked the minivan in the church parking lot. Sam was with Maria, the girls were in school, Frank was at work—and no one knew she was there.

She'd talked to Maria last week and brought up—or, more precisely, *tried* to bring up—reincarnation. Her older sister had looked at her like she'd just admitted she killed kittens for fun. Good thing she didn't bring up the question of Sam being a healer. It was time to ask a higher authority. Or at least someone who had more knowledge of the subject.

She locked the van and walked up to the parish door, where she rang the doorbell and waited. She rang again and was ready to give up when Father Keith opened the door.

"Hello, Father, I'm—"

"Sofia MacBride." He invited her in with a sweep of his hand. "I was just about to make myself some coffee. Would you like some?"

Sofia nodded. "That would be nice, thanks."

As they sat with their coffee, Father Keith asked about Sam. She told him he was doing fine, except that he still wasn't talking, and she mentioned her anxiety about him not reading.

"God sometimes works in ways we can't understand. Your boy is special—in ways you see and probably in ways you don't." He leaned forward, resting his elbows on his knees, and smiled kindly at her. "Everyone is special in their own way. We're all potentially godlike, as we're all made in the image of God. We merely have different layers of covering. I believe there are no bad people, just covered people who do bad things. I think your boy is very uncovered."

"Thank you, Father, I appreciate that."

"I'm just telling you what I perceive." He nodded slightly. "But you're worried about him, aren't you?"

"To be honest, yes."

"We can't know what kind of future our children will have. All we can know for sure is that they are in God's hands and are part of a bigger plan. Even when we don't know what that plan is," he explained. She loved his soothing voice. "As parents, you do your part, but so much is out of your realm of control. Worrying about what might go wrong usually causes more pain than the thing itself."

"I know, it's just …"

"You have something else you want to tell me, but you're worried I'll judge you."

When she looked at him quizzically, he chuckled. "Don't look so surprised. This is what I do." He leaned back in his chair. "Don't worry. Whatever you have to share with me won't go past these walls." His smile comforted her. "And I try my best not to judge."

Sofia decided to plunge right in. "I wonder if my son has been reincarnated. I know the Catholic Church is very much against the idea, but I wanted to ask you since you seem to have a good perspective on things."

"Sometimes 'things' are not what they seem."

"Which is why I wanted to talk to you. I feel a little confused." She told him the whole story, including her suspicions about Sam being a healer. She shook her head slightly. "I guess I'm feeling—I don't know—a little disloyal."

"Disloyal to who? God? Jesus? The Catholic Church? All the above?"

"I don't know, maybe. My sister told me even asking about these things was heresy."

He leaned back and sipped his coffee. The silence in the room lasted practically a full minute before he spoke. "I can't tell you what's right or wrong. I can only explain the way I understand things."

"That's all I would hope for."

Father Keith smiled. "So you suspect that your son can heal. Isn't that something Jesus did? Isn't that what made him so well-known? At least one of the major things? I think he came here to show us what was possible. Not just by healing others' bodies, but by showing the healing power of forgiveness, the strength of unconditional love, and the common divinity we all share, regardless of our beliefs."

"I like the sound of that," she said.

"Me too." He nodded. "I have no way of knowing whether your son has the ability to heal. But what I believe in my heart is that we all do. We may just not know how. You've heard of John of God, the healer in Brazil?"

"Yes. I've read quite a bit about him," she said enthusiastically. "His supporters claim he's healed thousands of people over the last couple of decades. Some—including those he's supposedly healed—say he's legit, but many others say he's a fraud."

Father Keith leaned forward again. "I've heard that too. I went to seminary with a priest named Father Matías, who was diagnosed with an aggressive brain tumor a few years ago. Doctors said he had only months to live—if that. He went to see John of God, and the tumor has been shrinking ever since." He ran his hand across his freshly shaved scalp. "Maybe it's coincidence. Or the power of positive thinking. I honestly don't know either way. There have been other healers at different times in different places who have apparently been effective, so why couldn't your son be one of them?" He tapped a finger on his lip. "Does he believe he heals people?"

"I'm pretty sure he does believe that."

"Then I'd say even if he didn't actually have the ability—just because he *thinks* he does makes him a better person, and he makes the world around him better." He waved his hand in the air. "If people who make that long pilgrimage to Brazil believe John of God heals them, there are apparently positive effects whether or not he directly causes the healing." He sat quietly for a few moments. "Personally, I have my doubts that he does, but I have no way of knowing for sure." He shook his head. "And as far as I'm concerned, it's fine either way as long as the results are there. I wouldn't discourage Sam from that path or worry about it if I were you. If his is an unrealistic fantasy, it may be the most healthy unrealistic fantasy anyone could have."

She pressed on the other point she'd raised. "So what about reincarnation?"

"Ah. Now that is quite a hot potato for us clergy folk. People don't want it in their laps. When it comes up, you'd be surprised at how swiftly the subject gets changed. Some of us take offense by the mere mention of that topic."

Sofia glanced at the door. "I'm sorry, it's just that I've been pretty confused about the subject. My friend—well, the mother of one of my daughter's friends—told me it was believed for hundreds of years after Jesus, but then the authorities of that era began condemning people to death for even talking about it." She sighed. "I should have researched it myself without bothering you. I'm sorry if I've offended you, Father."

"Please, I'm not offended in the least. I would call reincarnation the elephant in the room. Or in the church, more like it." He smiled. "It's rarely talked about—but in my opinion should be. Your friend is absolutely right, and in the middle of the first millennium, hundreds of years after Jesus walked among us, the Roman Empire declared that talking about reincarnation was indeed punishable by death—something they aggressively enforced." He looked at her over his cup as he took another long sip. "Did your friend mention the First Council of Nicaea?"

Sofia nodded. "I think so."

"That was what started the ball rolling," Father Keith continued, "and it was convened by the Romans—not the Church itself. Reincarnation was an accepted fact of life up to then throughout Christendom, but the Romans decided it would be much more difficult to rule if people thought they could actually get second—or third or fourth—chances. If the Church taught people they had only one chance to live, and the only options were either eternal damnation or eternal life with God, they'd be much easier to control. And then there's the question of church versus state politics. Many historians—and theologians, for that matter—believe the Roman Empire used the Christian Church to create order within their realm.

"The irony is that this is all clearly laid out by historical facts. There's not even a debate whether it all happened. Pope Vigilius was thrown into prison two hundred years after the Council of Nicaea because he continued to believe in and teach reincarnation. The only reason the Romans didn't put him to death was because they wisely understood that would've created a rebellion. He escaped with help from some faithful followers, and the result is that the Catholic Church never took an official position against reincarnation."

"That's amazing! I knew some of that, but I had no idea."

He nodded. "I agree, it is amazing. And the whole death penalty thing," he said and frowned, "well, that's a good way to make people stop talking about something." He shook his head. "We still live with the results of that today. There is a huge reluctance to discuss anything even remotely related to reincarnation, as you've noticed."

"I have. Besides my sister Maria, I tried to discuss it with my husband, who also absolutely rejected the idea."

Father Keith closed his eyes for a moment. "People believe and disbelieve all kinds of things, which doesn't make something true or not. Could your son be an incarnation of a healer from a past life?" He shrugged. "That's not for me to say either way. But my personal belief—and everything I know and have studied about God, religion, and the Church—says it is possible." He took a deep breath. "You've heard about our new pope?"

"Pope Francis? Of course."

"There are rumors he's going to denounce the concept of eternal damnation."

Sofia's eyes widened. "You're kidding!"

"It's only a rumor, but knowing him, it could be true. This is the pope who removed some of the most powerful cardinals in the church in his first year. Who only last month excommunicated the entire Mafia, ending decades of hypocrisy. He has made powerful enemies inside and outside the church—but he doesn't care. He wants to do God's work and serve not only his flock, but all humanity. Eternal damnation makes little sense if you believe in a merciful, kind, and just God." He smiled. "And the whole eternal damnation business came out of the same meetings and councils organized by the Roman Empire that made us stop thinking of reincarnation as a fact of life." He glanced at his watch. "I'd love to talk more, but I have a meeting with Father James in five minutes."

Sofia stood and smiled. "I'm grateful for your time, Father, and for sharing your views with me."

"Just remember those views are only my opinions, and I'm flawed like everyone else here on Earth." He looked upward and crossed himself. "Always examine facts on their individual merits, draw your own conclusions, and be open to not knowing all the answers." He gestured toward the door. "We live in a mysterious universe. We don't have all the answers, and hopefully we'll never stop looking for them."

CHAPTER TWENTY-SEVEN

SOFIA'S Journal. THIS IS PRIVATE. CLOSE IT NOW!

July 22, 2014

I'm journaling like a good girl. I journal when I want to, and don't when I'm not feeling it. I am in control of my journal writing destiny! This wasn't such a bad idea. For someone so young, Kim is very competent and focused. Was that a judgmental thing to say? I'm not going to tell Frank after all the whining I did about this, but I'm actually enjoying journaling.

He hasn't had a nightmare since last year. That is so wonderful. I wonder if his telling me about Italy had anything to do with that? I suspect it did.

I loved hearing what Father Keith had to say last week. Knowing there are people in the church who are open-minded and more concerned with spirituality than defining what's right and wrong is comforting and gives me hope. It also makes me wonder about our special little son.

Could he have been a healer in a past life? Could he have even had a past life?

Father Keith seems to think it was possible. Last week I downloaded a book called The Boy Who Knew Too Much onto my Kindle reader. It's an amazing story about this little boy who knew all these things about professional baseball he had no way of knowing. When the parents googled the information, it first appeared he was wrong, but later they found out he knew totally obscure details about names, relationships, and things that happened that weren't even on the internet!

I'm both intrigued and scared. What if Sam so identifies with some previous life of his that he wants nothing to do with us? Which is ridiculous, because he obviously loves us.

And once again I'm rambling. Why? Because I'm avoiding the assignment to write what I don't want to say. If I don't want to say something, it means I don't want to write it, either.

But here I go.

When I was a guidance counselor at Ben Franklin High, little Carl Chester was bullied at home and at school. He was smaller than most of the other kids his age but had a fearless heart, and he never told on anyone, even when I directly asked him who hurt him or tore his books. However, when he gave a bully a bloody nose for insulting his little sister, school rules forced me to call his mother to take him home. She yelled at him all the way down the hall and hit him many times. I saw this with my own eyes. Yet I did nothing. I'm a bad person. I should have called Child Protective Services. The principal told me to just let it go. Why did I listen to him? I still can't let it go twelve years later.

How's that, Kim? Once again, on your suggestion I wrote what I didn't want to say. Are you happy? I'm not. Was this supposed to make me feel better? It didn't work, not even a little bit. I am so not feeling good right now.

As they got ready for bed one night after a stressful day for them both, Sofia mentioned they hadn't gotten any new information from Sam's testing in over a year.

Frank wasn't in the best mood. "He'll talk one day—or he won't."

"You sound like Nonna Eve."

"Is that a bad thing?"

"No, it's just that she could be so optimistic and—"

"So being optimistic is a bad thing?"

"No! But it can be if you're a Pollyanna and ignore—"

"Pollyanna?" He was outraged. "This is good. Finally you say what you really think about Mamma."

She shook her head emphatically. "No, I loved your mamma. I still do. Nonna Eve was so—I don't know. She was more kind to me than my own parents ever were."

"Which doesn't say much."

"What's that supposed to mean?"

"It means we both know the truth of that." He gave her a pointed look. "You just don't want to hear it from me."

"I'm fine hearing it from you. I'm just saying Nonna Eve was not as—"

"Full of negativity." His hands flew as he paced the room. "Full of negativity in all they do." He added harshly, "And cold."

"That's not fair." Her eyes welled with tears. "My parents did the best they could. My father experienced the Spanish Civil War firsthand as a young boy. A neighbor murdered his father just because he disagreed with his support of Franco. His first wife died in a car accident a year and two weeks after they married and left him a baby to raise."

"Your sister Maria, I know."

She shook her head. "You go through things like that, there *is* no positive."

"*Amore mio.*" He took a deep breath. "I know he went through things. But so did Mamma. Worse things. You know."

"Nothing could be worse than that war."

Frank vividly recalled the scene in the dining room in Milan. "Maybe not, but there are things just as bad," he said softly.

Sam hadn't gone out at night for nearly a year. The alarm never reported any trouble or showed in its history that it had been disarmed. Then one warm September night, Frank woke to find the disarmed light on. He nudged Sofia, and together they searched the house but came up empty-handed.

Frank announced, "I'll drive around until I find him—or until he finds his way back."

"We should call the police."

"Really? You know they'll hate it. Anyway, it's warm out. He'll be fine and will come back soon."

She disagreed. "Frank MacBride, he is not fine. He's only eight and a half. He's out alone, God knows where, in a world where there are plenty of bad people who would love to do bad things to him." Her eyes filled with tears. "Does that sound fine to you?"

"No. It's just that this town is pretty safe and—"

"Please make the call," she said, her voice almost a whisper.

"Okay, sure. No need to yell." He smiled and pulled up the non-emergency number for the Eugene Police on his speed dial. "I'll drive around as I do this. Call me when he shows up."

She folded her arms across her chest and silently nodded as he went out the door.

"Eugene PD, Sergeant Kinzer here."

Frank explained the situation and wondered whether the sergeant ever took time off.

"Are you not setting your alarm system?" Kinzer asked.

"Well, yes, but he disarmed it."

"Why did you give him the code?"

"We didn't." Frank set his phone on the dash and put it on speaker. "I changed the master code and all the other codes when we went through this a year ago."

Kinzer cleared his throat. "I guarantee there's a logical explanation. Kids are notorious for watching their parents pin in a code and memorizing it. It's not that hard."

"Both my wife and I are very careful so that no one can see us enter our codes, especially Sam."

"What about one of your other kids? Maybe they gave it to him?"

"Impossible. They don't know our codes either."

"And yet he apparently knows it." Kinzer sounded paternal and condescending. "Did you check the alarm history?"

"Yes, and it showed him disarming the system at 2:37 a.m.—about an hour and a half ago."

"And you're sure it wasn't you?"

"Quite sure. Look, I know you want to help us, but it's not what you think. We've been very careful. This is our son who keeps putting himself in danger. We're trying hard to do something about it. Something strange is going on here."

"Yeah, I'm with you on that. Mr. MacBride, these things happen quite a bit. You let your guard down. One day you're a little tired, the kid sees you entering the code, or you write the code on a piece of paper or something—whatever, the kid finds it. Sometimes we don't notice things the way they do. Your son is obviously smart. I'm sure he picks up more than you're aware." The sergeant paused. "You know, I have two boys myself, and they continually surprise me with what they learn. The other day I heard my eight-year-old talking to my six-year-old about my gun, for God's sake. He knew it was a Glock, and he knew it was .40 caliber. That worried me. I never told him those things. Speaking of which, do you have any guns in the house?"

"No. No, we don't," Frank answered quickly. "Thanks for all that, Sergeant Kinzer, but right now we just need to find him. Can you send a couple of cars out to look for him?"

"I already sent a car over while we were talking. Modern technology is something, know what I mean? Can't send two tonight, as they have other duties. More likely than anything it's the same story as before. I do have to tell you, though, since this is the third time this has happened, we have to invoice you." He cleared his throat. "Department policy, you know."

"Yeah, whatever."

"I probably shouldn't be telling you this, but Child Protective Services left a memo on our board that if he goes missing again to notify them immediately."

"Hopefully you won't do that."

"I believe the best place for him is with his family. So I think I forgot about that memo—if anyone asks me."

"Thank you, Sergeant."

"However, I also believe his going out alone at night is way too dangerous. We won't be able to forget the next time this happens. Do you understand me?"

"I do."

"When he shows up, let us know immediately so we don't waste any more resources."

"Definitely," said Frank.

"You should go out and look for him too."

"Already doing that. I'm in my pickup now."

"And Mr. MacBride?"

"Yes?"

"Figure out how to keep that boy home. He's too young to be out on the streets at night."

Tell me something I don't know! "Got it, thanks."

Less than ten minutes later, Sofia called. "He's here." The relief in her voice was palpable. "And he's safe."

Frank knew his wife well enough to know when there was something else. "What is it, Sofia?"

"Well, he's such a sweet, wonderful boy. I don't know why he doesn't talk, and I sure don't know why he goes out or where. He seems to understand so much, and at other times he seems to understand so little. How does he not get that this is so unsafe?" She paused. "How can we make him understand? Should we punish him?"

"Maybe we should. I don't know, it's a tough call. He's always very contrite, he understands, he gets that he's not supposed to do it, and yet he does it again."

He sighed. "Maybe we spoil him, Sofia, and he thinks he can do anything he wants without consequence. Exactly what they said not to do in that parenting class we took when you were pregnant with Lisa. Remember that?"

"Of course. But Sam is so ... innocent. And why is he doing this? We don't know where he's going or what he's doing."

"I know. It's a mystery, but we're going to figure it out. And we're going to keep him safe. Please call the police and let them know. I'm about ten minutes out, and I'll see you as soon as I get back."

Eleven minutes later, when Frank opened and closed the front door, he noticed it didn't chime. It should have, since it was still disarmed. Odd.

He'd look into it tomorrow after work. Part of him wanted to take the day off so they could come to an understanding with Sam. Something had to change, but he knew Kingston would use any excuse he could to make him look bad. He had a breaker panel to replace at the water treatment plant, and he couldn't afford any more time off. Their confrontation with Sam would have to wait until the end of the day.

Chapter Twenty-Eight

When Frank opened the front door after work, he noticed the chime was back. He made a mental note to talk to the alarm company about it. First they had to sit down with Sam, however.

When they did, once again Sam understood they didn't want him to go out at night, and that it was dangerous. He wouldn't—or couldn't—tell them why he did it. Or how he got past the alarm system.

Maybe it *was* time for punishment. In their parenting class, they'd been taught that without consequences, there'd be no change. Frank knelt down by his son. "Buddy, I don't know how you are doing this, but it's dangerous for you, and it's driving your mom and me crazy."

He glanced at Sofia, who nodded slowly. He turned back to his son.

"You don't want us crazy, do you?"

Sam shook his head solemnly.

"Good. So you will stop this, right?"

Sam just stared at the wall.

Frank grasped his arm. "Sam, tell me you'll stop this," he said with an edge to his voice. He squeezed Sam's arm so he would understand the seriousness of the situation.

His son kept staring at the wall.

"*Sam—*"

"Frank, don't yell at him."

"Sofia, we have to get him to stop this. It's just too dangerous." He looked at his son. "You understand what a promise is, don't you?"

Sam nodded.

"Will you promise me you'll never do this again?"

He just looked at his father in his sincere way.

"Oh, for Christ's sake—"

"Frank!"

"Well, he understands, but he won't do anything about it. It's time we used a different tactic. The one we've been trying sure as hell hasn't been working."

Yet there was no punishment that day. They couldn't bring themselves to do it. Not to Sam.

That evening, Frank called the alarm company. "Remind me how to turn off the chime on my door."

"Easy. You log in with your master code and change the system setting for the chime."

"That's it?"

"Yep, easy as that."

As they got ready for bed, he spoke to Sofia about it. "So it's easy enough to turn the chime on and off. But how would he have figured that out?" Frank was puzzled. "And not only that, he would've needed to have the master code to get into the system settings. How could that have happened?"

"I have no clue."

Frank scratched his head. "That makes two of us. Unless it was something not working with the system itself. Otherwise, I don't understand how or why that happened."

"I think you need to have another talk with him tomorrow. Be gentle. It scares him when you're intense."

"I need to find out what will work with him."

"I'm just saying I don't want you to yell at our son again," said Sofia.

"Noted."

The next day, Frank sat down again with Sam. "Son, have you found ways to get around the alarm system so we don't know when you are out?"

He nodded.

"Do you know that creates a lot of worry for Mom and me?"

Nodding again.

"Do you care that it worries us?"

A very sincere nod.

Frank sighed. "I don't know where to take this, Son."

Sam gave a little shrug that melted Frank's heart.

Later that day, he called a locksmith and had dead bolts installed on the front and back doors that only opened with a key—inside and out. The locksmith tried to convince him to have a knob on the inside, that it was just too dangerous in case they had to leave in a hurry. But Frank was adamant. This was stopping now.

A week and a half after Lisa's middle school physical, Sofia received a call from the clinic.

"This is Margie from McKenzie Health Services. We need to discuss Lisa's test results with you."

Sofia caught her breath. "Anything to worry about?"

"Oh, no, but we need to get a few inconsistencies in her medical record cleared up. Can you come in at ten tomorrow morning?"

"What type of inconsistencies?" Sofia asked.

"Nothing of concern, but some things in the tests don't line up with her history, and Dr. Sturis asked to speak to you. She said it was important to get figured out."

"Sure, I'll be there."

"That's great. We need Lisa to come in with you, too."

Sofia didn't like the idea. "Why do you need her there? I can tell you every vaccine she's had and every—"

"I know it's more inconvenient, and she'll miss some school, but Dr. Sturis's note says it's important that both parent and child come in."

When they arrived the next morning, the doctor was all business and no warmth. "Mrs. MacBride, Lisa."

"What can we help you with, Doctor?" Sofia asked nervously.

"Well, first, as Margie said on the phone, there's nothing to worry about. Lisa is apparently in perfect health, and very fit."

"Then what was serious enough for us both to come down here?"

"Her records don't match her history."

"Margie indicated that on the phone. What does that mean, exactly?"

"Specifically, her medical records don't show she ever had Lyme disease, and something that serious must be—"

Sofia immediately saw the error. "I'm sorry, but she's never had Lyme disease."

"Her blood tests show positively that she did."

"The tests must be wrong."

"Not those tests, no. And we double-checked them." Dr. Sturis glanced at the papers in front of her. "This says ninety-four percent positive with only a two percent margin of error."

"No system is perfect. If you run the same test again—"

"Which is why we expressed the sample off to the National Center for Disease Control in Atlanta. We didn't want to take any chances on that not being correct, as serious as this is."

"Well," Sofia said, "maybe she only kind of got it, you know, in a minor way."

Dr. Sturis shook her head. "Not in this case. From Lisa's blood samples, we can gather that her immune system was under serious attack, and while I see no signs of nerve or other kinds of damage, I see signs of the initial attack on her system."

"Doesn't Lyme disease make you very sick?"

"Most of the time. Specifically in Lisa's case, her immune system was under attack, and it would have made her very ill. Did you have her treated with massive antibiotics? I'm surprised that it's not on Lisa's record. Or did you not get her treated for it? How long did it go on for?"

Sofia gave an exasperated sigh and didn't try to hide the roll of her eyes. "I'm trying to tell you she did not get sick from it. She's never had a major illness in her life, and we've never had a reason to give her antibiotics. She's only had a cold or the occasional flu, but nothing that lasted more than a day or two."

"I'm sorry, but that's not what her blood says."

Sofia turned to her daughter. "Lisa, have you ever been sick for more than a day or two at the most?"

Lisa thought about it. "Not that I can remember, no."

Sofia shrugged and gave the doctor a "there you go" look.

The doctor was insistent. "I don't know what to tell you, but I've been doing this for a long time with many people. I used to work for NCDC in Atlanta—the same place that retested Lisa's sample—and I saw dozens of Lyme's cases. Rarely have I seen a false positive. From a scientific standpoint, it's nearly impossible. You see—"

"Well," Sofia said as she looked at her daughter, "there was the time in fifth grade when you missed the field trip. And you stayed home the next day."

"Too long ago," said Dr. Sturis.

"What do you mean?"

"Well, the antibody count suggests it was more recent. It had to have been in the past eight to twelve months."

Sofia shook her head. "I don't know. I think the last time she was—"

"Mom." Lisa tugged on her arm. "Remember about a year ago when I had that high fever and you kept bringing me Tylenol?"

Sturis frowned. "How high was the fever?"

Sofia tried to recall. "A hundred and three. It may have hit a hundred and four at one point."

"And you didn't seek medical attention?"

"We did. I was on the phone with our pediatrician. She told us that when the fever got—*if* the fever got—to a hundred and five to call her immediately, or to take Lisa in to emergency if we couldn't reach her. That never happened, and by morning she was back to normal. I had her stay home from school just to rest, but that was it."

"How many days did that go on for?"

"It started one morning and was gone by the next morning."

"Gone?"

"By three or four in the morning, her fever was nearly gone, and by five, her temperature was back to normal. She slept most of the day, but I think that's to be expected considering the circumstances."

"I agree. That couldn't have been it. What other flus or fevers of any kind did she have this year or last?"

"None. That was the only time."

"Tylenol wouldn't have been enough to knock out Lyme Disease. Are you sure about everything you told me?" the doctor asked.

"Yes, I won't forget that day for the rest of my life. We have an autistic nine-year-old who stayed the whole night with her."

Lisa's eyes widened. "He did?"

"Yes. I thought you knew. We kept putting him in his room, but every time we went to check on you, he was back. Until your fever broke. Then he finally went to bed. I let you both sleep most of the next day."

Dr. Sturis chewed on her pencil. "Very interesting."

Sofia shot her a meaningful look. "Tell me about it."

"We'd like to run more tests, if that's all right with you."

"Yet you say she's perfectly healthy?"

"As far as I can tell, she's the very picture of health. I see nothing wrong with her whatsoever."

Sofia had reached the limit of her patience. "You know, we'd love to help you, but we have this thing with doctors and tests. Our family has had way too many of them." She rose to her feet and nodded to the doctor. "Thanks for your time. And concern."

They left the office with Doctor Sturis staring after them.

As they walked out into the sunshine, Sofia asked her daughter, "So, what do you think of that?"

Lisa shook her head. "I don't know. I mean, three kids from school had Lyme disease since fourth grade, and except for Kate Becklin, they were out for months. And Kate was out at least a couple of weeks." Lisa thought for a few moments. "So, either that doctor didn't know what she was talking about, or I'm some kind of freak. An anomaly, as Dad likes to say."

Sofia laughed. "I think our entire family is some kind of an anomaly."

"You can say that again." Lisa paused. "Um, Mom."

"What is it, *querida*?"

Lisa walked on in silence. Sofia frowned. "What's up, Lisa?" Her daughter's chin quivered, and worry shot through her.

"I left the gate open."

"What do you mean?" Sofia tried to imagine why that would be a problem. "It's okay, I'll just close it when I get home and—"

"No!" Her tone startled them both. "Sorry, I mean … no, that's not what I'm talking about."

"What are you—"

"I'm talking about Tracker," she said, tears running down her cheeks. Sofia tried to remember the last time she'd seen Lisa cry.

"Tracker?"

"Back in Portland, I left the gate open. I got him killed." She sobbed. "I broke Sam's heart."

"Oh, *querida*, that was a tough time for all of us." She put her arm around her daughter's shoulders and they walked along in silence. "We've all done things we wish we'd handled differently, but that's how we learn."

"But I wasn't honest," she said and sniffed, "and that just made things worse."

"Oh, I don't know, Lisa. It would have been bad no matter what. And that's part of the learning as well." She thought for a moment. "I mean, no one is honest all the time."

Lisa looked at her curiously. "No one?"

Sofia shook her head.

"Not even you and Dad?"

"No. We try our best, but sometimes we fall short."

"You mean you lie to us?"

"Not exactly. I mean, yes, if you count things like how if you don't do well in school you're guaranteed to have a messed-up life."

"Mom!"

"Well, that's almost true. We want you to keep your options open, and sometimes we put things in a way that is easier for you guys to understand."

"You mean you twist the truth?"

"No!" She paused. "Well, kind of. But always in a way that's to your advantage. And it is our exception, not our rule. And Lisa ..."

"What?"

"Telling the truth can be difficult and usually takes courage. What you just did took courage."

"But what will Sam think when he finds out?" Her chin trembled again. "What if he hates me for that?"

"He would never hate you, Leese. He adores you."

Lisa thought for a moment. "And he's one hundred percent honest, isn't he?"

"Yes." Sofia sighed. "Yes, he is."

They reached their minivan, and Sofia touched her daughter's arm. "Sam doesn't have to know. Telling him won't bring Tracker back."

Lisa opened her door and got in quietly. She didn't say a word until they were almost home. "I think he already knows."

Sofia shot her daughter a sideways glance. "What do you mean?"

"Well, you know Sam. He understands things." She twisted her lips. "Besides, I want to tell him. Until I do, I'm just living a lie."

Sofia was heartened by this sentiment. Where did she pick that up? "That's wonderful, Leese."

CHAPTER TWENTY-NINE

Frank whistled as he removed the top cover from his drone. He loved having the garage to himself. It was a space to work, and a place to get away. His man cave.

"Hey, thought I'd find you here."

Frank glanced up from his quadcopter. So much for getting away.

"What are you working on?" Sofia asked.

"Oh, trying to adjust this GPS. It keeps tracking about twenty feet off where it's supposed to be." He tried his best to smile away his annoyance. "What can I do for you, *amore mio*?"

"Remember when Lisa was sick last year and we got up every half hour to check on her?"

"No way I could ever forget that."

"Well, she had Lyme disease!"

"What?"

"We just got back from seeing a doctor who used to work with the National Center for Disease Control in Atlanta. She said Lisa had the signature of Lyme disease in her blood. The only time she's had a fever in the past three years was about a year ago, when she had that fever all night that was suddenly gone."

"That couldn't have been Lyme disease."

"Which is what the doctor said. Yet there is no other rational explanation. And Sam was there with her the whole night, remember?"

"Of course, but what does that prove?"

"Well, it proves that our daughter had a disease that can be extremely persistent and hard to get rid of and frequently puts people out of action for months or years. According to this hotshot doctor, she had it and got over it in one night. Which is essentially impossible."

"Let me see if I'm hearing you right." Frank set his screwdriver down. "You're saying she confirmed it but said it was impossible."

"Yeah, that's pretty much it. She said it made no sense, and that Lisa must have had Lyme disease, though we know in the last few years she's never even had the flu—except for that one night." She paused. "It may be that the good doctor just doesn't believe us. That she thinks Lisa had Lyme disease over its full course, for months—and we're just trying to hide that for some mysterious reason."

"So what are you hinting at? Do you think Sam had something to do with her getting better just because he was there in the room with her? Are we back to this crazy idea that he's some kind of healer?"

"It doesn't add up otherwise." She shrugged. "I see no other logical explanation."

Frank didn't see how her theory could be considered logical, either. "The thing with Lyme disease is strange. But it's quite a stretch to think Sam could have had anything to do with it. You've let your imagination overpower your common sense."

"Remember how he knew when Nonna Eve had passed? There is something special about our son that has nothing to do with common sense."

"I'll give you that. But that doesn't mean—"

"Like I said before, Jess thinks he was probably a healer in a previous life."

"Now you're just being ridiculous. How in the world could she know that? There are no such things as past lives. We've been over this. We're here once, and that's it." This is what happens when you hang out with flakes, he didn't add. You come up with flaky ideas.

"I don't know. I mean, when she told me last year it seemed absurd, but I've been reading about it."

"About reincarnation?" Frank asked.

"Yeah, and it makes more sense to me now than when she brought it up."

"You know the Catholic Church's stance on that is clear—"

"That's the funny thing. The Church's stance on it is actually *un*clear. Jess told me that for over three hundred years after Jesus' birth, reincarnation was widely accepted in the Christian world. It was only in 325 AD that the ruler of the Roman Empire decided to take that out of all Christian teachings. And the most interesting part is that the Catholic Church itself never really rejected reincarnation. People just *assume* that it's unacceptable to Catholic doctrine."

Frank shook his head. "I don't believe that for a second."

"Neither did I, so I visited Father Keith. He knew it off the top of his head. And he pointed out that it's all right there in the history books."

Frank frowned. "Why'd you go to him? Couldn't you just google it?"

"Why not? It's an important question, and I would like to get as accurate an answer as possible. He gave me a very balanced perspective, which helped me understand."

Frank still wasn't convinced. "Maybe you're trying too hard to come up with answers. I don't believe in this past-life business."

Sofia folded her arms across her chest. "Why not?"

"Well, this one life here on Earth is all there is. Then it's up to God, and we go to heaven or hell."

"How do you know this life is all there is?" she asked.

"It makes the most sense."

"I don't know about that." She paused. "You heard about that little girl in Pennsylvania who knew all those things that happened in the past? She knew places and people with no possible way of knowing them. Or that little boy who'd been a World War Two fighter pilot. He knew things he couldn't have known otherwise, including names of people and ships, types of airplanes, and even facts about equipment, battles, and maneuvers that weren't publicly known but only uncovered after years of research."

"Those are just anomalies," said Frank.

"If they *were* just anomalies, then that at least says it's possible. There's a part of us that's more than just matter. I believe our soul is the driver of a vehicle: our body. So why couldn't that soul go to another body after our current body dies?"

He couldn't believe his wife was so far gone. "How long have you been reading this stuff?"

"I don't know, I've just kind of been taking it in for a while. Today's session with the doctor and Lisa was a big wake-up call for me. There are things we don't understand—that our scientists don't even understand. There's some connection there I can't explain, and I think it has everything to do with Sam. I strongly suspect he heals people. Do I understand that? No. But reincarnation could explain why people come into this world with different attitudes and skills. I know a lot of it is upbringing, culture, genes, and all that, but it's been shown conclusively that a lot of things don't make logical sense."

"Conclusively by some New Age website? Maybe WackyAnswers.com?"

"Funny. No, by the University of Virginia. They have thousands of documented cases that point to reincarnation as the only logical answer."

The University of Virginia? Wasn't that supposed to be a good school? "I don't know about that. I say we're here once and that's it."

Sofia was quiet for a while. "Okay." More silence. "But *how* do you know? I think we like to dismiss what we don't understand. How do we know we didn't have different lives before this?"

"Do you remember any of your supposed past lives?"

"No, of course not."

"Well, there's your answer."

"I don't see why that's an answer," said Sofia.

"Because you'd remember."

"I don't know." More silence. "Jess says we're 'programmed' to forget so we don't remember all the pain and regrets from past lives, as well as the good things we may have had in the past that we don't have now. I can see how those remembrances would get in the way of us living fully in this life."

Frank sighed. "Maybe we should let this go for now."

"Maybe we should."

That night after dinner, Lisa asked the family into the living room, saying she had something important to share with them. When she told them about Tracker, Sam jumped up and flung himself into her arms. Sofia looked at her two beautiful children in their embrace, tears streaming down their faces. And now Jodie was also crying as she got up and hugged her siblings.

Soon the whole family was in tears.

School had only been back in session a few weeks when Jodie walked in and flopped down on the living room couch. "Mom, I need your help."

"With what, *querida*?"

"Everyone in our class has to give a presentation about someone who has shown compassion."

"Sure, what do you need help with? That sounds like it could be fun."

"Yeah," said Lisa. "That sounds like tons of fun. I wish *I* was doing it instead of you."

"Please shut up, dear little sister. Mom, they said if at all possible, it should be someone we know."

"That's it," said Lisa, "it's that *if at all possible* thing that's getting to you. I would just do it on Mother Teresa or somebody like that."

"Lisa, just stay out of this," Sofia said firmly, "and quit trying to irritate your sister." She sat next to her elder daughter. "Who do you know who's compassionate, Jodie? Or has shown compassion?" She rested a hand on her daughter's arm. "Or what about someone who inspires compassion in you?"

"That's my whole problem, isn't it?" Jodie huffed and stood up. "If I knew someone like that, I'd already *have* the answer."

"My, don't we have a couple of snippy girls today," Sofia shot back. "Honestly, sometimes I don't know why I bother trying to be helpful. And keep it down. Sam's taking a nap, and I don't want him to wake up yet. The last thing I want is *three* cranky kids in this house." She frowned at Jodie. "I'm sure the answer will come. When is this due?"

"In two months. I want to get a head start on it."

"That's my sister."

"Stop it right this second, Lisa!"

CHAPTER THIRTY

S ofia was having a great day. One thing she liked about Oregon was the variety of weather. The good days were amazing. She couldn't imagine living in a place that had good weather all year long. She'd get pretty bored with that.

The doorbell rang around two thirty. She opened the door to find a thin, unhappy-looking woman standing on her porch.

Sofia smiled. "Hi, how can I help you?"

With a grave expression, the woman handed her a card. "I'm Olivia Sconet, Oregon State Child Protective Services."

Sofia's smile faded along with her mood. "Yes?"

"May I come in?"

"May I see some ID, please?"

"I just gave you my card."

"So you did. I need to see an ID and hear what your business is before you set foot in my house."

With a loud sigh, the woman pulled her wallet out of her handbag and opened it to her Oregon State ID.

"And why are you here?" Sofia asked.

"I need to talk to you about your son, Sam."

Sofia stepped back out of the doorway and motioned her inside. "What exactly do you want to talk about?"

"About keeping your son safe."

"I beg your pardon?"

"He's been out wandering alone at night three times. That's way too risky for a nine-year-old, particularly one with special needs." She had an annoying habit of nodding rapidly when she made a point. "And for all we know, it's been more times than that."

"Look, it's only been three times over a three-year period. That's hardly enough to get you involved."

Olivia pulled out a spiral notebook with little ducks on the cover. She quickly opened it to an inside page. "February twenty-second, 2013; October twenty-third, 2013; and September ninth, 2014, earlier this month. That's three times in eighteen months." Her eyes narrowed. "Not exactly three years. Unless you and I have access to different information."

Sofia didn't like being corrected. "Sorry, that was off the top of my head. Still, only three times."

"Which is three times too many." There was the rapid nod again.

"What do you expect us to do, tie him up at night?"

"Whatever it takes to keep him safe."

"And if you took him away—which I can tell you right now will never happen—what would you do to keep him from going out? Would you lock him up?"

"Whatever it takes to keep him safe," repeated Olivia.

"Can you give me a non-robotic answer?"

"Look, Mrs. MacBride, I know you're upset—"

"I'm not just upset. I'm furious."

"… but we both want the same thing. You and I are both concerned for the well-being of your child. Going out to God-knows-where at night is not safe. I think we both know that."

"We know, and we're dealing with it. We installed dead bolts earlier this month." She pointed at the new lock on the front door.

Olivia nodded. "That's certainly a step in the right direction. However, I think if you were dealing with it, as you say, it wouldn't continue to happen."

She smiled thinly. "Consider this your final warning."

Later that week, all five MacBrides were having breakfast at the same time, an event that seemed to be more rare as time went on.

"Guess who's back in school?" asked Jodie.

"Duh, I give up," said Lisa.

"Tulasi Patel."

Sofia set a bowl of oatmeal in front of Sam. "That name rings a bell. Oh, wait, isn't she the girl who got in an accident with her mountain bike? Broke her back or something?"

Jodie nodded. "Her neck, and the doctors thought she might never walk again. I mean, they didn't know for sure, but she lost all feeling and movement in one of her legs and most of that side above her waist was numb."

Sam had stopped eating and was paying full attention.

"Right. I remember," said Lisa.

"And now she's walking just fine."

Sofia smiled. "Well, I'm glad she's back in school. And that the doctors were wrong. What her parents must have gone through—"

"That's not all," Jodie interrupted. "She thinks she saw an angel."

Lisa stopped her spoon halfway to her mouth. "No!"

"Seriously! She said it appeared next to her bed."

"Get out of here! Did it have wings and everything?" Lisa asked.

"Not sure what you mean by *everything*, and I don't know if it had wings. She said she could see it perfectly in the darkness, like she had this super night vision, but only on the angel."

"Wow!"

Jodie shrugged. "I don't know—sounds loopy to me. Who knows what all those painkillers can do to a person's head? But the very next morning, some of her numbness was gone. The day after that, she began to wiggle her toes on the leg that had been numb. Three weeks later, she could use a walker, and less than a month after that, she could walk without help. Now she's back in school."

Lisa looked up at Sofia. "That's what happens when you believe in angels, right, Mom?"

It was hard to tell when Lisa was being sarcastic. "Well, I can't say whether angels are real or not. But I guess if you *believe* they are real, then they truly *are* real. The power of belief is incredible."

"You mean, if I believed I was rich, I really would be?" asked Lisa.

"Well … sort of. If you truly believed it, you would 'live into' that. You would live your life in such a way that you would gradually become rich."

"Really?"

"Yeah, really. But let me tell you something else about belief," said Sofia.

"What's that?"

"Belief alone is not enough. You won't get what you want without a lot of hard work, focus, and dedication."

"Mom," said Lisa, "it's too early in the morning for a lecture."

Sofia was happy to have been handed the opportunity. "It's never too early for good advice, *querida*. One day you'll thank me. Perhaps in the distant future." She patted Lisa's hand. "Belief is one of the most powerful things we have going for us—and what a lot of people have going *against* them."

"And you know what Henry Ford said," Frank joined in.

"Actually no, Dad, I don't," said Lisa, rolling her eyes.

Frank continued, unfazed. "He said, 'If you believe you can do something, or believe you can't, you'll be right.' Or something like that."

Lisa rolled her eyes again. "May I be excused now?" Sofia looked at her younger daughter and sighed. Kids were supposed to resist good advice. It was part of the way things worked.

One of the relationship tools Frank and Sofia had learned from Kim in their counseling sessions was to reserve two nights a week exclusively for them. Tuesday nights they called State of the Union. It gave them time to discuss anything, no matter how long ago it had happened. The main rule was that no one could judge the other for bringing something up. If it was still not resolved in the mind of one of them, then it was not resolved.

The other suggestion was to have a date night. That meant every Friday night was also their night. It had to be out of the house and away from the kids. They both loved it and were grateful to have the time together. Maria was more than willing to babysit her nieces and nephew, and the kids enjoyed her, so it worked out well for everyone.

On this particular date night, the plan was to check out Eugene's Air and Space Museum, then go out for dinner. Sofia was surprised at how much she enjoyed the museum—which had been Frank's idea—and was impressed by the stories of courage and sacrifice displayed there. Next, dinner at Alfredo's was excellent. She loved Italian food, which was pretty much all they used to eat before they married. She was relieved that Frank didn't flirt with the beautiful young waitress who served them. Everything went perfectly, right up to the point of payment. The credit card Frank handed the waitress was declined, even though it had worked two hours earlier at the museum. The second card was also declined, as was the third. Fortunately, Sofia had an American Express card with no set limit in her purse, so they could pay for dinner.

On the ride home neither of them spoke for a long time. Finally Frank admitted, "Okay, I blew it."

"That was so embarrassing. How could you not know all our credit cards were maxed out?"

"I knew we had a lot on them. I just didn't know they were maxed. Come on, Sofia, what do you want me to do?"

"For starters, manage our cards. Know where we are in relation to our limits. That could just as easily have happened to me paying for food at the grocery store. I'm happy to take responsibility for them, but you said you wanted to." She got more agitated. "The biggest problem, though, is that you work for less than you're worth."

"How many times have we been over this?" asked Frank. "It's too bad that Kingston's a jerk, but that's reality."

"Yeah, and *our* reality is that we've got no financial breathing room," said Sofia. "We've got no more credit, no place we can borrow money from, and our cash is going out faster than it's coming in. That's pretty simple math. Aren't there agencies that deal with unfairness in the workplace? After all, you work for the city government. They must have some form of checks and balances."

"There are checks and balances—theoretically. They just don't always work," said Frank. He pulled over to the side of the road, put the car in park, and turned to his wife. "Should I quit? I can do that. I could resign and look for other work. I've done everything I can to get that raise. I've been good at work. Actually, I've been exceptional. I'm rarely late, I solve their problems—including the big, ugly ones—and I save them lots and lots of money. It's just that my supervisor is a total prick, and *his* supervisor, my ultimate boss, Rick Wilson, is the personification of apathy. He doesn't try to make my life worse the way Kingston does, but he couldn't care less about anything or anybody. And he's very aware of Kingston's family connections." Frank shook his head in disgust. "You just tell me. I'm ready to quit. Eventually, they'll have to give me that raise. Kingston can't keep denying it for no good reason. That I can appeal, cousin mayor or not." Frank paused. "Maybe we should cool it for a while with Sam's testing."

Sofia bristled. "No, we will *not* cool it. This is the well-being of our son we're talking about." Her voice rose in pitch and volume. "This is how we try to find him a normal life. Hoping that one of these overpaid professionals will figure out what's going on, what's wrong, and what we can do about it." She looked at him intensely. "We're the only chance he has."

Frank gave an exasperated sigh. "I know, but like we've talked about before, the only thing all these so-called experts agree on is that they have no clue. For all we know, he might talk tomorrow—or he might *never* speak. Or there might be one little trigger that will get him talking. We *know* he can talk. We found that out when Mamma died."

"But see, that's the point. What if one of those specialists came up with that trigger?"

Later that evening, Sofia lay in bed, reflecting on how their conversation had spiraled downward from that point. No matter what she did when they got into those arguments, sometimes things just got worse.

CHAPTER THIRTY-ONE

At dinner one night, Jodie asked her parents not to attend her upcoming school concert.

Sofia couldn't believe her ears. "*Querida*, we'd love to come support you and hear you play. You've spent months preparing for this."

Her daughter rolled her eyes. "Six months, if you must know. And it's such a cliché to have your family show up."

Frank set his fork down. "Cliché?"

"Yeah. As in you come only because I'm your daughter."

Sofia frowned. "So what's wrong with that?"

"Nothing is exactly wrong with it. I just want to get used to—"

"I would come anyway." Frank sipped his water.

"I don't think so."

He wagged his finger at her. "Oh, yes. If I'd never met you but heard about how much you practiced and how much of your soul you show through that cello, I would come hear you."

"You're just saying that."

"I swear on the name of Nonna Eve, that is true."

"Promise?"

"Promise!"

As they got ready for bed that night, Sofia looked at Frank admiringly. "Well played, MacBride!"

"Oh, that was easy. She wanted us to come all along."

"You think so?"

"I know so. She just needed to hear that we want to come for the right reasons."

On the way home from the concert, the entire family was almost giddy. Sofia smiled at her reflection in the passenger window and felt happier than she had in a long time. These were the moments parents lived for. She thought of Jodie's solo in *With or Without You* and played it in her head before she realized that someone was actually humming the tune. Lisa was talking to Jodie, and Frank had a deeper voice. Sofia turned to see Sam with a serene expression and a rare full smile on his face, looking out the window.

She listened carefully. She'd heard him hum before—but not like this. "Sam, why, that's beautiful."

His attention snapped to her. The smile left his face, and the humming stopped.

"Please keep going. I love hearing you hum."

Sam's face flushed, and Sofia immediately regretted having said anything. Why couldn't she have let him be? She turned back around, but it was too late. She looked over at Frank, frowning as he drove. Was he judging her? "What are you thinking?"

"Oh, just an idea I'm going to try when we get back. Remember when I told you I got a great deal on the alarm system from Amazon?"

"I think so."

"Well, one reason it was so cheap is because it uses DTMF."

"And that's supposed to mean something to me?"

He shook his head. "No, sorry. It means it uses the same technology as older push-button phones. More expensive alarm panels use either encoded signals or they mask the tones."

"You lost me before you even started."

"If my hunch is right, you'll see soon enough. But essentially it means each button on our panel has a distinct tone you can hear."

When they arrived home, Frank disarmed the alarm panel and asked Sam to close his eyes and face the opposite direction. The whole family crowded into the entrance area to watch. Frank hit a few random numbers on the control panel.

"Okay, buddy, what was the second button I pushed?"

Sam held up three fingers, and Sofia gasped. Frank gave her a knowing look and nodded, then turned back to Sam. "Great. What was the first button?"

He held up seven fingers. "No way!" said Lisa. She frowned at Sam. "How did he do that?"

"He hears and remembers the distinct tones." Frank then motioned for Sam to turn away again. He pressed five different numbers. "All right, Sam, what did I just do?"

Sam gave his dad a questioning look. Frank stepped back from the panel and motioned for him to try. He punched in the exact sequence his father had.

Sofia laughed. "Unbelievable!"

"I know," said Frank. "He taught himself the tone of each button. He must've listened to the patterns we entered and remembered the numbers."

Sofia looked at her son. "How is it you have such an amazing memory?"

He beamed at her, and she felt incredibly good for the second time that day. She looked at her husband, who also smiled. Their son would do just fine in the world.

Sam spent the rest of the afternoon in his room. He went to bed early and returned to his room immediately after breakfast the next morning. He came out to do schoolwork, but the family hardly saw him all day. Sofia asked him at dinner if everything was okay. He nodded and avoided her gaze.

"You're up to something, aren't you, young man?"

Sam stole a glance at Jodie and refocused his attention on his plate.

"Are we going to find out what you're doing?"

Sam smiled shyly and nodded.

They didn't have long to wait. As the family relaxed, checked email, or worked on their homework after dinner, Sam walked into the dining room, where Jodie had her books spread on the table, and motioned her to follow. He rounded up the entire family in the living room and handed a large manila envelope to his oldest sister.

Jodie pulled out the contents and gasped. It was an M.C. Escher-like drawing created with colored pencils. Sofia noted that it wasn't by a trained artist, but by someone with a good grasp of art and a playful sense of humor. Not the work of a typical nine-year-old. It was the work of her son, Sam MacBride.

Jodie teared up and hugged her brother. "Thank you, this is so wonderful. I absolutely love it."

It was on her wall before bedtime, having taken Pablo Casals' place, and it stayed there all summer.

During schooltime with Sam the next day, Sofia's phone rang. Frank's details appeared on her screen. "Hey, you," she answered.

"Hey. How's it going there?" he asked.

"Good. Sam and I are just getting a little schoolwork done."

"Great. Based on the revelation that Sam has had a lot more access to the alarm system than we gave him credit for, I did a little schoolwork of my own just now."

"What do you mean?"

"I found fascinating things in the alarm logs."

Sofia glanced at Sam and his innocent face. "Like what?"

"I'll print them out and show you when I get home."

"Okay. You better get some real work done so you don't get fired," she said.

"All right, then, I'll get back to it. See you later."

She hung up and sat down with her son.

When Frank arrived home, he could barely contain his excitement. "Look at this," he said, showing her the alarm system logs he'd printed.

"What am I looking at?"

"Well, it shows that someone has disarmed and rearmed the system five times in the last eighteen months."

"What's special about that? We set the alarm far more often than—"

"Sorry, I'm talking about five times late at night or early morning." He tapped his pen at the top of the page. "See, I set the search on this for eleven thirty p.m. to five thirty a.m. When we're all asleep." Frank got more excited by the second. "And they disabled both the entry and exit chimes."

"Unbelievable."

"Yeah, Sam has gone out more than we thought. It's right there in the logs. And there's a bright spot on the horizon." He pointed again at the entries. "The most recent log entry was over a year ago, before we installed the dead bolts. So they're working."

She shook her head. "At least we stopped it."

"Exactly what I was thinking."

A couple of weeks later, while in the grocery store with Sam, Sofia heard a baby crying hysterically in the natural foods aisle and wondered why the irresponsible parent didn't do something about it.

Sofia had been rattling on to Sam about apples and what was available, but when she turned to show him, he was gone. The panic she knew so well came rushing back as she ran to the front of the store and scanned the parking lot. No sign of him. "Have you seen a boy about this tall?" she asked the store manager, holding her hand out to indicate Sam's height.

"No, I haven't," he said with an unmistakable glimmer of disapproval in his eyes.

She finally found Sam in the natural foods aisle, standing next to a quiet baby in a stroller and a very grateful-looking mother.

Sofia approached them, forcing herself to smile. "You scared me, sweetie."

He looked at her with a smile that was half apology, half *this is what I do.*

"You know you need to tell me without just running off."

He nodded his sincere little nod, and Sofia felt a lump in her throat. Why couldn't she be mad at him?

"He's such a sweet little thing," the baby's mom said with a heavy southern drawl. "Y'all must just love him to death."

"We certainly do."

She knew he loved her. He loved everyone, as far as she could tell. Was his family more special to him than anyone else? Probably, but hard to say. He seemed to have no fear of others, so much so that it concerned her. There were people who wouldn't mind hurting an innocent child. And they didn't come more innocent than Sam. Sure, he had his little shows of temper, but he was their blessing in disguise.

Sofia put her hand on Sam's head. "He's very special to us."

The southern lady bent toward him. "I don't know how you made little Tommy stop crying, but thank you so much."

He smiled at her.

"He doesn't say much, does he?"

"No, he—"

"Sometimes when Tommy starts crying, nothing in the world can stop him." She looked up at Sofia, oblivious that she had just cut her off. "He can go for hours until he exhausts himself. The doctors say nothing's wrong with him, but they don't always understand—if you know what I mean."

Sofia nodded. "I know exactly what you mean. Some of those doctors have absolutely no clue."

"I know, right?" She looked back at Sam. "And this little angel—what's your name, pumpkin?"

Sam looked up at his mom. "Um," she cleared her throat. "He doesn't speak."

"Oh, I'm sorry."

"No, don't be." Tears welled in her eyes. Time to go. She wasn't about to cry in front of a complete stranger. "He communicates very well in his own way. Come on, Sam, say goodbye to the nice lady and Tommy."

He waved the way he liked to do.

As they walked away, Sofia heard the woman muttering to her baby. "That is the sweetest little boy on God's green earth."

Chapter Thirty-Two

SOFIA'S Journal. THIS IS PRIVATE. CLOSE IT NOW!

January 1, 2016

My New Year's Resolutions:
1) To have more fun and worry less!!
2) To write here more often.
3) To exercise twice a week for an hour or more.

    Frank took me to see The Big Short last week. He arranged in secret for Maria to watch the kids and made it a big surprise. Dinner and a movie. I have to admit I loved the movie, primarily for one reason: Ryan Gosling. He is one hot man. Be still, my beating heart!

    My man is hot too, and he hardly flirts anymore. He seems to have lost interest in other women, yet he pays more attention to me. Does that mean he's becoming domesticated? He's still wild in many ways. We made wonderful, passionate love last night. It's coming back for us, I think. More and better lovemaking. Much better. He's more present and considerate these days—both in and out of bed. Used to be he'd seem so far away. Not anymore! I'll take that as a win.

I'm not going to tell him I imagined he was Ryan Gosling, though.

Jodie's presentation was the last one of the morning. Frank had arranged time off work to attend. As was the MacBride custom, they always tried to have at least one parent at the kids' events. They knew this was a big deal for Jodie. She wouldn't tell them who she'd chosen as a person who exemplified compassion, but she wanted her dad there and asked him to video the presentation on his phone to share with the rest of the family.

Of the three presentations he'd seen before Jodie's turn, one was awful. That poor boy had tripped over his words and seemed extremely nervous. Frank had wished he could do something for him, but that was clearly out of the question. A girl gave a great portrayal of her grandmother and all she had done for others. She'd worked as a behind-the-lines supporting nurse before and during the Battle of the Bulge in World War II. She was an English citizen living in the United States and did not have to go into battlefield service, but she insisted.

The other presentation was okay. The girl presented all the reasons George W. Bush was compassionate. Frank couldn't help wondering if that was her idea or her parents'. And then it was Jodie's turn. He felt a flush of excitement as his daughter walked to the front of the room and started her PowerPoint presentation.

"I had a hard time picking someone for this." She looked around the classroom. "There are many compassionate people in our world. There are many compassionate people in history. There are compassionate people living today, and there are compassionate people in our family." She looked straight at Frank, who blushed. "I took my whole first week of this assignment thinking about not only who I'd pick—but also about what compassion is. Because I didn't understand it. I knew someone like Mother Teresa was compassionate. I knew Mahatma Gandhi was compassionate. I knew people who run homeless shelters and people like Florence Nightingale are all compassionate. And then there are people like Jesus or St. Francis of Assisi—and more recently, Albert Einstein and Martin Luther King who were compassionate. All in very different ways, and all in ways that affected not only people around them, but the entire world." She briefly showed a slide of each person she mentioned, and finally displayed an animated image of the world turning.

Frank shook his head and wondered where the heck she'd learned to speak like this. She seemed so calm up there, doing what he couldn't imagine doing himself. He looked around at the other students, who hung on her every word.

"My person of compassion is my little brother, Sam."

Frank's eyes widened. What a perfect choice!

Jodie explained to the class how his whole life he'd only said a single word—when his beloved Nonna Eve passed away. She explained that they didn't know why he wouldn't talk. Or why he didn't read or write. "But he hears everything," she said, "and notices things—more than most people." She paused. "He always thinks of others' well-being, comfort, and happiness before his own. Isn't that what compassion is? I believe he's a walking example of love." She took a deep breath. "Sometimes people do big, wonderful things and get recognized for them. And sometimes there are people we don't recognize as great, yet who are."

She came to the final slide, which showed Sam behind their house with his arms around both sisters and that lopsided smile on his face that said so much. Frank's eyes filled with tears. He felt deep love and pride for his kids.

Tulasi Patel gasped. "Oh, my God, he looks just like my angel."

"That's my brother," said Jodie. "He's no angel, but he's a sweet guy. I'm sure he'll be happy to know he looks like the angel in your dream."

"But it wasn't a dream. I saw a real angel, and it looked just like your brother."

Jodie looked puzzled, then shrugged and gave a little bow as the class applauded. Far more enthusiastically, Frank noticed, than they had for any of the others. As she walked back to her seat, Frank barely avoided hugging her in front of the class. When she met his gaze, though, he could feel her love all the way down to his toes.

"You'll never believe what happened at Jodie's presentation," Frank said as he walked into the house.

"Try me," said Sofia.

He explained what had taken place and how wonderfully their daughter had done. "It's funny that whatever Tulasi Patel saw, she thinks it looked like Sam." He had mused about that on the way home. "Of course, like Jodie said, with all the painkillers she was on, she could have seen a pink elephant and thought it was real."

"Our family seems to be a magnet for the unusual, doesn't it?"

Frank nodded. "All the more reason why I'm just gonna go do something normal. Like play with my toys in the garage. No point in going back to work for another hour and a half, especially with Kingston on my case. He's been riding me more than ever lately. Plus, my racing quadcopter has been begging me to finish it and get it up in the air."

"Maybe if you hadn't been flirting with his wife at the Christmas party three years ago, things would be different."

He frowned. "Thanks for bringing that up again. Maybe I should finally take your suggestion to heart and quit tomorrow."

"I would support you in that. I mean," she said, reconsidering, "we should probably have another plan first."

"Exactly. Which is why that wasn't a serious suggestion. We'd have to have Plan B in place first, but we don't even know what Plan B would look like."

"I know, but I believe there's an answer somewhere. We just don't know what it is." She gave him a hug. "Anyway, for now just forget about it, go work on your drone project, or whatever you feel like. Just relax." She smiled. "Sam and I will be right here if you need us."

Sofia sat down with Sam and his math flash cards. She'd hold up a card with an equation, and he'd write down the result. As usual, he was fast and flawless. How many ten-year-olds could handle high school math at Sam's speed? Or at any speed? What plagued her, though, was why he couldn't do the same with words. They'd gone through twenty cards when she got an idea. She picked up her phone and called the police nonemergency number.

"Eugene Police, Bishop speaking."

"Hi, if there was an incident reported that took place in someone's house, who can I ask to find out whose house it was in?"

"It's fairly simple. Just go to the Eugene City website, click on the police section of the menu, and look up dispatch. Then put in your date, and everything is right there."

"What if I don't know the date?" she asked.

"Then I would say good luck with that. It lists events by day, but you'd have to look through every single day until you find what you're looking for. Some days are quiet, and some days have dozens of entries. It can get tedious, trust me."

She thanked him and hung up. "Well, that's a project for a rainy day," she said to Sam.

Later that night as she tried to sleep, her mind spun. She went to check on her son, who slept peacefully. Her laptop sat where she left it on the kitchen counter. She considered going back to sleep, but decided it was a lost cause. She found the city of Eugene website and clicked on the police blotter. It was just as officer Bishop had said. Easy enough, but without knowing the date, she'd have to go through a lot of entries. She knew the event she was looking for had happened sometime early the previous spring, probably April or May, and she tried looking through the first part of that month but came up with nothing that seemed to match.

She tried again in the early hours of the morning. Her kids weren't the only ones in the family who were obsessive. Going through the whole month of May, then April, she still found nothing that matched what she was looking for. For all she knew, she had already overlooked it. She scanned hundreds of entries in the daily records with no luck until she got to March 10, where she saw a complaint from a family in the Parkhill subdivision that they had seen a young boy in their house. The house of Jagadish Patel. *Wow!*

And she found the call the police had made to their house, logged at 12:37

a.m., listed as a follow-up. Why hadn't they done a quick check on Sam the night the police called?

Once everyone had left the house—the girls off to school, Frank off to work—she sat down with Sam. "*Querido*, do you know who Tulasi Patel is?"

Sam gave her a puzzled look and shook his head.

"Oh, never mind, it was just a silly idea." As she said it, she wondered if she really *wanted* to know. Still, the incident bothered her. Could that have been Sam? "Just some coincidences, and I wondered if my very special son had anything to do with them." She knelt down and pulled him into a reluctant hug. "I know you don't like being hugged, but I'm your mother, and this is one of the side benefits of the job." When she let him go, he leaned his forehead against hers, which melted her heart.

CHAPTER THIRTY-THREE

Andrea took a long sip of her mocha latte and looked at Frank over the top of her Starbucks cup. "Thanks for meeting me. It's been way too long. What, something like two and a half years?"

"Something like that."

"I've missed you."

"Me too," he lied.

"You know, we have a lot in common."

"You think so?" No way in hell!

She nodded. "Absolutely. First of all, we're both good-looking people."

"You are."

"We both are, and you know it," Andrea said. "We're also good in bed and suffering through unhappy marriages."

"I'm not."

"Sure you are." She sipped her coffee and gave him a sultry look. "When's the last time you had sex with that cute little Spanish wife of yours?"

"Um. I don't know. A few weeks ago."

"Can I ask you a personal question?"

"I think you already did."

"Did she squeal with delight?" Andrea asked.

"That's classified information."

"Sure it is. I'll take that as 'No, she didn't.' See my point? You're telling me that's happy?" She smiled smugly. "I'm guessing you get it once a month, if that. Believe me, if your marriage was happy, you wouldn't have tried so hard to get into my panties in the first place."

"I wasn't trying to do anything. It just kind of happened."

"Of course you tried. Everyone tries." She touched his arm. "Nothing ever just 'kind of happens.' Look, we didn't plan for things to be like this, but here we are, so let's make the most of it." She smiled seductively. "If we don't have fun, we might as well be dead, right?"

"Not necessarily." Frank checked his watch. "You said you had something important to tell me."

"I do, but I don't want you to get the wrong idea."

"About what?"

She leaned back in her chair. "My therapist thinks I should tell Jeff about us. The whole story."

Exactly what he'd worried would happen. "What kind of therapist would tell you that?"

"The kind who has my best interest at heart."

Over the next couple of months, Frank waited for things to get dramatically worse at work. Once Andrea told Kingston, his job would be history. Yet Kingston was his usual unpleasant self, neither better nor worse. One day after Frank had loaded his tools onto the back of his truck and was about to get in, his phone chirped with an incoming text.

> Andi: *Just so you know, I haven't told Jeff yet, but the day is still young.*
> Frank: *What are you doing?*
> Andi: *Just touching in. Sofia says to say hi by the way*
> Frank: *WTF are you talking about?*
> Andi: *:)*

Sofia had been having a great day. The kids were cooperative and had only kind words for each other. They'd even had a surprise visit from Jeff Kingston's wife, Andrea, who brought them some hot blueberry muffins. She was warm and friendly, almost apologetic for her husband. Maybe she'd put in a good word for Frank. A woman that beautiful must have a lot of influence.

Later, while the girls focused on their homework, she wondered what it would be like if life was always so easy. She'd forgotten how quickly things could turn.

Frank arrived around six, and she could tell something was wrong. When she asked how his day was, he said it was fine, but something was obviously not fine.

"Anything you want to talk to me about?" she asked.

He nodded glumly, not looking her in the eye. "There is, actually."

Sofia was still in a good mood from the day she'd had. This couldn't be too bad. "Okay then, spill it."

"Sure, how about right after dinner?"

At that point, Sofia became concerned. Something about the tone of his voice.

He was quiet and sullen during dinner, hardly touching his food—which concerned her even more. By the time they were alone in the bedroom, she was genuinely worried. She looked at her husband questioningly, but he seemed unable to speak. "What is it, Frank? You know you can tell me anything."

He looked at her in silence for a few long moments before he spoke. "I had an affair."

"You what?"

Frank looked truly miserable. "I had an—"

"I heard what you said. How dare you?"

And there it was. Her greatest fears realized. That he could be bossy was one thing, though he'd gotten over most of that. Other aspects of their relationship were better than they'd been in the past. But this! This made all the progress they'd made meaningless. This was exactly what she'd sworn to herself she'd never tolerate. "How long?"

"Well, it's kind of complicated."

"So obviously, it was not just a one-night stand. Let's try an easier question. When did it start?"

"Almost three and a half years ago, at the expo in Portland."

"Three and a half years ago?"

"It's not what you think."

"It's *exactly* what I think. Three and a half years is a long time, Frank."

"But it ended over three years ago."

"Did it really? Or is that just when you stopped having sex?" She looked at him sideways. "It's all coming back to me. You returned from that expo acting strangely. It's still going on, isn't it?"

"No, definitely not!"

"When is the last time you saw her?"

"Recently, but—"

"Are you leaving us? Is that why you're bringing it up?"

"No. Never! *Amore mio*—"

"Don't call me that. Don't *ever* call me that!" She paused. "Do you love her?"

"No, and I never did. I only met with her because she demanded to see me. Honestly, I only did it to try to get her out of my life."

"*Honestly*? You are so not allowed to use that word."

"I don't know what else to say. I just got entangled and—"

"Entangled? Like you innocently walked into some gigantic spider's web and there was nothing you could do about it?"

"Not exactly, but yes, a little bit like that. I was drunk the first time and—"

"Stop." Sofia paced the room furiously as Frank sat on the bed, watching her with sad eyes. "Who was it?"

Frank sighed. "Andrea Kingston."

"You have *got* to be kidding me! The same Andrea Kingston who shared her hot blueberry muffins with me today?"

"What?"

"I was going to mention it before this drama took over our evening. She stopped by with home-baked blueberry muffins. It didn't even cross my mind how strange it was that she'd know my favorite food. I took it to be a lucky guess. Looks like she was luckier than I thought." She frowned. "But even stranger that you would bring this up the same day she stopped by."

"Not really that strange. She texted me."

"Really? What did she say that inspired you to so courageously bare your soul to me?"

"Nothing important. Just saying you said to say 'Hi.' I'm sure she was showing me how much power she has. And making a subtle threat. It's all pretty complicated. I was going to tell you anyway and—"

Sofia waved him off. "It's not so complicated. Let's see. She's younger than me by probably eight or nine years, and a beautiful woman with a perfect body. Probably hits the gym, what, four or five times a week? And fairly well endowed, at least compared to me. So flatter tummy and bigger breasts. She probably doesn't even have any stretch marks. Everything you've ever wanted in a woman, right?"

"No, that's not right. You're—"

"And the best part is that she's your boss's wife. The boss who gives you a hard time for what I thought was no good reason. Who at one point gave you a thousand-dollar bonus, but then inexplicably denied you raises, keeping us barely above the waterline, dog-paddling for dear life. All for motives I didn't understand. Until now." She looked at him ferociously. "Jeff Kingston already knows, doesn't he?"

"Not yet, but that was her threat. She's going to tell him today."

"I get it. Now we see the real reason you're coming to me with this. She's going to tell him, and you thought it would be smarter to let me know since I'd most likely find out anyway. Doesn't look like you were planning to tell me."

"I was waiting for the right time."

Which would be never. "You know you're making it worse, don't you? That every time you lie on top of a lie, you add more poison to the pond."

"I'm trying to give you the whole story. When she texted that you'd said 'Hi,' it scared the hell out of me. I've known for a long time Kingston might find out, and while I don't want to lose my job, that's nothing compared with how much

I don't want to lose you. Or the kids."

"Bet you wish you'd thought of that before, don't you?"

"I do. I've been sick with worry and regret over this for over three years."

She tilted her head and chewed her lower lip. "So if he doesn't know, why has Kingston become more hostile toward you?"

"At one point a couple of years ago, she told him I sometimes flirt with her."

"Ah, so we find another missing piece of the puzzle. Why would you flirt with her? Especially knowing that she's needy and unstable?"

"That's just it. I didn't flirt with her. I mean, not really, but—"

"Do you still think your flirting is harmless? That it means nothing?" She slowly shook her head. "You said you wouldn't lie to me anymore. Which was just another lie. I'm so stupid." She picked up an intricately detailed ceramic jewelry box from the dresser. Frank had given it to her on their first anniversary, many years before. She shook it in his face. "You meant you wouldn't lie unless it was a huge, terrible, relationship-destroying lie."

"Please, let me explain."

"You already have! The worst part is not you sleeping around. The worst part is you lying about it. You said when you told me about Italy that you would never lie to me again. I think you also said something like, 'Now you know everything.'" She glared at him. "But I didn't know everything, did I?"

He shook his head. "I'm sorry."

"And I'm obviously not enough for you."

"That's not it. Not it at all."

"I directly asked you if there was someone else."

"I took that to mean if there was someone else I was in love with."

"Oh, *please*! How stupid do you think I am?" she asked. "You just lied, plain and simple."

"I know you're not stupid. I know you're sharp as a razor. And it's not that I tried to lie. It's just—I didn't think it was the right time to tell you." He shrugged. "It was already over and done with. I was planning to tell you once things settled down."

"And how'd that work out for you? Almost three years later and you were still waiting for things to settle down."

"*Amore mio—*"

She threw the jewelry case to the floor, where it exploded into hundreds of pieces. "*Don't* call me that! You should have told me, especially when I asked you straight out."

"I know." He stared at the tiny pieces of enameled ceramic among his wife's jewelry all over the floor, and his face crumpled. "It was a very emotional thing telling you about Italy. I was—"

"Stop it! We lie or we don't. There's always a choice. You mostly choose lying." She shook her head in disgust. "And I was blind to it. You've been lying our whole marriage. This probably isn't even your first affair."

"It is!"

"Why should I believe you?"

"Because I wouldn't—"

"You're not supposed to answer that! It's what we call a rhetorical question. You lie whenever you feel like it. I don't believe anything anymore." She opened the bedroom door. "Right now I just need space." She gestured out into the hallway. He walked out and she slammed the door, then sat on the bed. How had she recreated this nightmare from her childhood? How had she been so blind? So trusting? So fucking stupid? The tears she'd been holding back streamed down her face, the taste of them salty in her mouth. After a few minutes, she wiped them dry and began packing her suitcase.

CHAPTER THIRTY-FOUR

When Frank put the kids to bed that night, the girls were much quieter than usual, and Sam was entirely unresponsive. Earlier, when he'd opened the door to the master bedroom and seen the jagged pieces of ceramic all over the floor still mixed with his wife's jewelry, he was almost knocked over by sadness. Something about her leaving her beloved jewelry on the floor among all the breakage got to him. He'd caused this mess, and it seemed possible that things could get a lot messier. For the first time that day, he faced the reality that he might not be able to make things right—which scared him profoundly.

Time slowed down, and each following day seemed to take forever. Sofia had been at her parents' over a week. He'd left voice messages, emails, and texts—but no response ever came back. He'd used up almost all his sick leave, and he would chew into his vacation time in two days. Kingston had been emailing him his displeasure almost daily. He didn't have much choice in the matter, but there was no way he would tell his boss that.

He had no idea the affair would lead to this. At least she called the kids every day. He could hear her on speakerphone with the three of them in the girls' room every evening.

She returned on the ninth day, around seven thirty in the evening. She didn't say a word to Frank as she hugged their kids, who were hugely relieved to see their mom.

"I've missed you guys. Dad and I are going to talk now. I want you all to go down to the family room and watch something."

Jodie looked at her earnestly. "We've already used up our four hours this week. Well, Lisa and I have."

"Then this will be extra." She walked toward the bedroom, Frank right behind.

He closed the door after them. "I cannot begin to tell you how sorry—"

"Save it. I'm here because of the kids."

"Okay, but I think—"

"I really don't want to hear it."

"Um, okay."

"Are you good sleeping on the couch?" she asked.

"If that's what you want."

"That's exactly what I want. I'll let you know when I'm ready to talk more."

"Okay, but I really think you need—"

"I need nothing from you right now." She opened the door and motioned him out with her head.

Frank obeyed at first and walked toward the doorway, then stopped and looked back at her. She shook her head firmly. He sighed and turned to go, then changed his mind and closed the door.

"I already told you I'm not—" she began.

"You have to listen to me. If you never want to speak to me again, that's your choice."

"I'm just not ready," she said.

"Understood. But hear what I have to say, then decide what you want."

"I already know what you're going to say."

"Actually, you don't," said Frank. "Give me five minutes to explain, then make whatever decision you think best."

"I don't know that I—"

"Please, just hear me out. If nothing else, for the sake of our children."

She sat on the edge of the bed and glanced at her watch. "Five minutes."

He told her the whole story, leaving nothing out.

"What a bitch!" she exclaimed.

Frank breathed a sigh of relief. "That's why I was trying to—"

"If you think for one second that puts you in the clear, you are dead wrong, mister." She shook a finger at him. "No one forced you to have sex with Miss Prima Donna. Especially three separate times. And you should have told me right away."

"I know, I just—"

"Worst of all, how dare you lie about it? Do you realize how much that has cost our relationship? Can you even *begin* to understand how deeply that has affected my ability to ever trust you again?"

"I think I do."

"Good! May I have some space now, please?"

"Thanks for meeting me on such short notice, Andrea."

"My pleasure. You know how much I enjoy our little meetings."

"I've told my wife everything about us."

"Congratulations. You should have brought her along so we could have a memorable threesome."

"This isn't funny."

"Who's being funny? That was a serious offer. I could make your cute wife happy in ways you've never even dreamed of. And you'd get to watch as an added bonus."

"Look, Andrea—"

"No, *you* look," she said sourly. "You can't just cut a girl off the way you did."

"I'd been trying to cut things off since we started."

"But obviously not trying very hard."

Frank's mouth tightened. "I'm trying to do the right thing now." He glared at her. "What were you thinking, showing up at our house like that? Blueberry muffins?"

"It was a nice thing to do. A peace offering."

"We weren't at war. You were threatening me. And our family."

"Can you please dial down the drama a bit? I think you've seen too many

Netflix specials. Does having a retarded child make you hypersensitive?"

"Sam is not retarded! He's—"

"Special needs. Sorry, wrong terminology."

He stood up, his blood boiling. "We're done here. Like I said, Sofia knows. This is over." He paused. "It's been over. She even knows I'm here talking to you."

"What a pussy!"

He was still fuming about what she'd said about Sam. "Call me whatever you want." He turned to leave. "Just don't call me on the phone."

"What about Jeff?"

He stopped. "What about him?"

She looked at him innocently. "What am I going to tell him?"

Frank wasn't sure where she was going with this. "There's no need to tell him anything." He frowned. "I thought you already told him."

"That was only a bluff. Didn't I spell it out for you in my text? I said I hadn't *yet* told him. How could it be that you're still working if I'd told him? He'd go ballistic. You give him *way* too much credit. Just like I've given you way too much credit. I thought you were smart, but you're just another Forrest Gump." She laughed. "An Italian Forrest Gump. That's rich!" Her smile faded. "Now I want to follow your shining example and come clean with my spouse."

"You know telling him wouldn't serve anyone, including you."

"Sure it would." She batted her eyelashes. "Jeff and I have been getting along much better these days. We've been way more honest with each other. Even if you hadn't brought this up, I would've told him anyway."

Frank narrowed his eyes. "We both know that's not what you would've done. You're simply threatening retaliation."

"Whatever makes you say that?" She clicked her tongue. "It's hard for a girl to get any respect around here."

"You must think you're being hilarious. We're talking about my job—and my future—at stake here."

"Maybe you should've thought of that before you tried to sleep with me."

"We both know that's not how it all went down."

"Part of it was you getting back at my husband for being such a prick."

Frank shook his head. There was only a tiny bit of truth in that. "Not at all!"

"You sure there wasn't a bit of 'Fuck you!' in all that for Jeff?"

"Totally sure."

"Right. And I'm the Queen of England." She stood up and smiled sweetly. "Nice of you to take the time this afternoon to catch me up."

"Hang on, we need to get this thing about telling your husband figured out."

"Oh, I think you've got it figured out already. Just remember that life is like a box of chocolates, Forrest. You never know what you're going to get." She started walking away, then looked back over her shoulder and smiled. "If you change your mind, call me. Or text me. But don't keep a girl waiting."

CHAPTER THIRTY-FIVE

Sam hadn't had one of his escapes in over two years. Now that he was eleven, he seemed to have grown out of his wandering phase. Or so Sofia thought until the night she went to check on him and found his bed empty.

Heart racing, she searched the house, then remembered the dead bolts. She went to the front door and stared at the key in the lock. A key that should have been in one of the nightstands next to their bed.

She woke Frank, who checked his nightstand drawer. No key. "Damn it!" He slammed it shut.

"Should we wake the girls?" Sofia asked.

"Not unless we need to. Lisa's got her big math test in the morning. Let's check the neighborhood first."

"What about the police?"

Frank scratched his head. "We should call."

The police said they'd keep a watch out, but they had a new policy and couldn't actually search until a person had been missing at least eight hours. Something to do with utilization of resources. Frank told them he understood, he didn't expect that, and Sam always came back within a few hours anyway. But not that night. By dawn, he still hadn't returned. Frank and Sofia had driven all over Eugene and part of Springfield in their separate vehicles looking for him, but they saw no sign of their son anywhere.

They convened in the kitchen, each on their fourth cup of coffee. Frank glanced at the kitchen clock. "The girls will be up soon. I'm going back out."

"Might as well. I'd go, too, but I need to help them get ready for school." She rubbed her forehead tiredly. "He's never done this before," she said as Lisa walked into the kitchen.

"Never done what before?" her daughter asked with a yawn.

"Sam took off again, and he's still not back. Dad and I are worried—"

Lisa looked as though someone had just slapped her. "Why didn't you wake us up?"

"*Querida*, we didn't want you to lose sleep, especially since you have a test—"

"Who cares about a stupid test? You should have woken us up. What, are we suddenly not part of this family anymore?"

"Of course you are, but Dad and I were out looking—"

"Yeah, and if we had twice as many eyes open, we might have seen him."

"Seen who?" Jodie walked in, her face softened by sleep.

"Sam," said Lisa. "He went missing last night and they didn't even tell us. Unbelievable."

Sofia set her coffee cup on the table. "Lisa, I know you're upset, but parents sometimes need to—"

"Don't give her that crap," said Jodie.

Frank held up a hand. "Jodie! Lisa! Don't talk to your mother like that."

Jodie glared at him. "Why didn't you wake us up?"

Frank sighed. "We thought it wasn't necessary, so we—"

Lisa chimed in again. "Wasn't necessary? You have *got* to be kidding." Her eyes filled with tears.

Sofia smiled sadly. "Girls, I'm really sorry. We're both sorry. I guess we thought he'd come back after a few hours like the other times. We didn't wake you up the last time two years ago, and it all worked out fine." She looked at Frank. "Anyway, we can't undo it, but we can move forward. We need to find him, okay?"

Both girls nodded.

Frank asked them, "Has anyone noticed anything different with Sam recently?" They all shook their heads.

Lisa spoke first. "He was his normal adorable self last night, and he fell asleep right after I read to him."

Sofia couldn't believe her ears. "You read to him?"

Lisa rolled her eyes. "Like, almost every night."

"How does he ask you?"

"He brings me a book and puts it in my hands."

"Really? How come you never mentioned this?"

Lisa glanced at her sister. "It's always after we're supposed to be asleep."

Jodie shook her head. "Thanks, Lisa. Didn't we agree we weren't going to mention it to Mom and Dad?"

Sofia's mouth hung open. "You do it too?"

Jodie rolled her eyes.

Somewhere out there was an innocent and vulnerable eleven-year-old boy who had his big sisters read to him.

Frank cleared his throat. "We need to focus and find Sam. You can keep reading to him, but this is urgent."

Sofia waved her hand at the kitchen clock. "They should get ready for school—"

Both girls opened their mouths to speak, but Frank beat them to it. "They're not going. Like Lisa said, two extra pairs of eyes will help. Besides, how much do you think they'll learn while worried sick about their brother?"

"What about Lisa's test?" asked Sofia.

"This is what's important right now." He nodded at his younger daughter. "It's her choice."

Lisa gave an exaggerated sigh. "You seriously have to ask? I'll worry about the test later."

They waited for Sofia's reaction. What was she supposed to say? "Okay, let's find him."

The morning dragged on, and the MacBrides' anxiety increased. Jodie had the next turn at home, and when Sofia called to check in, her daughter was testy with her. Both girls were upset with them, and not finding Sam just made it worse.

Frank called shortly after ten thirty. "They found him."

"Oh, thank God. Is he okay?" asked Sofia.

"She said he's mostly okay."

"What does 'mostly okay' mean? And who is 'she?'" Sofia asked.

"The police officer who picked him up. And, um, she asked if we wanted her to take him to the hospital."

Sofia felt as if her heart could stop at any moment. "Why would they do that? What's wrong?"

"Well, she said he looked very bedraggled and worn out. No signs of any damage, though. I said if he doesn't look like he needs anything urgently, bring him home and we'll take care of him." Frank added firmly, "I think we need to see him and if we have to take him in, we can do that then."

"Good call. I'm about twelve minutes away. Make that ten. The hell with speed limits."

Frank paused. "Well, that's the other thing."

"What's the other thing?"

"He's with the Springfield police. They picked him up in North Springfield."

"What? How'd he get all the way over there?" asked Sofia.

"Not sure, but I suspect he runs. We know he's a great runner and hardly gets winded. We can try to find out from Sam, but that's later. For now, I want to make sure he's safely home with us. I'll be there in eight or nine minutes. You might as well take your time, because we'll both be there long before him."

It seemed to take forever, but eleven minutes after they had both arrived, a police car pulled up to the curb.

They all ran out as the policewoman opened the back door of the car to let Sam out. He looked happy but run-down. He ran first to Lisa and hugged her tightly.

The officer stood with hands on her hips. "Found him walking on Pioneer Parkway, and he fit the description of the missing minor. When I stopped to ask him where he was going, he wouldn't talk to me."

Frank nodded. "Sorry, he doesn't talk."

"Yeah, that's what they told me when I called dispatch. They gave me your number." She removed her cap and scratched her head. "I'd like to know how he got all the way to Springfield."

Frank watched Sam hug Jodie and Sofia. "So do we, Officer."

"Dispatch says he's done this before."

"Yes, a few times. But it's been over two years since it happened last. And he's never been that far away. At least not that we know of."

"Well, if I were you, I'd do what I can to keep him home. It's a dangerous world out there." She seemed uneasy. "There's something else I need to tell you."

"What's that?"

"Eugene Police said they had to alert Child Protective Services. They told me to let you know."

"Thanks, Officer." Frank was too tired to comment on that. They'd deal with CPS when the time came. And evidently, it would come. Was there a way to keep Sam from wandering? Hiding the dead bolt keys might work, but that would be more unsafe. Maybe they could sleep with the keys around their necks. If they knew what he was up to, maybe they'd have a chance.

Sam slept most of the day, as did the rest of the family. Frank had to go in at 2:30 to meet with his subordinates. He didn't want to, but he knew the kids would be fine with Sofia. He'd hoped to be there when Sam woke up, but he'd just have to talk to him later. He started his truck and sat for a few minutes staring out the windshield. At least Sam was safe. At least he came home. He put the pickup in drive and took off. This *had* a solution, and he was determined to find it.

Frank called a family conference when he got home from work. "Sam, we're glad we found you. And you already know this, but it worried us sick."

Sam nodded sincerely.

"... and you know we can't let this continue."

Another nod.

Sofia sighed. "We're responsible for your safety, *querido*. And you heard the policewoman who brought you home. It's a dangerous world out there. There are bad people who hurt kids."

Sam nodded.

This is what they had always gotten from him. Agreement and understanding—yet he still went out. This would stop now. Frank shifted in his chair. "We don't want to lock you in your room. That wouldn't be safe in case there was a fire or something. Plus, this is our home, not a jail." He motioned toward his daughters, who paid close attention. "Your sisters were worried sick as well. We're not being paranoid. Bad things can happen and sometimes they do. Today, we have to find a solution to this."

Sam nodded again.

"Let's start with where you went last night."

Sam just stared at him. Not openly defiant, but not compliant, either.

"I need you to tell us."

No reaction.

"Son, you have to tell us."

Sam picked up a pen from the coffee table, wrote something on the back of a World Soccer magazine, and handed it to his father. Frank looked at what he wrote, his eyes wide. He handed the magazine to Sofia, who gasped. "You can write!" she said.

Sam nodded, as though writing was the most natural thing in the world for him.

Sofia continued to study what Sam had written. "What do you mean by 'Sacred Heart'? Do you mean the hospital in Springfield?"

He nodded again.

Sofia couldn't believe it. "That's where you went last night?"

Another nod.

"How long have you been able to write?" asked Sofia.

Sam shrugged.

"This is unbelievable," Frank said. "Why did you go to the hospital?"

When he didn't react, Frank handed him back the pen and magazine, but Sam just set them down.

"Sam," asked Jodie, "did you go there to help someone?"

He nodded.

Sofia frowned. "When you have gone out before, did you go to help people?"

He nodded again.

She sighed. "Look, *querido*, we like that you want to help people, but it's too dangerous for you to go out in the middle of the night. Besides, the doctors and nurses in the hospital know what they're doing."

Sam didn't respond.

"April's mom says he heals people," said Lisa.

"Is that true, Son?" Frank asked.

Another nod. Sofia and Frank exchanged a quick glance.

"Do you go inside people's houses sometimes?" Sofia asked.

He hesitated, then nodded.

Frank knelt down in front of his son. "Do you understand how dangerous that is? People have guns, and they could think you are coming to hurt them. They might hurt you." He frowned. "Or kill you."

Sam swallowed.

"We can't let you do that," said Frank. "It's way too dangerous. It's great that you want to help people … and heal them, but we can't let you do what's unsafe." He tried to figure out the best way to handle the situation. "We'll meet you halfway. If you want to go visit someone in the hospital, tell me and I'll take you. Wake me up any time of the night, and we'll go. If you need to go during the day, then Mom will take you." He glanced at Sofia, who nodded. "And no more going into people's houses. Ever. Does that sound like something you can agree to?"

Sam nodded solemnly.

"Part of the deal is that you have to promise, as long as you live here with us, you will never leave the house without us knowing. Or," he added, "whatever adult is looking after you at the time."

Sam considered that for a while, then nodded.

Frank looked hopefully at Sofia. "We may have just had a breakthrough."

CHAPTER THIRTY-SIX

A month after Sam's escape, Sofia had thought they'd dodged the bullet of the Oregon Child Protective Services. Maybe the police hadn't told them.

Early one December afternoon, a knock on the door dashed her hopes.

"Sofia MacBride?"

"You know who I am. We've met before, remember?"

"I'm here again on behalf of the Oregon State Child Protective Services."

"How surprising."

"This is a courtesy visit to let you know—"

"Courtesy visit? Do you honestly think this has anything to do with courtesy? I can tell you up front you're not taking our son away."

"We gave you every opportunity. And we've seen the need to become involved."

Sofia wasn't about to give in. "It's been two years. Two whole years since it happened last time."

"Making it at least the fourth time he's run away, and the fourth time you've had to involve the police."

"Okay. But are you telling me this never happens to anyone else?"

"It does. Which is why we're so concerned. We know what can happen. Once we become aware, it's our duty to monitor the situation and act if need be."

"You couldn't possibly take any action that will put him in a better environment than we can provide here." She had to give this hard woman more of an explanation. "We found out he feels the need to comfort people in the hospital." And he heals them—but there's no way in hell I'm telling you that.

"In the middle of the night, without letting you know?"

"Pretty much, yeah. He has a heart bigger than the state of Oregon." Sofia's eyes brimmed with tears.

Olivia looked at her for a few moments. "May I see him?"

"Is that necessary?"

"For someone identified as a high-risk youth, yes. Otherwise, we can proceed as planned."

"Since you put it that way." She opened the door wider and motioned her in. "Sam, can you come in here, please?" she called out.

He walked in, wide-eyed, looking from his mom to the CPS lady and back.

"Hello, Sam," said Olivia.

He nodded, staring out the front door.

"I want to make sure you are okay. You know that's my job, right? To keep children like you safe."

He nodded again.

Sofia folded her arms across her chest. "There's no need to talk slow. He's not retarded."

Olivia shot her a quick glare and continued with the same slow approach. "You know the other day when the police brought you home?"

He nodded.

"Can you look at me when I talk to you, dear?"

To Sofia's surprise, he looked Olivia right in the eye.

"Did you go to the hospital to help people?"

He nodded again.

She glanced at Sofia, then turned her attention back to Sam. "Do you know it's dangerous for a young person like yourself to go out unprotected at night?"

Another nod.

"I need you to promise me you won't go out without telling your parents.

Otherwise, I have to take you to a place away from your family where you won't be able to get out. Do you understand and agree?"

He nodded solemnly.

Sofia added, "We had a similar talk with him. He's promised us as well, and he always honors his promises."

Olivia began to retreat toward the front door. "That's good. Because I would hate to put him in a secure facility." She turned to go. "But that's what I'd do if I thought it in his best interest."

"I have no doubt."

The big surprise that Christmas came in a small package from Sofia's parents. They typically gave each of the MacBrides something, which could be anything from creative toys to books or practical tools. But not this time. This time they had given a present for the entire family.

It was a card offering them a vacation to anywhere they wanted in the world. Eduardo had to buy the tickets before the end of the year, so they had less than a week to decide together where they wanted to go and when.

First, they all cheered. Then reality sank in. Even with tickets to get to where they wanted, vacations could be expensive. Things had been financially tighter than ever for them.

No doubt this had something to do with Eduardo's 2016 tax year about to end. But Frank tried to not be cynical about it. After all, a gift was a gift. "Hard to believe these are the same parents who refused to loan us money the last couple of times we've asked them for help," he mentioned to Sofia.

She gave him a dark look. "My father needs to feel he's in control. If we ask him, he feels powerful saying 'no.' But if he's feeling generous and it's his idea, he gives us ten times more in the form of a vacation. I'm happy to accept it."

The second big surprise that day happened when she called to thank her parents. Sofia mentioned they might have to wait until they could afford accommodations and the other expenses of the vacation.

"I forgot to mention on the card we're giving you three thousand dollars for food and lodging," said Isabel.

Sofia almost dropped the phone. She knew her parents were wealthy and had always been so, but her father in particular was very frugal. Maybe he'd decided he didn't want to die with ten million dollars unused in his bank account. Or maybe Madre put her foot down and said they had to use some of the money for a good cause—or else.

Frank looked up his paid time off on the public works team calendar and found out they could go in March. Spring break was not available, but the calendar showed an opening two weeks earlier. "We could make it a ten-day trip," he said. "I'd miss a full week of work, and we'd take the weekends on both sides plus the following Monday. Do you think the girls can miss that much time from school?"

"I think they could if we set the right conditions—that they have their assignments done in advance and catch up whatever they missed within a couple weeks of our return. This is too good an opportunity to pass up," said Sofia.

Frank loved seeing his wife so genuinely excited.

Though Sofia's parents had said they could go anywhere they wanted, the MacBrides still needed to decide when and where. Making the choice seemed simple, but it wasn't that easy in practice. The girls wanted Hawaii, Frank wanted New Zealand, Sofia wanted Egypt, and Sam wanted Nepal. Sofia told herself it undoubtedly had something to do with him thinking that was where he was born. The subject hadn't come up in over a year. But it was certainly up now. Thus began the family negotiations, each presenting to the others the advantages of where they wanted to go. Sofia would've been fine with any of the destinations.

Finally, she proposed they put it to a vote. They could vote for any of the destinations except the one they originally wanted, and they'd see what destination had the most interest. In this second round, Jodie voted for Australia, both Lisa and Sam voted for Nepal, and Frank and Sofia voted for Hawaii.

"Okay," said Frank. "Looks like we have a tie. There's five of us, and we're all going to vote between either Hawaii or Nepal. The place with the most votes wins."

"Dad, that's not really fair," Jodie complained. "Sam voted for Nepal again—which he wasn't supposed to do. Besides, since both Lisa and I originally wanted Hawaii, we couldn't opt for it in this vote. But if you look at things logically, most people wanted Hawaii as their first or second choice."

Frank cleared his throat. "Good point, Jodie, and since we have a tie, it has to go one way or the other. I propose we agree as a family to go to Hawaii. It'll be a wonderful vacation we'll all love." He put his hand on Sam's shoulder. "What do you say to that, buddy?"

Sam shook his head and pointed to Nepal on the list.

"Look, Son, I know that's where you want to go, but we have to find a compromise. And since most people voted for Hawaii as their first or second choice, I think that's what we should do. We can swim with dolphins and sea turtles, see an active volcano, go paddleboarding, and play in the waves. Or just lie on the beach and bake in the warm sun. It'll be wonderful. Maybe we'll even see whales."

Jodie had a sudden inspiration. "Do I have the right to change my vote?"

"Of course you do, but why—"

"I vote for Nepal."

Sofia's eyebrows went up. "Didn't you just say that Hawaii should be the destination, since more people wanted that as their first or second choice?"

"Yep, but I want to change my vote to Nepal."

Sam smiled broadly. A full, rarely seen smile.

Sofia slowly shook her head. "Looks like we're going to Nepal."

SOFIA'S Journal. THIS IS PRIVATE. CLOSE IT NOW!
Move along, there's nothing to see here!

January 4, 2017

My New Year's Resolutions:
1) To do something I normally wouldn't dare.
2) To write here more often.
3) To exercise at least twice a week for an hour or more.
4) To cut way down on sugar.
5) Every night before bed, to ask myself what I let go of that day.

Of all these, #5 will be the hardest. It's also going to be the best thing in the world for me. I'm not quite ready to let go of some things, which Kim says is normal. She says it all has to happen at the proper time, which only I can decide, but it's also good to nudge myself. #5 is my daily nudge.

Frank last cheated—as far as I know—three and a half years ago. But I've only known for seven months, so it still feels raw. I've seen a deliberate effort on his part to be more transparent, honest, and straightforward. Sometimes he'll tell me things I don't need to know that could fall into the category of TMI. I don't need to know that he didn't fill out a report properly or accidentally added his hours wrong. But the important thing is that he's trying and making progress.

Four days in to this beautiful new year, and I've already completed resolution number one. Whoop whoop!! I think I channeled Nonna Eve when I did something totally crazy today. Crazy and illegal. I did one of those people finder searches for Carl Chester and called him. You're not supposed to contact former students, at least not in Oregon. Borrowing one of Frank's favorite sayings, I said 'Fuck the rules!' and just did it, which felt pretty damn good.

Anyway, I apologized to Carl for not doing anything to help him when I was his guidance counselor, but he said it was all right. And he meant it. What a sweetie! He told me my successor at Ben Franklin High called Child Protective Services when Carl came to school one day his junior year with a black eye and visible bruises—which eventually led to him getting placed in a foster home. A great one, fortunately. He eventually went to Portland Community College and started a successful business showing local artists and musicians how to market themselves. He's got a girlfriend and they have a loft in Northwest Portland. Apparently, he couldn't be happier.

Some stories do have happy endings. I only wish I'd looked for Carl sooner. It would have saved me a lot of guilt, worry, and stress. After we hung up, Sam came up to where I sat at the dining room table and leaned his forehead against my shoulder. After a few minutes he even put his arms around me. I felt so good I cried until I ran out of tears.

What a perfect day!

Kathmandu was an exotic mixture of sights, smells, and sounds. Many buildings were still in ruins from the 2015 earthquake two years before, but people seemed to have an enthusiastic spirit of rebuilding their city. Frank had a hard time understanding the bizarre mixture of poverty, peacefulness, and sense of well-being. They often crossed paths with beggars and discovered quickly that the more they gave, the more beggars would surround them. Whenever Frank said no, however, Sam would insist they be generous, and he frequently got his way.

The four separate flights they took to get there had been grueling but worth the effort. True, Hawaii would've been nice, but this was more of a cultural experience. Sofia had found their hotel online the month before. The description and photos made it sound good, but Frank had his doubts—until he saw it. Better in real life than it looked on the internet, it was a simple, clean, rustic beauty of a hotel on the side of a hill. It had a large balcony with breathtaking views of the Mahabharata mountain range as well as the city. They had gotten the family suite, with an inner room for the kids and an outer room for the parents' privacy and sanity. The inner room was nicer, probably designed to be the master bedroom, but Frank wasn't about to take any chances in case Sam's urge to go night wandering came back. Not in a strange foreign country where people had been known to disappear—never to be seen again.

They all enjoyed visiting the exotically different temples in and around the city, though none as much as Sam. The vegetarians in the family—everyone but Frank—were delighted by the simple meat-free restaurants that seemed to be everywhere. Even Frank had to admit they were pretty good.

The second afternoon of their visit, the family was getting over their jet lag and decided to go for a walk in the city. The girls were a little cranky, but that was to be expected. Going halfway around the world to a totally different time zone took some adjustment. But Sam seemed unfazed. He was completely attentive to everything around him and seemed to have twice his normal energy.

"You enjoying yourself?" Frank asked Sofia as the three kids went off exploring ahead.

"Yes, and I will enjoy myself a lot more when I've had a nice hot soak and a good night's rest." She smiled. "And some cozy alone time with my hubby."

CHAPTER THIRTY-SEVEN

The next day they visited more temples and shrines and bought things at some of the bazaars to take home. Frank had been warned ahead of time, but he had to see it in practice: nothing sold at the price originally requested. Haggling and negotiating was part of the game all the locals seemed to enjoy playing. The negotiations were fun at first, but they soon became tiring.

Everyone's favorite place was the Monkey Temple, an ancient temple compound with many buildings—and monkeys—on top of a hill outside Kathmandu. It was a long hike and climb for them all, but they loved the place. Overall, it had been an exciting but exhausting day. Frank looked forward to getting back to their hotel and putting his feet up. The girls were getting grumpy and tired. But not Sam—he wanted more of everything. They finally chose to turn back, though Sam kept pointing at another temple on top of a distant hill.

"Not tonight, buddy," his dad said. "We've visited enough hill temples today. That Monkey Temple was exciting, wasn't it?" Sam didn't budge. "Let's go back to the hotel. We're heading up into the mountains tomorrow on a very special tour. It'll be exciting. We need to get some good rest, or we'll never make it through the day without collapsing. So let's go."

Sam didn't move.

Sofia smiled at her son. "We've had a great day, but now it's time to head on home, *querido*. I think you've tired us all out."

They started walking back toward the hotel. After a few dozen steps, Frank turned around and saw Sam standing still, watching them impassively.

"Come on, Son, we've got a long walk ahead of us." Sam watched his family for a few moments—his dad lingering, his mom and sisters walking on. Then he ran like the wind in the opposite direction, toward the temple on the hill.

"*Sam! Stop! Come back!*" Frank yelled after his son, but his words went unheeded.

Locals and tourists alike stared. Sam ran like someone possessed and showed no sign of slowing down.

Frank gave his wife and daughters an exasperated look. Muttering angrily, he took off at a slow jog after Sam. "Meet you back at the hotel," he called back over his shoulder. The main thing was to keep Sam in sight—if possible. He'd seen the kid run. No way he could catch him unless he wanted to be caught. At that moment it didn't seem likely. At least Frank had a good idea where he was heading.

Frank jogged for more than half an hour to reach the temple, just as the sun began setting behind the Mahabharata Range. Any other time, he would have taken in the view—but he had to find Sam, whom he'd lost sight of about halfway up. Why did he think he could run off like that, especially in a foreign land? Frank would definitely give him a piece of his mind.

Everyone he passed he would ask, "Boy?" and hold out his hand at about Sam's height. All he got was shrugs and head shakes. The temple itself was larger than it looked from a distance, especially since part of the hillside had been excavated to accommodate it. He saw many beautiful and ornate wood carvings wherever he went, along with magnificent paintings of mythical animals and people. If he hadn't been so upset about losing sight of his son, he would have spent more time admiring the art.

He followed a wide passageway paved with yellow sandstone tiles accented with red trims. Occasional small pots of incense smoldered lazily in little alcoves next to the passage, creating a beautiful and subtle fragrance Frank had never experienced before. Small trees planted in strategically placed locations gave a powerful sense of life, and they created a blend of privacy and openness. His anxiety gradually increasing, Frank looked behind every shrine, column, and tree, desperately hoping to find his son. Was he hiding?

His anger turned to worry, then outright fear bordering on panic. The growing darkness made the situation far worse. What if he ran off from here? Could Sam find his way back to their hotel? Did he even want to? What if he'd already left the complex?

He approached an old man wearing a simple monk's robe, standing at the far end of a large open-sky courtyard.

"Boy, boy?" he asked, but received only a shrug and a slight smile from the old man. "Do you speak English?" Frank asked.

The old man raised his palms upward and showed more of a smile. Frank heard someone loudly proclaim, "Ah!" and turned toward one of the most beautiful sights he'd ever see: his son running across the courtyard toward them. Frank's anxiety melted away as if it had never been.

He felt more love for his son at that moment than he'd probably felt for anyone his entire life. Not his mom, not Uncle Gino. Not even Sofia. Then Sam ran straight into the open arms of the old man.

What the hell? Sam had never met—or even seen—this man. They'd been with him every moment since touching down at Tribhuvan Airport two days earlier. Not that the old monk looked mobile enough to be moving around, anyway.

Frank stared open-mouthed as they hugged for what turned into minutes.

"We need to go, Son." But his words were unheard—or at least not acknowledged. Frank experienced a strange mixture of awe and worry. "Sam, it's late, and we need to go find your mom and sisters. They'll be worried sick."

Without letting go, Sam turned his head toward his father and gave him the biggest smile he'd ever seen from the boy.

Frank felt conflicting tidal waves of emotion. Seeing Sam in the arms of this old man, he wondered if he was about to lose him. What if Sam wanted to stay here? He wasn't about to let that happen. His son's place was with his family. He'd carry him over his shoulder if he had to. As unlikely as that scenario seemed, and for reasons he couldn't even begin to understand, he burst into tears.

They finally let go of each other, and the old man gave Sam a bow, which the boy returned, folding his hands in a gesture of respect.

A couple of younger men in monks' robes entered the courtyard, and as they walked past, they turned and bowed to the older man, who returned their respect. Sam then turned and bowed to them. They seemed surprised at the young Westerner showing them respect in their traditional way, but probably not as surprised as Frank. They offered and received a few more bows all around, then turned to go.

"Excuse me," said Frank. The young monks glanced at each other before turning to face him. "Do either of you speak English?"

"A little," said one monk, pinching two fingers almost together.

"Can you tell me where this is?"

They glanced at each other again, then back at Frank. "What you mean?"

"I mean, what is this place?"

"Oh, this," the monk who spoke a little English gestured around him, "is Temple of Sun."

"And if I may ask, who is this man?"

The other young monk said something in Hindi that Frank couldn't understand. The English-speaking monk responded in a way that sounded a lot like scolding before turning back to Frank. He motioned to the older man. "This is Jayadeva, temple guru. Advanced much in God-connection." He bowed again to the old man.

"He doesn't speak English, does he?"

The young monk laughed softly. "Jayadeva speak nothing. He take silence vow fifty-two year running." He nodded his head deferentially toward Jayadeva. "But understand all. English including."

"How does he know my son?"

"Oh, Jayadeva—he know everybody. He show everyone how connect to God."

"If you say so." He turned toward the old monk and made a slight bow with his hands folded as he'd seen the others do. "Well, nice to meet you, Mr. Jayadeva, and thank you for greeting my son so warmly." He turned to the English-speaking monk. "And thank you for explaining so I can understand."

Honestly, though, he didn't understand much of anything. What he'd just seen happen between his son and the old monk seemed amazing. His head believed what the younger monk said, but his heart told him something else had occurred.

Sam had spoken when he'd seen him in the courtyard—the second word he'd spoken his entire life. He'd distinctly said "Ah." Frank began to cry again, in front of his son and three adult strangers, all of whom looked at him with kindness and compassion.

"Heart open," said the young English-speaking monk.

Frank didn't know how to respond to that. He wiped his tearstained face with the back of his hand. What a strange day it had been! "Come on, Sam, are you ready?"

Sam looked into the eyes of the old man and bowed once more. He then stepped back and bowed to all three monks, who returned the bow.

Frank was momentarily puzzled by the thought that Sam had looked everyone in the eye since he'd entered the courtyard. How strange!

As they turned to leave, Sam's hand in his, Frank turned back to the young monks. "How many of you practice this vow of silence? "

"Oh, only one presently. Only Jayadeva."

Frank thought about that. "One presently. So have there been others?"

"Oh, yes, different times different peoples doing. At one time, beside Jayadeva, there was other in silence vow. Also great connector to God. Pavana cross over …" He conversed in rapid Hindi with the other young monk. "He young man, cross over more than twenty years ago, before we came here, but we hear many time how he was loved. Die by accident, fall from roof trying to save monkey who got hand stuck in vent. He care for everything, everyone. People very sad. Pavana so much loved. Like Jayadeva." He nodded at the old man. "And the two great friends."

"I see," Frank said, even though he didn't. "What does everyone *do* here?"

"Many things. We have full community. So many things need done. Cleaners, cookers, artists, repairmans."

Frank nodded. "If I may ask, what does Jayadeva do?"

"He is teacher. I thought we told, he is guru."

"How does he teach if he doesn't speak?"

He translated that into Hindi for the other monk. They all laughed, including Jayadeva. Apparently a vow of silence doesn't mean you can't laugh. "Is funny, and I tell you why." He gestured at Jayadeva. "How long you here with him?"

"I don't know, maybe fifteen minutes, more or less."

"And have you learned here?"

"I'm not sure exactly what I've learned."

"Not ask *what* learned. Ask *have* learned."

"I think so. But it doesn't quite make sense."

"Narada Muni say, 'All make sense in time.'"

"Who?"

"Much wise man. Many years ago."

"I hope it makes sense." He had another thought. "Was Pav—um, the other vow of silence person also a guru?"

"Yes and no. He was guru in own way, but main thing other job." Jayadeva nodded and smiled as the young monk continued. "He was healer. Heal you from any sicken. He know before people come something wrong. Nobody here sick long."

As they walked down the path back to town, Sam positively glowed. Frank had never seen his son happier. With a sudden shock, he realized he was still holding hands with this son of theirs who avoided physical contact of all kinds unless he himself reached out. Even then, it was always brief. Who is this boy we've raised? He had to admit he had no idea.

Later that evening, after everyone else had gone to bed, Frank and Sofia sat on a little outdoor sofa on the balcony, admiring the beauty of the moonlight on the mountains.

"Thanks for getting Sam," she said.

He smiled ruefully. "It's part of my job description. If I hadn't, I don't know if we would have ever seen him again."

"You really think so?"

"Honestly, I don't know." He shook his head. "He probably would have been very content there."

"But he left with you."

Frank nodded. "He did, and I didn't have to force him."

She snuggled close and leaned her head on his shoulder. "There's your answer, then. He's chosen to be with us."

On the flight back to the U.S., Frank kept turning back in his seat to look at Sam, a row behind them and across the aisle. Finally Sofia asked him what was wrong.

"Nothing. I just can't get over Sam."

"I know. He's special, isn't he?"

"Yes, but … that was such a strange experience with the old man in the temple."

"You know Sam. He loves everyone."

"Yeah, but it was more than that. They seemed to know each other," said Frank.

"I doubt that temple guru has ever been to Oregon."

"I know. That couldn't have happened."

She studied her husband's face. "You're not thinking Sam knew him from a previous life, are you?"

He glanced back at Sam again. "I don't know what to think."

Sofia noticed how subdued the family was once they got back home. Everyone seemed so introspective, including the kids. Travel will do that, especially when the experiences were so exotic.

Spilling over with curiosity, she called a past-life regression therapist named Julie she found online, who patiently answered her questions. Sofia learned that when someone dies young and violently, they are more likely to remember that previous life in their next life—most commonly from the ages of two to six. Conscious past-life memories and behavior—if remembered—are usually forgotten by the age of eight, sometimes ten, and more rarely by the time they're twelve or even up to fifteen. When she asked Julie if she thought Sam not speaking could perhaps have something to do with remembering a vow of silence from a previous life, she answered that while it could be possible, she'd have no way of knowing. A regression session might help if he could talk, but that wasn't practical if he didn't.

Sofia thanked her but felt disappointed. She'd learned some interesting information, but nothing that would change Sam's situation. It seemed like yet another dead end. Julie may have sensed that, and she told her that if his silence *was* remembered from a previous life, then that memory might fade at some point and he could begin talking.

The observation at least gave her some hope. If he never talked, Sam would still be fine, though she would have to learn to release some of her expectations.

CHAPTER THIRTY-EIGHT

Frank checked his watch, sighed, and sped up. He was being loaned out to Lane County Public Works. Again. He'd been about to clock out Friday afternoon, ready for a relaxing weekend, when he saw the unsigned memo on his desk: LCPW 8:30 a.m. Saturday.

Couldn't Kingston have asked him if he had other plans? Or at least tell him in person? Apparently not. And now he was late. He'd already clocked in at the Eugene shop, at Kingston's insistence. Either so he could keep closer tabs on Frank or just to punish him. Maybe both. It added another fifteen minutes to his travel to go to the Eugene shop before heading over to Lane County Public Works. That affair with Andrea had been such a mistake. It was bad enough he had to work on Saturday; Kingston would surely use his being late against him.

He glanced at his speedometer. Twenty-three miles per hour over the speed limit. They couldn't afford a ticket, but it would be a disaster to come in late to work again. Just last week Kingston had given him a stern warning, writing him up for starting five minutes late. Today, he'd be nearly twenty minutes late. Things were not looking good. He knew if Kingston could, he'd cut Frank's pay. Or maybe fire him outright.

He and Sofia had a heated argument that morning about his having to work Saturdays, and he'd totally lost track of time. It wasn't pretty, and the kids doubtless had heard, even though they were in their bedrooms with the doors closed. He'd skipped breakfast when he realized how late it was.

He slowed down as he saw flashing blue and red lights ahead. An Oregon State Police cruiser had stopped behind a battered old Chevy pickup. Frank checked his speedometer to be sure he was going well under the speed limit as he passed.

Weird. No sign of the cop or the driver of the Chevy. A guardrail separated the edge of the shoulder from a steep embankment before the beginning of some fairly dense woods. He eyed the flashing lights in his rearview mirror. He tried to tell himself it was none of his business. Yet he got only a few hundred yards down the road before making a fast and illegal U-turn. The driver behind had to slam on his brakes and laid on his horn to express his displeasure.

Frank parked on the opposite shoulder from the state trooper's car and the battered Chevy. He's most likely chasing someone, and the trooper probably already radioed in for help. Maybe they even called in a helicopter. He scanned the sky but saw nothing. The feeling in his gut said something wasn't right. He sat watching the flashing lights for another few seconds, then punched 9-1-1 into his cell phone.

"Nine-one-one, what is your life-threatening emergency?"

"Well, it's probably not life-threatening, but there's a state patrol car here on Crest Drive, just east of Chambers Street, with lights flashing and no one in it. I'm wondering if there's some kind of trouble. I don't know if—"

"I'm sure the officer has it under control. I'm showing a routine traffic stop at eight thirteen a.m. Six minutes ago. Tags checked out. I've got nothing here on my screen to say anything is amiss."

"You mean he didn't radio in to say he's chasing a suspect?" Frank asked.

The irritation was clear in the dispatcher's voice. "No, and I'm sure everything is fine. Look, we appreciate you trying to help, but I need to keep this line clear for actual emergencies. So if—"

"What makes you sure everything is fine, if he didn't say he was chasing a suspect and he's not in his car?"

"I'll have Eugene PD check it out. There's a car five minutes away," the dispatcher said tersely.

Frank ended the call. Five minutes could be a long time. Against his better judgment, he got out and walked across the busy road. Past the edge of the shoulder, at the bottom of the embankment, he spotted two men wrestling. One man was huge—he must've been over six feet tall and pushing two hundred and fifty pounds—and much of his bulk appeared to be muscle. The other man wore an Oregon State Police uniform. A great deal of blood covered them both. The trooper saw Frank and yelled for help. The bigger man was trying to grab the trooper's gun. It didn't look as though things would end well. Heart pounding in his ears, Frank ran back to his car, threw the door open, reached under his seat, and grabbed his .45. He got back to the top of the embankment just as the bigger man took control of the trooper's gun.

Frank hesitated, frozen by the sudden understanding that his entire life was about to turn upside down. Then he took aim and fired.

The argument that morning had been upsetting. But the result was that they'd cleared the air. Frank had to do something about that awful job of his.

Sofia made an uneventful trip with the kids to the grocery store. The girls had surprised her by asking to come along and by being nice to each other, like they were best friends. No crying babies in the store this time, either.

As she pulled into the driveway, an unlisted number popped up on her phone. She briefly considered not answering but finally picked up. "Hello?"

"Sofia, it's me. I'm in trouble."

"Why? What happened?"

"I'm at the main police station on Country Club Road. I'll tell you all about it when you get here. I just need you to get Josh—"

"Josh Goldstein, our lawyer?"

"Yes, and get down here as fast as possible. The kids can watch each other—just tell them to stay home. Get Josh on the phone first, though, and tell him it's an emergency."

"Frank, you're scaring me. Tell me what happened."

"It's complicated. I'll tell you as soon as—"

"Frank, *please* tell me." All three kids stared at her with worried expressions.

"I need to tell you in person."

"I'm waiting." She covered the phone and told the kids to go inside the house.

There was a long pause. "I—I killed a man today."

"No!" For a moment Sofia felt as though she would faint.

"That's why I wanted to tell you in person."

"What happened?"

"I can't give you the details over the phone. When you come down with Josh, I'll explain. Like I said, it's complicated—but I also saved someone's life. I need you here as soon as you can make it. Just call Josh."

"I'll get right on it and be there as soon as I can."

"Oh, and after Josh, call Kingston and tell him I can't make it over to Lane County today."

"What do you want me to tell him?"

"Say I'm not well."

She hung up and called Josh, who told Sofia he didn't work Saturdays—especially since he had plans with his family after he caught up with stuff from the office.

"Frank killed someone."

"What? No way! What happened?"

"I don't know. He said for you to get down to the main station on Country Club Road as quickly as possible."

"Hmm. Maybe I can get Jeffrey to cover for me. Even still, it will take me at least an hour to wrap up here. I have a deposition first thing Monday morning and then a hearing at noon. I have to hand things off to my paralegals so they can put everything in order. You should go down there right away and see him. Tell him I'm coming. They don't have to let you see him, so be ready for that. I'll be there as soon as I can. Make sure you don't answer any questions. Be nice."

"Of course."

"And tell Frank to do the same, if you get a chance. Especially to not answer any questions before I get there."

Chapter Thirty-Nine

When she told the desk sergeant her name, a hush fell over the station. When she asked to see her husband, the sergeant told her to wait until he checked with Lieutenant Conklin. He came back a minute later and smiled, which gave her hope.

"The lieutenant said, 'Of course.' I hope you don't mind. I had to check."

"Sure." This was the opposite of what she expected. Why were they being nice to her?

Frank was seated in a sparsely furnished police interview room. One table, three chairs, and a wastebasket. At least he wasn't handcuffed like she'd seen in the movies. He was obviously stressed—and very relieved to see her.

"Did you talk to Josh?"

"I did. He'll be here as soon as he can. He said not to answer any questions."

"Well, too late for that. But on the bright side, they're treating me like a celebrity here."

"How is that?" This didn't add up.

"The short version is that I shot someone who was trying to kill a cop."

"No!"

"Yes, but I did it with an unregistered, unlawfully concealed, illegal weapon."

"Illegal how?"

"Well, for one thing, it has the serial number ground off."

"The gun you carry in your truck and keep in your nightstand?" She didn't know if she could stand any more surprises. "Why is that?"

"It was Uncle Gino's idea. I don't know why; that's just the gun he got for me. I couldn't get one myself since I didn't want to be fingerprinted. You know why. So now I've been charged with at least four firearm violations, and three are felonies."

"Oh, no."

"Well, that part may not be as bad as it sounds. Every step of the way, they've been extra nice to me. They are treating me like I'm some kind of hero." He looked at the floor. "Which I'm not."

"But you *are* a hero. Josh will get you out of this, I'm sure."

"That's not what I'm worried about. The cops keep saying—almost apologetically—stuff like, 'Sorry, we have to do this.' It looks like they're planning to have the charges dismissed. It'll be up to the D.A. and the city prosecutor, but the cops think it's not a problem. They're sure the charges will all go away. What I'm worried about is that I've been fingerprinted, and now my prints are in an international database. So if anyone's watching on that side—"

"You don't think after all these years …"

He sighed heavily. "I don't know what to think."

Josh came in, greeted the MacBrides, then went to see the lieutenant. They waited anxiously for twenty minutes before he returned.

"Looks like we don't have anything to worry about," said Josh.

"How's that?"

"They're going to make sure the charges are dismissed. Besides being very grateful to you for saving one of their own, they don't want the news that the gun was illegal to go public. It would send the wrong message."

"That's great, but—"

"No *buts*! They're going to make sure you get a free walk here." Josh's smile faded as he took in their expressions. "Okay, what am I missing?"

Husband and wife glanced at each other, then back at Josh. "Well," said Frank, "you'd better sit down for this." He told him the main parts of the story.

"That's serious." Josh rubbed his chin. "If they wanted to, they could deport you. You're technically an illegal alien, and with the Trump government's aggressive anti-immigration stance, that's not a good thing to be right now."

"Thanks for reminding me."

"But from what you say, deportation is not the big issue anyway."

"No, and if they have a price on my head, I wouldn't last long."

"Right. But weren't you sixteen when you left?"

"Seventeen."

"Still, that's what? Twenty-six years ago, or something like that. I'm sure you're not interesting to them."

"You don't understand. I'm interesting to them because I got away. They hate that. Even worse, we took the money my father stole from them. They are always thinking about examples that get set. And so many of the police over there are in their pocket. All they'd have to do is to have a flag set up in their system. When I—or my fingerprints—appear, they would just let the Concino family know."

Josh stood. "Look, you know the Italian Mafia is not as vicious as it once was. I'd be a lot more concerned if they were Russians."

"You and me both." Frank cleared his throat. "Can you ask the lieutenant something for me?"

"Sure, you name it."

"Can you ask them to keep me anonymous?"

"I can tell you right now that'll be very difficult. Everyone will want to know who you are."

"Yeah," said Sofia. "Let the world know the kind of man you are."

Frank shook his head. "I'm the kind of man who needs to keep a low profile for the safety of his family."

Josh shrugged. "I can try, but I won't promise they'll be able to do it. All someone would have to do would be to look up your arrest records."

"But they wouldn't even know there was an arrest."

"True, but I'm just saying it's a roll of the dice," he said and shook his head, "and the odds are not in your favor."

Within hours, they had released Frank on $50,000 bail. Josh told them that part was pretty much unavoidable. Until they dropped the charges, they had to go by the book. For what he had been charged with, though, the bail was on the low end of the scale—another good sign. Sofia had gone to a bail bondsman, who agreed to post the full amount as long as she put up at least $5,000 cash. She was grateful she still had that much available on her Amex card.

A very long day was finally ending. Sofia listened to Frank's gentle breathing—his "almost-snore," as she liked to call it.

How he could fall asleep after all that had happened was beyond her. Nonna Eve loved to say the best drug for sleep was a clear conscience. Her husband was very innocent in many ways. He'd shot and killed a man earlier that day, but more than that, he did the right thing. In all the years they'd been married, they had their challenges, but what marriage didn't have at least some of those? There was no one in the world she'd rather be married to. Especially now. Forgiveness was another matter. She was moving in that direction, but it would take time, though she genuinely felt the affair was behind them and all secrets were finally out in the open. He was probably right to not tell her about the Mafia before. But at least now they were in on the same secrets. Most of the same secrets, anyway.

They'd made an important decision that day. Not just to keep Frank anonymous, but to keep what had happened from the kids for the time being. It would be hard for them to keep that news quiet.

For the next few days, the anonymous hero was all Lisa and Jodie talked about. Whenever the topic came up at the table—which was fairly often—Sofia would shoot Frank a knowing glance, and he'd suddenly find whatever was on his plate very interesting.

A huge buzz went around school about the act of heroism, and it was all anyone spoke of at work. Except Frank, who had nothing to say on the subject. They made a big deal in the papers and on all the social media sites of the good Samaritan shooting the druggie high on methamphetamine who almost killed an Oregon State Trooper. The police wouldn't release the Samaritan's name, saying he had the right to remain anonymous, which just made people more interested. Rewards were offered left and right. Free dinners, free hotel stays, and one Portland car dealer even offered whoever it was a "pre-owned" car.

Like anything, it would eventually blow over. The excitement would fade, and people would forget.

Sofia knew Frank couldn't wait for that to happen.

Exactly one week after the shooting, Frank got a call from Lieutenant Conklin.

"Are you able to come down to the station, Mr. MacBride?"

"Sure. Do I need my lawyer with me?"

"That shouldn't be necessary. We just need to do some routine follow-up."

"Can you tell me what you mean by that?"

"I can, but I need to tell you in person."

Frank drove to the station with a sinking feeling in his stomach. When he walked in, the duty sergeant escorted him to the lieutenant's office, who offered him a seat.

"We seem to have a problem with your processing, Mr. MacBride."

Frank frowned. "What sort of problem?"

"Unfortunately, your fingerprints got overwritten."

"How is that possible? I know how careful you are with those kinds of things."

"I know. It seems unbelievable. But it happens rarely."

"How rarely?" asked Frank.

"Well, this is the first time I know of."

"Oh."

The lieutenant cleared his throat. "And we'd never intentionally listen to a conversation between a lawyer and his client, but sometimes microphones accidentally get left on ..."

"Like in an interview room?"

"Exactly. So all I'm saying is—"

"That you need to fingerprint me again?"

"Not at all. You are neither under arrest nor under suspicion of a crime. I just wanted to explain the unfortunate and irrevocable loss of your prints." He looked meaningfully at Frank. "And that you can relax, since your prints won't show up in Italy, either."

"Ah."

"Yeah," said the lieutenant. "So what the hell were you thinking?"

"What do you mean?"

"You know. When you saw Trooper Correy's car with the lights on and no one in it. You turned around."

Frank shrugged. "It just seemed that something wasn't right, that's all."

"No, something sure wasn't right. But you did something right. Do you know Correy has two small kids? And a devoted wife?"

"I think I read that."

"How many people do you think would have turned around? Or pulled that trigger? Or called an ambulance afterward instead of running for cover?"

"I have no idea, Lieutenant."

"I don't either." The lieutenant stared at Frank in genuine admiration. "I don't think many. Maybe one in a million. This is the least we can do for you." He stood up and shook his hand. "Let me know if there's anything else you need. Anything at all."

Chapter Forty

Frank found a note on his desk the following Monday morning. All it said was "See me." He groaned. Kingston's handwriting, of course.

He knocked on his boss's open door. Kingston kept his head down while writing something, and he waited a good long time before acknowledging Frank with a terse, "Sit!"

"I got your note."

"Good thing." He pressed a button on the recorder sitting on his desk. "Just so you know, this is being recorded."

"What for?"

He gave Frank a shrewd look. "So, you weren't well a week ago Saturday?"

"I have a lot of sick days, which I rarely use, and I needed one that day."

"Sure. MacBride, what do you do for fun?"

"Sir?"

"You know, what are your hobbies?"

"Well, I'm kind of an inventor. I make things that—"

"Want to know what I do?" he interrupted.

"Okay."

"I like to look up things and see what's happening in this town. Especially the police dispatch record, which is fascinating. Sometimes I get behind with work and all, but I eventually catch up. Guess what I found out over the weekend?"

"I think we both know."

Kingston smirked. "We sure do. Says here they arrested you Saturday before last on several firearms violations. The same day you supposedly weren't well."

"There's more to the story you—"

Kingston held up his hand in a *stop* gesture and continued reading. He frowned. "Let's see, now. Looks like we've got 'unlawful concealment' and 'possession of an un-serialed firearm.'" Kingston let out a low whistle. "MacBride, those are serious charges. Felonies."

"And they were both dismissed, along with the other charges."

Kingston turned his attention back to the police report. "So I see," he said, as if he hadn't already read that. He shook his head.

"I think they appreciated what I did," said Frank.

"It would seem so." His eyes narrowed. "And in this moment of so-called bravery, where were you going?"

Frank was losing patience fast. "You already know I was on my way to Lane County Public Works."

"Ah, yes, on your way to work with an illegal firearm, illegally concealed, in a department-owned truck. After you clocked in here. Thanks for your honesty around that, at least." Kingston opened a manual on his desk. Without being able to read it from where he sat, Frank knew what it said. He'd just fallen into a trap. He could have said he was going on a picnic. That he was supposed to work but changed his mind. Or better, that he had gone home to get the gun after he clocked in.

"Let's see … Oregon Revised Statute ORS 410.22.9 says, 'No employee of the state may have a concealed firearm on or about their person while on government property, including any government-owned vehicles, unless they are in possession of a valid concealed-carry permit.' And," he continued, "'that shall be allowed only with the written permission of said employee's supervisor.' That's me." Kingston was enjoying himself. "And not only did I *not* give you permission, I think it is already clearly established that you do not have a permit."

"No, but as I already said, they dismissed all the charges, and—"

"Hang on—I'm not done yet. Now, where was I?" He looked down at the manual again. "Here it is. 'Violation of the above is considered a Class C felony under Oregon law—'"

Frank stood up, his face flushed. "The charges were all dismissed! I committed no crime."

Kingston smiled and continued reading. "Wait, we're almost there … 'and is just cause and grounds for immediate dismissal, with no compensation of any kind for the dismissed employee.'" He looked gleefully at Frank. And that's not even talking about the weapon being illegal. You'd be toast even if it was fully registered with a genuine serial number."

"You wouldn't dare!"

"Hold on, I need to change these batteries. They're getting low." He clicked off the recorder. "You know, Andrea told me everything over a month ago. This would have happened anyway, but on a different time schedule. You know what they say about how revenge is a dish best served cold. Maybe my revenge is not as cold, but it will be much better than I'd planned. You've not only sped things up, you've made it much easier."

Frank rolled his eyes. "What's not easy about letting someone go?"

Kingston smiled thinly. "You'll see. But first, I have good news for you."

"What would that be?"

"I'm not pressing charges. Your buddies at the police station would undoubtedly help you out of that, which might make me look bad. We can't have that, now, can we?"

Frank glared at his boss.

Kingston went on, "You fucked my wife. I'm going to return the favor." He shook his head slightly. "You look upset. Maybe you'd like to take a swing at me. That would feel so good, wouldn't it? I'd love nothing more than to go a couple of rounds with you. Right here and right now—you arrogant little dago." He was obviously delighted with himself. "No? Smart choice. You know I'd have you for assault." He grinned menacingly. "Even though I'd knock the living shit out of you."

"Just hang on a minute …"

"But as hugely satisfying as kicking your little guinea ass would be, that could get complicated."

Frank shook his head. "You should know that what happened with Andrea was not—"

"Save your breath. I'm getting rid of that bitch."

"She told me you had an open marriage."

He laughed bitterly. "And you were stupid enough to believe her." He narrowed his eyes. "But in truth, you probably didn't. That's just what you pretended to believe. If you really thought it were true, you would have asked me."

"It's not like we had frequent chats over a couple of cold brews."

"That's funny, MacBride." He shook his head. "You apparently think she was irresistibly attracted to you, but you were nothing more than a little pawn in her game. You weren't the first, and you won't be the last. But I'm getting off that merry-go-round of hers—at the right moment when she least expects it."

"If you give me a chance to explain—"

Kingston abruptly restarted the recorder. "MacBride, your threats are being taken seriously." He picked up his desk phone and pressed seven, the number for internal security. "Jenkins, get down here to my office on the double. Bring Adams. Code three."

Frank couldn't believe what was happening. "What are you doing?"

Kingston glared at him. "Just stay right where you are. You are being dismissed, and security will escort you off the property. All your personal belongings will be gathered up and sent to you at a later date."

"You're not serious!"

"Serious as a heart attack, MacBride. Remember how you thought I'd fire you way back when? Well, my friend, your day has come." He smirked again. "In a very big way, I might add. You've created this situation for yourself, so you might as well—"

Jenkins burst in, hand on his sidearm, scanning the room. "I got here as fast as I could, sir. Adams is on break." He looked around for the threat. "What seems to be the problem?"

"We have an employee who brought an illegal firearm on the premises, has been making threats, and needs to be escorted off the property."

"Where can I find him?" Jenkins paused. "Or her?"

Kingston nodded at Frank. "He's right here."

"Sir, this is Frank MacBride. You can't—"

"I know exactly who this is, Jenkins, and unless you also want to be escorted off, you'd better do as I say."

Jenkins glanced at Frank before turning his attention back to Kingston. "Sir, could you tell me what this is about?"

"No. My first priority here is safety, and I need him off the property. Now."

Jenkins hesitated, then sighed. "Sorry, Frank, you heard the man." He shot a glare at Kingston. "Let's pick up your stuff and get you off-premises."

Kingston stood abruptly. "*Did you not hear a word I said, Jenkins?*" he yelled, spittle forming on his lips. "You take him straight off the property. Do not allow him to touch anything or talk to anyone." As they walked through the door, Kingston called out behind them, "And don't forget to collect his keys."

So ended the worst day of Frank's nearly six years with Eugene Public Works. That evening was not a happy one in the MacBride household.

Sofia had picked him up outside the gates, with Sam in the car. He was happy to see his dad, but she looked worried. "We'll make this work," she said. "Just get another job. It's what we've wanted all this time."

The rest of the drive home was quiet.

Frank sighed heavily as they walked into the house. It felt strange being home mid-morning on a weekday. "The big problem is that I just got fired for cause. For a serious cause. Plus, you know that idiot Kingston will give anybody who asks about me the worst possible review."

"You can at least try."

"Of course I'll try, but I'm pretty well screwed. That's my work history for the past six years—all washed out. Worse, actually. That history is now going to work against me. It'll be difficult to convince anyone to hire me."

"Just tell them the truth."

"Which part? "

"The part where they dismissed the charges."

"That wouldn't work. It's not about the charges being dismissed. Kingston tricked me into admitting on tape that the gun was in the truck I used at work."

"Then it's time for you to come out and admit you were the one who saved that trooper."

Frank didn't want to go that route. "We've talked about that. You know it would increase the chance they'll find me, or inspire some snoopy reporter to look into my past and find out that some things don't add up. The less I'm in the public eye, the better."

"But we need to do something. You need to work. If you let—"

"Look, I know, all right? I understand what you're saying. But I will not put you and our kids at greater risk by going public with this." He shook his head emphatically. "That's just not going to happen."

She was equally as adamant. "It's up to you, but I just want you to consider—"

"I *have* considered, and I'll *keep* considering. I'm just telling you straight up it's not going to happen."

She'd never seen him so on edge. "If I need to, I'll go back to work."

He frowned at her. "You'd put Sam in public school?"

"If we have to. They have this Oregon Special Needs Integration Program in some of the public schools. OSNIP for short. It's supposed to be a good compromise between full-on special needs and regular public school."

"You think that might work for Sam?"

"Honestly, I have no idea," she said with a pained expression. "It's not my first choice, but I want what's best for all of us."

"Well, so do I." He rubbed his face. "Right now I'm going to see what I can get. We don't even know what will happen. There are other options. We might have to move elsewhere if I can't find work around here. Salem is a long commute. It'd take me over an hour to get there. But it's a possibility. I'm going to look. I want you to take care of Sam."

But the next few weeks just brought up one "no" after another. A couple of companies were interested, even after Frank was up front about his relationship with his ex-boss. They seemed to understand. But after they called Kingston or the Eugene Public Works HR department, they'd come back with a polite "no." Always for other reasons.

Sofia was supportive, but Frank could feel her fear and anxiety. They'd asked Sofia's parents for a loan—which they declined. Of course. They generously gave them thousands of dollars for their vacation but couldn't loan them one red cent.

Their credit cards maxed, their savings gone, they cut back wherever they could. For the time being, tests for Sam were out of the question.

Frank found some good things about not working, though. He was able to spend more time with his family. In particular, he loved taking walks with Sam. He felt his love for his son grow every day he spent with him.

He talked to Sofia about it one night after the first week. "I know I'm not supposed to have favorites, but Sam is so special."

"He certainly is."

"Remember how Mamma used to tell us to stop worrying? That whether or not he talks, he's an amazing little human being—who will eventually grow into an amazing full-sized human being."

"Of course I remember that. I replay that pretty often. Nonna Eve was so wise." She took his hand. "And she had such a connection with Sam."

They discussed strategies, the best jobs to apply for. They talked about why people said no. They tried to figure out the reasons behind the rejections but were working with very little information. Apparently, some so-called legal wisdom said that if you turned someone down for a job, make sure you give them a very safe reason why—a reason that may have very little to do with the truth. They discussed different options, but none of them seemed viable, especially going public. It relieved Frank that Sofia finally let the idea drop. He simply needed to find work. Once that was in place, things would look a lot brighter.

One evening, Sofia suggested a different strategy. "What if I worked and you took care of the kids?"

Frank gave it some careful thought. "I didn't think that would be an option for you."

"It hasn't been. Mainly so I could take care of Sam." She paused. "But we could switch roles. You'd be an excellent teacher."

"I wouldn't have your patience."

"Yeah, there's that," she admitted. "But it'd be better than him going to public school."

"Which might be something we should consider."

"Not as our first option."

"But it could be. You mentioned it yourself last week."

"Well, maybe I changed my mind. No, I would say I'm still open to that—but only as a last choice." She closed her eyes for a moment. "We'll find a way to make things work. Besides," she said and shrugged, "we only need to find something for right now. We can make adjustments later if we need to."

"I'm with you on that. Let's say if I don't find work in the next two weeks—at a level that will sustain us—we switch, and you start hunting. Fair enough?"

Sofia smiled more brightly than she felt. She loved working with Sam and didn't want to lose that. Sam and Frank got along wonderfully, but she doubted he'd do as well teaching their son.

A couple of nights later, Frank woke to being shaken gently by Sam. He squinted at the time on the alarm panel. "It's after midnight, buddy. What's up?"

His son stood there in silence for a few moments before it dawned on Frank. He spoke quietly so as not to wake Sofia. "Do you want me to take you to the hospital?"

He could barely see his son nod in the dim glow. Frank sighed and put his feet on the floor. A deal was a deal. This was definitely better than Sam sneaking out, but not how he'd planned to spend his night, either. He had a job interview in Salem later that morning.

After starting the minivan, Frank asked his son if he wanted to go to Sacred Heart in Springfield.

Sam shook his head.

"McKenzie-Willamette in Eugene?"

Sam nodded.

That was better—at least it was only a ten-minute drive. Frank parked in the hospital's main lot. He started getting out of the van, but Sam grabbed his arm. "What is it?" he asked his son.

Sam made a gesture of him staying in the van.

"I need to go with you, buddy." Sam held on to his father's arm and shook his head decisively. Frank closed his eyes for a moment. What was the right thing to do? "You can't just walk around inside the hospital by yourself without an adult."

Sam again motioned for him to stay. Sometimes he seemed so grown-up. Most of the time, actually. Frank pulled his door shut and sighed. At least this was better than the alternative. "All right. I'm here if you need me."

Sam got out, and with a wave jogged across the parking lot and walked through the front entrance. Frank watched the doors for quite some time until he felt sleepy. Was he doing the right thing? He didn't remember drifting off, but he woke to the sound of the car door opening. Sam was back. The sky was already lightening.

"What the … ?" Frank looked at his watch. Four fifty-seven. They'd been there over four hours. "That was a long time, Sam."

His son nodded, visibly exhausted.

"Ready to go home?"

He nodded again and was asleep before they left the parking lot.

CHAPTER FORTY-ONE

Three weeks and four days after being fired, he got the call.

"Frank MacBride?"

"That's me." Frank's heart raced. He was hoping for a call back from one of the six interviews the previous week. He'd been as far north as Salem and as far south as Sutherlin.

"This is Sergeant Granland of the Oregon State Police."

Frank tensed. They were going to charge him, after all. "Yes?"

"We have someone on their way to speak to you and wanted to make sure you were home."

Frank felt his mouth go dry. "I'm home. Do I need to have my lawyer present?"

"That's up to you, sir, but I don't think it will be necessary."

"Okay, thanks." He hung up and turned to Sofia, who looked at him questioningly. "The state police are on their way to ask me some questions." He hit Josh's number on speed dial. "I'm telling Josh to get his ass over here."

"Can we afford him right now?" Their finances were lower than ever, their credit cards maxed out, and they had no extra spending money. No extra anything money. Savings had dried up weeks before.

"We can't *not* afford him," he said nervously. As he waited for Josh to pick up, an Oregon State Trooper pulled up in front of their house, lights flashing.

"That didn't take long. They must have been close by." He walked to the window, still holding the phone to his ear. "This is more serious than I thought."

Just then Josh's outgoing voice message came on. *Sorry, but I'm in court today. Please leave a message—* Frank hung up as a second state police car pulled up. Then a third and a fourth. He looked at his wife. "Will you come visit me?"

"Don't talk like that. Josh will—" Two black Chevy Suburbans stopped in the middle of the street, followed by a media van and another two patrol cars. Several motorcycle police blocked the street from either direction. "Oh, this can't be good," she said.

Frank looked up and down the street at all the vehicles. "I'm thinking either jail or sending me back to Italy, or both. If they send me back, I'm toast. But that might be better than rotting in jail."

"Don't say that!" Sofia put her arms around him and squeezed, tears filling her eyes. "I love you so much."

Two men in suits got out of a Suburban and walked toward the house along with two uniformed troopers.

"They have all kinds of plainclothes here. They're sending me back." He glanced around the room. "Where's Sam?"

"Taking a nap."

"Can you get him, please? I might not see him for a long while."

She was out of the room before he finished the sentence.

When the doorbell rang, Frank slowly walked to the door and opened it wide just as Sofia and Sam hurried into the room. He took a long look at them before addressing the quartet of police on his doorstep.

"Officers?"

"Frank MacBride?" The officer who spoke seemed familiar.

"That's me."

The other uniformed officer unclipped a gadget from his belt that resembled the electronic wands used for airport security. "If you don't mind, sir, please step outside and raise both hands above your head."

Frank did so. He expected this, but not the politeness. Must be the new way of doing business.

When the police officer finished with the wand, he started a pat-down. They must have decided he was especially dangerous, with all these police present. Either that or they wanted to make a good show for the press.

When the officer had finished his pat-down, he gave a quick thumbs-up to one of the plainclothes officers, who then held his hand high.

Frank looked at his wife, tears streaming down her cheeks, and down at Sam, who looked at him lovingly, not bothered in the least by what was going on. So much for him being so tuned in.

Frank noticed movement out of the corner of his eye and saw a TV crew and at least a couple of photographers fanning out across the lawn. This is great. Let's add some humiliation for good measure.

Two more plainclothes cops got out of one of the Suburbans and walked back to the other SUV, standing in front of and behind the rear side door. They opened it and yet another plainclothesman stepped out, wearing a light blue suit with a sheen to it. He appeared older than the other cops. The three of them walked toward the porch, and Frank had a vague feeling he was part of some alternative reality.

As they approached, the other officers stood aside for the older man, who walked up to Frank and held out his hand. "Frank MacBride?"

"Yes?" The man had a warm, firm grip.

"On behalf of the state of Oregon, I want to thank you."

Frank's mouth fell open as the man in the blue suit turned sideways, still firmly clasping Frank's hand. "Let's give the cameras a good angle, shall we?" He glanced at Frank. "You might want to close that mouth a bit. It'll show better on the news."

One of the camera operators called out, "Governor, can you turn your head slightly toward Mr. MacBride, please?"

Frank's mind spun. Governor? He did look a lot like Governor Lindsey, whose picture was up in the Eugene Public Works offices.

"Mr. MacBride, can we get a shot with you and Trooper Correy?"

That's why he looks so familiar! Correy shook Frank's hand. "Thanks for saving my life. My wife says to tell you we're naming our next child after you. Unless it's a girl. Then it could be Frances."

Frank felt his face get hot. "I'm sure you would have done the same for me."

"Yeah, but not with an illegal gun I'd get busted for. You knew you could have gotten in trouble for that, and you chose to do the right thing. Not to mention having the courage to check on me in the first place."

They all turned toward the cameras and shook hands again.

With his deft politician's charm, the governor nodded to Sofia. "You must be very proud."

"I certainly am."

He shook her hand and turned to Sam. "And who is this big guy?"

Sofia beamed. "That's Sam. He's our eleven-year-old, Governor Lindsey."

The governor moved so the video camera could get a good angle. Sam came up to the middle of his chest. "Would you like to have a picture taken with your parents and Trooper Correy and me?"

Sam nodded earnestly.

As they took their places, Frank asked Correy what happened to his anonymity.

"Oh," answered one plainclothesman. "See that guy in the blue shirt bossing those camera people around?"

"Yeah, he sort of sticks out."

"Well, he called the governor's office two days ago asking for a statement about you being the anonymous hero. We made a quick deal with him and said if he would wait for today, we'd give him and his station an exclusive and let him come along on the parade. Or circus, more like it. It worked out fine, since Governor Lindsey had business here anyway. He just got it all moved up a couple of days."

"And there we are," said the governor. "You all done here?" he asked the man in the blue shirt.

"Can we get one more shot with you and the family?"

"Love to, but I'm already behind schedule. I'm sure you can use what you've got." With a big smile, he walked back toward his SUV, surrounded by his detail. The uniformed troopers followed close behind, with Correy giving the MacBrides a wave.

That evening, the family watched the news together. They only got a short segment, but it showed Sofia, Sam, and Frank with Trooper Correy and the governor. There was a brief mention that Frank lost his job because of the shooting. Both girls were beside themselves that he was the anonymous hero.

"I can't wait to tell the kids on the team," said Lisa.

"I don't think you have to. We're not the only ones who get the news, you know," said Jodie, tears running down her face.

For once, Lisa was too happy to fire back a retort.

As they climbed into bed that night, Sofia asked Frank what they were going to do about the Mafia.

He shrugged. "One option is we throw some necessities in the van and drive out of here before sunrise. Go somewhere else and change our names. We'd be giving up the house and most of our things." He sighed. "And they might find us anyway. If they are even looking."

"What if you left for a while and laid low?"

"You and the kids would stay here?"

"Sure. Whatever works."

"Leaving you as an offering for the wolves." He shook his head emphatically. "No way in hell am I doing that."

"I'm ready to pack what we can fit in the van and leave tonight, if that's what you want."

He looked at her for a long minute. "What I want is the best life possible for us. I don't want to uproot you and have you live in constant fear. They may not have seen the news. They may not recognize me, and they may not care. They may not have even been looking for me after Italy. Either way, I say we stay right here. I'm done living in fear of what might be."

"Are you sure?"

"One hundred and fifty percent."

She snuggled up to him. "I'm beginning to think you're the right man for me, Frank MacBride, even if you're obviously not great with percentages."

"I'm for sure the right man for you, *amore mio*." He paused. "And it's definitely one hundred and fifty percent."

Frank's phone rang all the next day. After forty-seven job offers from as far away as Houston, Texas, they lost count. Frank asked everyone who called to email him their proposal. He wondered at first how they got his number, but he realized that anyone with internet access could find it. So much for privacy.

He sat in the little room that served as their home office, sifting through the emails that had poured in. He called out to his wife, "Sofia, some of these offers are for well over a hundred thousand per year. Plus benefits."

"Seriously?"

"I am unbelievably serious. Oh, wow, look at this—$125,000 per year, with benefits including three full weeks per year paid vacation time."

She came into the office. "What would you do?"

"Let's see. Production management." He shrugged. "Whatever that means."

She read the email over his shoulder. "The pay is good. Though the cost of living would be far higher there in LA."

"I doubt any of us would like living there, and the work doesn't seem appealing, either. I'd rather work for less, as long as I loved it and we lived in a place we all liked. That was the thing about Eugene Public Works. Apart from my interaction with Kingston, I enjoyed it. I got to do new things, solve difficult problems, and meet interesting people."

"Some of those interesting people were cute, no doubt."

"Sure, but not nearly as cute as you."

"Good answer, MacBride."

Two days later, he got another important call.

"Hey, Frank, this is Rick Wilson from the Eugene City Council. I wanted to call and thank you for saving Trooper Correy's life. We haven't met, but—

"We have met." Frank thought it was too bad Wilson couldn't see him rolling his eyes. "At the department Christmas party two years ago."

"I meant lately," Wilson said without missing a beat. "Look, I know things were not good between you and Jeff Kingston, and that's partially my fault. He was too much of a micromanager, and I was too hands-off. I should have seen what was going on there. You emailed me and tried to let me know, but I didn't listen. Part of the problem was that he put out a lot of static, saying how much trouble you made and so on. Anyway, I apologize."

"Apology accepted. I appreciate you calling. I know it took a real effort on your part to pick up the phone."

"Sure. Just trying to do the right thing."

And not get fired yourself, Frank thought.

"Anyway, the city of Eugene would love to rehire you."

"Oh, thanks for the offer. But you know, I've got so many offers coming in from different places—"

"I fired Jeff Kingston."

"Really?" Now he had one hundred percent of Frank's attention.

"Yeah, something that should have been done long ago. He was the reason there was so much turnover in the department. But he's gone now, fired for cause. Deliberately misleading us, harassing employees. You'd know better than anyone. Would you consider coming back to work for us? We need someone to fill the supervisor post, and everyone in the department likes you."

Frank couldn't believe his ears. "Email me your offer and I'll get back to you."

"Sure, I'll do that. Are you good to give me an answer by noon Monday at the latest? If it doesn't work for you, we need to put an ad in every paper in the Pacific Northwest."

"Will do." Frank hung up feeling better than he had in a long time.

The email from Wilson arrived the next day. They offered to pay him for all the time he missed after being fired, at the new rate—nearly twice what they'd been paying him before.

He wouldn't do as much hands-on work as he had with his old job, but it was time for a change, anyway. Plus, he'd have a lot more interaction with people. Sofia told him he'd be crazy to say no.

The next day after dinner, Sofia asked Frank if they could have a word in private. He said, "Of course," but she could tell he was a little nervous. Once alone in the bedroom, she told him about Ben Franklin High and Carl Chester. He was attentive and glad to hear the story had a happy ending, but he didn't say more than a word or two the whole time.

Then she told him the story of her last day in the Barcelona public school system and why her father shipped her off to Santa Angelina. Halfway through the story, she began crying when she spoke about her father's emotional and physical abuse. But the tears didn't stop her. She told him how she'd been convinced she was incapable of lasting friendships and why she was incompetent to provide guidance and protection. She also told him she was slowly getting over the problem but still had a long way to go.

Frank had tears rolling down his cheeks well before she finished. They held each other for a long time before either of them spoke. Finally, he smiled. "Thanks for sharing that. You are my forever."

She was ready for him to do his guy thing and try to make her feel better, fix her pain, and teach her how to see things with a better perspective. Or to at least say he'd suspected some of that all along. Which he probably did. But he did none of that, only telling her she was his forever.

She wiped her face with her hand. "And you are mine, *cariño*. You are mine."

From: AndiKing117@gmail.com
Sent: May 23, 2017 2:15 PM
To: frank.macbride@yahoo.com
Subject: My Hero!

Hey there, Frank, saw you on the news! I wanted to reach out and say congratulations for what you did. That took a lot of guts.

Sorry things got so weird between us, though I have to say overall, I benefited from our relationship. I think we both did.

Jeff is in a total funk over being let go. I keep telling him it's his own doing for being such a jerk, but he won't listen. You know what he's like. At least you're not married to him!

Let's meet for coffee and have closure. What do you say? Love,

Andi

From: frank.macbride@yahoo.com
Sent: May 23, 2017 4:37 PM
To: AndiKing117@gmail.com
CC: Josh.Goldstein412@gmail.com
Subject: RE: My Hero!

I appreciate your congratulations, Andrea. I did what I felt was right.

Regarding closure, I wish you and Jeff the best. I genuinely do. Respectfully, though, I don't want to ever hear from or see either of you again. I'm not sure how you got my personal email address. Please don't call, text, or email me again. Don't show up at my house or place of work, and don't send me anything in the mail.

That is all the closure I need.

Sincerely wishing you the best,

Frank MacBride
CC: Goldstein & Fitzhugh, Attorneys at Law

Chapter Forty-Two

Sofia had gotten into the habit of rising before the sun and sitting—sometimes meditating, sometimes praying, sometimes simply feeling gratitude. Something had changed in her toward her husband. She was proud of what he had done, but the feeling extended further. Maybe deeper forgiveness for his affair. Maybe seeing more of who he really was. Not the flirty Italian who had cheated on and lied to her, but a brave man who'd taken a great risk to save the life of a stranger. Time really does heal wounds. Over four years since he'd cheated, and fifteen months since he'd lied about it.

Her biggest fear—that her husband would cheat—now seemed nearly inconsequential. She slept better than she had her entire life, worried less, and as a result, felt far less stressed. Like Father Keith had said, "Worrying about what might go wrong usually causes more pain than the problem itself." How true! Her biggest worry had always been Sam, and she was gradually learning to come to peace with his situation.

She was of two minds about the South Eugene High Juniors' Labor Day picnic that coming Saturday, however. She wasn't looking forward to lots of questions full of hidden statements about her family, but she was ready to make the best of it. In any case, she liked the idea of getting out and seeing other parents and knew going would be the best thing for the kids.

Whatever his reasons for not speaking, being around others didn't seem to faze Sam. Nor was he bothered that other people would sometimes stare or occasionally talk slowly and loudly, as if he was hard of hearing or stupid. It bothered Sofia far more.

When they arrived, Jodie promptly walked off. Lisa spotted April almost as quickly and trotted over to her. Sofia sighed. Both girls were at an age when not being seen with their parents when peers were around was important. She liked that her kids were social, including Sam. Not what she had expected, but definitely the way he rolled. Just like Nonna Eve said, he would be fine. She was the one who needed to adjust.

Sofia didn't receive many questions, except "How's Sam?" "How are the girls?" and that sort of thing. Not nearly as bad as she'd anticipated. People she'd never met came up and talked to her like she was their best friend, almost as if the entire family had reached minor celebrity status. She took a deep breath. That's what happens when you're married to a hero. Since they'd gotten back from Nepal, Frank had been quieter and more likely to listen than talk. That might have concerned Sofia a year before. But now something seemed right about it.

The picnic took place in the field behind the high school, surrounded by the athletic track. A huge shade awning had been set up, which was perfect for the warm and sunny September day.

"Hey, stranger. Long time, no see."

Sofia turned to see an attractive woman in sunglasses and designer sweats, her ponytail pulled through the back of a white NY Yankees cap.

"I'm sorry, I—"

"It's me, Jess."

"Oh, my goodness. I didn't recognize you with the sunglasses." Sofia took in the other obvious difference about her. "Plus, you've lost a lot of weight."

"Fifty-seven pounds."

"You look terrific."

"Thanks. You're not looking so bad yourself."

Sofia shook her head. This is not the Jess I remember. "How have you been?"

"Great. I have joint custody of April now. Seems Kevin wanted to teach me a lesson more than anything else. He didn't realize how much work parenting is."

"Tell me about it." She smiled. "Looks like you got yourself a whole new image."

"I know, right?" Jess stepped closer and lowered her voice. "But it's the same old me inside."

"May I have your attention, please?" A voice with a distinct Texas drawl came over the PA system. "We are about to start the all-age race—once around the track, or four hundred meters."

"Well, that's my cue. Let's have coffee again sometime." Jess gave her a quick wave and jogged off.

"I'd love that," Sofia called after her.

The announcer continued, "The finish line will be the same for everyone, but according to age and ability, some of y'all will get a head start—specifically if you are under high school age or over thirty." A stir of excitement rose from the group, and at least a dozen high school students walked, strutted, or jogged over to the starting line. Eight or nine middle schoolers—including Sam— walked to the designated head-start marker, about eighty meters ahead of the regular starting line. A few parents lined up, surely part of the daily jogger set. Some of them—including Jess—started with the high schoolers.

"Go, Lisa! Go, Sam!" Jodie called out. Sofia jumped. She hadn't seen her daughter come up behind them. "This will be interesting," she said, watching her younger children with great pride. Without taking her eyes off them, Sofia asked Jodie if she wanted to run.

"Nope, but thanks for asking, Mom."

Sam trotted back toward Lisa and the other high schoolers. Sofia frowned. What's he doing? She watched him give his sister a quick hug, then stand next to her at the starting line. The organizer walked over and said something to them that Sofia couldn't hear. Sam shook his head and Lisa shrugged. The organizer walked back over to the side, raised his starting pistol in the air, and spoke into his wireless headset mic. "Okay, here's what we're going to do. Once around the track. You high schoolers and brave souls with them, y'all will end up right where you are now. Everyone else, you finish where the high schoolers are. Understood?" Nods all around. "Okay then, here we go. Runners take your mark! Set!" The entire group moved as one at the crack of the starting pistol.

Sofia swelled with pride as she watched Lisa pull ahead. A little more than a third of the way around, she had passed all the middle schoolers and many of the adults and high schoolers in the head-start group. Frank put his arm around his wife's waist, who at that exact moment felt a degree of happiness she couldn't remember experiencing, ever. Watching their daughter run was so special. About halfway around the track, some of the other high school kids passed her. She probably started out too fast, but that didn't reduce Sofia's pride, not by one drop. She screamed encouragement until she was almost hoarse. When Lisa was about three-quarters of the way around the track, Sofia saw Sam out of the corner of her eye, passing some of the high school kids, then passing most. "This is unbelievable," a man said a few yards off to Sofia's right. "Look at that little kid go! He's passing everyone."

Frank turned to the man and said—louder than he needed to—"That's our son!"

Lisa came in sixth, having kicked it the last fifty meters. But the surprise of the day was that Sam came in tenth, a twelve-year-old besting over a dozen high school runners, many of them athletes. Lisa stood with her arm around her brother's shoulders. An excited group of runners encircled them, which they both seemed to enjoy. Frank, Sofia, and Jodie jogged over to congratulate their son and brother. Sofia wiped her eyes on the way. She didn't mind people noticing her tears but didn't want to embarrass her kids.

Sam and Lisa radiated joy when Sofia told them how proud she was. It was an intensely happy moment for the MacBride family. The man who had started the race walked over to them.

"I assume these are your kids?"

Frank nodded. "They sure are. This is Lisa, this is Sam, and this is Jodie, who graduated from South Eugene last year. This most beautiful human being is my wife Sofia." He paused. "I'm Frank."

The man nodded and shook his extended hand. "Pleased to meet y'all. I'm Coach Howard. I run the PE department here and coach the track team." He looked from one MacBride to the next. "You know, folks, y'all got some pretty fast kids here."

Sofia's smile widened. "Yeah, we know it."

Coach Howard directed his attention toward Lisa. "Do you go to school here?"

She nodded, shy for a change. "I'm a junior."

"Then why in the world aren't you on the track team?"

"Well, I've been kind of busy with other things. I, um, play on the soccer team—"

"Hang on, you're a starting forward, aren't you?"

"I am."

"I've seen y'all play. You're not only fast. You change direction like a Texas tornado."

Lisa reddened as Coach Howard continued, "Y'all should go out for the track team. I can think of a few things you'd be great at. One is hurdles, and another is the two-hundred-meter sprint. A little work, and I believe you'd be unstoppable. We could really use you right now."

Lisa looked surprised. "Oh, but didn't you already start the season, like mid-August?"

"We started a few weeks back. But that's the point—you just beat three of my varsity runners. With some training, you would be almost as good as the two stars who finished in front of you. And you might be much better. Main thing, we gotta get you out there and see what you can do. Y'all are definitely state champion material. And you're only a junior." He included Frank and Sofia as he added, "I can tell you we're talking serious scholarship opportunity here."

Frank frowned. "She loves playing soccer, though, and her team kind of depends on her."

"Sure. I understand that. But I'm tight with Beth Wilkers, the girls' soccer coach. I'm sure we could arrange a split practice schedule so she can do both. There might be a few meet-match conflicts, but mostly those are on different days of the week. There are no school rules against being on two different varsity sports at the same time. What do y'all think about that?"

Sofia and Frank were both in.

Lisa beamed. "I'd love that."

"Okay, then. Stop by my office tomorrow and we'll come up with a plan. And you!" Coach Howard said to Sam. "How old are you, partner?"

Sam looked at Sofia, who cleared her throat and felt the faint but familiar pressure of tears that wanted to come forth. Sam's fine, and he has a great life in front of him. This isn't sad at all. "He doesn't speak," she clarified. "He turned twelve the first of the month."

"Oh, my God, aren't you—" he pointed a finger at Frank's chest. "Are you the guy who saved the state trooper from that psycho?"

Frank gave a reluctant nod, and Coach Howard vigorously shook his hand again. "Great to meet a local hero." He turned back to Sam. "Yeah, I heard about you, mainly because of your daddy. I'm fine with you not talking, partner, because most people talk way too much. Know what I mean?"

Sam smiled and nodded.

"Do you like running?"

Sam's smile widened and he gave a big, enthusiastic nod.

"How would you like to run on my track team when you come to high school?"

An even bigger nod.

"We're actually homeschooling him," Sofia said.

"That's okay, we get a lot of kids that come in from homeschooling. They tend to do well."

"But I don't know if he will go to high school. I was thinking about homeschooling him all the way through."

"Y'all can't be serious!"

Sofia was caught off guard. "I'm just trying to do what's best for our son. I can't stand the thought of him being teased in school. Besides not speaking, he's been a late starter with reading and writing."

"I understand. I know how it is being a parent. You're always worried about your kid—whether they'll be treated fairly, whether other kids might bully them. Stuff like that." He smiled gently at her. "And I can relate, since my older daughter got heckled when she was goin' through high school." He shook his head. "But you know, life is like that. And it won't change. I admire you for homeschooling, and I know you're doing the best you can for your son, but being around other kids might not be as bad as you think. In fact, it might not be bad at all for Sam. Look at how he relates to people, and how people relate to him. He's got a magnetic personality." The coach shrugged. "He's just different. Anyway, it's something to consider. You might think I'm biased because I'd love to have another track star on my team. But I also believe that letting him go to school might be the best thing for him."

"But he doesn't talk."

"That's true, but you and I both know keeping him home won't get him talking. I'm sure you know about the Oregon Special Needs Integration Program. South Eugene is an active participant in that. We had a blind boy from OSNIP on the wrestling team a few years back, and he won third place in State. There's an autistic girl from the program who's a senior this year and the starting center on our basketball team. Not that it's all about sports—but in my experience, that can be a big help for *any* youngster, and they'll never get that being homeschooled. Public school might be precisely what the boy needs."

He smiled at Sam. "He seems to be a great listener, which is a big part of gettin' along." He frowned. "You can't protect him forever, you know." He looked from mother to son. "The real world will come crashing down on his doorstep sooner than you think, and there's not a single thing you can do to stop that. You can help him be more ready for it, though." He smiled warmly, perhaps to soften the intensity of his words. "If he's as smart as he looks, then give him a shot. Having a skill like that will help him in school. Sure, it would be a risk, but it might just be a worthy risk. There's far more to gain than to lose, if you ask me." He winked at Sam, who just stared back. "Think about it, folks."

He nodded to Lisa. "I'll see you in my office tomorrow, young lady. Right after lunch is a good time." He waved to them and walked across the field.

The family watched him in stunned silence. Sofia sighed. "Well, that's what I'd call a hard sell." She put her hand on her son's head. "Sam?"

He looked up at her.

"What do you think about trying school? Maybe next year? You know, there might be bullies, and—"

He spoke so softly that Sofia wondered if she'd imagined it. She glanced at Frank and the girls, who all stared at Sam with open mouths.

Sofia took a deep breath. "What did you say, *querido*?"

He looked her in the eye and said—this time loud enough for all four of them to hear—"I would love to try that."

~

THANK YOU!

Thanks for taking the time to read this book. That means a lot to me.

I'd absolutely love it if you left a review so others can know what you thought of *Different*. I made a conscious decision to self-publish instead of going the traditional publishing route, so reviews and word of mouth are the main ways people can find out about this book:

ReviewDifferent.com

Last but not least, please tell people about this book. If you liked it, chances are they will too. And I would be even more thankful.

With gratitude,

Datta Groover
Golden, Colorado
February 19th, 2019
P.S. This is my first novel, but I am already enjoying the process of writing another. Your review (see the link above) will encourage me ;)
Stay tuned by liking my author page on Facebook:
Facebook.com/DattaGrooverAuthor

You can also connect with me at: **DattaGroover.com**

Resources

Datta's Facebook Author Page: **Facebook.com/DattaGrooverAuthor**

The Groovers' Book page (published and upcoming books from both Datta and Rachael Jayne Groover): **GrooverBooks.com**

GrooverSeminars.com/TheAwakening: The Groovers' yearly event (held in Denver and Melbourne) where they show people how to become world-changers and make a life and business out of it.

TheAwakenedSpeaker.com: Datta's world-class speaker training

Interesting reading about reincarnation:
   Life after Life by Ian Stevens
and
   The Boy Who Knew Too Much by Cathy Byrd

If you'd like to know about The Council of Nicea and other events in the early Christian Church (Jess and Father Keith were right—it really *is* all there in the history books), feel free to do internet searches on that subject.

For great relationship suggestions (for example, State of the Union and Date Night), google the work of Dr. John Gottman.

ACKNOWLEDGMENTS

Ever heard the saying "It takes a village to create a book?" Okay, maybe I just made that up, but it's nonetheless true.

My profound thanks to the "village" that has supported me in the process of writing this book.

First I want to thank Team Groover—I couldn't have done this without you. Your encouragement as well as emotional and practical support has been invlauable to me.

Thanks to my editors: Mary Rosenblum and John Paine.

Thanks to my book creation support team: my proof readers, beta readers, and cover designer, Patrick Knowles.

Thanks to my writing coaches: especially Donald Maass, Delores Cavallo, Robert McKee, and Tom Bird.

Thanks to all my friends, supporters, and others who believed in me: you know who you are, and you made more difference to me than you could possibly know.

Thanks to my family: The Kennedys, Groovers, Freemans—and extensions thereof. You all helped make me who I am.

Thanks to my dear sons: your belief and trust in me was at times all that kept me going through life.

Thanks to my mentors: George Horan, Gary Ferguson, Furman Riley, Jayananda, Swami Prabhupada.

Thanks to the extended family of courageous souls I've had the honor of working with as clients and friends.

Thanks to my wife, who has given me more support and encouragement than could ever be measured: Rachael Jayne Groover, you are my best friend, the love of my life, visionary business partner, and travel buddy on the road through life—all rolled in to one.

Just for Fun

I travel extensively in my training work, and people have asked where I wrote *"Different."* I thought it would be fun to list all those places. I would like to think that a bit of each place has found its way into the book.

The places where I worked on this book, in alphabetical order:

Apollo Bay Australia, Ashland Oregon, Banff National Park Canada, Big Island of Hawai'i, Breitenbush Hot Springs Oregon, Brisbane Australia, Calgary Canada, Canby Oregon, Denver Colorado, Detroit Oregon, Evergreen Colorado, Fort Collins Colorado, Frankston Australia, Golden Colorado, Great Otway National Park Australia, Greely Colorado, North Shore of Maui, Hakone Japan, Tasmania Australia, Honolulu Hawai'i, Houston Texas, Kauai Hawai'i, Island of Lanai Hawai'i, Kiyosato Highland Japan, Jannali Australia, Los Angeles California, Loveland Colorado, Lower Plenty Australia, Medford Oregon, Melbourne Australia, Mooloolaba Australia, Newcastle Australia, Newport Oregon, Noosa Heads Australia, North shore Oahu Hawai'i, Parsley Bay Australia, Phoenix Arizona, Portland Oregon, Rocky Mountain National Park Colorado, Salem Oregon, Scottsdale Arizona, Sedona Arizona, Summit of Haleakala Maui Hawai'i, Sydney Australia, Tampa Bay Florida, Tokyo Japan, Wailea Maui Hawai'i, and on the bank of the Yarra River in Victoria Australia.

- Datta Groover

ABOUT THE AUTHOR

Datta Groover is the founder of The Awakened Speaker™ training and has been honored to train and coach some of the best speakers in the world. In addition to his lifetime love for writing, he hosts transformational events around the world with his wife Rachael Jayne.

He also loves dance, photography, hiking, exploring, meditation, and playing music—all of which energize his writing. He firmly believes that any one thing we do is always influenced by every other thing we do and by the people we hang out with. Therefore, he says, we should pick our activities and associations carefully.

When they're not on the road, the Groovers live in the hills outside Loveland, Colorado with their dog Dakota, surrounded by lots of wild critters and vast natural beauty.

Like Datta's Author page on Facebook: **Facebook.com/DattaGrooverAuthor**
Connect with Datta: **DattaGroover.com**